M000232910

SILENT
CHILDREN

ALSO BY CAROL WYER

THE
SILENT
CHILDREN

CAROL WYER

bookouture

Published by Bookouture in 2017
An imprint of StoryFire Ltd.
Carmelite House
50 Victoria Embankment
London EC4Y 0DZ

www.bookouture.com

ISBN: 978-1-78681-328-2
eBook ISBN: 978-1-78681-327-5

PROLOGUE

Aiden Moore's chubby legs couldn't carry him any faster. His brother Kyle was ahead of him, whooping loudly as he raced along the trail, flattening tiny blades of grass as he tore through the woods, waving the mobile phone.

'Wait!' yelled Aiden, but Kyle either didn't hear or didn't want to hear.

Grandma Hannah was way behind them now. She struggled with walking fast and had to stop regularly to take a breath from her inhaler. It made a funny, wheezing noise when she used it, like the plastic trumpet Aiden got for Christmas that Kyle had broken. It had been her idea to come on the Gruffalo Spotting Trail on Cannock Chase. Ever since she'd told them about it, Aiden had thought of nothing else. He loved *The Gruffalo*, and with the app they'd downloaded onto Grandma's phone, he and Kyle were going to find footprints, spot Gruffalo characters and get their photos taken with them. Kyle knew more about it than him because Kyle had been here before with some school friends.

It seemed he'd been waiting for this day for forever, yet it had only been two weeks since Grandma had visited and told the boys about the treat she had in store for them. Mummy had left her to explain and gone into the kitchen while Grandma had sat with the boys.

'What happens when you find the footprints?' Aiden had asked, staring at the mobile phone, his comfort blanket gripped in his small fist.

Grandma smiled. 'You point the phone at a marker and the character comes to life so it's in the forest with you.'

'Will I be able to speak to it?'

Grandma laughed, then coughed and coughed. Eventually she spoke. 'No, Aidy. They're cartoon-alive not real-person-alive, but I'll take your photograph with them and you'll be able to see them on the app.'

'They're alive,' said Kyle, who'd been watching the television at the time.

Grandma Hannah gave him a look. 'Not properly alive,' she said.

'They *are*,' he whined. 'I've seen them.'

Grandma opened her mouth to speak but Kyle suddenly bounced off the sofa and raced off to kick a ball outside. He could never settle to any task for long. He was always twitchy. Mummy had tried to explain he had an attention disorder but Aiden didn't understand what that meant. Grandma coughed again and turned back to Aiden.

'You'll be able to see yourself with the characters.'

'Owl?'

She nodded. 'And the others.'

'And the Gruffalo.'

'Definitely the Gruffalo.' She ruffled his hair like she always did when she was about to stand up and leave.

Aiden couldn't believe it. Mummy had read the story about the Gruffalo to him at bedtime, almost every night for the last month. He would so love to actually see the Gruffalo in the forest. He'd had to wait for Kyle to finish school for half-term before they could go. Mummy hadn't been keen on their outing because Aiden had had a sniffle for three days and it was a really cold day when Grandma turned up in her old silver Honda to take them to Cannock Chase.

'I don't think the forecast is good for today,' Mummy said. 'Maybe you should go another day? I don't want Aiden to get worse.'

Kyle wailed, 'No! Today. We're going today. I want to see the Gruffalo.' He kicked out at the wall in the kitchen. 'I want to see… the Gruffalo.' Kyle always kicked walls and doors when he was cross. Mummy pulled him away and tried to explain that they could go another day when the weather was better. Kyle crossed his arms and began crying, loud noises that made Aiden want to stick his fingers in his ears. Kyle could really wail when he wanted to.

'Stop that now, Kyle. It's not necessary. You've been before. You can go another day when it's nicer out.'

Aiden's heart sank into his stomach. He'd been waiting for this day so patiently. He didn't even feel sick and his nose wasn't running as badly as it had been and he really wanted to go Gruffalo spotting. Tears brimmed over his thick, dark eyelashes and sobs rose in his throat. He'd thought about nothing else since Grandma said she'd take them to Cannock Chase. It was too much to bear. He'd really wanted to see the Gruffalo.

Mummy glared at Kyle, who shrugged, his tantrum now forgotten. Grandma hugged Aiden and wiped his snotty nose. 'We'll go, but we won't stay for too long. I don't want you to become ill either. We can go again another day too.'

It took ages for Kyle to get ready. He had lost the trainers he wanted to wear and wouldn't go until they were found. They got stuck in a huge traffic jam going through Stafford, and then Grandma got lost trying to find the correct car park on Cannock Chase. By the time they arrived at the starting point, it was after lunch and the café was empty of visitors. Kyle decided he wanted some food and Grandma had to buy him a sandwich and crisps. Aiden wasn't hungry but Grandma insisted he had a sandwich too. She ordered a coffee for herself and seemed to take forever to drink it. Eventually, they got activity bags and were ready to start Gruffalo-spotting. Aiden held his own activity bag tightly in his hand. It contained cards about the animals they might find, including Snake and Owl. He also had a magnifying glass and a special ruler. He didn't want to lose any of the bag's contents.

Outside, the temperature had dropped further. The skies had become black and Grandma was worried it would snow. Aiden thought it'd be great if it snowed. Maybe he could build a Gruffalo out of snow. Grandma wasn't as excited as she had been. Now she looked fed up. She made them wait by the activity centre building and wrapped them up in coats and scarves and woollen hats. Kyle had twisted about and pulled his hat off. 'I don't want it. I want to go hunting for characters.'

He'd scampered on ahead, joining a group of three children, and screamed in delight when they found a marker. Grandma had followed with Aiden, who eagerly pulled at her hand.

'Come on, Grandma,' he urged.

The other children stood beside a marker point and grinned as their mother took their photograph. Kyle hopped from one foot to the other, eager to take their place. Grandma aimed the phone at the marker and lifted it so Aiden and Kyle could see the short animation. Aiden's mouth dropped open as he watched a 3D Mouse appear from behind a stump of a tree trunk and run across it. Afterwards, Grandma photographed the pair of them with Mouse. Aiden couldn't have been happier. Kyle became increasingly impatient and bounded on again. Grandma took out her inhaler.

'I have to stop for a minute,' she said.

Kyle came skipping back. 'Can we go ahead, Grandma? I'll show Aidy the animals and take the photographs. I know what to do with it. I did it before when I came with James.'

Grandma gave a tired sigh. 'Go on. You go ahead and look for footprints and markers, but you hold Aiden's hand while you're walking and don't let go of it. Don't go out of my sight. Under-stand? You wait for me and make sure you can always see me. I don't want you getting lost in the woods. Promise?'

'Yes, yes. Promise. Come on, Aidy. Let's find the Gruffalo.'

Kyle grabbed Aiden's mittened hand in his own and tugged him along. At first, Aiden had been able to keep pace with his brother but suddenly Kyle dropped his hand and began walking faster. 'I'm a hunter,' he shouted. 'I'm going to track down the Gruffalo and shoot it,' he said, pretending he had a gun.

Aiden's eyes filled with tears. 'Don't shoot it.'

Kyle laughed at his misery and began to make whooping noises.

Aiden slowed his pace, his breath now coming out in white, misty clouds. He blew into the air and watched as they drifted away. He wondered if the Gruffalo could make white breath clouds too. Kyle had found a stick and was prodding at the ground with it. Aiden was torn between looking for the footprints and feeling scared Kyle would hurt the Gruffalo. Kyle could be cruel at times. He'd pull legs off spiders and laugh. He didn't seem to care. Kyle looked across, waved at Grandma who was walking towards them slowly, and shouted, 'It's okay, Aidy. I won't hunt it. I'm only joking. Let's find a footprint.'

At that moment, Aiden couldn't find any of the other animals or markers. Kyle had scooted ahead, even though Grandma had told him to stay with his brother. The trouble with Kyle was that he wouldn't listen. He just did what he wanted to. Grandma had told him off for kicking the back of her seat while she was driving to Cannock Chase. He'd beamed at her and said sorry, but he did it again and again. He wasn't being naughty. He was just Kyle. He never sat still and he would often become very impatient with his younger brother, who, at five years old, struggled to keep up with seven-year-old Kyle.

'Come *on*, Aidy,' urged his brother, now stooped over something on the ground. He waved the mobile at it and shook his head. 'No. Not here. Hurry up.'

Aiden trotted quickly to catch up, then remembered his grandmother. He turned to check she was still in sight. She was some way behind. He waved at her and she waved back, her hands beckoning him to return to her, huge sweeping gestures that were unmistakable. Her mouth opened and closed, but he couldn't catch her words. She waved her hands more agitatedly, but Aiden wasn't going to return to her. He hadn't found Snake, Owl, Fox or the Gruffalo yet. He scampered in the direction his brother had taken. The path twisted and turned between trees and suddenly Aiden came across a clear footprint. It was huge. How could Kyle have missed it? It must belong to the Gruffalo. He concentrated on looking for more prints and a marker point. The Gruffalo would be there. He found another large footprint and spun around, desperate to find Kyle and the mobile phone that would allow them to bring the creature to life. His brother had disappeared and Aiden had wandered further into the woods than he intended. He couldn't spot the trail they'd been on. He turned and tried to retrace his steps but ended up completely lost. Black clouds that scurried across the sky suddenly turned day in the direction of night.

'Kyle,' he called. There was no reply. He brushed through the undergrowth and startled a bird that chattered angrily at him, making him jump. 'Kyle,' he said again, this time more uncertain of himself. The woods didn't seem to be quite as friendly.

He began to shake with cold and anxiety. There were no markers here – the big arrows he'd been told to follow. Then he remembered the Gruffalo was friendly and would help him find his way out of the woods. He just had to find it.

He stumbled on in the gloom, nudging past some tall ferns and a few trees. All the while, he clutched his activity bag to his chest. He could hear rustling ahead and then… he saw feet – feet and legs. The Gruffalo was hiding under a bush, near a clearing.

'Hello,' he whispered. The Gruffalo didn't answer or move. Aiden wondered if maybe he was angry for some reason, or playing hide-and-seek. The wind moaned quietly through the trees, frightening Aiden, now suddenly anxious that the Gruffalo would leap out and try to scare him. Kyle sometimes did that and Aiden hated it. He wanted to go home. He backed away from the bush and further into the clearing, and when he turned, there in front of him was a car – a red car exactly like Mummy's. Mummy had come to find him. He trotted up to it and stood on tiptoe to let Mummy see him. He wondered if Kyle was already inside.

He tapped on the window and pressed his face against it. For a moment his mind couldn't process what he was seeing. This wasn't Mummy's car. It belonged to a man – a man with his swollen tongue hanging from his mouth, and red-veined eyes wide open, staring at Aiden. The activity bag tumbled to the ground; cards, ruler and magnifying glass spilled out. Aiden let out a terrible wail and began to call desperately for his grandmother.

CHAPTER ONE

DAY ONE – TUESDAY, 14 FEBRUARY, AFTERNOON

'Who are they from?' Sergeant Mitz Patel stared at the enormous bunch of scarlet anemone blooms on the desk.

DI Robyn Carter shrugged. 'I have no idea.'

'How romantic,' said PC Anna Shamash, pushing her face closer to them and inhaling deeply. 'They don't have any scent but they're absolutely beautiful. Well, whoever it is, they've spent a fortune on you. Must be smitten.'

Robyn snorted in an unladylike manner, her attention on a report she was reading. 'I can't think why,' she mumbled.

'Maybe they're from DCI Flint as a thank you for all your hard work.' PC David Marker grinned and waited for a response from his superior.

Robyn grunted. She wasn't even listening.

'Have you got any plans for tonight, David?' Anna's dark eyebrows were raised and a smile played across her lips.

David shrugged good-naturedly. 'I forgot it was Valentine's Day and got the big freeze from the ball and chain so I nipped out at lunchtime and bought her a charm bracelet. She's been hankering after one for ages. I'll give it to her tonight and pretend I haven't forgotten at all, that I was waiting to surprise her. I also booked a table for two at that new posh place in Stafford.'

'It's always fully booked – how did you get in there?' Anna asked.

David spun on his chair, twirling his pencil. 'I was really lucky. There'd been a cancellation. I'm going to be husband of the year after tonight. Might get some peace and quiet now when I try to watch the football, instead of, "Can you put up those shelves?" or, "The dustbin needs emptying."'

Mitz shook his head. 'You're such a romantic, David.'

'You wait until you're married, Sarge. It'll change your life.' David winked.

It had recently come to light that Mitz had begun dating Anna. Both were keeping it quiet and behaving professionally in the office, but the entire team was aware of the fledgling relationship.

'Can you lot get on with some work, please?' Robyn was uncharacteristically snappy. Mitz looked across at Anna, who shrugged. Anna slid into her seat and began wrestling with a burglary report that had to be completed. The office fell quiet. Robyn tapped at her keyboard and deleted what she'd written, then swivelled to face the window. She was about to speak when DI Tom Shearer banged on the open door once and leant against the doorframe, hands in his pockets.

His gaze lit on the floral display. 'Flint wants us, that is, if you're not too busy. Taken up flower arranging, DI Carter?'

She ignored his comment, collected her phone and walked towards the door. Shearer let her go ahead and faced Mitz. 'She okay?' he mouthed.

Mitz shook his head. 'No.'

Shearer nodded and strode after her, catching up with her as she reached the stairs.

'Sorry about the flower-arranging quip. That's me – open mouth, say something stupid, brain catches up later.'

She paused for a moment, looked at Shearer. 'It's not like you to be bothered about what you say, Tom. You're renowned for your sarcastic wit. That was quite a good comment by your standards.'

He smiled. 'I thought I'd been less than sensitive, what with Valentine's Day and Davies and everything,' he said, his words drying up. 'Shit, I'm no good at this sort of thing. Look, I'm sorry, okay?'

She buried a pang of hurt. 'It's been two years, Tom. I'm fine. Today is just another day. You didn't upset me.'

'Good. Glad that's settled,' he said.

Detective Chief Inspector Flint's office was much more sterile since he'd taken it over. It had once belonged to DCI Louisa Mulholland, who had worked and lived in there, rarely leaving to go home and always arriving early, way before her officers. Gone was the collection of memorabilia that had been on windowsills. The ornaments and Corgi police car Louisa had received for a birthday had gone with her to Yorkshire, where she'd taken up a new position. The large number of photographs that had adorned the wall had been removed, leaving several dark patches as a reminder. Flint's desk was impossibly tidy with only a leather desk blotter and matching square pen pot and business card holder on display. A tray containing documents had been pushed to one side of the desk, and in front of it was a silver-framed photograph of him and his wife taken at a police ball.

'Tom, Robyn, sit down.' Flint was as red-faced as usual. A roll of fat hung over his collar. He loosened the blue tie he was wearing as if it was choking him, and he swallowed. 'I wanted to give you the heads up about the latest development at the station. As you are aware, the counterterrorism department has increased over the last year, and the powers that be have decided it requires more operational space. We looked at all the possibilities, but with the constraints we have on our budget, the only viable option is to increase their current space by knocking through into the room next door, which is currently Tom's office.'

Robyn had a feeling she knew where this was going. Flint eased back into his chair, one leg draped over the other. His trousers rode up to reveal dark socks bearing the Batman logo.

'That raises the issue of where to house Tom and his team. Robyn, your office has sufficient space to accommodate another three members of staff and equipment. This will only be a temporary situation as we're considering other possibilities for Tom, and I appreciate it isn't ideal for you both, but I also have confidence you'll manage. You're both resourceful officers.'

Regardless of the sudden sinking feeling in her stomach, Robyn maintained a poker face. This was all she needed, snarky Tom Shearer in her space every single day. There was nothing she could do about it. Flint, or the super, had made the decision. If she started griping, it would reflect badly on her, especially as Tom was looking quite calm about it. This was most unlike him. She couldn't be bothered to argue. The decision had been made.

Flint studied his officers. 'You'll need to shift your gear out by start of the day tomorrow, Tom. We want to get the workmen in as soon as possible.'

Shearer spoke. 'Yes, sir.'

Flint's eyebrows disappeared into his hairline. 'Okay, that was easier than I expected. I thought you might have issues with this decision?'

'No, sir. I'm fine about it. Robyn?'

Robyn nodded her accord.

Flint looked relieved. 'Okay. That's it. Thank you for your cooperation.'

Outside again in the corridor, Robyn faced Shearer. 'What's with all the "yes, sir", "no, sir" nonsense? You're going to hate sharing your space with me. We have very different ways of doing things.'

'You'll hate it more,' he said with a smirk. 'We'll have to make the best of it. I'm not keen, but it'll only be for a short while. We could draw chalk marks on the floor and divide the place up so we don't get in each other's way. Bagsy I get the side with the coffee machine.'

'No way! That stays in my section. You and your officers can keep your hands off it.'

The corners of his mouth twitched upwards. 'That's better. More like your old self. It was like you were in another world or time zone in Flint's office. Normally you'd have created seven bells about sharing with me. What's going on?'

She shook her head. 'Nothing. I'm having an off day, that's all.'

'Can't say I've ever noticed you having one of those before. You're like Wonder Woman most days. You whirl into the station, spin about and whirl out.'

'Now you're going to be in my face every day, you'll probably see more of my off days.' She attempted a small grin. 'Wonder Woman?'

Shearer laughed. 'I could have described you like the Looney Tunes Tasmanian devil, but you're in a bad enough mood.'

'You'd better not come out with any of this sort of stuff in front of my officers, DI Shearer, or you'll really see my bad side.'

'Don't tempt me. You know I can't resist a challenge,' he said.

'I mean it. It's one thing to be sarcastic out of earshot and another if you undermine me in front of my officers.' She threw him a steely gaze.

He gave a grunt. 'Okay. I can see you really have got out of the wrong side of bed today. I'll leave you to it.'

CHAPTER TWO

The office was buzzing quietly with activity. Sergeant Matt Higham had arrived and was attempting to coax the photocopier into life by thumping it.

'Listen up, everyone.' Robyn's voice made them all look up. 'We've got to shift the furniture around and make room for company. DI Shearer and his team are moving in with us for an indefinite period.'

Mitz let out a long groan. 'Please tell us you're joking.'

She shook her head. 'It's come from upstairs. Counterterrorism is expanding into DI Shearer's office and he's being moved in with us. I don't like it any more than you do, but we're all adults and can get along, can't we? You've all worked with him and his officers on various cases. There shouldn't be an issue here.'

Mitz voiced all their thoughts. 'Working with them is different to having to share our space with them every day.'

'Sorry, Mitz. Like it or not, they're moving in.'

Matt thumped the photocopier once more. 'Better move the biscuits to a better hiding place,' he said, looking at Anna. 'If I can find them, that lot will.'

Anna's mouth opened. 'I knew it was you who was eating them.'

He gave a winning smile. 'Man cannot survive on coffee alone.'

An officer knocked on the door and waved a piece of paper. 'Excuse me, ma'am. This has come through. Forensics called it in. They're at the scene.'

Robyn read through the information at speed. 'It looks like a murder's taken place on Cannock Chase. Male, in his thirties, shot in the neck. Okay, team, let's go check it out.'

※

Daylight was fading as Robyn pulled off the road and drove towards the blue lights of parked squad cars. The area was crawling with white-suited officers. A makeshift screen had been erected, hiding the car and occupant, and floodlights now lit the grassy space and woods beyond. Robyn and her team made themselves known to the officer standing in front of the cordon stretching far into the woods, before donning the protective clothing and dipping under the yellow tape. A figure handed over a plastic bag to another officer and, with a wave of his hand, beckoned them over.

Connor Richards, originally from Dublin, was in charge of the forensic team. He'd had fifteen years' experience in Ireland before taking up his position in Stafford. Robyn had heard colleagues commenting that his easy manner and soft Irish accent made the unpleasant act of examining a crime scene seem more bearable. At the moment, nothing could be seen of Connor other than his eyes, the colour of Wedgwood blue. He acknowledged the trio and lowered his face mask to speak.

'We haven't got too much at this stage for you, Robyn. We're still collecting evidence. Found his driving licence in his wallet along with a credit card and twenty pounds. The victim is Henry Gregson, aged thirty-three, and lives in Brocton. He's wearing a wedding ring, and judging by the logo on his shirt, he works at the MiniMarkt convenience store in Lichfield. We think he was murdered sometime between 1 and 3 p.m.' He shook his head as he spoke. 'It was a little lad who found him. Must have been a heck of a shock for him.'

Mitz made a tutting noise. 'Awful,' he said, quietly.

'The pathologist's confirmed Gregson received a single fatal gunshot to the neck that punctured the carotid, the main artery in the neck, and undoubtedly death was instantaneous. We found no evidence of a struggle inside the car. There's no damage or scuff marks; in fact, little sign of movement, suggesting Gregson died immediately. The passenger window was lowered at the time of the shot, which allowed the bullet to enter the car unimpeded.' He squinted at an almost invisible speck on the ground. 'So far, we haven't uncovered any prints on the passenger side of the vehicle. Indeed, it appears the passenger door, handle and seat have all been wiped clean. Gregson's injuries and the extent of tissue damage surrounding the wound suggest the weapon wasn't fired at close range. More likely the assailant was approximately three yards away. The bullet entered the left side of his neck, and, as there's no obvious exit hole, I assume it's lodged inside his body.'

'He's still in situ?' Robyn asked.

'Sure he is, we waited for you. Follow me.' Connor pulled up his mask again. He picked his way carefully towards the screen. Behind it was a red Kia Sportage. The doors were open, and sitting in the driver's seat was Henry Gregson, his head tilted back against the headrest, his tongue out and eyes open. Robyn studied the circular hole with abraded skin, crusted with bright red blood. The stain had spilled down onto the collar of his white shirt to form a crimson bib around his neck. His hands, palms facing upwards, were resting on his thighs, and Robyn noted the wedding band on his ring finger. Henry Gregson had been undoubtedly classically good-looking, clean-shaven, with dark wavy hair, olive eyes, a slightly Roman nose, white teeth and a strong square jaw. A tie was coiled neatly on the passenger seat beside him as if it had recently been removed. Robyn cast a look around the interior. Connor was right. There was no sign of a struggle. Henry's car was immaculately clean: the dark plastic dashboard was free of smudges and smears. He'd even got a microfibre cloth in the door pocket to keep it spotless.

'It's a clean shot. I'd suggest whoever did this is used to firing weapons,' said Connor.

Anna appeared by Robyn's side. 'He's not wearing a seatbelt,' she said.

Connor shook his head. 'He wasn't wearing one when we found him. The radio was on though – tuned to Classic FM. It appears he was either taking time out to enjoy some solitude here on the Chase or he was waiting for somebody.'

Robyn looked at the thick padded jacket lying on the back seat. 'It's been a cold day. Not the sort of day to come out to the Chase for a walk.'

'He might have wanted some time to think. I usually take Rascal for a walk when I want to mull things over,' said Anna.

'That's quite possible,' Robyn replied. 'This isn't a car park, is it?' She looked around the grassed area.

Connor spoke. 'The main car park is over by the activity centre. This is just a clearing, accessible only by the route you took from the main road.'

Robyn looked at the body again then moved to the rear of the vehicle. There was a sticker on his back windscreen – 'Baby on Board' – and she shivered, not from cold but from the knowledge that a child was now fatherless, and his partner or wife would have to learn the horrible truth that her man was never coming home again. *Today of all days.*

Connor joined her and spoke again. 'I think you'll be interested in evidence bag F101. It contains Gregson's mobile phone. We suspect he was using it when he got shot. We found it under the passenger seat, hidden from view. It was tricky to coax it out. Had to use a piece of wire and ingenuity to reach it. I'll make sure you get it pronto. Just need to check it over for prints first. If you don't mind, I'd better get on. We've a large area to cover.'

She nodded her appreciation. 'I'll see you back at the station later.'

'I expect that's messed up any Valentine's Day plans you've made,' he said with a light shrug of his shoulders. 'I called Kate to explain I'd been called out. She wasn't best pleased. Sometimes, I worry this job will mess up every relationship I attempt.'

Connor had been with florist Kate for six months; she was a good-time girl who loved partying and letting her hair down. Robyn had met her at a police event and noted her self-centred attitude, the looks she threw Connor when he was talking to others and paying her insufficient attention, and the way she clung to his arm in a proprietorial manner whenever they were together. Robyn was sure Kate would get fed up of the broken-off engagements and abandoned plans. It was tough being in a relationship with anyone in this line of work. She took a deep breath to prevent herself dwelling on thoughts of Davies again. She couldn't afford to think about him at a time like this.

She walked some of the area, head down, noting the position of the vehicle before checking the car again and taking a last look at Henry Gregson. Then she ducked back under the crime scene tape, removed the protective clothing, dropping it in the bin provided, and strode to the squad car. Mitz and Anna had shadowed her movements in silence. Standing beside the squad car, Robyn pinched her nostrils together then spoke. 'Mitz, is the little boy who found Gregson still here?'

Mitz shook his head. 'No, guv. He was taken home. I have the address. Mrs Price, his grandmother, gave a statement before leaving. The boy, Aiden Moore, was following the Gruffalo Spotting Trail with his older brother.' Seeing the puzzled look on Robyn's face, he explained. 'It's basically a route that allows children to search for characters from the book *The Gruffalo*. Once they find special markers, they're able to point a mobile phone at them and watch the characters appear on their screens. The markers activate a 3D animation of that character, making it seem to come to life in the forest.'

'I understand. Sort of,' Robyn said, wrinkling her brow further.

Mitz continued, 'Aiden and his brother, Kyle, went on ahead. Mrs Price suffers from asthma and was struggling to keep up with them. She told them not to go too far. Aiden strayed off the route and came across this clearing where he spotted the car. It's identical to his mother's car and, he approached it thinking it was hers.'

'Is he okay?' Robyn asked.

'I had a quick word with one of the other officers while you were with Connor. He said Aiden was painfully shy and didn't want to speak. He kept trying to hide behind his grandmother. He didn't know if that was normal behaviour for the boy or if he'd been frightened by what he'd seen.' Mitz put his notebook in his pocket and waited for instructions. They were quick in arriving.

'Right, let's start with the grandmother and see how best to proceed. I don't want the little boy put under any duress and we need to find out what state he's in. We'll interview her, Mitz. Anna, please get hold of the statements made from those working here today. Check them through and ask David to run background checks on all the staff. We'll be investigating anybody who might have been in the vicinity between 1 and 3 p.m., and that includes staff, dog-walkers and visitors.'

Anna scribbled down the requests. They came faster now.

'Use the CCTV footage and list the vehicle registrations of the cars in the car park today. Given it was a very cold day, we might be fortunate and only have a handful to check out. Locate the owners of those cars and we'll run background checks on them too. Ask Matt to dig up everything he can on Henry Gregson, his family, work colleagues and friends. Find out which officers were dispatched to break the news of his death to his family. Have a word with them first and get an idea of how the news was received. We'll pay them a visit after we've spoken to Mrs Price,' Robyn added, nodding at Mitz. 'And, Anna, make sure you get hold of Henry Gregson's phone. I want to know if he was using it when he was shot and a list of any people he contacted that morning.'

Anna wrote quickly then stubbed a final full stop and looked up in case there was more to follow.

Robyn shook her head. 'That's it for now.'

Mitz looked across at the crime scene. Lights bobbed up and down as officers continued with their searches. 'A man chooses to park up in a secluded part of Cannock Chase for no apparent reason, then, again for no apparent reason, winds down the passenger window and is shot. It makes no sense.'

Robyn opened the car door. 'This type of crime rarely makes sense but once we've got sufficient evidence, hopefully we'll track down his killer. It's all we can do. And we'll start by gathering some facts.'

Mitz hurried to the driver's side. Robyn was right. It was all they could do.

CHAPTER THREE

THEN

'Stop it. Stop it!' she screams. 'He's only ten. You'll kill him!' She pulls at her husband's beefy arm, her painted nails raking across his massive bicep, leaving raised red marks. He stares at them for a brief instant, then raises his huge, leather belt once again, bringing it down hard. She screams again, the noise deafening the boy, who cowers on the floor. Each slap of the belt intensifies the pain, which now radiates in ever-increasing circles over his back. The boy wishes it would stop. He tries to concentrate on something other than the slapping of the belt and his nerves that scream in agony.

His mother yanks on the arm again. His father flicks her away and she crashes against the kitchen table, lets out a loud groan and flops to the floor like a rag doll. He turns his attention back to the boy, a sneer on his face, eyes mere slits, narrowed by cruelty. He lifts the belt again; the shining buckle in the shape of a skull glints menacingly and the boy shrinks into the smallest ball he can make. This is going to hurt even more than the strap.

'Stand up, you little shit. Behave like a man.' His father's voice is flat, emotionless, and his words slurred by the alcohol he's consumed.

'I'm sorry,' says the boy, hoping his words will end this torture.

'No, you're not sorry… yet,' replies his father, 'but you soon will be.'

The boy pulls his arms over his head. It'll soon be over. His father's rage will cease as it has started. He'll go to bed and sleep off the effects *of his latest drinking spree and tomorrow it'll be like none of this ever happened, apart from the marks and bruises. Mum will put ointment on them, kiss him, hold him tightly in her arms, and cradle him until he stops crying, her eyes warning him to keep the secret. Above all else he must remain silent and keep the secret. In the morning, she'll disguise her own bruises then apply thick concealer to the purple mark on his cheekbone. She'll walk him and his eight-year-old sister to school while their father will whistle along to a song on the radio and behave as if he's done nothing wrong.*

His mother lets out a moan of despair. His sister, hiding under the kitchen table, now crawls towards their mother, tugs at her torn sleeve and is scooped up in her arm. He wishes he could join them, but he can't. It's his turn to be singled out and he has to take the punishment. If he doesn't, his sister will be next. His sister is watching him with huge eyes; an unspoken understanding passes between them. He gives her a brave smile to let her know she'll be okay.

CHAPTER FOUR

DAY ONE – TUESDAY, 14 FEBRUARY, EVENING

Hannah Price was in her early sixties, but the deep frown lines and thin face made her seem older. She eased onto a kitchen chair next to a pine table, on which stood a mug of tea, her inhaler and a romance novel.

'Poor little mite,' she said, shaking her head.

'Aiden's your younger grandson?' Robyn asked.

Hannah smiled, the corners of her eyes creasing. 'He is. Kyle's older. He's totally different to Aiden. He suffers from a mild form of autism so he can be a bit of a handful at times. Kyle shot off as soon as we got on that trail. I ought to have known. I thought it'd be a nice, easy walk, but it was bitterly cold in the wind, and I couldn't keep up with the pair of them jumping and racing about. I told them they could go on ahead if they stayed within sight. I wouldn't forgive myself if something happened to either of them.' She gave a small shudder. 'Kyle went off like a rocket, but I could still see Aiden. He turned and waved at me, and I shouted for him to wait up, but he continued. I hurried up the path after him, but I had to stop to take my inhaler. Once I start getting breathing difficulties, I need to stop for a minute. Anyhow, I heard a noise – a high-pitched howl – then Kyle came bounding back and asked where Aiden was. I panicked, which made my asthma worse. I didn't know what to do. I grabbed Kyle's hand and told him to stay beside me and we both started shouting Aiden's name. We called out five or six times and he suddenly appeared, near some trees. His face was so white I knew something dreadful had happened. I asked him what was wrong and he wouldn't answer. Then Kyle told him he was an idiot to rush off and Aiden began to cry. He said there was a scary man in a car like his mum's. I asked him if the man had touched him or spoken to him, and he shook his head. I began to wonder if he'd been mistaken. Little boys can have vivid imaginations at times. Then, I spotted a glimpse of red through the bushes. I pushed through them into a clearing and saw the car. From where I was standing I could see exactly what had frightened Aiden. I dialled nine-nine-nine immediately and reported it.'

'You didn't move closer to the vehicle, Mrs Price?'

The woman shuddered. 'Absolutely not. I walked the boys back to the café at the beginning of the trail and told a member of the staff what I'd seen. She phoned her manager. It all went crazy after that. Within a few minutes the police arrived. I wanted to get the boys back home as soon as possible. I made a statement and Aiden was asked some questions but to be honest he wasn't up to answering them. The officer agreed it was best for us to leave.'

'Did you notice anyone else near or around the car at the time?' Robyn asked.

Hannah rubbed her lips together in concentration. 'The police asked me that, and since then I've been racking my brains, but I didn't see anyone. I was anxious about Kyle and Aiden so I didn't really look as hard as maybe I ought to have. Do you think the killer was still about?'

Robyn shook her head. 'I doubt it. I think they'd already left. Were there many people on the trail with you?'

'There was a mother and three children, but they were on the way back to the car park when we met them. They were taking photographs at the first marker. I didn't see anyone else at all,' Hannah answered. 'I shouldn't have taken the boys. The weather wasn't good. Emma, that's their mum, wasn't keen for them to go and yet I insisted. I should have listened to her and gone on a different day.'

'What time did you arrive at Cannock Chase, Mrs Price?' asked Robyn.

'We were later than I'd hoped. Had trouble getting Kyle ready and then traffic was bad. There was a broken-down vehicle on a roundabout coming out of Stafford, and to cap it all I couldn't find the right entrance to the trail. The Chase is so big. I went to the wrong car park at first. We got there about one fifteen. By the time we had lunch, collected the activity packs from the café and headed off on the trail, it was one forty-five.'

'I don't suppose you heard anything like gunfire or a car exhaust backfiring at any time, did you?'

Hannah breathed in, lips pressed together, and thought. Eventually, she replied. 'No. I didn't. I'm pretty sure I didn't hear anything.'

'And finally, could you tell me what time it was when Aiden discovered the car?' Robyn asked.

'I can't be certain. I'd guess sometime between two and two-fifteen.'

✳

As they drove back in the direction of Stafford, Robyn was already assimilating what she'd learned. The pathologist had put Henry Gregson's death at between one and three. Hannah Price's statement had corroborated that he was dead at about 2 p.m. and she hadn't heard any gunshot while in the vicinity. Based on that information, Henry Gregson had been murdered sometime before 2 p.m. Robyn needed to know who was on the Chase before that time. Not only did she want to talk to Aiden, she wanted to interview the family of three who were returning to the car park when Hannah and her grandchildren were beginning the Gruffalo Trail. She called Anna.

'Nobody knew who they were,' said Anna. 'They came into the café at twelve thirty, bought some drinks, paid in cash and left. They didn't get an activity pack. The staff at the café didn't see them leave either, or their vehicle. I'm about to check the security camera footage to see if we can spot their car in the car park.'

Robyn let out a soft huff of annoyance. It would have been easier to trace the family if they'd used a card as payment. 'Okay, keep me informed.'

Mitz spoke without shifting his gaze from the road. 'That family were taking pictures at the first marker point, which must mean they were using the Gruffalo Spotter application. Those photos will have been automatically added to the device's gallery and can be shared via social media using the hashtag GruffaloSpotters. If we search recent additions on Instagram or Twitter, we might stand a chance of finding them.'

'Good thinking, Mitz. Can you look into that further?' She was interrupted by her mobile. 'Robyn Carter.'

'I've left all the information I could find on Henry Gregson on your desk. He was squeaky clean. Worked in the local convenience store in Lichfield. Is there anything else you need from me tonight, only I've got a table booked…' David Marker's voice trailed off.

'No, David. You get off. See you in the morning.'

CHAPTER FIVE

As Robyn bundled into the station with Mitz in tow, she spotted one of Shearer's men ahead of them, dragging a chair down the corridor, and sighed. There'd be little peace in her office for the next few days or weeks, or however long it took to find somewhere to house Tom and his team. She hoped her patience would hold out.

The anemones displayed elegantly in a red, plastic-lined box on her desk served to remind her of why she was feeling less than her usual feisty self. She ought to be pleased that someone was showering her with affection and generous gestures but her heart ached and her mind was in turmoil. She hadn't the foggiest who'd sent them. There was one possibility, but she didn't dare consider it. In spite of her efforts, she was overwhelmed by a memory that refused to be quashed, of her and Davies's last Valentine's Day together…

※

The house is in darkness when she returns from her shift. She's had a tough few days and today has been no different. She's struggling to find sufficient evidence linking a pair of suspects to a burglary. She's had to admit failure and now the case will go in front of a jury. She slots her key into the lock, heart heavy and with an ache in between her shoulders. As she opens the door, she's met by silence. She shouts Davies's name but there's no reply. She drops her bag, along with her keys, onto the table, slips off her shoes and pads towards the sitting room, wondering if he's been called away at the last minute.

She pushes open the door and is met with a sight that makes her mouth drop open. Before her, dressed in a toga and sandals, is Davies. He bows to her then lifts a child's plastic recorder to his lips and plays a terrible rendition of the theme tune to Love Story. *She can't stop the grin spreading across her face.*

'Happy Valentine's Day,' he says after murdering the tune.

'What's all this? Why the sheet and whistle?'

He fakes indignation. 'I'll have you know I'm a Greek god – Pan. And this "whistle" is supposed to represent his pipes. After all, Valentine's Day originated in Greece. I'm staying true to the original idea, and getting into character. Come on, I've got a costume for you too.' He holds out a hand and drags her towards the settee where he's laid out a simple tunic purchased from a fancy dress shop.

'You'll have to disrobe completely, of course,' he says, giving her a wink. 'And then I'll feed you grapes – well, a glass of wine – and we'll amuse ourselves with romantic Greek games.'

'What games would they be?' she asks, slipping out of her shirt and pulling the tunic over her head.

He points towards the large set of wooden blocks stacked in one corner of the room. 'Love Jenga,' he says with satisfaction. 'Each block has a love command on it. If you pull a block out and the others tumble, you have to pay the forfeit written on the block.'

She marvels at how he comes up with such innovative ideas. 'They'd better be good forfeits or I'm not playing. None of them involve you playing that recorder again, do they? My eardrums can't take another song.'

He gives her a cheeky grin and suddenly she doesn't feel so weary.

米

Robyn gently rubbed the band of the engagement ring that she still wore and thought about what was really troubling her. For three weeks, she'd been trying to get to the bottom of the mystery surrounding her fiancé Davies' death. She'd always believed he'd been murdered in an ambush, in the foothills of the Atlas Mountains. That was until she'd received a photograph that contradicted everything she'd been told, and as she rubbed her ring, she wondered for the umpteenth time if he was still alive, and if it had been him who'd sent the photograph to absolve her of her guilt.

Davies had been an intelligence officer, although to all who knew him he worked for a company specialising in microchip technology. His secret life was very much that, and Robyn had always been kept in the dark about any missions. It was for both their safety. That last fateful trip had broken the rules. She had joined him at his request. He'd insisted it wasn't a covert or dangerous mission. He'd been sent to Marrakesh purely to meet with an informant, and there was every chance the man wouldn't show. It had been his suggestion she come along, convinced there was nothing to worry about.

At first, Robyn had refused, but Davies was a persuasive man and wheedled and cajoled until she agreed to accompany him. As he reasoned, he wouldn't have asked her if there had been any risk at all.

Having recently discovered she was pregnant, Robyn had decided to break the news during this impromptu short break in Marrakesh, a city that had always fascinated her.

On the second day of the trip, Davies had been instructed to meet the informant, and set out on the three-hour drive to the meeting point, except he never made it. His vehicle had been involved in an ambush. From that day, she'd carried a mountain of guilt, convinced she had drawn attention to him through her presence. It was because of her that his vehicle had been targeted and bombed.

The photograph had landed on her desk just over three weeks ago, while she was in the middle of a serious murder case, and she'd therefore been unable to fully consider its implications. Since then, her attempts to check its validity and work out why she'd received it, had been hampered by work. She was hoping to grab a few days' leave so she could hunt down Davies' superior at the time of his death, Peter Cross, and tackle him about it. She'd had no luck locating him to date and was keen to talk to him. For the moment, though, she had to concentrate on police work and it was proving difficult.

She squared her shoulders. It was still her office, after all, and she wasn't going to let Tom Shearer get too comfortable there.

Tom and his men had already made themselves at home, and the office was filled with furniture, computers and boxes, arranged in a higgledy-piggledy fashion. To the far side of the room, four desks had been arranged in offset rows, facing the whiteboard at the front of the room. Matt looked up from his own desk that was wedged in the corner next to the coffee machine and grinned. He pointed to the machine and gave a thumbs up to Mitz. Robyn clambered over PC Gareth Murray, an exuberant youngster who'd joined Tom's team three months earlier, now on his knees, searching for sockets.

The young man leapt up to attention. 'Ma'am,' he said, as Robyn slid into her seat, trying hard to ignore the fact it had been moved extremely close to both Anna's and Mitz's desks, to make room for the new arrivals. The bouquet of anemones was still on it. She shifted it aside.

'PC Murray, if you're going to be sharing this office with us for a while, please refrain from calling me ma'am.'

'Understood,' he replied, almost clicking his heels together and standing straighter.

Tom appeared, a box of files in his arms. He nodded at Robyn. 'It's okay if we squash in over there, isn't it? I know it's in front of the window, but there wasn't much choice.' He dropped the box onto his desk and began sorting through it. 'Gareth, make sure those tech guys are on their way to set up the computers, will you? I'm getting way behind with investigations thanks to this farce. You'd have thought Flint would have got somebody in to help us move. I don't recall seeing the words "removal man" on my last CV. You got enough space, DI Carter?' He spotted the irritated look on Robyn's face and studied her, head cocked, a smile tugging at the corner of his mouth. 'I could get Gareth to sit on my knee if you'd like some more.'

She didn't respond with a smile and instead shrugged. 'It's fine. We'll get by, but I need the whiteboard.'

Tom sniffed. 'Suits me. I don't use those old things any more myself. Bit antiquated.'

Robyn bit her tongue. She had her methods and it had no bearing if they were regarded as antiquated or otherwise by the likes of Tom Shearer. They worked for her and for her team. Mitz didn't need to be asked to collect it. He knew the routine. Robyn would want to thrash out what they'd uncovered before deciding how best to approach the investigation. He dragged the board across to their section of the room and stood it beside Robyn's desk. It acted as a small screen, shielding her slightly from Tom, who was now grumbling on the phone. She wrote down a few words and then stood, marker pen in hand.

'This is what we have so far – murder victim is thirty-three-year-old Henry Gregson, currently living in rented accommodation in Alford Lane, Brocton. Married to Lauren Gregson, an estate agent. Mrs Gregson has been informed. Police officers say she reacted very badly to the news and a doctor had to be called out to sedate her. She's not in a fit state to talk to anyone else tonight. Officers say she had no idea Gregson wasn't at work. He'd texted her that morning from MiniMarkt Convenience Store in Lichfield, where he works. Matt, what else did you find?'

Matt rummaged through his notes, cleared his throat and spoke. 'There's nothing about him on our databases. Ergo, no previous convictions. Born 30 March 1983 in Stoke-on-Trent. His sister, Libby, and their mother still live there. He left school in 1998 with a handful of GCSEs. Not got anything on employment record up until more recently. Worked for a large chain of supermarkets in a variety of roles: shelf-stacker, checkout operative and team leader. Studied and passed his Level 3 NVQ Diploma in Management a couple of years ago. No idea why he might have been targeted as yet, guv. His sister, Libby, cares for their mother, who's suffering from early-onset Alzheimer's. She can't travel without making arrangements for her mother, so I told her we'd go over and speak to her tomorrow.'

'That's good. I might go myself if there's time.'

'She said she's an early bird, so if you want to go first thing, that'd be fine.'

Robyn checked her watch. It was coming up to quarter to eight. They'd been in since eight that morning. She wanted to send them home, but she had to start on the investigation. Anna arrived, carrying Gregson's iPhone in a plastic evidence bag. She handed it to Robyn, who examined it for a minute before returning it.

'Make sure the tech boys get this pronto. I want to know who he was calling or texting at the time he was shot. As soon as we finish here, okay?'

Robyn wrote 'telephone' and 'gun'. She replaced the cap on her pen and tapped it against her chin thoughtfully.

'The body was discovered by a minor – Aiden Moore. His grandmother, Mrs Hannah Price, and his older brother, Kyle, are our only witnesses and they didn't hear any gunfire. From that, I could deduce the murderer used a silencer on his weapon, but until we've tracked down and spoken to other possible witnesses, we won't know. Mitz, I'll leave it to you to trace the family who were there before Mrs Price began walking the trail. Your hashtag GruffaloSpotters idea was a good one. Anna, get anywhere with the other vehicles at the car park?'

'Got registrations for seven vehicles. CCTV footage wasn't much use. The family walked across the car park and out the other side. They must have been parked elsewhere – maybe along the road.'

Robyn unscrewed the cap on her pen once more. Tom shuffled towards the door, disappearing into the corridor. 'Okay, this is how I'd like to play it: Mitz, chase up those car registration numbers. See if any of those owners caught a glimpse of something out of the ordinary. You know the drill. Matt, talk to friends, neighbours, people he knew. Anna, tomorrow morning, I'd like you to accompany me to interview Henry Gregson's widow, followed by his sister, and then we'll go to his place of work. Also, we need to find out as much as possible about him, see if he uses social media, and anything that might help. We need to ascertain if this was a random killing or a deliberate murder. If it's the latter, why? Any first thoughts?'

'Nothing new from me, guv,' said Matt. The others shook their heads in unison.

'We've got plenty to get on with,' said Robyn. She glanced at her watch again. 'Right, that's it for tonight. It's almost eight. Go home, folks.'

They shuffled towards the door, donning their coats and picking up scarves. Anna was first out, hastening down the corridor to find somebody to examine the telephone. Matt was last out. 'You going home, guv?' he asked.

She looked up. 'In a mo. Just going through your notes first. See if I can work out any reason he might have been murdered.'

'It's certainly seems to be a premeditated murder,' Matt replied. 'You don't ordinarily wander about Cannock Chase with a gun. Not unless you intend shooting someone or something. It's full of walkers, cyclists, tourists and day-trippers.'

'True. Have good evening.'

'Yeah, you too, boss.'

The ringing footsteps of her officers departed down the corridor and through the fire door. As it swung shut, silence fell. She began reading the file Matt had left her. There was nothing extraordinary about Henry Gregson, a local man who lived in a small village near Stafford. On the surface, he was an upstanding citizen with no convictions, not even a parking ticket. Robyn sighed and shifted to get comfortable on her chair. She eased back her shoulders, which had stiffened up. It'd been a long day and she could do with going home too. She was drawn back to the photograph of the pleasant-faced man. Who would want him dead and why? She scribbled a note on a neon-green Post-it: *Is shooting allowed on Cannock Chase? Make list of local farmers.*

She stood and stretched. She might have a quick run before she showered and went to bed. The Ironman event was in June, only four months away, and she needed to keep up her training. She shuffled the files to put them away.

She shouldered her bag. As she prepared to turn off the lights, the door swung open and Tom Shearer stumbled through, a box of files in his arms, and collided with her. The box dropped onto the floor with a clatter and the files tumbled out.

'Oh, for crying out loud,' he began. 'Sorry, Robyn.'

As she helped him gather up his files, Shearer seemed to recover his composure. 'Cheers. Er, don't suppose you fancy a drink, do you? I'm parched after all this lifting and carrying.'

'Sorry, Tom, I've got to get off. Another time.' She scooped up the anemones, careful not to damage them.

'Yeah, sure, whatever.' He marched over to his desk and let the box land with a thump. 'No probs. Got a load to sort out here, but it can wait. I'm off for a pint.' He nodded at the flowers. 'My ex-missus used to get in a right strop if I didn't buy her a dozen roses on Valentine's Day. Bloody expensive they were, too. Seems such a waste of money now when I think back. It would have paid for quite a few pints. Night, Robyn.' He turned his attention back to his box.

Robyn drew up outside her house at the end of Leafy Lane. It was neither a lane nor leafy but it was a relatively quiet street with well-kept semi-detached houses. A soft glow shone from behind her kitchen blinds. The automatic timers she'd fitted had illuminated the lamps in the sitting room so she no longer came into a dark and empty house. With flowers held awkwardly under an arm, she felt in her bag for her house keys and cursed the fact the bulb above her front door had gone out again. It must be faulty. This was the third bulb in as many weeks. She'd have to get it looked at.

She dropped her bag onto the floor in the hallway and tossed the car key onto a console table before heading directly for the sitting room. She placed the flowers on the dining table, pulled out the envelope postmarked London and withdrew the photograph of Davies taken at three thirty on the fifteenth of March 2015, the very same time she was in a room in Marrakesh, being told by his superior Peter Cross that Davies had been murdered on his way to rendezvous with an informant on the other side of the Atlas Mountains.

The flowers had rattled her. Davies had been the only person who'd ever sent her anemones on Valentine's Day…

※

The Jenga bricks are in a heap over the carpet. Robyn drops a grape into Davies' mouth and he chews, eyes closed.

'I like having a slave,' he says.

She thumps him on the arm. 'That's it. I'm done with this game. Your forfeits stink.'

'Oh, come on. You liked having your feet bathed.'

'Yeah, that one was okay.'

She moves across to the bouquet of anemones on the table; rich crimson petals open to reveal dark stamens. She can't describe the perfume. It's unusual.'

Davies studies her movements and speaks. 'It's part of the Greek theme. They're more romantic than roses. After jealous gods murdered her lover Adonis, Aphrodite cried tears on his grave. Those tears grew into anemone flowers. The flowers are forever linked to the forsaken, or those left behind.'

※

Robyn stared at the bouquet. First the photograph and now the flowers. If Davies were alive, he might have sent her both, but the question remained as to why? Why hide from her and send cryptic messages? That led her to consider other, more sinister options. Somebody was aware Davies bought her anemones each Valentine's Day and – or – knew about the Greek myths that gave the flower the dual meanings of the arrival of spring winds and the loss of a loved one to death. Could they be sending her a veiled threat, or even a warning? Far from wondering if Davies was behind the gesture, she now wondered if she might be in danger, from somebody who either had captured Davies or was following up a vendetta against him.

She searched the anemones again for a card and found none. Sitting down with her mobile, she searched for local florists, writing down their contact details. She'd ring them when she had a chance. The arrangement had come inside a plastic bag filled with water and placed in a lined, red box. Maybe this sort of display was particular to only one or two florists.

She stroked a silken petal gently. It was yet another mystery, one that caused a chill to run through her.

CHAPTER SIX

THEN

Happy Hippo's mouth opens and shuts at speed as his sister tries to capture the marbles spinning about the old, red plastic tray. He's working Henry the blue hippo's mouth for all its worth, and the marbles dive in all directions, clattering against the sides. There are two remaining marbles, and his sister is concentrating hard, tongue between her lips. The pink hippo grabs them and she hoots with delight. The boy shrugs. Normally he's a dab hand at this game and can trounce her, but today, she's won fair and square. Her eyes sparkle in jubilation.

'Want another game?' she asks.

He shakes his head. 'Later maybe.'

'Sore loser,' she says. She puffs out her cheeks like one of the hippos they've been playing with and waddles around the kitchen, arms held wide by her side. 'I'm Happy Hippo.'

'Yeah, you're about the size of a hippo,' he teases.

She blows a loud raspberry in response that makes them both snigger. She pulls another face and crosses her eyes before packing up the game and taking it upstairs. He reaches for the unfinished sandwich in front of him on the table.

'You didn't take any money out of the jar, did you?' His mother appears, a crease developing between her eyes. 'I won't be angry.'

He shakes his head, chops full of bread and jam. There had been no butter again and the bread was dry, but when he complained, his mother replied, 'Drier where there's none,' as she plonked it down in front of him.

He always eats whatever he is given. Some days they have half-decent food, usually after his father gets paid. Mum will treat him to something nice. He likes fish and chips, but recently they don't even get fish, just chips: fat, crispy chips with lots of ketchup. He smacks his lips at the thought. He'd been really hungry today and wolfed down the first sandwich as soon as he got it before his sister had insisted on a game of Hungry Hungry Hippos. They'd played football at school and he'd run about like crazy, chasing after the ball and eventually scoring. One day, he'll become a top footballer and earn so much money he'll never have to eat dry bread and strawberry jam again. And he'll take his mum and sister to a mansion, far away from his father and his temper that is fast spiralling out of control.

Both he and his sister have taken to hiding in their bedrooms as soon as they hear their father's key in the door. It is best to hide, especially when he's been drinking, which he seems to be doing more and more often. His sister hadn't been quick enough to race upstairs last time Dad'd come in, stinking of alcohol and with a mean look on his face.

The boy hates it when his father takes his rage out on his sister. She is so little and frail, but nevertheless, each time she falls foul of his mood, the boy jams his fingers in his ears to block out her shrieks, afraid to challenge the man that is supposed to care about them. He will save them when he gets older and bigger. He'll become a footballer and take them far away.

That reminds him – he needs another plaster from the medicine cabinet. His blood blisters are really big now and the largest burst during the match, splattering warm blood into his sock and making his foot squelchy. His football boots are too small for him and press on his feet. He'd squeezed them on again today but he'll be in danger of breaking his toes soon. There is no way he is going to be able to get new ones, not unless he steals some.

He'd considered asking his mother for a pair of second-hand boots from one of the numerous charity shops that are in the area, but now the emergency money has gone, that isn't likely to happen. He'll have to work out how to steal a pair.

'I wouldn't take the money,' he says finally, wiping his finger around the plate, scooping up the last of the sticky strawberry jam.

His mother shakes her head. 'Yeah. I know you wouldn't. I had to ask though.' Her words are carried on a breath of air that comes from deep inside and keeps escaping. Her head and shoulders drop. It's like she's deflating.

He sticks the finger in his mouth, sucks at it until the final sugary residue has gone. His mother doesn't speak again. She stares out of the window onto the street, where two women are chatting animatedly while two small girls run around the lamp post, giggling wildly. He puts his plate in the sink. He's still hungry but it'll be pointless to ask for more food. If the money's gone then his father must have taken it. His mother's been saving that money for ages – a little each week.

He pads to the small box room that serves as his bedroom, and stares out of the window onto the street below. The two girls are now further along the road and still laughing. A little dog has joined them and they're taking it in turns to throw a ball for it. It pirouettes for the ball to be thrown and darts after it, tail high. Suddenly he spots his father rounding the corner and striding down the road, scowling like he does when he's had a bad day, and he's immediately aware of how miserable and dark it feels in his world. Outside is freedom. Inside is a prison he can't escape.

Outside is another world. As far away as the moon.

CHAPTER SEVEN

Lauren Gregson was still in a state of shock and her cheeks were drained of colour. She wore a delicate chain and silver heart around her slender neck, and a pale pink baggy sweater that swamped her frame. She tugged at the sleeves, pulling them over her hands so only her long fingers were visible, and looked up. Robyn had seen others wearing the same haunted look, not yet fully comprehending the enormity of what they'd learned, carrying on as normally as they could until they were suddenly side-swiped by it and crumbled. Lauren was close to the edge. The family liaison officer, Sheryl Morris, a veteran in this line of work, was making tea in the tiny cottage kitchen. Robyn heard the whine of the kettle as it boiled and the gentle tinkling of spoons against china as she prepared the drinks. She glanced towards Anna Shamash, who exuded calm and compassion – qualities required for this part of their job.

'I keep expecting Henry to walk through the door.' Lauren looked towards Robyn. 'And thinking it's all a huge mistake and you've identified the wrong man.' Her voice was soft. She blinked back a tear that had formed.

The woman's fragility was palpable. Robyn understood what she was going through. She'd experienced the same emotions and thoughts when she'd learned Davies was dead.

'Here we go.' Sheryl placed mugs of tea in front of Robyn and Anna and handed another to Lauren before settling down beside her on the settee. Sheryl's presence was welcome and helped make the situation less awkward. Lauren sipped her tea, clutching the mug between her hands so tightly her knuckles turned white, and gave a nod.

'Are you feeling up to talking to us?' Robyn asked.

Sheryl gave the woman a smile of encouragement. 'You're doing really well,' she said.

Lauren breathed in shaky, small gulps of air then nodded again.

'I'm going to ask a few questions and if at any time you want to stop, just say the word. Okay?'

Lauren's head moved up and down slowly as if in a daze. She looked at Sheryl, who gave another smile.

Robyn spoke again. 'What can you tell us about yesterday, before Henry left to go out?'

'Not much. I was a bit miffed because it was our first Valentine's Day together in our home, and I'd taken the day off from work – I'm an estate agent – and planned on cooking us a special meal together, but he'd swapped shifts at work at the last minute without consulting me. He knew I was upset about it so he made me a special breakfast in bed to make up for it.' She wiped away more tears that had formed. 'He bought me this necklace. I… I…'

She fingered the chain bearing a silver heart and there was a moment of silence as Lauren struggled to regain control. 'He texted me as soon as he got to work. Said he was sorry about the meal and he'd make it up to me.'

'And that was about what time?'

'Just before ten. His shift began at ten.'

'You said he swapped shifts?'

Lauren bit her lip. 'Yes, it was last minute. He swapped with Daisy.'

'Daisy?'

'She's one of his colleagues. Been there a couple of years, I think. Single mum. She usually works on stock control, shelf-stacking, that sort of thing. She asked him last minute if he'd cover for her. Her childminder couldn't have the kids as planned. That's why he went in. To cover for Daisy.' She paused and looked about, eyebrows raised and lowered in confusion.

'Had Henry seemed concerned or anxious about anything at all?'

'He was quieter than usual but that was because of personal issues. We've been trying for children without success. The doctor suggested we had tests to make sure everything was working normally, and Henry was pretty anxious about his results. He was convinced it was his fault, especially as mine showed I was healthy and able to conceive. Henry went to the fertility clinic in Tamworth last Friday. His results are due this week.' Her face crumpled. 'This can't be happening,' she wailed.

Sheryl patted her hand.

'I don't understand why Henry was found on Cannock Chase. He was at the store. He texted me saying he was at the store. He couldn't have been on Cannock Chase.' Her voice rose and she clutched the mug more tightly.

'Lauren, we're going to talk to the store manager about it. Henry might have been sent out for some reason and stopped off on the Chase,' Robyn said.

'Liam. Liam's the store manager. He's a good friend of ours too. We see a lot of him and his girlfriend, Ella. Henry is godfather to their daughter Astra. They'll be devastated.' The words came automatically, without true comprehension of what was being said. Finally, Lauren lifted her head to Sheryl and whispered, 'He's really gone, hasn't he?'

The silent sobs seemed to rise from her core, and her chest lifted and dropped several times as she fought to regain control. 'What am I going to do without him? I can't cope on my own. This place. Our home. I can't stay here. It was okay with both of us paying the rent but now… What will I do?'

Robyn felt her heart sink further. The woman would have so much more to deal with than the loss of her husband. They waited until she'd calmed down.

'We won't trouble you any further, Lauren. I'm very sorry to have put you through this. I have only one more question. Do you own a computer or laptop?'

'We do. It's in the spare room. Why?'

'If you don't mind, we'd like to take it with us.'

Lauren nodded. 'Go ahead. I don't use it much. You can ask me about Henry again. I want to help. Please ask.'

'Did he mention falling out with anybody?'

'Fall out with Henry?' Lauren gave a short laugh. 'There were a few people he didn't get along with, but who gets on with everybody? A couple of the neighbours got sniffy about Henry parking too close to their houses and there were a few arguments about it. Where else are we supposed to park? It's not a private road. Anybody should be able to park there, especially people who live here who don't have a front driveway. They got really stupid about it and put plastic bollards in front of their houses, but Henry took them down and parked there anyway.' She shrugged.

'One of the cricket dads was majorly annoyed Henry hadn't played his son in a match last year, and had a right go at him in front of everybody, but apart from that, I can't think of anyone else. We didn't row that often either, only over silly little things. If we did, we always made up. He used to say we should never go to sleep on an argument. I was huffy with him about Valentine's Day. I never really thanked him for buying me a present. I should have been more grateful. That's the thing about life, isn't it? You don't appreciate what you have until it's too late.'

'What about his mother and sister?'

Lauren grimaced. 'Henry didn't have anything to do with either of them, so I don't know them very well at all. His mum's got Parkinson's, or Alzheimer's, or some other awful illness that's transformed her. He refused to even talk about her – I don't think he could – it hurt him too much to think of her as she is now. I suggested visiting them on a few occasions but he wouldn't go. Said whenever he'd visited in the past, she hadn't recognised him and it was too heartbreaking to go through that. He wanted to remember her as she used to be. She's in a care home in Stoke-on-Trent. As for Libby, I've only spoken to her on the phone, and she's always been curt with me. I invited her to our wedding but she didn't come. Apparently, she's got a drugs problem and Henry preferred to keep his distance from her. She's done some wacky things in the past, took an overdose and phoned him at the last minute, so he'd save her. Again, he rarely talked about her. I think he found it too embarrassing.'

'Did you speak to her a couple of weeks ago?'

'No, but she rang here. I was upstairs and heard Henry yelling at her. She was badgering him over something and he told her to go to hell. He was pretty upset afterwards. I can't tell you any more than that.'

'Did he have any other friends, other than Liam and Ella?'

'He knew a few people in the village through cricket. He plays for the village team and he coaches the young cricket team players too. I wouldn't say they were friends as such. He gets along with them and sometimes has a drink with them in the pub, but he doesn't have many close friends.'

'Does he not have any old school friends or other acquaintances?'

Lauren shook her head. 'He had a fairly shitty upbringing on a council estate in Stoke-on-Trent. From what he told me, he didn't much enjoy his childhood. He couldn't wait to get away from the place, and as soon as he was able to, he took off. Went to London for a while, but found it too full-on. Then he moved back up to Staffordshire and worked in various towns at various jobs – didn't put down any roots until we met. He was searching for somewhere cheap to rent. I showed him around a few properties and we hit it off. I found him a really nice, reasonably priced flat, and he took me out to dinner to celebrate.' She smiled at the memory. 'I found this cottage for us too; one of the perks of working at an estate agency – you hear of bargain-priced houses and rented accommodation before they're officially advertised. It's not very big but we both adored it – the setting, the village – it was perfect for us. He loved living here, said it was like being on holiday all the time.'

She handed over a framed photograph of them as newly-weds. In it, Henry had shorter hair but the same wide smile that stretched across his face. He looked content. Robyn could see this was a man happy with his lot in life. His arm was wrapped around his bride and both were bathed in a glow of happiness. It was such a shame his life had been snatched from them.

Robyn needed to eliminate Lauren as a possible suspect. There was no easy way of putting her next question. 'After Henry went to work, what did you do?'

Lauren looked dazed. 'You surely don't think…' Her words dried on her lips and she stared open-eyed at Robyn. 'I loved him,' she said almost in a whisper.

Robyn gave an apologetic nod. 'We have to ask.'

Lauren drew a shaky breath. 'I arrived at the John Lewis car park at about eleven twenty. I mooched about the store for a while and then made my way through Touchwood Shopping Centre, stopping at French Connection to try on a pair of trousers. Then I went to Café Rouge for a salad and coffee.' Her head seemed to bounce with each sentence as she thought about her movements. 'I've got a receipt for that. It'll show the time on it. After lunch, I went to the House of Fraser and had a mini beauty makeover at the Clarins counter so I'd look nice for the evening, when Henry came home. And then, I left sometime before four. I got back at just after five. No sooner had I got in than the officers arrived to tell me they'd found Henry.'

'And you were alone all day?'

'No. I was in a town full of people. What are you getting at?'

'You didn't meet up with anybody who can confirm you were there?'

Lauren's eyes filled. 'No. But if you ask at the make-up counter in House of Fraser, they'll remember me. You can't possibly think I've anything to do with Henry's death.' She began to sob. Robyn wouldn't be able to ask any further questions. Sheryl put a friendly arm on the woman's shoulder to comfort her, and Robyn decided it was time to go. As they left the cottage, Anna cast a look behind her.

'She's not much older than me,' she said, shaking her head slowly. 'What a shit thing to happen. I expect they'd made all sorts of plans for the future and now—'

'We have to keep an open mind, Anna. We still have to check that her alibi is sound. We can only work with facts, not our personal feelings, and hope we get it right.'

Anna slipped into the driver's seat. 'Yes, guv. I can't help but feel sorry for her though.'

Robyn looked at the cottage as they pulled away. 'I wonder if he'd been planning a clandestine meeting on Cannock Chase. It happens,' she said, catching a look from Anna. 'He wouldn't be the first man to lead a double life.'

'You saw his wife. She's beautiful. Do you really think he'd want to have sex on the side?'

Robyn shrugged. 'He might. She might. You heard what she said about trying for a baby. What if she, like Henry, believed he was impotent and had become involved with somebody else who was able to make her pregnant? At this stage we have to consider every possibility, no matter how wild it might seem. We'll know more once the techies have looked at his phone and we've seen what's on his computer. We need to have hers checked out too. Until that happens, we have to consider all angles, even if they seem distasteful or wrong.'

'I suppose so. People can behave strangely.'

CHAPTER EIGHT

Anna and Robyn headed back to the station. Connor Richards, head of Forensics, was set up and expecting them, his warm smile a sharp contrast to Tom's scowl as he bashed away at his computer keyboard, ignoring them all. As soon as Robyn was ready, she tipped Connor the nod and he began.

'It's early days and there's still a lot to check. We completed a thorough search of all of the immediate surrounding area, and there was indeed evidence of trampled grass at the scene, in some bushes approximately five metres from the car. We collected a cigarette end, crisp packet and dark fibres from clothing made of a cotton and polyester mix. They might be relevant. As for footprints, there are quite a few of varying sizes along the trail as you can imagine. It was a very large area to search and we covered all the car park and the trail itself.

'These are the most important finds to date: fingerprints on Gregson's Kia belonging to him and his wife Lauren, and a third set of prints, yet to be identified.'

He passed out a copy of the fingerprints, the loops and whorls clearly visible.

'There were partials and an entire, clear print on the passenger door handle, and two more belonging to the same anonymous person on the door itself. There were also partial prints belonging to Mrs Gregson on the steering wheel. We collected several hairs and fibres, which we believe belong to the victim and his wife. We're still testing them.' Connor illuminated the overhead projector and slid in a transparency. A map of the clearing and surrounding area appeared on the screen.

'Fragments of the bullet that killed Henry Gregson have now been removed from his body and we've identified it as a .455 cartridge. They've been sent for further forensic examination. Although we were unable to locate the weapon used, we found evidence of several areas of trampled grass especially here, about three metres from the vehicle.' He pointed towards the spot marked on the map with an X.

'Based on the angle of the victim's body, the entry wound and the blood spatters, it's possible to conclude the bullet followed a trajectory from this vicinity into the vehicle.' His finger followed the arc he'd drawn on the transparency.

'The cross, marked on the map as A, is where we found a small area of trampled grass. It is in and around a Scots pine tree.'

Robyn recalled the open space. The attacker could have had a good view of the car's passenger side from there and remain unnoticed by the driver.

Connor searched the officers' faces, waiting for questions. Mitz had one.

'Could he have seen his attacker?'

'I can't answer that but it would make sense for the offender to step to one side to fire the pistol. As I said, it's a clean shot and the perp must have had a good visual on his victim.'

Robyn kept silent. Mitz's comment had her thinking. If Henry Gregson had seen his assailant and not leapt from the car, or driven away, he must have known them. Unless it all happened so quickly he couldn't react. That made her consider a second question. Had

Gregson recognised his assailant's intent at the last minute and deliberately thrown his mobile under his seat to conceal it?

'We discovered dark fibres on the tree trunk where an individual had rubbed against the bark. These matched fibres under the bush marked B, where we located footprints. There were no other matching fibres in the area, or in the car.

'Finally, in spite of the heavy rain, we found five distinct footprints along the Gruffalo Trail itself, close to where the boy strayed. Two prints definitely belong to children. The third footprint is a size seven print, made by a hiking boot. The fourth is a size six ladies' Rieker shoe print, and the last is most definitely made by a size ten trainer. This final print was identical to other prints found in the undergrowth, particularly under the bush marked B, where we found the clothing fibres. We believe this trainer to be a Nike LunarGlide 8. As you can see, it has a distinct, simplistic sole pattern, like a topographical map, and bears the Nike logo.' He flicked on the overhead projector and flashed up a picture of a cast of the trainer, followed by a photograph of the side, overhead and sole.

'Based on the size of the shoe and the stride length, you're probably searching for somebody five foot ten or eleven. The depth of the print indicated that person was running before they turned off the trail. Examination of the wear pattern on the shoe – or rather, lack of wear pattern – shows these were brand new shoes.' He turned off the overhead projector.

'Thank you, Connor.'

'I know it's not as much as you hoped for. We're still working on it. I'll be in touch as soon as I have more for you.'

As soon as Connor had left, Robyn searched for information online about .455 cartridges. It appeared that such a cartridge was used in Smith & Wesson Webley revolvers, weapons that had been standard issue for the armed forces up until 1963. There weren't many such cartridges in circulation, which made it all the more curious. There were more popular weapons, with more readily available ammunition. Was the perpetrator an ex-serviceman still in possession of their firearm, or had they bought it on the street? Such weapons, along with a host of others, including converted replicas, were easily acquired on the streets these days.

With that in mind, she tackled the list of Henry Gregson's acquaintances using the general database to establish if any were ex-military. Her efforts were in vain, and having turned up nothing of note, she turned her attention to the list of those who were in some way connected to Henry Gregson. It appeared on the surface to be an insurmountable task, but she had patience, and no task was too daunting. She'd do it after she'd spoken to Libby Gregson.

☀

It was almost midday when Robyn and Anna pulled into Longdon Road and knocked at flat number fifty-five – a downstairs apartment in a dingy block. Libby Gregson, the victim's sister, dark-eyed and pale-faced, opened the door and ushered them into a sitting room, where a skinny woman in her fifties, dressed in an overlarge, pink cardigan, skirt, thick tights and large furry slippers, sat staring vacantly into space, an open magazine on her knees. She turned to look at them; as she did so, the cardigan slipped from her shoulder.

'This is my mother, Kath,' Libby said as she moved across the room with the grace of a dancer, pulled her mother's cardigan back over her shoulder, did up the top button and stroked her hair in a gentle gesture. 'Mum, these detectives have come to talk about Henry,' she said.

The silver-haired woman nodded, her eyes darting left to right in confusion. When she spoke, her voice was thin and reedy. 'We went to see him yesterday.'

Libby shook her head. 'No, we didn't, Mum.'

'I'm sure we did. We went in the car to see Henry.' She smiled and Robyn could see that once she'd been a good-looking woman.

Libby let out a huff of exasperation. 'We didn't see Henry. You haven't seen him in ages. He doesn't come any more.' She moved away from her mother, brows furrowed. 'She gets confused easily. She hasn't seen Henry for two years. Not since she was diagnosed with Alzheimer's. He said he couldn't bear to watch her decline. He stopped visiting. Mum constantly thinks he's been when he hasn't.'

The tone of her voice implied frustration and irritation but she maintained a steady gaze. 'Come into the kitchen. She'll be okay in here. Mum, I'm going in the kitchen with these officers.'

'Is Henry coming to visit today?' her mother asked.

'*No*, Mum. He isn't.'

Kath's face took on a fresh look of bewilderment.

'Why don't you read your magazine and I'll come in with a cup of tea in a minute?' Libby moved them into the adjacent kitchen and sighed. 'It's true then,' she said with a finality that cut through Robyn.

'I'm very sorry, Miss Gregson.'

Libby pressed her lips together in an attempt to control her emotions. Her face was very like Henry's but with softer features, and her hair, slightly darker than his, hung in ringlets around her neat face. Looking at her, Robyn put her in her late twenties.

'Mum doesn't understand what's happened. I told her but she can't accept it. It's the illness. She can't remember much. Some days, she thinks Henry is still a boy and is going to come home from school. She's no idea who I am half of the time. It's hard.' She reached for a cigarette packet, pulled one out and held it up. 'Okay if I smoke?'

Robyn nodded. Libby lit it and dragged deeply. Pale grey smoke curled from her nostrils upwards to the ceiling, and she let out another sigh.

'If there's any way we can be of assistance, please let us know. Mrs Gregson has a liaison officer with her. If you require any—' Robyn didn't get to finish. Libby shook her head vehemently.

'We'll be fine. I haven't seen him in so long, it's not like we were close any more. We used to be. Before we grew up and apart. That seems such a long time ago. What can you tell me? Your officer only gave me a few details – that Henry had been found dead on Cannock Chase.'

'We're waiting for the pathology report this morning and then we'll let you know more.'

'How did he die? I want to know.' Libby cast a furtive look through the open door at her mother in the next room.

'I'm afraid he was shot.'

Libby drew a breath and let it out slowly. 'Poor Henry. I hope he didn't suffer.' She took a second to compose herself before speaking calmly. 'He took off when he was eighteen. Never liked it around these parts. He'd come back now and again, but like I said, once Mum took ill, he stopped visiting. I was still living at home and was working as a nurse, so the job of looking after her fell to me. One of us had to do our duty and stand by her. So, while Henry was off enjoying his life, and shirking his responsibilities, I was here.' She sucked on the cigarette greedily, inhaling deeply, and then stubbed it out on an ashtray.

'Stress,' she said, by way of an explanation, looking at the unfinished cigarette end. 'I managed to kick the habit. Didn't touch one for a whole eighteen months, then Mum became more of a handful and I took it back up again this year. So, as I was saying, Henry hasn't been in our lives much. He and I had an almighty row about it. I told him I was sick of him coming around only when it suited him. I was tired of him waltzing up here to play the doting son, bring her chocolates, flowers, get her all excited, and disappear again, leaving her more confused. I had to put up with her talking endlessly about how wonderful he was, and yet it's me who's been here for her every day. It's me who's had no life to call my own because she needs me. It's like looking after a child and sometimes an angry child at that.

'Henry didn't care. He just did his own thing. Like he always did. He dossed about, going from one place to another, and then he met Lauren. Didn't hear from him for ages, then suddenly I got a call to say he was getting married. We got an invite to the wedding but we couldn't go. Mum took a bad turn at the time and was too ill. I could have left her in day care and gone alone and buried the hatchet, but what difference would it have made? He'd have still been Henry – selfish, irresponsible Henry.'

Robyn mulled over what Lauren Gregson had told her. Lauren's version differed greatly to what she was seeing here. Lauren believed Kath to be in a care home. It appeared that Henry had lied to his wife.

Libby continued her monologue. 'He didn't bring Lauren to visit us – not once. I offered to drive across with Mum a couple of times, but he made excuses about them being busy and so on. I gave up. It was transparently obvious he didn't want either of us over. I've never understood why Lauren didn't want to make any contact with us though – try to persuade him – or even visit on her own. We're related, after all. I asked Henry about that and his response was they'd both decided it was better for Mum if they didn't visit and confuse her. Bloody liars!

'I spoke to him two weeks ago. I phoned him because Mum's been getting really needy recently, as you may have noticed. She's been talking about him more than usual, and the Alzheimer's is really taking hold. She'll have to be admitted into full-time care very soon. I can't look after her alone any longer. I thought I ought to let him know. I needn't have bothered. He told me to do whatever I wanted to do. Just like that. How selfish is that?'

She turned sad eyes on Robyn. 'I was so angry with him I slammed the phone down. Now… Well, now I wish it had turned out differently.'

Anna, who'd been standing quietly, gave her an understanding smile. Robyn rested her gaze on Kath in the chair in the next room. Her eyelids were drooping shut and her head was falling backwards as she began to doze.

'So you never met or spoke about Lauren – Mrs Gregson – with Henry?'

Libby looked away briefly. 'I spoke to her on the phone – a few words. He mentioned her a couple of times, but to be honest, I wasn't interested in her. Had her down as a self-centred bitch.'

'What did he say about her?'

'Just they were having a few problems. He rang me for some sympathy.' She tutted. 'That was Henry – always the needy one. He was feeling low and needed me to make sympathetic noises. Funny that, because he never made any time for me, not when I was feeling upset or sick of looking after Mum. Just left me to get on with it. Honestly, some days, I could've—' She pressed her lips together to halt the words.

'I gave up everything to look after our mother. I put my career on hold to become her full-time carer. I often ask myself why I did that. Henry certainly wouldn't have. But I did. And you know why? Because she's my mother and I didn't want some stranger tending to her personal needs, somebody who had no idea of the love she'd shown us over the years, or who really cared about her. I gave up a social life – boyfriends and opportunities – to be here with her, washing her, feeding her and watching her fade away, a little more every day. And I'd do it all again if I had to. You only get one mother. She's mine. I wish Henry had felt more that way.

'When I first became her carer, I thought it would only be for a short while, but it's been much longer than I expected, and all the while, Henry was elsewhere, not even thinking about us. He found a new love – Lauren. He was going to have a new family and then that didn't happen. They didn't have the children they hoped for. He rang me one afternoon and cried because Lauren blamed him for her not falling pregnant. He asked me if I thought it was likely to be his fault.'

'That seems a strange thing to ask your sister.'

Libby shook her head. 'No. You misunderstand. He wanted to ask my professional opinion, as a nurse. I told him it was possible his fertility had been threatened by the damage he sustained years ago, but unlikely, and recommended he see a specialist in these matters. He was involved in a fight years ago, and got kicked in the groin. I don't know how bad it was – we never discussed it. We were both a lot younger then and it wasn't the sort of stuff we shared. However, it was bad enough for him to be taken to hospital. He hadn't told Lauren about the incident. He was too scared to. Can you believe that? Too scared to tell his own wife.'

'So, you think he and Lauren had fallen out over this?'

'Definitely. She made him sleep on the settee. Was even talking of splitting up with him. That's why he was upset when he called me. I tried to be sympathetic, but I have enough to handle here without listening to my brother's reproductive problems.'

Robyn digested this information before continuing. 'Bearing in mind what you've just told us, Miss Gregson, can you think of any incident or anybody from his past that you think might be significant? Had he ever had any trouble with an individual or individuals?'

'He rubbed one or two people up when he was a teenager, but nothing serious. He was one of a gang of kids from around here who got up to mischief. There wasn't much else to do in those days. I think that's one of the reasons he left – boredom. You think somebody deliberately killed him?'

'We're investigating all possibilities. It might have been an accident. We can't say for sure yet.'

Libby looked at the cigarette end again and shook her head. 'You must think I'm such a cow. I've done nothing but slag him off. I don't mean to sound like I don't care about what's happened. Of course I care. He always looked out for me when I was younger. He was my big brother.' Her voice finally cracked.

❋

Anna drove from Longdon Road, leaving Robyn in the passenger seat to dwell on what she'd heard and observed. Henry had lied to his wife about his mother being in a home, but had he also lied to her about Libby being on drugs and about saving her after she overdosed? Something else didn't add up. Surely, Libby wouldn't have given up everything in her life to care for her mother. While Libby had been dealing with Kath, who'd suddenly called out, her mobile, on the table in front of them, had lit up with a message. Although it had only been visible for a moment or two, Robyn had noticed the name of the sender – Tarik Akar – and had read the message before it disappeared:

> *Remember – just keep quiet about it and it'll be okay*
> *Luv U*

She pondered its significance. What was Libby to keep quiet about? Was it linked in any way to their visit, or was she reading too much into it?

'Anna, what did you make of her claim she had no life?'

Anna considered the question, and without taking her eyes from the road, she said, 'It was nonsense. She was wearing a trendy jumper and designer jeans, and make-up. She wouldn't sit around the house all day with her mum dressed like that. She must have friends, and there's support for carers in similar situations so they can have free time. She doesn't sit in that house day after day, does she? She must have some life.'

'My thoughts exactly. When we get back, will you do a little digging on her, please? And find out if she has any friends called Tarik. Try the clinic where she used to work, and social media.'

'Sure. You think she might have gone after her own brother?'

'She definitely bore a grudge against him for leaving her to support and look after Kath alone.'

Anna's face screwed in concentration, and with eyes still trained on the road, she voiced her thoughts. 'Do you think it's possible that last phone conversation they had pushed her over the edge? Lauren said she heard Henry shouting at Libby. And he told Lauren that Libby takes drugs. If she was high, or not thinking straight through drug usage, she might have decided to kill him – or it could even have been an accident and she hadn't meant to actually kill him, just scare him.'

'It's conceivable. Libby has no concrete alibi for her whereabouts yesterday, only her word she was at home all day with her mother.'

'Her mother insisted they saw Henry yesterday. What if they did? What if Libby drove her mother to visit him?'

'We'll check to see if her Toyota passed through any of the ANPR points in the Stafford area. That'll answer that question. Her mother has Alzheimer's. It's likely she doesn't have any idea if she did or didn't see Henry. I don't think we can take what she says too seriously. However, we'll check. I never take anything for granted.'

Anna grunted a response. Robyn was glad Anna felt the same way as her. Her instincts rarely let her down, and for now, she wasn't 100 per cent convinced Libby Gregson was who or what she made herself out to be.

CHAPTER NINE

DAY TWO – WEDNESDAY, 15 FEBRUARY, AFTERNOON

They stopped at the station to drop off Anna. Tech-savvy Anna had worked in computing before joining the force and Robyn wanted her to check out the Gregsons' computer, as well as find out everything she could about Libby and the mysterious Tarik.

'Get into any social media accounts the Gregsons might have, search Henry and Lauren's browsing history and see if either was signed up to any dating websites, or if there's any suspicious online activity. They can't be perfect. None of us is perfect. There has to be some reason he's been murdered and there may be some online trail that will enlighten us.'

Anna's face brightened slightly. She always appeared to be most content when hunting online for information.

❀

The twenty-five-minute journey passed quickly. Robyn checked her rear-view mirror and turned into Beacon Street. As she did so, she caught a glimpse of the three spires of Lichfield Cathedral. The last time she'd driven down this street was when she was following one of her famous hunches and chasing after a perp the media had named the Lichfield Leopard. It brought back memories of the night when she was unsure of herself but guided by her instinct she'd found her killer. Davies had always said she had phenomenal instinct yet it had let her down the day he supposedly left for his rendezvous in Morocco. *Stop it!* She had to put Davies out of her mind for a while. She couldn't let him dominate her thoughts.

She drew up outside the convenience store Henry had worked at and, having found a suitable parking space, headed towards the store. The door opened and a woman with a buggy emerged, a full plastic bag dangling from one hand. Robyn held open the door. She waited as the buggy was manoeuvred through, her gaze resting on a small, serious face in a woollen hat staring up from under a fluffy blanket. The woman departed and Robyn entered. The inside of the store was brightly lit and smelt of warm bread. Several aisles were in front of her, to the right were two checkout tills, and to the left, a kiosk and counter where cigarettes and lottery tickets were sold.

Liam Carrington, the store manager and Henry Gregson's best friend, was at the back of the store, talking to a woman in her late fifties who was wearing a white shop uniform bearing the MiniMarkt logo and a blue hair protector. The smell of baked bread was strongest here, causing Robyn's stomach to gurgle. The memory of eating warm croissants on a balcony in Paris with Davies threatened to overtake her, but she drove it back into the recesses of her mind and strode towards Liam. He looked up, acknowledged her with a nod, said something to the woman and joined Robyn.

'You must be DI Carter,' he said, holding out his hand. 'PC Marker phoned me and told me to expect you.'

'Thank you for taking time to speak to me. Can I say how sorry I am about Henry Gregson? I understand you were close.'

Liam's mouth turned downwards and his shoulders slumped. 'He was like a brother. He was such a good chap. Wouldn't harm a fly. He's godfather to my daughter Astra, you know? Took his role really seriously. He and Lauren saw Astra almost every week. Sometimes they'd take her to the park or zoo. Lauren even bought one of those little stickers for his car – 'Baby on Board'. They loved her to bits. Astra will miss him badly.' He shook his head sadly. 'One in a million. How's Lauren? Ella is going around to see her later. How's she bearing up?'

'It hasn't quite sunk in yet. She's got an officer with her at the moment. Ella's your girlfriend?'

'We live together,' he said distantly, staring at a couple in their late seventies now approaching them. The husband, wizened, with hair so thin his liver-spotted scalp was visible, was guiding his wife by the elbow, holding her gently as if she were porcelain. Her face was peculiar to look at – one side a darker shade than the other – and slightly distorted, as if she'd had an accident that had shattered the cheekbone. She shuffled forward, barely able to cover the distance across the floor.

'Look, shall we go out back? It's more private.'

Robyn agreed and was shown into a tiny kitchen come staff-room. There was a long bench against one wall behind a table, and opposite, a kettle and an array of white cups and mugs. Liam pulled a mug forwards.

'Tea?'

She shook her head. 'I just had one.'

Liam boiled the kettle and rested against the kitchen top, facing her. He was rangy and lean-faced, tiny pockmarked scars visible on his cheeks in the fluorescent lighting of the restroom. His hair was thinning and his hairline had receded to reveal a long forehead. He removed his round glasses and looked myopically at her. His hands trembled as he polished the lenses with the sleeve of his shirt.

Robyn spoke. 'I understand Henry swapped shifts with another staff member – Daisy – and was working yesterday. Can you tell me what time he clocked off?

Liam shook his head. 'No. No, he didn't come in yesterday. He didn't swap shifts with anybody. Daisy was here all day. I'd have known about it if he had.' As the kettle reached its boiling point, Liam's shoulders slumped again and Robyn watched his face crumple. He turned away from her and tears dripped onto the kitchen top. Robyn was once again helpless. She'd seen so much grief, and every time it ate into her soul. A person's life affected so many others. Their death, even more so. Robyn waited for him to regain control. When he finally faced her, his eyes were red-rimmed. He sniffed back tears and passed her a mug of tea.

'Did you want sugar?' he asked.

She shook her head and thanked him even though she'd already refused the drink. 'When did you last see Henry?'

Liam sniffed a couple of times. 'Erm, Monday. Monday morning. We were both in then. I left at eleven to go to the distribution warehouse in Stoke, to discuss a problem with a delivery. Henry was here when I left. I didn't get back until six, and by then, he'd gone off shift.'

'Did he seem okay to you that day?'

Liam nodded. 'Fine.'

'Lauren told me you're his best friend. Has he spoken to you about any troubles he was having – any problems or anxieties?'

Liam pondered the question. 'He wasn't worried about anything major – nobody threatening him or anything like that, if that's what you mean?'

'I was thinking along the lines of more personal problems. Was everything okay with his marriage? Did he ever talk to you about his relationship with Lauren?'

Liam shrugged. 'Well, yes. But I don't think that's relevant. He and Lauren were sound. They had a few differences but what couple doesn't?'

'I understand they had a minor fallout that upset Henry – it was about children.' Robyn hoped she wasn't being too pushy. Liam's face suggested she was treading on thin ice.

'They wanted children. As I said, they regularly took Astra out to the park, or out for the day. Lauren is desperate – no, make that obsessed – with getting pregnant, but they've had a few problems. One night, Lauren got overemotional and they rowed big time about it. Stupid things were said in the heat of the argument – she said he wasn't committed to her or to their relationship, and even accused him of seeing other women. She was wrong – very wrong. He loved Lauren and he'd have loved a baby. Maybe not immediately, but he wanted one in time. He didn't think they could afford a child, especially if Lauren became a stay-at-home mother like Ella. He asked me how I manage on my salary and I told him the truth – I barely do, but we get by. That was why they had a fallout. All couples row about stuff. Nobody has a perfect, lovey-dovey relationship. Do you, Detective?'

For a second, Robyn thought back to Davies – an angry Davies, red-faced through shouting – turning his back on her and marching towards the door, and an equally angry Robyn hurling a plate of uneaten food at the wall behind his retreating form. She shut her mind to it.

'I'm sorry to have to ask you such personal questions. It's important I get a complete picture of Henry. He didn't confide anything else? Anything else you can tell me that would throw light on why he was on Cannock Chase yesterday afternoon?'

He wiped his glasses absent-mindedly with some kitchen roll and checked for smudges before putting them back on.

'I can't think of any reason.'

'You say you went to Stoke on Monday. Did you ever meet Libby?'

He looked blankly at her. 'Who's Libby?'

'Henry's sister.'

'No – that can't be right. He told me he was an only child. His parents died a few years ago, in a boating accident while on holiday in Spain. He couldn't bear to talk about it.'

Robyn gave a sad shake of her head. 'That's not true. His sister lives with their sick mother, in Stoke-on-Trent.'

Liam's mouth flapped open. 'I had no idea. Why wouldn't he tell me that? I was his best friend. It makes no sense. I thought he was an honest sort of guy.'

'I'm sure he was honest. From what I can gather, his mother has a serious degenerative illness that caused her to no longer recognise her son. I expect he didn't want to burden you with his anxieties. He and his sister didn't get along too well either, so that would explain his reluctance to tell you.'

Liam nodded dumbly. 'I suppose so. We blokes don't like to wear our hearts on our sleeves. Henry was no different to most. I'd have listened though. If he'd needed to talk to me, I'd have listened. I really liked him. I don't have many friends and none like him. I'm going to miss him so much.'

'What did you talk about?'

'The usual: sport, work, life in general, news and all sorts of other stuff. We just got along. Some people do, don't they? You don't need to be talking all the time – sometimes it's a shared laugh at something, a few pints after work and a moan about how the team played at the weekend that makes a good friendship.'

'Did you talk about your families?'

He nodded. 'Mostly about Astra. She's always up to something to make me smile.' He gave a proud father smile that changed almost immediately. 'It's going to create a gaping hole in my little girl's life. She loves Henry and Lauren.' His head lowered again. Silence hung for a minute, then he spoke softly. 'It's going to be a huge loss to us all.'

Robyn left with the distinct impression Henry Gregson was a secretive individual. He'd lied to his best friend, family and wife. She wondered what else he'd lied about and if a lie had led to his death.

CHAPTER TEN

DAY TWO – WEDNESDAY, 15 FEBRUARY,
LATE AFTERNOON

Robyn tapped on the whiteboard with her black pen and summarised the information she'd given her team. Her heart was heavy at the thought of the phone call she'd just taken. Lauren Gregson had called to ask if there was any progress and to find out when her husband's body would be released. She wanted to make funeral arrangements. Her voice was weary and distant, as if the very act of phoning was too great a chore to handle. Robyn was again reminded of the pain she'd felt when she'd lost Davies. The urge to find Henry's killer was even greater now.

'To recap, all the occupants of those cars present in Cannock Chase car park yesterday have been interviewed, and none of them saw Gregson's car or Henry Gregson himself, or observed any unusual activity. Lauren Gregson believed her husband to be at work and received a text from him at just before ten in the morning to say he'd arrived at MiniMarkt. After that, she went shopping for the rest of the day. We have car park CCTV footage showing her arriving at John Lewis car park in Solihull at 11.21 a.m. and departing at 4.50 p.m. She can account for her movements and there are witnesses who will corroborate them. She stopped at a café for lunch and has a receipt for it, and she had a mini beauty makeover at a counter in the House of Fraser.' She paused to allow her officers to process the information.

'Henry Gregson lied to his wife about his mother being in a home and about his whereabouts yesterday,' Robyn said. She took a sip from a bottle of water before continuing.

'His friend and the manager of MiniMarkt, Liam Carrington, told me Gregson definitely took the day off from work yesterday and didn't come in to replace anybody. Carrington wasn't at the store himself but those on duty verified Gregson did not appear all day. Therefore, Gregson must have lied to his wife. Why? Where was he all morning and what was he doing on the Chase at lunchtime?'

Robyn looked around the room at her officers and continued. 'Gregson has an unblemished record at work, was well thought of and respected among the other members of staff. I spoke to two others who confirmed that Gregson was a unique man, caring and obliging. None of them knew of his whereabouts yesterday and assumed he was with his wife. Mitz, what have you got?'

'We monitored the hashtag GruffaloSpotters, and photographs were uploaded late yesterday afternoon by a Mrs Jane Dean. I followed them up and established that these were photographs taken by the family who were on Cannock Chase the same time as Mrs Price and her grandchildren. I took a statement from them earlier today – Mrs Dean heard a noise that sounded like a car backfiring or a firecracker. She didn't pay any attention to it at the time, but it was shortly before they left the park around 1.45 p.m. She also believes she caught a glimpse of a jogger ahead of her on the path. She described that person as wearing a dark hooded top and jogging bottoms. She couldn't elaborate or identify them as male or female.'

Robyn folded her arms. 'Good work, Mitz. So, we might have a sighting of our perp?'

'It seems that's possible. The children don't remember seeing anybody other than Mrs Price, Kyle and Aiden.' Mitz leant forward on his desk, studying the whiteboard.

Robyn unfolded her arms, wrote 'jogger' and folded them again. 'Anna?'

Anna, sitting on her desk at the back of the room, shook her head. 'Still working through the Gregsons' website history, caches and cookies. They use the computer for storing photographs, online shopping, watching YouTube videos, and for general searches. There are loads of searches to do with having children, reproductive health websites and forums, women's health, online sexual health sites and fertility treatments. I've also traced cookies to numerous marketplace sites that sell baby items: specialist sites, department stores, Amazon and Etsy sites that specialise in baby clothes and toys, christening gifts and so on. What was interesting was that the browsing history for all these sites has been deleted. Other searches – mostly for sports websites – are most likely her husband's. There are other websites but nothing that indicates they're anything other than squeaky clean.'

The door flew open and Shearer strode in, a sandwich in his hand, jaw moving up and down. He halted and chewed faster.

'Sorry,' he said, wiping a crumb from his face. 'Don't mind me.' He dropped onto his chair and began tapping at his keyboard, his dark eyebrows furrowed.

Robyn tried to ignore him. 'David, you talk to the tech department?'

'They had a rush on some other equipment but they're working on his mobile now. However, I've got a log of the calls Gregson made over the last month and those he made yesterday.' He held up a list. 'I'm about to check them out. Techies say he didn't finish typing his last text message and there's no recipient. This is what he typed.'

Robyn collected the paper and read it out. 'I can't keep this secret. Will have to—' She wrote the words out on the board. 'I imagine he didn't finish typing because at that moment, he was shot, or surprised, and dropped his mobile. What do you think?' She caught Shearer looking across. It was unnerving knowing he was listening to her and no doubt judging how she operated.

'Gregson was keeping a secret. That leaves it wide open. It could be any sort of secret. An affair, for example?' said Matt.

'I don't want to jump to any conclusions, so while we might have our own theories as to what the secret might be, all we know for sure is Gregson was keeping one.'

Robyn folded her arms. 'Imagine this scenario and feel free to disagree with it: Gregson arranged to meet his killer to discuss this secret. The killer arrived ahead of the scheduled meeting and lay in wait for him. Gregson pulled up and waited. While he was waiting he began to type a message. For some reason, he lowered his passenger window, at which point he was shot. Might he have been texting because he thought the killer wasn't going to show up?' She waited for a second to check all were following her argument. When no one spoke, she continued.

'The phone flew out of his hand and landed underneath his seat. Did the attacker open the car door and try to locate Gregson's mobile because it might have incriminating evidence on it, or did he leave it and attempt to flee the scene?'

Mitz breathed in and spoke. 'That's a likely scenario. I'd like to add another possibility, that Gregson spotted his assailant while he was texting, lowered the window to call to him, and was shot.'

'I like that idea. That works well and explains why the window was lowered on a cold, wet day. I also wondered if he might not have deliberately attempted to conceal his mobile at the last minute to protect evidence.'

'But he didn't write in the name of the person he was contacting. There is no evidence. Normally, I choose a contact and then message them; I don't write a message and then decide who to send it to,' said Anna.

'Ah, but you might if you didn't know their number. What if it wasn't somebody already in your contact list, or was an unfamiliar number? You might write out a message and then add the number, wouldn't you?' shouted Matt, delighted with himself.

'Good. Yes. So, let's move on from the theories and look at what we know for sure. A jogger was spotted in the area and we need to track him or her down. That could be a difficult task. It could be somebody who lives nearby, or a regular jogger. I run over the Chase some weekends. All I'll say is it was either a keen jogger, because as we know yesterday was a very cold and wet day, or maybe even the killer. Matt, it's a long shot, but would you talk to occupants of houses in the area in case it was one of them running?'

Robyn thought about her friend, Tricia, who sometimes trained with her. She knew Tricia through her local gym and had become friends with her after solving a case involving one of Tricia's friends. Robyn liked to run alone but they'd occasionally run together and often over on Cannock Chase. 'And try a few local gyms and running clubs. It's possible the lone jogger was a member of a group who regularly used the Chase. Another long shot, but what else can we do?' She shrugged an apology.

'As for suspects, we've got his sister, Libby, who was supposedly at home in Stoke-on-Trent with her sick mother. She says she didn't leave the house all day. We're checking to see if that bears out.

'Then there's Liam Carrington, his co-worker, who lives in the village of Yoxall, ten miles from Lichfield. He was off work yesterday, looking after his three-year-old daughter, Astra, while his partner, Ella, visited a friend in hospital. He watched television with Astra for most of the morning. Just before lunchtime, he took her to the playground and onto the butcher's shop in the village, so no doubt somebody will confirm his whereabouts between 1 and 3 p.m. We'll verify that.'

She thought briefly of Liam, tears flowing down his cheeks in the back room at MiniMarkt, trying to be strong, but failing.

Shearer finished his sandwich, balled the plastic wrapper and threw it into the waste bin with a self-satisfied smile. Again, Robyn ignored him.

'Matt, find out what you can about Carrington – go to Yoxall and double-check his alibi. Anna, you've got your instructions and if you find anything that'd help prove Lauren was having an affair, let me know immediately. Mitz, I know it's highly unlikely because they use rifles that don't take .455 cartridges, but talk to the Forestry Commission anyway to see if they've been shooting muntjac deer. I know they culled some a few years ago. Speak to the park ranger and establish who is allowed to shoot on the Chase and when they're allowed to. There's an outside chance this was an accident. I thought about checking with farmers in the area. Can you handle that?'

'Certainly can,' replied Mitz.

'Good, and request his financial records, in case there've been any larger sums paid into or come out of his account. I'm going to talk to the little boy who found Gregson. David, you ready? Time to put your recent training in handling children in these situations to good use. Let's see if we can wind this up soon, folks.'

She put down her pen and gathered her coat and bag. She avoided looking at Shearer, who she sensed was watching her. As she moved in front of the door, it flew open again, causing her to sidestep to prevent being hit, and Gareth Murray bowled through, a box of documents in his arms.

'Sorry, ma'am. I didn't know you were standing behind the door,' he said, trying to squeeze against the wall to allow her to pass.

She threw him a steely look. 'May I remind you of how many people are now occupying this office? In all likelihood, one of us will be near the door at any given time.'

She stomped down the corridor, wishing Flint would hurry up and find somewhere to house Shearer. She didn't like having him in her space. It stifled her thought process.

It was chilly outside; what her mother would have called 'fresh'. She didn't think often enough about her parents and she ought to. She had happy memories of them. For a moment she wished they were still alive and she wondered what they'd make of the mystery surrounding Davies. She felt a stab of sorrow. She couldn't carry on like this. She needed to solve this case and she needed to find out if Davies was alive. There was one person she could talk to. As much as she didn't want to involve her cousin Ross, she might have to. Ross was exactly the person to ask. The ex-policeman was now a personal investigator, and this was what he excelled at – finding lost people. She needed another opinion, and his would be the best. He'd know what she ought to do.

※

Eyes the colour of a perfect summer's day, fringed with lengthy sooty eyelashes, dominated Aiden Moore's cherub-like face. Wavy blond hair that tumbled to his shoulders added to the angelic impression. One hand clutched a soft toy Gruffalo; the thumb of the other was planted in his mouth as he sat beside his mother, nestled closely as if welded to her. His older brother, Kyle, a lean, sharp-featured boy who'd been jumping up and down on the well-worn settee, was now squirming about on a large chair, pulling at a thread that had come loose on the arm. His mother, Emma, oozed fatigue. Kyle had bombarded them all with question after question in the space of only a few minutes, and Robyn was under the impression life with him was one constant barrage of questions punctuated by wild antics.

David Marker was attempting to coax information from Aiden, who refused to speak and wriggled even closer to his mother's side.

Kyle pushed himself up onto his knees and spoke out. 'I don't have to stay inside, do I?'

David smiled at him. 'You've helped us a lot, Kyle.'

He twisted about and looked out of the window. 'Can I go outside now?' He got up without waiting for an answer. Emma looked at Robyn, who nodded.

'Yes, but you stay in the garden, understand? It's dark out there. Stay near the house,' said his mother.

Kyle jumped up and bounded out of the room.

Emma heaved a deep sigh and gave Aiden a squeeze. 'You okay, matey?' she asked. 'Want some juice?'

Aiden shook his head. Since his brother had given his version of what had happened along the path, Aiden had tightened his grasp on the toy Gruffalo. He pulled it tighter to him. Robyn had read up on the story the night before in readiness to talk to the boys. She had to find some common ground to connect with Aiden.

Robyn spoke gently. 'I love the Gruffalo because he looks scary with his claws and tusks and poisonous wart, but he isn't scary at all, is he? He's actually frightened of the little mouse. You see, things that look scary sometimes aren't at all. Did you see Mouse in the woods when you went with your granny?'

Aiden managed to nod. Slowly, he removed his thumb. 'On a tree trunk,' he said.

David picked up from Robyn's cue. 'And did you see Fox? Fox is my favourite. I love his bushy tail.'

Aiden shook his head.

'That might be because Fox saw you coming and ran away from you. Maybe you were scary like the Gruffalo. Or maybe Kyle frightened him away.' David smiled at the boy and the child gave another serious nod.

'Did you see the Gruffalo?' David pointed at his toy.

Aiden looked at it and gave a small nod.

'You saw the Gruffalo?' he said, with fake enthusiasm. 'Kyle said he didn't find the Gruffalo print. Did you find it?'

'I saw it and then I saw him.'

Robyn felt a tingle of anticipation. Neither boy was near the Gruffalo section at the time. Aiden couldn't have seen the Gruffalo footprint unless he was confused, or he meant he'd found a real footprint. She remained silent, allowing David to draw the information from the child.

'Was it on the path?'

'Yes.'

Robyn knew the Gruffalo footprint sign was further up the track. She'd studied the map of the route Anna had drawn. The character stops were marked, as was the point where Mrs Price had to slow down to catch her breath and where she lost sight of her grandchildren, and the exact spot where she and Kyle had found Aiden. Robyn had placed an X where the Kia had been stationed, about fifteen metres from the path in the clearing. David spoke again.

'Do you think the Gruffalo was hiding behind a tree because he was scared of you?'

Aiden shook his head, a small furrow across his brow.

'He might have been in the bushes, too frightened to come out and talk to you,' David said.

A look of concern flashed across the boy's face. David spotted it and fell silent. At that moment, the child's lips trembled. 'Not me. Not scared of me. He was scared of the man.'

Robyn caught David's eye and shook her head. They'd have to leave it for the moment. Aiden was hugging his toy again. Emma didn't want them to continue questioning him, and Robyn agreed. She didn't want to cause the little boy any undue stress. She left David to make arrangements for them to talk again. Aiden had seen something hiding in the bushes near him. Could it have been the killer? She'd have to wait until Aiden was able to tell them more.

CHAPTER ELEVEN

THEN

His sister is whimpering in her room. His father had been in a filthy mood this evening. His dinner had dried out in the oven while he'd been at the pub, and when he'd finally turned up to eat it, he was displeased. The boy had been watching the television when he heard the familiar sounds of raised voices and scraping chairs as his father laid into their mother. His sister had thrown him a look and they'd been about to melt away when they heard a sickening crash followed by silence. The boy had raced to the kitchen and found his mother on the floor, blood pouring from her face. His father was glowering at her.

'She's fine,' he'd growled as the boy threw himself onto the floor. 'Leave her.'

His sister, standing in the doorway, had started to cry.

'Mum.'

'I said leave her.'

His mother had struggled to sit up, a crimson ribbon of blood falling from her nose. She had pinched the bridge of her nose and winced. Her voice was thick. 'It's okay. Go,' she said.

He'd not wanted to leave. He'd wanted to help her. His father had ignored them all, pulled out a chair and began eating his dried dinner, stabbing at it angrily. He'd waved his fork at them. 'Shove off,' he'd said, mouth full of potato.

He'd taken his sister upstairs and cuddled her while she cried herself to sleep.

Now she's whimpering again. It happens frequently. He slips into her bedroom and sits on the bed.

'It's okay,' he says, stroking her hair. She's not asleep.

'He's going to kill her,' she says through gulps of air.

'No, he won't,' the boy replies, but his insides turn upside down at the thought. His mother accepts the blows and the shouting, too afraid to speak out about the man who beats her and her children.

They all live in perpetual fear in this silent house, and nobody outside it knows what goes on behind its walls.

CHAPTER TWELVE

Tom Shearer was lounging at his desk, shirt sleeves rolled up to his elbow. He exuded confidence but his face had darkened when he'd read the message that had been sent through for him, and Robyn could almost see his thought processes as his face twitched uncomfortably. His cocky attitude and supreme confidence only served to disguise how he truly felt about his job. He'd divulged as much one rare night when, after attending the funeral of an old school friend, he'd let his guard down and confessed he was a results man who hated the atrocities he faced.

He cleared his throat. 'Right. Listen up. An assault has taken place in Hurst Lane. There are two victims believed to be from the same family and both female. One is aged twenty-nine, the other in her sixties. Police are in situ but the attacker's taken a hostage and is holed up inside the house. Get to the incident room for a full briefing.'

Shearer, like Robyn, had a team of four working with him. The room was filled with the immediate scraping of chairs as they gathered up their necessary kit and hurtled out of the office, the drumming of boots on the floor like cattle running. Shearer followed swiftly behind, his face grim.

Robyn had been reading through Mitz's notes on Henry Gregson. She shifted from side to side in her chair. There wasn't anything in the notes that pointed to why Gregson had been killed. His bank accounts held no answers.

Her mind wouldn't settle. This wasn't like her. Ordinarily, she'd have leads and ideas and direction. At the moment, she felt stumped and she didn't like that feeling. She surveyed the mess of files and boxes at the far side of the room. She preferred order in her life, and having several more bodies cluttering the office was affecting her concentration and adding to her frustration. Or was she still half-thinking about Davies? She needed to get out of the office.

The door opened and Anna marched in, waving a file.

'Gregson's mobile,' she said, placing the file on Robyn's desk with a small smile of satisfaction. 'Both mobile and computer are clean – no current social media accounts, dating websites, porn, gambling sites, nothing.'

'You're kidding,' said David, looking up from his own computer. 'That's not possible. Surely there must be something – he's thirty-three. He must be on social media. I'm ten years older than him and I'm on it.'

'He had a Facebook account but he hasn't bothered with it for well over a year. There's not much of interest on his wall, mostly comments about football games, some sports clips taken off the web. He rarely posted on it. He had four friends. I contacted them and one has closed his account altogether, one knew him through football and two attended the same school as him. Nobody has heard from him in ages.'

'And what guy doesn't have some porn on his computer?' David muttered.

Anna shook her head. 'He's squeaky clean. Mainly visits sports and news websites, technology sites, forums about sport. I went through his deleted history too – nothing.'

Robyn found it difficult to believe. Henry had had a life before Lauren. He hadn't lived like a monk. And surely there'd been friends, acquaintances and other women in his life? He wouldn't have shut himself away and only watched sport. It didn't add up. Maybe he'd deliberately kept off such websites in case Lauren found out, and instead accessed them from a different computer. He was a man who kept secrets and who told lies; he'd be able to cover his trail if he had been accessing sites he didn't want his wife to know about. No, Henry Gregson wasn't as morally pure as he made out, she was sure of it.

Anna continued. 'He used WhatsApp messaging from his mobile. The details are in the file along with all the calls he made and received. That's Liam Carrington's number.' She indicated another number, highlighted in green. 'That's Carrington's partner's number – Ella. He rings or messages them regularly. He's godfather to their child, isn't he?'

'Yes. Liam Carrington said Gregson took that duty seriously and even looked after Astra on weekends. I expect that's why he phoned them so frequently,' said Robyn, running her finger down the list. 'Have you identified all these numbers?'

'All but that one,' said Anna, indicating the number. 'The tech department say it's a pay-as-you-go phone and it isn't operating any more.'

Robyn tapped the number with one finger. 'Gregson rang this number the morning of the fourteenth at ten past ten. And it appears to have rung him several times during the last fortnight.'

'Six times in total, and we can't throw any light on who owns the mobile, guv.'

Robyn tutted. 'This is ringing alarm bells. Pay-as-you-go numbers that are suddenly no longer in use seem highly suspicious to me.'

David spoke up. 'Might be a girlfriend's phone.'

Robyn's face pulled into a grimace. 'You could be right. Maybe his whole goody-goody image is a front. No prints on that mobile?'

'Only his.'

Anna interjected with a slight cough. 'Lauren Gregson is a big Snapchat user. She's got a Facebook account but she only uses it these days to play games. Looks like she used it far more before she met Henry. Posts trail off about eighteen months ago.'

'Glean much from her account?' Robyn asked.

'Only that she had several boyfriends before Henry – six of them in the three years she was using Facebook. She has loads of friends on Snapchat.'

'Stick with it. See what else you can learn. Mitz?'

'I've just got off the phone with a chap from the Forestry Commission. There's been no deer culling anywhere on Cannock Chase recently. He says that's not part of the Chase they tend to shoot in, especially given the Gruffalo Trail is in the vicinity. And it's unlikely a hunter would be in that area. The official was quite clear on rules and regulations on the Chase. Moreover, they definitely don't use .455 cartridges.'

Robyn's nostrils flared as she breathed out noisily. 'I think we can unequivocally say Gregson was murdered.' She rose and stood in front of the whiteboard, rubbed out 'accidental death'.

'Keep digging?' asked David.

She waved a finger at him. 'You got it. Anyone know where Matt is?'

'Yoxall. He's verifying Liam Carrington's story. Think he also planned on buying some juicy steaks at the butcher's while he was there. I put in my order too. You want anything bringing back, guv?' David grinned.

Robyn smiled back. Sometimes a little light-heartedness did them all good. 'Only evidence pointing to our killer,' she replied.

'I've got something interesting on Libby Gregson too,' said Anna. 'Unlike her brother, she's very active on Facebook. She's got over two hundred friends, most of whom live in or around Stoke, and several who were work colleagues. She's big on selfies. She must post pictures of herself at least twice a day. She never mentions her mother in any of her status updates. They're usually about television programmes, celebs, magazines or funnies from the Internet. She discusses various shows and has a laugh with her girlfriends. She's also into tattoos. Recently – the last six months – she's been posting pictures of the tattoos she's had done all over her body. Some of the pictures were taken down from the site due to complaints, and she fired off angrily at the so-called friends who reported them as pornographic.' Anna handed over a printout taken from Facebook. 'That's the latest one.'

Robyn looked at the pictures of a semi-naked Libby, back to the camera and wearing only a thong. Her back was a collage of red, black and blue stars and swirls that started at the base of her shoulder blade and travelled over her hips and buttocks and down the back of her legs. There was a large tattoo of a skull with angel wings across her spine, and under it the word 'Mother'. Anna pointed to a photograph, showing the underside of Libby's left forearm, and the fresh tattoo of a handgun shooting flowers.

Robyn looked up at Anna, who nodded. 'Might be something. Might be nothing.' Robyn had hauled in a suspect during the investigation into missing girls earlier that year because the man had hunting tattoos on his body and she was searching for a man calling himself Hunter. It had been the wrong call to make, and she wasn't keen to repeat the mistake. The tattoos might have no relevance. However, they proved Libby had another side to her personality and was not the put-upon and obedient daughter she painted herself to be. She'd posted this photograph late Monday afternoon, before Henry was shot.

'Either way, we'll need to talk to her again. Anything on Tarik?'

Anna nodded. 'I think so. There's a Tarik Akar who's one of her friends on Facebook. He's a car mechanic in the centre of Hanley

– works for Mike's Motors. Attended the same secondary school as Libby and Henry. Married. Got a younger brother and a younger sister, both of whom went to the same school.'

'Look into their backgrounds before we go dashing off to Stoke-on-Trent to interview them both.'

She turned her attention back to the list of numbers and began studying the dates and times of the calls. The buzzing of her mobile broke her concentration.

'Carter,' she said, writing as she spoke.

'It's Emma Moore, Aiden's mum.' Her voice was quiet. 'Can you come over? Aiden told me why he thought the Gruffalo was hiding in the bushes. He said it was frightened of the man in the car. He also said the Gruffalo was wearing shoes and trousers. DI Carter, I think he might have seen the person who killed that man.'

CHAPTER THIRTEEN

DAY THREE – THURSDAY, 16 FEBRUARY,
LATE MORNING

Aiden was colouring in a picture of a house, lost in his own world, when Robyn turned up. Emma acknowledged Robyn and David but stayed seated on the edge of her chair, watching her son protectively.

'Hi, Aiden,' said Robyn.

The boy looked up for a second, gave a brief smile, then returned to the picture, his small hand clutching a red crayon and scooting it over the shape in front of him in untidy lines.

'You remember me and Robyn, don't you?' said David, dropping down onto the floor beside Aiden. 'We came yesterday.'

'Yes.'

David gave Robyn a small nod to encourage her to speak.

'Do you want to play a game?' Robyn said.

Aiden looked quizzically at her.

'It's a memory game. Are you good at remembering things? I bet you are.'

Aiden held on to his crayon but stopped colouring.

'Yesterday you told me you saw the Gruffalo. I've never seen him and I'd really like to know what he looks like. I've only seen pictures. He's very big, isn't he? Is he as big as a tree?'

Aiden gave a serious shake of the head.

'But he's big, isn't he? Is he taller than me?'

Aiden looked at her and nodded.

'That's really big. Oh, and he's got big claws. Did you see his claws?'

'No. He was wearing shoes.'

'I expect that was because it was raining and he didn't want to get his feet dirty. Did he have big slippers like those?' Robyn smiled warmly at the child.

He studied his red slippers for a moment. 'No, these aren't for outside. I have shoes for outside.'

'Are they like my shoes?' asked Robyn.

Aiden looked at her black, flat-heeled shoes and shook his head. 'I have trainers. The Gruffalo has trainers too.'

Robyn leant forward and spoke in awe. 'You saw the Gruffalo's trainers?'

He nodded again and smiled. 'But they weren't the same colour as mine.'

'What colour were they?' asked Robyn. 'Pink?'

Aiden gave a sudden giggle. 'No. That's silly. Not pink. Black. Big black ones.'

'Of course. The Gruffalo wouldn't wear pink shoes. How silly of me,' said Robyn, slapping her forehead with the palm of her hand. 'So, you saw his big black trainers, and was he wearing trousers, or did he have hairy legs and hairy brown knees?'

Aiden put his crayon down, shuffled forwards on the floor and giggled again. 'He had dark trousers like Daddy wears when he goes running. They have elastic at the bottom.'

'So, you saw his big, hairy ankles?'

'No,' he spluttered with a smile. 'He had socks.'

'Wow, what a good memory you have. Can you remember what colour socks he had?'

His brow furrowed a little. 'I don't know. I think they were stripy ones.'

'Well done. I'd never have remembered that. So, when you saw the Gruffalo, he wasn't hiding behind a tree, was he? I expect he's too big to hide properly behind a tree, isn't he? His big, hairy tummy will stick out.'

A smile and another shake of the head, then in a tiny voice he whispered, 'He was in the bush.'

'Did he speak to you?'

'No.' He shifted on his bottom uncomfortably and picked up his crayon again.

'Aiden, was this before you saw the red car?'

Aiden hesitated and looked towards his mother, who spoke. 'It's okay, matey. Tell Robyn exactly what you saw. Can you do that? Tell her what happened after you lost Kyle. He ran on without you, didn't he?'

His lips pouted as he considered the request. He spoke, deliberately and slowly. 'I saw a big footprint by the path. It was the Gruffalo's footprint. I wanted Kyle to see it and I called him, but he had gone away. I thought I heard the Gruffalo and I went to find him in the woods. I saw his feet under a bush, and then I got scared in case he jumped out at me, like Kyle does sometimes. I don't like it when he does that. I said hello but he didn't speak. I couldn't see Kyle. Or Granny. And I got frightened of the Gruffalo because he didn't say anything. I saw Mummy's car and I ran to it. But it wasn't Mummy's car.'

David spoke words of encouragement. 'You're a very brave boy. I bet the Gruffalo thought you were brave too. Did he stay under the bush or did he run away?'

'I think he ran away. He was scared of the man in the car. He disappeared back into his woods.'

Robyn observed David as he continued talking and engaging the boy. Now they knew for certain somebody else had been in the vicinity of Gregson's car. It might have been the jogger the family had seen. If so, why had that person hidden in the undergrowth?

She had to locate whoever it was. They were either a valuable witness or guilty of murdering Henry Gregson.

✳

Robyn clattered up the corridor with determination. Matt was standing by his desk, paper cup of tea in his hand.

'The butcher remembers Liam Carrington and his daughter Astra in his shop, but he has no idea what time that was. He'd been busy sorting out the freezer and lost track of time. One eyewitness spotted Carrington in the park, pushing his daughter on a swing, but again he wasn't sure when, and said it could have been about twelve. Can't find anyone else in Yoxall who saw him,' Matt said. 'His partner, Ella Fox, returned earlier than she expected, and claims Carrington was in the house at 2 p.m. If Jane Dean heard a shot at one forty-five, there's no way Carrington could have committed the crime and returned from Cannock Chase by then.'

Robyn linked her hands behind her neck and groaned. 'Not Carrington. Who could want Gregson dead? Lauren has an airtight alibi but she might have asked somebody else to shoot him – a boyfriend, or even hired somebody. We might also have to look more closely at Libby Gregson and her friend Tarik Akar. I can't discount the possibility they were somehow in this together, although I'm thin on evidence at the moment. Anna, any more on either of them?'

'Still working on it.'

'Okay, David, try Gregson's work colleagues and anyone he plays cricket with, and his neighbours. Until we find out who might have a motive, we'll have to talk to everyone, no matter how unlikely a suspect they seem.'

Robyn struck through Liam Carrington's name and sidled past the desks to her own. Lauren was still a potential suspect, although they had little reason to suspect her. There was no proof she was seeing another man. For now, Robyn was left with only two potential suspects – Libby and Tarik – and a weak motive for murdering a sibling – jealousy.

No sooner had she sat down than her phone rang. It was the front desk.

'There's a man to see you at reception, name of Carrington.'

Robyn was surprised. 'Put him in interview room two and I'll meet him there.'

She hastened from the office, hoping Liam Carrington had some new information for her. She opened the door to the interview room and was met by soft sobbing and a small, crumpled face. Tears hung from the little girl's eyelashes as she studied Robyn.

'Hello,' said Robyn, crouching down to face the pretty child. 'I'm Robyn. Who are you?'

The child turned away, bottom lip trembling, and scampered across the room to her father, burying her head in his lap. He attempted to lift her away without success.

'This is Astra. Astra, say hello to the nice lady.'

Eventually, the child raised her head and managed a shy smile, but remained close to her father, clutching his fingers with her tiny hand. Liam Carrington had dark purple bags under his eyes and the look of a haunted man. 'I'm sorry. She wouldn't let me leave the house without her. Henry was supposed to be taking her out today and I had to explain he couldn't, because, well, you know, and she's been like this ever since – frightened to let me out of her sight. She's taken it badly.'

On cue, and hearing his name, the little girl whispered, 'Henry?'

Robyn's heart sank at hearing the hope in the small voice. Carrington looked at her in despair.

'Is Henry here?' she said.

'Sweetie, he isn't. He had an accident.' Robyn spoke as gently as she could.

The girl's lip trembled uncontrollably. 'No Henry,' she stammered.

Her father drew her to him and planted a kiss on her head. He gazed across at Robyn, his hand resting on the child's hair. 'I came to see if you'd got anywhere in the investigation. I couldn't sleep last night. I hoped maybe you could give me some news.'

Robyn stood again and let out a gentle sigh. 'Not yet but I'll let you know as soon as we make progress. We will find whoever did this.'

He nodded but his face remained unconvinced. 'Thanks. I'd better get Astra home. Shall we go home and see Mummy?'

Astra blinked back more tears. 'Henry? Bouncy balls?'

He shrugged at Robyn. 'He takes her to the bouncy ball pit at Wolseley Bridge on Thursday afternoons. It's a cage filled with soft balls and slides for the kiddies. She loves it.' He looked down on his daughter. 'Astra, shall Daddy take you to the bouncy balls?'

She hung her head and her little shoulders began to shake as she sobbed. 'No Daddy. I want Henry.'

⁂

Robyn retraced her steps to the office and threw herself behind the desk. As she did so, she realised she was functioning more clearly. Davies had finally taken a back seat in her mind.

CHAPTER FOURTEEN

THURSDAY, 16 FEBRUARY, EARLY MORNING

Tessa Hall padded down the stairs into her kitchen, flicked the light switch and blinked away the sleepy dust in her eyes. She tugged at the fleece, pulling it over her ample chest and belly, and shivered.

The boiler hadn't yet kicked in so the air in the kitchen was cool, her nose and cheeks chilly to the touch. It was a bitterly cold morning and she was mad. Mad to be up at this ungodly hour to pound the streets. She should still be tucked up in bed, fast asleep under her warm duvet, with Schrödinger, her kitten, beside her. For a minute she considered heading back upstairs and joining him. It was a tempting thought. Then she heaved a sigh. She'd made the New Year's resolution to get into shape for a good reason, and it was paying off. She had to stick to it, no matter if it was bloody awful getting up before 6 a.m. three times a week to jog miles along wet or slippery pavements while the world slumbered on. At first, she'd struggled to manage even half a mile, her breath coming in painful, ragged gasps with each step, but now she could keep up a decent pace for about five miles and was pleased with her efforts. It hadn't been easy, and she'd hated every minute of it, but she had a goal – a reason for all this punishment.

She caught sight of her reflection in the kitchen window and thought she was looking fitter and healthier. She smoothed her stomach with one hand and smiled to herself. The reason for her interest in exercise would be here tomorrow night, and she couldn't wait.

Tessa's thoughts drifted to their last liaison, and she squirmed at the delicious memory. He'd had to spend Valentine's Day at home, which was a bummer, but what could she expect? The jealous cow would be sure to suspect him of an affair if he'd been out on that particular night. It didn't matter. Tessa looked at the huge display of flowers he'd sent her. She was winning. He was becoming more and more besotted. It wouldn't be much longer before he'd dump the miserable cow; after all, Tessa had a trump card – one she'd kept close to her chest. She was biding her time before she played it, and when she did – he'd be amazed, delighted and wholly hers.

It would be worth it – all the deceit, all the clandestine meetings. The future was looking remarkably brighter. She checked her iPhone to make sure her running music was set up. The music was the only thing that kept her going some mornings. She'd get this over with, do some stretching back home, grab a shower and maybe stop off at the drive-in Costa on her way to work. She'd pick up a hot chocolate – one naughty treat wouldn't hurt.

She'd have to buy some drinks for tomorrow night too. She planned on sharing her news at last and they'd have some serious celebrating to do.

Tessa attached the iPhone to her upper arm, over the fleece, and picked up her running shoes. As she did so, somebody knocked at her front door – a gentle tap. It couldn't be him, could it? He sometimes surprised her by stopping off on his way to work. He'd done so last week. He'd arrived at six thirty, desperate to see her. They'd had eager, passionate sex on the kitchen table before he'd had to leave. Her insides squirmed at the thought of it. Of course it would be him, desperate for her. Like her, he couldn't wait for tomorrow. She eagerly drew back the bolt and opened the door but was disappointed to find it was not who she was expecting.

'What are you doing here?'

'I had to see you. It's urgent.'

'Look, I've made my position clear on this subject.'

'I'll only be a minute. Please let me in. It's freezing out here.'

Tessa sighed. 'Make it quick. I want to get a run in before I go to work.' She moved aside to let her visitor in and then shut the door.

'Won't you reconsider?'

'I'm not changing my mind about this,' she said, folding her arms. 'I told you on the phone. I've made my mind up and that's that. So, it doesn't matter what you say, I won't back down.'

'Tessa, I'm asking nicely.'

'How many times do I have to tell you no?'

'I'm begging you to reconsider.'

A soft meow made Tessa look up. Her kitten was at the top of the stairs, seeking attention. He called again but did not move.

'I don't have to beg, do I, Tessa?'

The voice was angrier this time and irked Tessa. She wasn't in the mood to put up with any intimidation. Besides, she'd made up her mind. She looked away from the kitten and shook her head crossly. 'I have to get going.'

She turned back to open the door again but stopped in mid-action. Her eyes widened with surprise as an object swung towards her and warm liquid spilled down her cheek. Then the pain exploded in her head. There was no time to assimilate what had happened. There was nothing but blackness as she slipped to the floor. The kitten called out plaintively.

Her visitor checked for a pulse then stepped over her body, reached for the door handle and slid out into the darkness.

CHAPTER FIFTEEN

THEN

The hammering on the door echoes throughout the house – a thud, thud, thud of urgency. The boy lifts his head from the pillow, eyes heavy with sleep, and listens. His head still throbs. The day before, he'd been kicking his football against the kitchen wall, practising his moves, doing keepie uppies and then kicking it hard, as if scoring a goal, when his father had come thundering outside in a blind fury and whacked his head against the brick wall so hard he'd seen stars.

'Keep the noise down. It's doing my bloody head in listening to you. I can't hear the telly.'

He'd spent the day at home in bed with the curtains drawn. His mother had sat with him on and off. Told him he wasn't to mention it at school when he went back, and he was to say he'd tripped up. He wasn't to tell anyone, no one at all. She made him promise, and kissed him on the cheek and told him it would be okay. They both knew it was never okay. He might still be alive this time but what would happen the next?

Now he's awake. His head isn't hurting as badly and his senses are on full alert. His parents' bedroom door creaks open and he hears his mother descend the stairs, one at a time, hesitating until the thumps begin again and a voice calls her name. She scurries lightly down the last few stairs and the door opens.

He gets out of his bed and pads to the door. His sister hasn't woken. She sleeps so badly at night she needs a good shake every day to get up. She's wrapped up in a faded duvet covered in lambs, no doubt lost in a magical world far away from parents who scream at each other, where plaster crumbles from the ceiling to leave light flurries of snow-like grey dust on their bedding, and where large damp patches of mould spread up the bedroom wall. She lets out a soft sigh. He leaves her sleeping. He knows it is much better to be asleep. When you're sleeping you don't feel the hunger that rumbles like a caged tiger or the anxiety that you wear like a heavy cloak.

The voices below are mumbled then his mother cries, 'No!' A deeper voice speaks and the door closes again, the voices moving into the kitchen.

He creeps down the stairs and hovers outside the door, not daring to enter but desperate to know what has made his mother cry out. He can't hear what's being said. He walks silently to the front window and peers outside. The police squad car is difficult to miss in its fluorescent yellow and blue. His heart thumps against his rib cage as he thinks about why the police might be behind the kitchen door. The day before, before he'd had his head smacked against the wall, he'd gone into Mr Bridge's local shop. It hadn't been planned. He'd been going home from school with Johnny Hounslow, whose dad owns a factory in Birmingham. Johnny, who gets loads of pocket money, decided to buy some crisps. While Johnny was hunting through the various flavours in a large box next to the counter, he'd wandered down the aisles. Mr Bridges had been so busy watching Johnny, he didn't spot the theft of a king-sized chocolate bar. Neither did Johnny. What if it had been caught on camera and now the police were here to tell his mother? It wasn't the first item he'd stolen.

The sound of a kitchen chair scraping on the floor makes him draw back up the stairs. The door opens. His mother emerges, her face ghostly white. She spots him and signals for him to return upstairs. Two uniformed officers head for the front door, speaking in hushed tones.

'Someone will be in touch soon.'

His mother shuts the door behind them and stands with her back against it.

'What's happened?' he asks. 'What did the cops want?'

'Your dad. He got into trouble. Looks like he'll be going to prison for quite a while.'

He takes in her words. No more drunken beatings. The relief is palpable and he wants to shout hurray, then he notes the silent tears.

'Why are you crying? If he's in prison, he won't be able to hurt you any more.'

She shakes her head, sniffling so badly, snot runs down her face. 'He can't hurt us but I don't know how I'll manage. I don't have a job and the rent is overdue on this place again, and I've not even got the emergency money.' The words trail away, overtaken by sobs. 'If I can't look after you, they'll take you away…'

He doesn't understand. 'It's okay. You can get a job and I'll look after my sister when you're out. I'll get a job too. Maybe I could deliver papers.'

Her shoulders shake up and down like she's laughing hysterically. The tears fall faster. She can't speak. The look on her face makes his blood run cold. He senses it's going to be worse without his father.

CHAPTER SIXTEEN

Robyn was working through the information on Gregson's mobile when her phone rang for the second time. It was the desk sergeant again.

'DCI Flint asked me to pass this to you. DI Shearer's not available and it's urgent. There's been an incident at Barton-under-Needwood. Victim's a young woman. Don't have any other details. Paramedics called it in. Head injuries.'

Robyn got everyone's attention. 'We've got another case to handle. We'll need to split the team for the moment. Matt, stay on this, and Anna, see if you can trace Henry Gregson's Kia before it headed to Cannock Chase. Keep me in the loop. David, Mitz – with me.'

※

Robyn gritted her teeth as they attempted to navigate the popular village of Barton-under-Needwood, populated by commuters working in nearby Lichfield, Tamworth and Burton-upon-Trent. Even with the siren blaring, it took several minutes to circumnavigate the lunchtime traffic and reach the terraced house situated in a side road, near the Tudor church of St James.

Robyn slipped on the obligatory crime scene paper suit behind the squad car and studied the front of the house, separated from the road by a foot of pavement and accessed by a paved driveway to the left. It was a small, brown-brick property, with a wooden door painted in duck-egg blue and windowsills to match. Window boxes filled with pale pink and purple pansies, damp and limp from the recent rain, had been recently tended and deadheaded. Slatted cream blinds hung halfway down sparkling windows, and on the window ledge was a black kitten, its head turning this way and that, attracted by all the outside activity. Robyn showed her ID to the PC standing at the entrance to the drive, and entered the property. The kitten watched her, its golden gaze following her as she stepped cautiously over the threshold.

The front door led directly into the kitchen that doubled as a dining room. Tessa Hall, in jogging bottoms and a fleece, was lying near the foot of a staircase that rose from the side of the room. The tiled floor was splattered with bright-red stains. Several tiny droplets of blood had splattered onto the kitchen cupboards and some even onto the white wooden banister behind her. Her head was a bloodied mess surrounded by a crimson halo. Several forensic officers were working silently in the kitchen, and the photographer was in the doorway separating the kitchen from a sitting room, checking through what he'd already captured. Connor Richards, already in situ, raised his hands helplessly when he saw Robyn.

'Horrible,' he said.

'What are we dealing with here?' asked Robyn.

'Female in her twenties. Head injury. Might have been due to a nasty fall. Or more likely it was an attack. Harry McKenzie is on his way. He'll be able to verify if it was deliberate.'

On cue, Harry McKenzie, the pathologist, entered, his medical case gripped tightly, brows furrowed. He didn't greet them; instead, he nodded in their direction and heaved a sigh at the spectacle before him. A small, neat man in his fifties, with greying temples, pale face and delicate features, Harry had a gentle bedside manner.

Robyn liked his methodical approach combined with the kindness that exuded from him.

He unpacked his case in silence and set about examining Tessa, gently checking her injuries. Robyn turned away from the sight of the woman and looked around the impossibly tidy kitchen. Tessa looked after her home. Porcelain jars marked coffee, tea and sugar stood beside a gleaming kettle and a mug bearing a picture of a cat in a bow tie. Other animal mugs were hanging from wooden pegs under kitchen units, and a magnificent display of flowers rested upon the table at the far end of the kitchen. Beside it stood a large card bearing a velvet red heart. A small beanbag cushion balanced on a kitchen chair was presumably for the cat. A litter tray and a blue food bowl bearing the name Schrödinger stood by the door. One of the forensic team had removed the kitten from the windowsill and it was now shut in a cage by the door, still fixated on Robyn. It meowed at her – a weak, lost cry – and a rush of sadness overcame Robyn, for both the house-proud young woman and her small companion.

Mitz joined them, notepad in hand.

'Victim is Tessa Hall. Twenty-six years old. Single. She was a nurse and worked in Tamworth. The neighbours on either side are currently out at work. I've just spoken to the woman who found her, Mrs Frances Shields. She came around to drop off a copy of the local newsletter and heard the cat yowling. She thought it might have been injured, peered through the letter box, caught sight of Tessa lying on the floor, and called the emergency services. We're getting a full statement from her now.' He looked up from his pad.

'Can you arrange for house-to-house enquiries?'

'Sure.' David glanced at the body of Tessa Hall and winced. 'You want me to start now?'

'As soon as we've finished here. I don't want to get in the way of the forensic team.' Robyn looked around the room. There didn't appear to be any obvious signs of a struggle. Forensics would be able to ascertain if there had been one. Her eyes lit upon the iPhone still attached to Tessa's arm and the running shoes on the floor. 'It looks like she'd been getting ready to go out jogging. Maybe she surprised an intruder. This could be an attempted burglary that went wrong or a random attack. Connor, can I take that phone with me?'

'Sure.' Connor removed it to examine it and dust it for prints.

'I'd say she's been struck across the temple by a blunt weapon,' said Harry McKenzie. 'It's a particularly fragile part of the skull. It's almost certainly what killed her.'

Robyn examined the front door, checking for damage. 'There's no sign of forced entry so we can assume she opened her door to somebody. She might or might not have known her assailant. If she was about to leave, she probably wasn't expecting a visitor, unless it was a running buddy.'

Her gaze was drawn to a black leather purse next to a handbag. She moved quickly towards it. 'Connor, can you look at this, please?'

Connor's eyebrows rose high as he leafed through the notes filling the purse. 'You might rule out a burglary or robbery. There's about £500 in it,' he said.

'That's a fair amount of cash,' said Robyn as she examined the kitchen top, looking for anything untoward. 'Most people use cards these days to pay for stuff. I can't think why she'd have that amount, unless somebody had given it to her – or paid her for something in cash.' She moved towards the kitchen table and the window that looked out onto a six-foot hedge providing the house with privacy. It would be impossible for anybody to gain entry from that direction. She turned a full circle.

'I can't see any obvious damage or anything out of place in here.'

Mitz agreed. 'It appears robbery can't be the motive, not if the killer left all that money behind.'

Robyn glanced across at Tessa's body. Harry was checking her core temperature to work out time of death.

'Harry, what are your initial thoughts?'

'I'd say death occurred about four, five hours ago. There's little evidence of rigor, although there's some recent stiffening of the neck muscles commensurate with the approximate time of death. Her core temperature hasn't dropped a huge amount and indicates death was sometime this morning. Around six or seven.'

The kitten let out a plaintive yowl.

'What's happening to the cat?' asked Robyn.

One of the forensic team spoke. 'We've contacted the local cats' home but they haven't got anyone free to come and collect it yet.'

The kitten meowed again and pawed at the cage. Davies' daughter, Amélie, who lived with her mother, Brigitte, was cat-crazy. Her grandmother, who was in France, owned a Siamese, and Amélie always talked at length about the animal after her visits there.

'Schrödinger's a weird name,' said David, who'd been upstairs and was now standing by the door, quietly observing the proceedings.

A puff of air escaped Robyn's nose in a light snort. 'I'm assuming it's after the Schrödinger cat experiment. Don't ask. I don't understand the concept. Look, if no one's coming to collect that poor animal, I'm taking it with me. David, anything upstairs?'

'No, guv. No sign of any tussle or attack.'

A lengthy sigh escaped Robyn's lips. 'Okay, it's time to find a witness, collect some statements and leave this crime scene to the forensic chaps. Harry?'

'There's blunt force trauma to the temple and fractures to the right cheekbone. There's a skull fracture to the back of the head that might have occurred when she fell, or from a direct blow to the head. I'm sure my examination will show the skull casing has been fractured here,' he said, pointing to an area above her hairline. 'It's possible fragments might have made their way into the brain and caused haemorrhaging. I'll confirm my findings later today.'

Robyn took another look about the home. Access to the French windows was impossible from the other side of the wall unless the killer had used a ladder, and there was no obvious damage to them. Whoever had attacked Tessa must have come through the front door. A wind-up toy mouse lay in Robyn's path. She stepped over it and strode back into the kitchen. The space seemed impossibly small, filled, as it now was, with investigators in white suits.

'David, I'd like you to remain behind to gather as many statements as possible from neighbours and begin questioning other locals in the area who might have seen or heard something unusual. Mitz, let's see if we can find out more about Tessa Hall.'

Connor handed over an evidence bag containing the phone. 'Nothing but her fingerprints on it. There's an iPad in the other room. I'll get it to you later today. Have to debrief the team on the other incident on Cannock Chase first.'

'Of course. I'd almost forgotten about that.'

'Somehow, I doubt that,' said Connor.

'Harry, can you get onto this immediately, please?'

'Most definitely. You'll get my full report as soon as possible.'

Robyn stood by the doorstep to remove her protective clothing, placed it in the bin and picked up the cage containing Schrödinger.

'What are you going to do with the lucky black cat?' asked Mitz as they climbed back into the squad car.

'I have absolutely no idea,' said Robyn, wondering why she'd acted on a whim. It was most unlike her. The vision of Amélie's face drifted into her head. Maybe part of her did know.

CHAPTER SEVENTEEN

Back at the station, Robyn and Mitz relocated to an interview room to pool their findings. The office was far too busy for them to collate information with Shearer barking instructions to his men.

Robyn was perplexed. 'There's nothing on her phone – nothing at all except some downloaded music: no photographs, only a few game apps, and not one phone number in her contact list. She must have deleted all the information. I've contacted her provider to get details of her phone activity.'

Mitz gave a shrug. 'That could be a genuine blip. It happened to me. I downloaded updates onto my iPhone, and when it rebooted, I'd lost all the information on it. It was a right pain. I had to input it all manually.'

'That would explain why her contact list is empty. What have you found out?'

Mitz ran through his information quickly. 'No convictions or anything we ought to be concerned about. Parents live near Solihull – her father's a watch repairer working on high-value items. Has his own workshop and shop in Solihull. Mother's a doctor – paediatrician. Tessa worked at the fertility clinic in Tamworth.'

Robyn pursed her lips and huffed. 'Tamworth clinic? Isn't that where the Gregsons went for tests?'

Mitz nodded. 'It's the main fertility clinic in the area.'

'Might be a coincidence but I'll talk to Lauren and see if she knew this woman.'

'The house in Barton is in her name. She bought it last June.'

'I don't know many young people, especially nurses, who can afford to buy their own property. She must have had some help with a deposit at least. Best to check that out. There were flowers on the table in the kitchen and a Valentine's card, so I'm guessing there's someone in her life. I'd like to find out who that someone is.'

'Not had too much time to contact colleagues or friends but she has an online presence, so once I have a moment, and her iPad, I'll look into that in more detail. Might need Anna's help.'

Robyn nodded in agreement. 'Definitely. The sooner the better. Okay, what are we dealing with here? Tessa's assailant attacked her and left her for dead, but apparently stole nothing of worth. Are we looking at a random attack without any motive? Or could she have upset or angered somebody?'

The interview room was devoid of all furniture bar the table in front of them and three plastic chairs. Robyn wriggled forwards on her chair, unrolled a large sheet of paper onto the table, anchored it down with her elbow and began writing the key words that would be their starting points.

'Can you talk to her parents? They might know about Tessa's love life and be the ones who helped her out with a deposit for the house. If not, I'm curious as to how she could afford it. After that, we'll need to speak to her work colleagues. With that and David collecting statements, and Anna looking into Tessa's online activities, we might be able to build up a picture of what's happened here. The fact she worked at the same clinic Henry and Lauren attended is bugging me. I'll call on Lauren Gregson and ask her a few more questions. Okay, let's get back to the madhouse.'

Mitz stepped forwards. 'You want me to handle this with David? You can't be racing between the two cases.'

Robyn's cheeks lifted. 'You're not trying to fast-track to DI are you, Sergeant Patel?'

He laughed. 'Well, if there was a way…'

'If anyone can, you can,' she said, shuffling her notes into a neat pile. 'Thanks, but I want to oversee both cases. It keeps me on my toes and my mind from wandering.'

'Talking of wandering… You might have to keep an eye on your new pet. I think Anna's got her eye on it. She was making cooing noises at it earlier.'

✳

Robyn returned to the chaos in her office and a bad-tempered Shearer.

'It's like a bloody pet shop in here,' grumbled Shearer. 'First it was a florist, now it's a pet shop. Lord knows how you ever get any work done.'

'We'd all get more done if we didn't keep falling over all your clobber,' retorted Robyn, kicking at the box file on which she'd just stubbed her toe. 'It's no good complaining. We're all in the same boat.'

'More like Noah's ark,' said Shearer, returning his attention to his laptop and typing methodically with two fingers. 'Get a wriggle on, Gareth. I want to get this completed before the bastard's brief comes in again and he starts shouting about his client's diminished responsibility.'

Gareth pulled a face. 'Almost done, sir. It's a bit hard to concentrate, what with all the comings and goings.'

Matt piped up. 'Mostly from you lot. It'd help us if you didn't keep leaping about the place. You're like jack-in-the-boxes. Up and down every five minutes with paperwork and dashing about.'

Gareth mumbled, 'It's called police work.'

'What's that you said?' said Matt, bristling. He scraped back his chair, ready to have a go at the young policeman.

Robyn's voice rose. 'Whoa! That's enough.' The tension was palpable. She hadn't time for tantrums and distractions. She threw Shearer a look but he was otherwise occupied.

'Where are we with the Gregsons? Anna?'

'I've identified more websites Lauren Gregson visited. She told us she wasn't online frequently, but she was – more often than she led us to believe. I get the impression she was completely obsessed with having children and didn't want her husband to be aware of her fixation, hence all the deleted browsing history.'

'That correlates with what Liam Carrington told me, that Henry was less keen than Lauren to have children. I'm going over to visit her after this meeting and will try to find out more about that. Have you found out where Gregson disappeared to the morning he was killed?'

'No. I've been through all the automatic number plate recognition camera footage from Gregson's house to Cannock Chase. His Kia passed a point on the A51 shortly after leaving his house in Brocton, headed in the direction of Lichfield, which is exactly the route we'd expect him to take to go to work. However, it doesn't pass through a second point on the route that leads to MiniMarkt, so he definitely didn't go into work that way. The Kia doesn't appear on any other number plate recognition cameras in Lichfield and doesn't show again until it passes the one situated a mile from Cannock Chase. It's hugely frustrating but I can't pinpoint his movements for that morning.'

'Matt?'

'Same here. Been hitting a brick wall. Interviewed his friends and connections at the cricket and football village clubs. Nothing.' He waved at a pile of papers on his desk. 'And no fix on that pay-as-you-go mobile.'

Robyn bounced the tips of her fingers together lightly. It was all too frustrating for words. She had two cases and couldn't get leverage on either. Was it because her mind was elsewhere? Was she letting her concerns about Davies dominate her thoughts? She certainly wasn't getting anywhere at the moment. And to cap it all, sharing the office with Shearer was hindering her ability to work. She blinked into the distance, wishing Shearer would vanish and free up her office.

The door flew open, barely avoiding hitting Matt, who threw the culprit a harsh stare.

'Sir, DCI Flint requested we follow this up immediately.'

'I've got twenty-twenty vision but even I can't read what's on that scrap of paper from over here, and I'm not a bloody mind reader. What are we to follow up?'

'Suspected arson attack.'

Shearer pulled down his rolled-up sleeves and lifted his jacket from the back of his chair. 'Gareth, drop that. It can wait until we get back.' He sauntered off, whistling Rag'n'Bone Man's 'Human', leaving Robyn torn between shouting something after him or sighing with relief that he'd vacated the office.

Matt headed for the coffee machine and cleared away the sloppy mess left by Shearer's men, and then set a cup under the spout. He folded his arms as he waited for the bubbling to begin.

'What next?' he asked.

'I think we're going to have to call forward witnesses. I'll speak to DCI Flint and ask if we can put out a television appeal and ask the press for help.'

Matt groaned. 'Not Amy Walters. That woman is horrendous. She's like an irritating wasp. You swipe at her and she buzzes off only to return later, and you're never sure when she'll sting you.'

Robyn felt that was an apt description of her. 'I don't like her any more than you do, but she'll probably help out. She owes me a favour.'

Amy Walters was in her late twenties, single and driven solely by work. It was her ambition to be picked up by one of the national papers and even move into television reporting. She was currently writing a book about serial killers, based on real cases, and it was to be her one shot at grabbing the headlines herself. Robyn had given the young woman two lengthy interviews for chapters in the book in exchange for information. Amy was only a nuisance in that she never let go of anything. In fact, it was surprising she hadn't already attempted to contact Robyn. Maybe she was too busy with her book. Robyn shook herself free of those thoughts and turned back to the whiteboard.

'Have we identified the mysterious jogger, seen running along the Gruffalo Trail?'

'Checked all the homes in the area – no one was out running on Cannock Chase on Tuesday,' said Matt. 'I've got a list of running clubs and gyms in the immediate vicinity. I've phoned Chase Warriors, a running group a mile away, but none of their members were out either. I've still got to check out the other clubs and gyms.'

Robyn's frustration mounted. Trying to find somebody spotted running in such a wide public place was almost impossible. They could have come from anywhere nearby, and the Chase had many entrances accessible to joggers. The individual might even have driven to a spot nearby, parked up and then gone running.

'I think we'll waste valuable time trying to track them down this way. An appeal is probably the only way to go. I hope I don't have to ask for another one in the Tessa Hall case.'

'DCI Flint will love that – talk about spooking the public.' Matt grinned.

'I know.' Robyn scratched her head. 'As for Henry Gregson, I've been putting off interviewing his sister Libby again, but I think it's time to talk to her and Tarik Akar.'

Anna spoke: 'I've been looking into their backgrounds. I can't find anything on Libby, certainly nothing that would indicate she was on drugs as her brother suggested, or any attempts at suicide. Tarik Akar is another matter. He's got previous, for assault. He and a friend were accused of attacking a twenty-year-old man they believed to be vandalising Akar's vehicle. They chased after him and set about him with fists. Case went to magistrates' court but was dropped due to insufficient evidence. The victim claimed he'd been drinking heavily and stumbled from the pavement into the car, and wasn't vandalising it. He'd been too drunk to identify either of his assailants with any accuracy.'

'So, Henry was probably lying about his sister, much like he lied about his mother. I wonder why he was so keen to keep Lauren and Libby apart. And Tarik might be a man with a short fuse. I'm keeping an open mind about him. He could be involved, although I've yet to work out a genuine motive, or prove he was on Cannock Chase that day. Matt, do you want to talk to DCI Flint about the appeal and do it?'

'You know how much I love cameras, guv. I ought to have been a movie star with my looks, not a policeman.' He pretended to lick his hand and wet down his absent hair. 'My pleasure.'

The kitten unfurled and stretched, then curled up again with a small sigh, a soft bundle of black fur. Robyn knew Amélie would adore it. Was that really why she'd brought it away with her? She rubbed her forehead. The pain above her right eye had begun to travel down her neck. She had to make some progress. She might be going out on a limb chasing after Tarik, but what choice did she have?

CHAPTER EIGHTEEN

Lauren Gregson wore the look of a lost soul. Robyn had seen it before – the thousand-yard stare usually associated with soldiers but applicable to any victim of trauma. Lauren didn't appear to recognise Robyn when she opened the door, and beckoned her in without a word.

The kitchen was in disarray: paperwork littered the kitchen tops along with the contents of kitchen drawers. An orange ceramic dish covered in cling film stood on the table, its contents untouched. Lauren slipped onto a stool and lifted a half-empty glass of wine to her lips, downing it in one.

'Want one?' she asked.

Robyn shook her head. 'No thanks. Driving.'

'Fair enough.' Lauren picked up the bottle and refilled her glass. 'I couldn't face any more today. I've been trying to get affairs in order. I have to have all sorts of paperwork to register Henry's death. I was given loads of leaflets to supposedly help me through this process but all they've done is make me feel like crap. Why do you have to go through so much aggro when somebody dies? Isn't it bad enough losing them without all this as well? I have to get a death certificate before I can do anything. That could be ages, and all the time, I can't let go of him. He's here but not here, if you know what I mean.'

Robyn understood exactly what she meant. It had been the same for her when Davies had been killed, except Peter Cross had told her not to concern herself. He'd dealt with all of the paperwork and organised the funeral. At the time Robyn had been glad to leave it to someone else but now she questioned Peter's motives. Had he really organised a funeral or had it all been a sham?

'I understand, Lauren. I've lost people I love too and this is such a difficult period. You are getting support, aren't you? Have you got friends or relatives to help you?'

Lauren gulped some wine and nodded.

'I hope you don't mind me troubling you again?' Robyn asked, wondering if Lauren was sober enough to answer her questions.

'No trouble. Not like I've got anything else to do. I didn't fancy any company. People keep tipping up to say how sorry they are to hear about Henry. Even brought me food in case I can't manage to cook,' she said, nodding at the dish on the table. 'I can't take any more at the moment. I want to pretend it isn't happening. Their long faces and quiet voices and looks of pity just remind me it's all real.'

'It's about the clinic at Tamworth.'

Lauren's face took on a faraway look.

'Did either you or Henry have any contact with a nurse called Tessa Hall during your visits?'

'There were a few nurses at the clinic. I was seen by at least three different ones. None of them was called Tessa. I don't know about Henry. I don't know which nurse dealt with him. His appointment was with a consultant called Galloway. He didn't mention the nurses.'

'You didn't accompany him?'

'No. I was at work that day. I'd already taken time off on a few occasions for my own appointments. Besides, he said he'd prefer to go alone.'

Robyn passed across a photograph of Tessa Hall downloaded from the clinic website. 'Do you recognise her at all?'

Lauren squinted at the picture. 'I might have seen her there. I can't be certain. I was so nervous.'

Robyn left the photograph on the table but Lauren had lost interest in it. She took another sip of her wine. Robyn waited for Lauren to ask why she'd been asked about Tessa, but she didn't.

'I don't know what I'll do,' said Lauren after a few minutes. 'Mum and Dad are coming to help me sort out everything. They liked Henry. He was the first boyfriend they really took to. He and Dad would talk for ages about the bloody football. Ignored both Mum and me. Used to drive me crazy. Mum just laughed about it and said I was lucky to have found Henry, especially after Nick. Nick dumped me for no good reason and broke my heart. Henry mended it.' Her eyes slid across to an unopened parcel on the kitchen top. 'I don't think I could go through all that again. I can't face more heartbreak. I wish I'd had something to remind me of our love – a baby. As it is, I have nothing.'

Robyn tried one last time. 'You really can't remember Tessa Hall?'

Lauren shook her head. 'There are so many nurses and doctors at that place.'

'Can I ask you about Liam? Did he know the truth about Henry's mother and sister?'

'I doubt it. It's not the sort of thing you shout about. Henry's sister is a screwed-up junkie, and his mother's so ill she doesn't recognise her own son. Henry rarely spoke to me about them, let alone anyone else.'

'Liam must have talked about family at some stage. He and Henry were good friends.'

Lauren shrugged. 'Probably made up something, or changed the subject. He was good at that.'

'What do you mean, Lauren?'

Lauren stared at her wine glass. 'He'd change the subject if he didn't want to talk about something. It was his way of getting out of an argument or a sticky situation. I used to get cross with him sometimes about that. It doesn't seem important now.'

'You're friends with Liam's girlfriend, Ella – did you not mention Henry's sister or mother in conversation?'

'Why would I?' Lauren looked blankly at her wine glass. 'Ella's hard work – I mean, she isn't the sort of person you'd want to share a bottle of wine with and have a girlie night. I like her, but she only ever wants to talk about Astra, which is fine. I love Astra. I'd really love a little girl just like her. But Ella's intense. She hangs on Liam's every word and doesn't get involved in conversations. I find it hard to open up to her. It'll be harder still now Henry isn't here.'

Robyn looked at her watch. She ought to get home. Lauren looked up and opened her mouth to speak, then closed it again.

'I'll be in touch again soon. When are your parents coming?' Robyn stood to leave.

'Sometime this evening. I told them I was okay and not to fuss but Mum insisted. I wanted some time to be alone. I wanted to feel his presence here and be with him for a while longer. Mum wouldn't have that. Said it was too maudlin and I needed company. I don't think I can face her. She can be so overbearing sometimes. Makes me feel like I'm only fifteen.'

'She means well. She'll be worried about you. And she'll be upset about Henry too. You're her daughter. Of course she wants to look after you.'

Lauren nodded dumbly. Robyn moved towards the door, glancing at the parcel as she left. The sender's address was clearly printed. Lauren had received a parcel from Mothercare, a store specialising in baby items. Robyn hastened into the bitter cold, wondering how fixated Lauren was on having a child.

CHAPTER NINETEEN

Anna called Robyn across to her computer screen as soon as she walked through the door.

'I don't know if this is significant but I came across it when I was searching through the ANPR points. Mr Akar works there, doesn't he?'

She handed over a photograph, a still captured from one of the cameras on the route to Cannock Chase, of a white van with blue writing along its side that read 'Mike's Motors'. She looked at the time it was taken, twelve thirty, and tapped it.

'Good work, Anna. We'll start with Mr Akar and Mike's Motors. What time do they shut?'

'It's late night on a Thursday. Six thirty, guv. I phoned up and checked. We've just got time to catch them there.'

Robyn gave Anna a warm smile. The woman would go the extra mile to catch a criminal. She loved that about all her team. 'Let's see what Libby and Tarik have to say.'

⁂

It took twenty-eight minutes to reach the industrial estate in Hanley. The garage, a bland, concrete building with a tin roof, looked like all the other buildings lined up beside each other, row after row on the estate. They passed electrical stores, furniture outlets, decorating stores and clothing outlets before they came across it at the end of the fifth row. There was no sign to make it stand out. Only the several cars lined up outside gave it away as a garage.

Robyn and Anna made their way around the building to the side, which turned out to be a large entrance to the workshop. A VW Passat faced them, bonnet open, a figure leaning over it. Loud, tinny music that Robyn identified as Britney Spears came from somewhere at the back of the garage, where somebody was whistling tunelessly along with the song and bashing metal noisily. She ducked under the metal shutter hanging a third of the way down, and walked into the workshop. The smell of grease was overpowering and she carefully trod around a dark puddle of what looked like oil, towards a man working underneath a Range Rover, jacked up on a ramp. He soon caught sight of her and shouted.

'Office is round the other side, love.'

She held up her warrant card. 'We'd like a word with one of the mechanics, please.'

The man approached, wiping his black hands on a filthy rag. 'I'm Mike of Mike's Motors. What's this all about? We run a clean ship here. No dodgy dealings.' He scowled at her as if to make a point.

'Just a friendly word with Mr Akar, please. Nothing related to your premises. Just after some information.'

His eyes narrowed. 'Tarik?'

'Is he here?'

'At the back. Hang on.' He bellowed in the direction of the music and the whistling stopped.

Tarik appeared, a well-built man with a solid chest, in blue overalls stained black at the knees, hands as dirty as Mike's.

'Yeah?'

'For you,' said Mike, indicating Robyn with his head and moving back towards the Range Rover.

'Sorry to bother you at work but we're investigating a murder and would like to ask for your help.'

'Murder?' Tarik's dark eyebrows rose in surprise.

'We understand you know the victim's sister – Libby Gregson.' Robyn watched his reaction carefully.

'Oh yeah. She told me. Her brother. Don't see how I can help. Never met the bloke.'

He folded his arms, veins bulging on his biceps as he did so. Tarik Akar was obviously keen on bodybuilding.

'It's just to clear up a few things. I understand you went to the same school as Mr Gregson.'

'I did but I wasn't in the same year. I'd left before him and his sister joined the school. My brother was in Henry's class but they didn't hang out together.'

'And your brother is?'

'Nadir. Don't see how that's important. He never hung about with Henry. He went out with Libby for a few months after they left school.'

'And you know Miss Gregson through your brother?'

'Sort of. She brings her car here for servicing.'

'And you're friends with Miss Gregson?'

Tarik gave a light shrug and stared hard at Robyn. 'Yeah. I suppose so. We chat and stuff. She hangs about here waiting for her car when it's in, or sometimes I give her a lift home and take the car back for her when it's done. It's difficult like, what with her mum being sick and all that. She doesn't get out like she used to.'

'And did you see her yesterday?'

'Nah. I was here all day. Why would I see her?'

'Maybe to give her support. After all, her brother had died.'

He shrugged again. 'They weren't that close. He left the area years ago. He was a bit of a prick, to be honest. He used to hang about with a rough gang of lads. They were always into trouble, shoplifting, underage drinking, and fights. One time, he and his fellow thugs took Nadir down an alley and thumped the crap out of him. Nadir didn't let on who'd done it until I wrung it out of him. He didn't want no trouble. Said Henry had egged the others on. I wanted to flatten the little shit but Nadir said it would only make things worse. Made me promise to stay out of it. I didn't want to. I don't like people messing with my family. Family's important. That's water under the bridge now. Libby's nothing like her brother.'

Robyn gave a nod. 'You were here at work all day?'

He cocked his head. 'Yeah. Why?'

Robyn pulled out the still from a folder and held it up. 'So it wasn't you driving this van yesterday at twelve thirty?'

'Oh yeah, that,' he said, scrubbing at his chin. 'I forgot I had to fetch some spare parts from outside Cannock. We needed them for the Passat, isn't that right, Mike?'

Mike stopped working and looked up. 'What?'

'I had to fetch spare parts for the Passat?'

Mike nodded. 'Yes. I sent him. It needed a new carburettor. The guys at Cannock had one.'

'And what is the name of the garage in Cannock?'

'It's just a small workshop. They tinker about with various cars and have parts, but not for sale to the public. JJ Parts. It's called JJ Parts.' He ran his tongue over his lips.

'And what time did you return from JJ Parts?'

'I don't know. I had to hang about a while. They couldn't find it, and when they did, it was the wrong one, so I had to wait for them to get the right one delivered from their other workshop. Probably about four-ish.' Tarik spoke quickly, his eyes never leaving Mike. 'Mike?'

Mike shrugged. 'I wasn't clock-watching. About four.' He turned away and lifted a wrench, and then disappeared under the car once more.

'They'll confirm it. Ring Brett. He'll be there until seven. He'll tell you. So, if that's everything, I have to get back to work.'

Robyn glanced at his heavy work boots. 'Can I ask you what size shoes you take, Mr Akar?'

'What?'

'Shoes, sir.'

'Ten. Why?'

Robyn ignored the question.

'Thank you, sir.' She watched as he strode to the back of the workshop. The prints found at the crime scene on Cannock Chase were a size ten. There were unidentified fingerprints on the Kia's passenger door. If they were lucky, the prints might match Akar's.

'How soon can we get his fingerprints? They are on file, aren't they?' Robyn asked Anna.

'Yes. I asked for them to be sent directly to Connor, as you requested. Should get them later today or by tomorrow morning at the latest.'

'Here's hoping they do. In the meantime, we'll talk to Libby again.'

※

Libby was dressed in black leather trousers and a red silken blouse more suited to an evening out than sitting at home, caring for her mother.

'Mum isn't well at all today. I don't want to upset her by inviting you in.'

'I'm sorry to hear that. We won't keep you.'

Robyn stood her ground until Libby allowed them entry. Kath was wearing the same outfit as the day before and a coat unbuttoned and hanging open. Her face brightened when she saw Robyn.

'Have you come to take me out?' She began to fumble with the large black buttons on her coat.

Robyn shook her head. 'Sorry, Mrs Gregson. I'm here to talk to Libby.'

'Libby? Libby's at school. She won't be home until tea time.'

Libby walked across to her mother and knelt in front of her, hands resting on her mother's knees. 'It's DI Carter, Mum. She's here about Henry.'

Kath's face clouded further. 'Henry. When's Henry coming? He promised to take me to the park.' She stood up. Libby coaxed her back into the chair, where she sat and fiddled once more with the buttons on her coat.

'She won't take off the coat,' said Libby. 'Sometimes she sits in it all day. I used to take her out to the park but I daren't now. She gets so stressed and won't even get out of the car.' She gave a sad smile.

'I'm sorry to disturb you yet again. I've got a couple of questions. You might want to talk in private.'

Libby sighed and moved into the kitchen, where she rested against the kitchen top, keeping Robyn and Anna standing.

'What is it?'

'It's about the tattoos you have.'

Libby barked a laugh. 'What of them?'

'It's coincidental you have a new tattoo of a gun shooting flowers you posted on your Facebook wall the day before your brother was shot.'

Libby was incredulous, her mouth agape. It was a moment before she spoke.

'You accessed my Facebook page? Why?'

'We look into the backgrounds of everyone connected with the victim, Miss Gregson. You weren't singled out. I'd like to clear up why you posted a photograph of the tattoo. You can see how strange that would look to us.'

Libby reached for the packet of cigarettes near the kettle and lit one before speaking. 'Let's get this straight. I like tattoos. I've been getting them done since I was a teenager. When Mum became ill, I developed an interest in "darker" tattoos. You've seen the one of the skull with angel wings on my back? That represents my mother. She's alive but dead. Have you any idea what it's like to watch somebody you love with every bone in your body fade away, to be nothing more than a shell, to know they don't remember you, or share the memories of your life together? I look at my mother and remember her kissing my knee better when I fell over, being there for me every time I needed her, us shopping together, or sitting on the settee together sharing a box of tissues while we both sobbed at a sad film. She looks at me today and can't remember any of it. It's horrible knowing she can't remember Christmases or birthdays, or even who I am some days. And she'll get worse. She'll forget how to eat, to wash herself, or even how to use the toilet, and everything that made her the caring, loving, gentle woman I loved so much will be gone, but she'll still be there – a frail, helpless shadow.

'The tattoo was a release. It's my way of dealing with this. The gun wasn't for Henry! It represents me shooting my own mother – not in hate, but with love – with flowers.' She stubbed the cigarette out angrily, grinding it until it split and remnants of tobacco crumbled from the paper into the saucer.

'I understand,' said Robyn softly. 'I'm truly sorry. You see why I had to ask you?'

Libby nodded dumbly then drew herself back up on her chair. 'Is that it? The podiatrist is coming in a while to cut her nails. Mum won't let me near them. I'd rather you left so I can get her prepared.'

'Can I ask you one other thing, about Tarik Akar?'

The dark expression that crossed Libby's face indicated she'd struck a nerve.

'What about him?'

'You know him?'

'I've known him most of my life. I went out with his brother, Nadir, when I was younger. He helps out sometimes when I can't leave Mum – picks up shopping, calls by, that sort of thing. His sister, Kiraz, watches Mum for me when I need to go out for an appointment, shopping or a quick coffee with friends, that sort of thing. It's never for too long.'

'So, he's a good friend?'

Libby raised her shoulders in a nonchalant shrug.

'You wouldn't say it was more than a friendship?'

'He's married and his wife's expecting. Does that answer your question?' Libby folded her arms and glared at Robyn.

'Not really. I believe he sent you a text asking you to keep quiet about something. Forgive me for asking, but what was he referring to?'

Libby's mouth fell wide open. Her words were a gasp of astonishment. 'You read my texts?'

'Your phone lit up when I was sat next to it. I only glanced at it.'

'That's an invasion of my privacy. I'd like you to leave now.' Libby's face darkened further and she marched towards the front door, opening it wide.

'Miss Gregson, I don't wish to pry. I'm merely ensuring we can track down the person guilty of murdering your brother.'

'You think Tarik killed him?' Her voice rose in indignation.

'His van was captured on a camera near the area where your brother was discovered. I have to follow up on that, eliminate him from our enquiries, and find whoever is responsible.'

Libby floundered. 'He can't have been there. He was at work.'

'Could you explain the gist of the text, please? At the moment, it incriminates him.'

Libby let out the longest sigh. 'Okay, okay. I *have* been having an affair with him. I've always held a torch for him. I know he's married and he'll never leave his wife, but I'm so lonely. I was in other relationships prior to looking after Mum full time, and they all ended up disastrously. I'm rubbish at finding the right bloke. Tarik's different. I know it can't be anything other than it is, but

I need him. The text was about our affair. Tarik comes over when Mum's asleep, and recently, his wife's started to question his movements. The text was about me keeping it under wraps if his wife asks me any searching questions. Of course, I'd never let on. And that's all there is to it.' Her lips turned downwards. 'He wouldn't do anything to hurt Henry.'

'Thank you, Miss Gregson. I'm truly sorry to have caused you any distress.'

'So, you'll leave Tarik alone?'

Robyn avoided answering. 'I appreciate your honesty and I'll do everything I can to track down your brother's murderer.'

Anna waited until they were on the road back to Stafford before asking if Tarik was no longer to be considered a suspect.

Robyn chewed her lip before responding. 'Not sure. I think I'd like to talk to that chap Brett at JJ Parts first. There was something about the way Tarik dragged Mike into the conversation to back him up that didn't seem right. Okay, let's head back – I'll call Brett on the way, let's hope he's working late. Connor is due in at eight, and if we're lucky, we should just make it in time.'

※

Connor, dressed casually in a navy jumper and jeans, arrived at 8 p.m. on the dot, looking fresh-faced as if he'd been relaxing on holiday rather than working a crime scene all day. He meandered into the office, beamed at Anna and pointed at the sleeping feline in the cage next to her desk.

'Is it bring-a-pet-to-work day, PC Shamash?'

Her face broke into a rare smile. 'Highly amusing. If it were, my ferocious hound, Razzle, would be sitting faithfully by my side.'

'I've met Razzle and the only thing ferocious about him is his appetite. Am I over there?' He waved at a table at the front of the room sandwiched in between two desks, right in front of the whiteboard.

'That's you. Sorry it's a bit of a squeeze. We've got squatters,' said Anna.

'I'll manage. There's not a great deal to report. Apologies for the casual dress,' he said as Robyn lifted her head. 'Got to meet up with a certain person and take her out to make up for missing Valentine's Day.'

Matt let out a groan. 'If you cave in to her now, man, you'll be under her thumb forever. Take it from one who knows.'

Connor laughed and organised his notes.

'The floor's yours,' said Robyn.

'Firstly, I have bad news regarding the fingerprints I received. Tarik Akar's fingerprints don't match the one we found on the door of the Kia.' He caught Robyn's look and smiled apologetically. 'As for Tessa Hall, we're still securing the crime scene. I have a list of tagged and bagged items so far.' He passed over three sheets of paper and Robyn read through them quickly.

'So far we haven't located the weapon used in the attack. With regard to fingerprints – there are quite a few. Most of them belong to Tessa, but there are a few that don't. There are partials and full fingerprints in the kitchen, on the kitchen table, and in the downstairs toilet. We used fingerprint identification technology to establish the gender of the prints, and a quick male/female response revealed one set of these prints, found on a kitchen stool and over surfaces in the sitting room – television control, television buttons and CDs – belonged to a male. Prints lifted from the Valentine's card in the kitchen matched those we found elsewhere. We're still working through the rest of the house.' He put up a series of transparencies showing the fingerprints.

'Her boyfriend must have left them,' Mitz said.

Robyn agreed. She read through the items taken from the house and stabbed at the paper. 'Fingernail?'

'It's being tested for DNA to see if it belongs to Miss Hall. It was found under a piece of loose skirting board near the fridge and might have been there for years. Right. I'd best be off. I'll be back in touch as soon as I have more.'

Connor collected up his documents and, with a wink at Anna, left the office. Robyn took over.

'I know we're working two cases here but it's nothing we can't handle. Let's go back to Henry Gregson for a minute. We're excluding Libby Gregson from our enquiries for now. Tarik Akar is still a person of interest. He was in the area at the time of the murder, has size ten feet to match the prints at the murder scene, and although his alibi holds up, I believe he's hiding something.' Robyn thought back to the phone call she'd made to JJ Parts. Brett had sounded vague and evasive when she'd questioned him. Tarik Akar was involved in something. Her instinct told her so, and even under duress, her instinct was rarely wrong.

CHAPTER TWENTY

DAY THREE – THURSDAY, 16 FEBRUARY, EVENING

The Skype call was the antidote Robyn needed. Amélie's voice shrieked in excitement once she saw the kitten. 'Oh-mi-gosh. He's so adorable.' She ran her hand down her screen, and Schrödinger pawed at it. 'I want to stroke him.'

Robyn studied the face of the excited girl, so like Davies'. She had the same chestnut-brown hair, snub nose and wide smile. Amélie had accepted Robyn in her life as if it were the most natural thing in the world to have her there.

A surge of affection rose like a powerful wave and threatened to overcome her. After her father's death, Robyn had taken it upon herself to watch over her, support her and be a friend. In her free time, she arranged trips out with Amélie and Amélie's best friend, Florence. The girls both confided in Robyn, treating her as an older sister, or aunt. While their relationship was strong, nothing changed the fact that Amélie was not hers: she was Davies' and Brigitte's, and had a family who adored her. In many ways, Robyn would do better to sever links and move on with her own life, yet however much she might want to, Robyn couldn't detach herself emotionally from this bright, enthusiastic teenager who reminded her more each day of the man she'd loved.

'So, what's he called?'

'Schrödinger, after a Nobel Prize-winning Austrian physicist.'

'That's a bit weird, isn't it? I'd call him Shadow.'

The cat pawed at the screen again.

'See, he prefers Shadow.'

Robyn smiled. 'In that case, I'll have to change his name. So, when do you want to come around and meet him properly?'

'It's half-term this week and I'm going to Birmingham with Florence and her mum tomorrow, but we'll be back by six. Can I come around in the evening?'

'Sure. How about eight? I should be back by then. You can stay over if you fancy.'

'Great. Want me to bring a DVD to watch?'

'Why not? You choose.'

Ending the call, Robyn stroked the kitten, now standing on the edge of the dining table. The animal turned and rubbed his head against her hand.

'Better get you settled in.' She lifted him and placed him on the floor. He raced off to the other side of the room and back again, making her smile.

It was good Amélie was coming. She hadn't stayed over for a while and it would give them plenty of time to talk. She rubbed her neck. The muscles were bunched up and sore to the touch. Her gaze fell on the red anemones. She ought to start phoning florists and ask about them. No. She was working an investigation. There was no point in chasing after ghosts or hoax photographs. Davies couldn't have sent the anemones. It might be no more than a generous gesture from one of her team to lift her spirits. She refused to consider any other explanation. She shut her eyes, but a vision of Tessa's bloodied face made them fly open again. Her restlessness was due to frustration. She wasn't making sufficient progress in either case. Her brain was swollen with possibilities and the seemingly impossible task ahead.

It was going to require a marathon effort from all her team to interview everyone known to both victims, and without motive or suspects they would inevitably become demoralised. DCI Flint would be waiting for her to nosedive. He might be polite to her face and seemingly respectful, but she could sense the undercurrent of loathing under that façade. She slumped back onto her chair. That was nonsense. Of course Flint didn't loathe her. Where was all this negativity coming from? What was the matter with her? This self-pitying attitude was unlike her, and why did she suddenly care what DCI Flint, or anybody, thought of her? She needed to regain her grip on reality.

The answer was the same as it had been the last few weeks – Davies. The cat leapt gently onto her knee and headbutted her. As she caressed Schrödinger's head, she questioned her motives for inviting Amélie over and for bringing the cat home. Was it simply because she cared about the girl, or was she somehow unconsciously trying to lure Davies out in the open and to her?

CHAPTER TWENTY-ONE

THEN

The boy opens the front door to a weedy man with long arms. His smile reminds the boy of a predator – a crocodile.

He holds out a milky-white hand and says, 'Hello. I'm Clark. I've come about the room.' Clark's voice is soft and lilting, from a place the boy has never visited – southern Ireland. He wears round spectacles that make his insipid blue eyes look distorted and washed out, and he tugs repeatedly at a pale ginger moustache that barely covers his top lip.

The boy doesn't take Clark's outstretched hand. Instead, he opens the door wide and says, 'Mum's in the kitchen.'

He's cheesed off about the whole thing. He doesn't want a lodger to be using his room, especially someone who looks like Clark.

'I don't know how else I'm supposed to pay the rent,' his mother had said, arms folded and a determined expression on her face, when he'd protested about giving up his room. 'If we don't take somebody in, we'll all be out on the streets.'

He'd had no choice and carried his meagre pile of belongings to his sister's room. His mother got a mattress from the charity shop and laid it on the floor next to his sister's bed. It smelt of sweat and was covered in stains, but they're now hidden under a sheet, and he'll spend each night on it, listening to his sister's soft breathing while Clark sleeps in his old room.

His mother is all over the man, almost curtsying at the sight of him. He's equally polite, complimenting her on her clean house and charming son. She's bought a sponge cake especially for him, to make him feel welcome, and cuts him a generous slice. The boy watches as Clark breaks off small pieces with his slim, ladylike fingers, and pops them one by one into his mouth, making appreciative noises as if his mother had baked the cake herself.

His sister is called downstairs and she enters the kitchen with a skip until she sees the man at the table, then she is suddenly shy and says hello in the quietest voice before sitting at her place, opposite her brother. Their mother cuts them both small slices of cake but for once the boy has no appetite.

Clark licks the crumbs from his fingers, all the while never taking his eyes from his sister, and then says how lovely it is to be part of a family. His mother simpers in an irritating fashion and thanks him before making another pot of tea. As she turns away, she doesn't see what the boy sees – Clark staring at his sister, like he'd rather eat her instead of the cake.

When the boy's mother returns, Clark smiles at her again and thanks her. The boy notices the smile never reaches his hooded eyes, and he is suddenly anxious for them all. What has his mother let into their house?

CHAPTER TWENTY-TWO

Even though a sharp frost had fallen overnight, it was unbearably stuffy in the office. Robyn had been forced to scrape ice from her windscreen before leaving home and travelling the fifteen minutes to work. In spite of taking painkillers, she still had a dull headache. Normally, she'd have ignored it and gone for a run, but she'd spent the time instead ensuring everything was ready for Amélie later that day, and all evidence of her search for Davies locked away in a cupboard. She'd set up a clean litter tray and bowls of food and water for her new lodger, who appeared to be house-trained, and left Schrödinger sitting on the back of the settee, staring out of the window. It would be nice to have someone to welcome her when she returned.

It was very early but she wanted to get started before any of her officers arrived. She picked up the list of Gregson's contacts and double-checked none had been ex-military or had any history of shooting. It was a task she'd not wanted to put off for so long but it yielded no positive results.

A siren wailed in the distance. The sound increased as it approached, and she moved across to the window to watch the blue light of an ambulance as it sped past the station in the direction of the hospital. Two more cars had pulled into spaces in the car park below. It wouldn't be long until it was full and some latecomers would have to use the car park ten minutes away by foot.

She spun around. The door had opened. Shearer, face unshaven, walked in.

'Should have guessed you'd be here,' he said with a wry grin.

'Says the man who looks like he's slept in the cells all night.'

'Sleep is a luxury I can't afford. Thought I'd come in and get started.'

'Great minds,' said Robyn. 'Fancy a coffee? I was about to kick the machine into life.'

Shearer yawned and stretched. 'Sounds like a great idea. I've run out of milk at home. Don't suppose you've got a bacon roll hiding anywhere?'

She laughed. 'I can only offer coffee.'

'That'll do. I'll pick up something later. I'm not interrupting you, am I?'

'Yes, but I can manage. I needed some peace and quiet to order my thoughts. I managed that and now I'm ready to tackle the cases.'

'Yeah, handling two cases simultaneously is a bit crap. I'd offer to help out but we're still tidying up the assault in Stafford. Can't believe how some people behave. It's mad out there.'

Robyn was only half-listening, thinking instead of how best to approach each investigation. She'd probably keep Matt and Anna working together on the Gregson case.

Shearer took a sip and winced. 'That is mega-hot. What is it with this machine? It either produces stuff that tastes like soap or it scalds your tongue off.'

'It's decent coffee. Blow on it and stop moaning.' Robyn marched back to her desk.

He blew on the coffee and scowled at it then took a tentative sip. 'This is still hot.'

'You really are an old grouch, aren't you? Want me to blow on it for you?' Robyn crossed her arms and pursed her lips.

Shearer snorted in a friendlier manner. 'I'll manage. And of course I'm a grouch. I had two hours' sleep last night. I've got a stack of paperwork to sift through, a case to close, a disgusting individual who held a woman and baby hostage to interview again, and I've got to appease my boss. And to top it all, I'll have to try and prevent PC Murray from knocking into you every two minutes. It's going to be a long day.' He stomped to his desk and, dropping onto his chair, plonked his mug down and grabbed at a file. 'Cheers for the coffee. It's just what I needed,' he muttered.

Robyn smiled to herself.

※

At just before eight, Robyn checked her watch. She'd been so busy she'd not noticed the time tick by. She had arranged a visit to the fertility clinic in Tamworth, and she'd need to get going if she was to reach the place before nine.

The clinic looked like an ordinary, brown-brick office block rather than a place that could transform people's lives. Robyn felt an instant of sorrow as she pressed the buzzer outside the door. She hadn't needed to attend such a place, but she understood the pain of desperately wanting a child.

She waited in the bright, cheerful reception before being escorted along a thick, carpeted corridor to an office at the far end. Mr Galloway, the consultant who'd seen Henry Gregson, was small and lean, and he leapt to his feet with an energetic burst when Robyn entered.

'Sit down, Ms Carter,' he said smoothly, as if she were one of his patients. 'Such a terrible thing to happen. Tessa was a joy to work with: bubbly, hard-working and compassionate. She'll be sorely missed.'

'Thank you for sparing time to talk to me,' said Robyn.

'I don't know how I can be of much assistance to you. We don't get much time to socialise or chat in this job, I'm afraid, other than to ask the nurses for various medical information or assistance. I know little about the staff here.'

'I understand. Can you tell me anything about Tessa at all?'

'Only to reiterate what I've already told you. She worked efficiently. She was invariably cheerful. We like our staff to be upbeat and caring. It's important. We deal with so many people for whom we are their last hope of having children, and it's good to have friendly nurses like Tessa on board.'

'She didn't appear anxious about anything, maybe less focused or distracted recently?'

'Far from it. She was assisting me on Monday and was quite ebullient. I remarked on it and she said she was looking forward to something "major" happening. I didn't pry. I was on a tight schedule and had several patients to see. I suggest you talk to some of the others here. They have more opportunity to gossip.'

'My officers have interviewed those who were her friends, but I might talk to one or two.'

'Try Juliet Fallows. She's one of her closest friends.'

'Can I ask you about a patient?'

He pursed his lips. 'Patient confidentiality. I won't be at liberty to assist you on that.'

'The patient in question is deceased. He was murdered on Tuesday.'

'I still can't reveal medical information. You know the score.'

'I do. This isn't so much about that. I wondered which nurse was dealing with him. He had an appointment with you, and I wondered if Tessa was assisting you that day.'

'Who's the unfortunate person?' He folded his hands in front of him and gave her a clear-eyed look.

'Henry Gregson. He had a consultation with you a couple of weeks ago. His wife Lauren has been here too.'

He nodded. 'I know the Gregsons. Henry did consult me. Let me see when it was.' He clicked his computer mouse and dragged up his appointment schedule. 'He attended the clinic on Tuesday the seventh. Just over a week ago.'

'Was Tessa working with you that day?'

He glanced at the screen again. 'Yes, she was. Is there some connection between their deaths?'

Robyn returned his steady gaze. 'I can't comment on that, sir. I'd appreciate it if you could keep this conversation between us for now.'

'I'm very good at keeping confidences, and I wish you luck. I wouldn't want your job. Must be quite demoralising some days.'

Robyn didn't respond. Her mind was whirring again with possibilities.

He stood to see her out of the office and spoke once more as they stood by the door. 'You might want to ask Juliet about the team.'

'Team?'

'She and Tessa got involved in a quiz team together. Tessa was revising for a quiz a while back. I overheard her and Juliet testing each other on all the bones in the human body. The others on the team might be able to assist with your enquiries.'

'You don't know who they are?'

'Sorry. Not a clue. I know Tessa was pretty keen on the quiz nights. Struck me as unusual – quiz nights aren't my idea of a fun night out. Thought it strange two young women would think otherwise. Shouldn't they be out at nightclubs, pubs or out on the town? I certainly was when I was their age. Mind you, nowadays, I give anything for a quiet night in with a decent Burgundy.'

Robyn headed back to reception, hoping to catch Juliet Fallows, but she wasn't at work. She got details of her address in Hamstall

Ridware – just outside Yoxall – and left the clinic, musing on Galloway's words. It wasn't that strange for two women to join a local quiz team. Both lived in rural communities. There wasn't much in the way of nightlife for single women. She should know. She hadn't had a fun night out or any social life for two years.

CHAPTER TWENTY-THREE

It had been pandemonium in the office all morning, and after 1 p.m. Shearer finally decamped to an interview room, along with Gareth Murray, to give Robyn a chance to make headway on her cases.

She'd never experienced such disorganisation and so many distractions. Everybody was under duress, not helped by DCI Flint, who'd been in three times asking for updates on all the cases. Tom Shearer looked like she felt – baggy-eyed, hung-over with work and the demands being placed on him. She had no time to feel sorry for him. Following a television appeal for witnesses to the assault made on Henry Gregson, the phones had been ringing non-stop.

Moving about the office had been a tightly choreographed procedure with each of them side-stepping and shuffling to get to drawers, cupboards, files and the coffee machine, which had been refilled three times.

Forensics had dropped off Tessa Hall's iPad, so Robyn had swapped the teams about. David was now searching through car registrations in the vicinity of Cannock Chase on the fourteenth of February, while Anna examined the device.

'You okay with that, Anna?' Robyn asked.

Anna, glued to the screen, was tapping it repeatedly. Suddenly she realised she was being spoken to, stopped to tidy a strand of hair behind her ear. 'Sure. Sorry. It's a little unusual. Tessa appears to have deleted her browsing history and cookies.'

Robyn scrunched her nose. 'You'll be able to fish out any deleted history, won't you?'

'Of course. Leave it to me. I'm trying to get into her emails at the moment. Need a password.'

'Try Schrödinger.'

'I tried that first. It doesn't work. I'll crack it. Give me a few minutes.' She lowered her face, her long, straight fingers flying over keys, fully concentrated on her task. The series of codes flying across the screen were a mystery to Robyn. She straightened her back and decided she needed to fit some training into her schedule. She'd been planning on doing the Ironman event in June and up until January had been in great shape for it. Since the arrival of the photograph, she'd dropped a few of her gym sessions and it was becoming obvious. She'd have to fit some training back in, even if it meant less sleep, or drop out of the event altogether.

Robyn had always looked after her body. A sugar-free diet and daily exercise kept her in physical and mental shape. She missed the regular rush of endorphins that came with her early-morning runs or cycle rides. She mentally chastised herself. She ought to have gone this morning.

'Guv, you definitely want to see this,' said Matt, waving Harry McKenzie's pathology report on Tessa Hall.

'Go on,' she said.

'Tessa died due to a blow to the head resulting in a fractured skull and a massive haemorrhage to the brain, as we suspected. But get this… she was expecting a baby. Harry reckons the foetus is about two months old.'

Robyn took a sharp breath. 'Do we know who she was going out with?'

Matt winced. 'No. None of her friends or work colleagues knew about any steady boyfriend. She didn't tell a soul about the mysterious man.'

'Did you speak to Juliet Fallows?'

'I interviewed her,' said Mitz. 'She said the same as the others. Tessa hadn't mentioned any new boyfriend.'

'That can't be right. The only reason I can think she'd keep a relationship quiet would be because she was seeing a married man. We must establish who that man might have been. Has nobody come forward? Surely if he cared about her, he'd have wanted to know who killed her?'

'Unless he killed her because she was pregnant,' said Anna.

Robyn rubbed her forehead in dismay. 'As much as I hate that idea, it's possible. That makes it even more imperative we identify him. I'm seeing Juliet Fallows about another matter in half an hour. I'll see if she knows any more. Talk to her parents, relatives, anybody. We have to locate this man.' She took a step backwards as another idea struck her. 'Tessa had five hundred pounds in her purse, which I found odd. I've just had a rather unsavoury thought. Her boyfriend or somebody – maybe even his wife – might have given it to her towards an abortion.'

'I'm in,' said Anna. 'Oh. She hasn't got any emails. She's deleted them all. That isn't normal. There ought to be one or two hanging about in the trash at least. Who deletes every email?'

Robyn came across and looked over her shoulder. 'Somebody who's trying to hide something.'

'An affair?'

Robyn wasn't so sure. It seemed peculiar to delete all email history. 'I don't know. You'd delete them if you were hiding them from somebody, but she lived alone. Who'd see them? Is there no correspondence between her and her lover?'

'Nothing. I can't retrieve a thing. Someone with excellent computer skills has deleted them all, or told her how to.'

'Maybe the killer deleted them.' Mitz's suggestion rang true for Robyn.

'Is she on any social media sites?'

'She was. She's deleted her Facebook account.'

'When?'

'Two weeks ago. And she's closed her Twitter and Instagram accounts,' Anna said, as she pulled up the information on her own computer, which she was using in tandem with the iPad.

'That's really strange. She's been described as bubbly, and yet she'd dropped out of all social media activity. That doesn't make any sense. Keep checking, Anna.'

Robyn checked her watch. It was coming up for 4 p.m. and she had only an hour or two left to make headway before she clocked off. Tonight, Amélie was coming over, and she had to finish before six.

She dragged up Harry McKenzie's post-mortem report on Henry Gregson and reminded herself of the details. Henry had been killed by a .455 cartridge that entered the left side of his neck and into his spine at C6/7. The tissue and organ damage corroborated Connor's findings. She thought once more about Henry's sister, Libby, and her boyfriend, Tarik. Even though she'd been trying to establish a connection between Henry, Lauren and Tessa, she hadn't completely ruled out Tarik, who had history with Henry and knew his sister well. Had he or Libby also known Tessa? She made a note to talk to them both again, and stuck it on her desk to remind her. She was about to leave when Anna sidled up to her.

'You might be right about the money in Tessa's purse. I just checked out the cost of a private abortion and it's about £500.'

Robyn winced at the news. 'Thanks, Anna. It gives us another avenue to pursue.' As she darted from the office to rendezvous with Juliet Fallows, she wondered if there could possibly be a link between the secretive, pregnant young nurse who knew Henry Gregson, and his wife, who desperately wanted a child.

CHAPTER TWENTY-FOUR

DAY FOUR – FRIDAY, 17 FEBRUARY, LATE AFTERNOON

Juliet Fallows, with hair the colour of stewed plums, pulled at the ends of a cardigan dragged over a beige woollen dress that stretched over ample hips. Her tights matched her hair, and beige, furry slippers completed the picture. She didn't smile but instead bustled Robyn into the kitchen, shutting the door and talking quietly.

Loud noises came from the sitting room.

'My kids,' she said by way of an explanation for the machine gun fire that suddenly blasted from next door. No sooner had she spoken than the kitchen door opened and a boy in his mid-teens swaggered in, jeans low on his waist, the peak of his baseball cap facing backwards. He nodded at the adults, said hi, crossed the room to the fridge, pulled out a carton of juice and headed back to the door.

'No you don't. Use a glass,' said Juliet.

'No point. I'll drink it all. Saves on washing up.' The boy gave a sly smile and disappeared, leaving the door wide open. Juliet shut it.

'He's diabetic. He needs to keep up his sugar levels,' she said by way of an explanation.

'I'm sorry to disturb you, and for your loss. I understand you and Tessa were good friends.'

Juliet walked across to the sink, ran the tap cold and poured a glass of water, which she drank slowly. 'We were. I liked Tessa. She was a breath of fresh air. Get to my age, you've seen your fair share of disappointments and become disillusioned with life, but Tessa was vibrant. I took to her the first day I met her at work. She'd moved to Barton-under-Needwood and was asking about places to go out. I told her I didn't socialise at all, that I'd split up from my ex and had two teenagers, and quite honestly wasn't up to going out. It's really hard to find your feet again once you've been in a long-term relationship. I'm not exactly a great catch, and to be honest, I'd suffered a bit of a confidence knock after Gerry. Tessa was a great listener.'

'I heard you played on the same quiz team,' Robyn said.

Juliet nodded. 'When she found out we were living only a few miles apart, she suggested we went out together. She was a real go-for-it type. Barton's only a few miles up the road from here, so we agreed to meet at the pub in Yoxall because it's midway between the two of us. That night there was a quiz on in the pub and the place was packed. While Tessa was at the bar getting us drinks, she got talking to this guy Anthony who was hoping to play but had been let down by two of his team. He asked her if we'd like to join him, so we did. It was one of the best nights I'd had in ages. We won the prize fund of forty pounds that night. Anthony decided we were his lucky mascots and invited us to join them again at the next quiz night.

'By the end of last year, we'd had enough of going along to quiz nights. Anthony was too serious about the whole thing. We preferred the social side of it – enjoyed a few drinks and giggles. It got me out and because of those evenings, I met some nice people who I see now and again. I've got Tessa to thank for dragging me out of my shell and helping me find my mojo again.'

'I'd like to talk to the others on the team, too, if you have their contact details.'

Juliet's eyebrows rose high on her forehead. 'I don't have them any more. I deleted them after I stopped going to the quiz nights. There seemed no point in hanging on to them.'

'Not to worry. I'll find them. You spoke to Sergeant Patel about Tessa, but I'm going to ask again if you suspected she'd been worried about somebody maybe stalking her, or bothering her, or if she'd mentioned anybody new in her life.'

'No. Nothing. She hit it off with most people. She was so enthusiastic about everything – her job, her life – everything. I really can't imagine who'd kill her.'

'We believe she was seeing somebody – possibly a married man. Did she say anything to you about meeting up with a boyfriend, or give any hints about a new man in her life?'

Juliet looked downwards before speaking. 'This is going to sound nasty but I really don't mean it to be that way. Tessa was a charming, good-looking girl. She flirted outrageously with anyone who glanced in her direction, and she had a few admirers. She was sexually uninhibited. Her mantra was carpe diem, and she lived her life as she wanted. She had one-night stands with at least one of the guys on the quiz team, and some of the blokes we met in various pubs. She told me once that she'd been in a long-term relationship before she moved to Barton and it had become too claustrophobic for her, so she'd broken it off to "have some fun" while she was still young. She didn't say anything about a new man, or a married one, to me. Although, come to think of it, she did seem bouncier than usual on Monday. She was singing. I remember she was singing. I've only seen her at work since we stopped the quiz nights. In fact, I haven't seen any of the others since last December. That's all I can tell you.'

'I understand. You haven't spoken to any of the team at all?'

She shook her head. 'No need to talk to them. I don't suppose Tessa did either.'

The door opened again. This time a girl, about eighteen, came into the kitchen. Like her brother, she exuded an air of confidence and was unfazed by seeing Robyn in the room. 'You seen my fags, Mum? Terence says he hasn't got them, but I left them by the telly,' she said, gazing at Robyn with almond eyes. 'You a copper?'

Robyn nodded.

'I haven't seen them,' said Juliet. 'Ask him again.'

'I will. He can't keep his thieving hands off anything,' she said, eyes still on Robyn. She directed her next sentence at Robyn, ignoring the look on her mother's face. 'We could have done with you when my dad was bashing my mum up.' With that, she wandered off. Raised voices joined the sound of gunfire and then it went quiet.

Robyn caught the look in Juliet's eyes. She'd seen it before in the eyes of other victims of abuse. 'He beat you?' she asked, quietly.

Juliet twisted at her cardigan and nodded. 'It's over now. I left him. I don't want to talk about it again – ever.'

'Did you report him?'

'No. I left him.' She stared hard at Robyn. 'And that's that. Steph, my girl, still has issues about it as you can tell, but I've got on with my life. Gerry is no longer part of it. I'm getting over it in my own good time.'

Robyn paused in case the woman wanted to say more but she clamped her lips tightly shut and wrapped her arms protectively around her body. This wasn't the time to talk further about an abusive husband.

'One last question. Do you know this couple?' She pulled out photographs of Lauren and Henry Gregson from a file she'd been holding, and showed them to Juliet.

'I recognise them. They've visited the clinic. I've seen them in the waiting room there.'

'Did you have any dealings with either of them?'

'No, they weren't my patients.'

Robyn returned the photographs to the file and sighed inwardly. She'd hit another dead end.

'Tessa had a relationship with at least one of the team members. Do you know who?'

Juliet gave a light shrug. 'She didn't tell me who. We were chatting in the staffroom and she let it slip, but when I asked her who she'd slept with, she put her finger to her lips and giggled.'

'You said Anthony asked you to join the team.'

'Yes, that's right. He was older than the rest of us. He was quite flirty with Tessa. I doubt she slept with him. She was always taking the piss about him behind his back. Besides, he's old enough to be her father and I don't think he's her type.'

'Does he live in Yoxall?'

'No. Stafford way, I think.'

'You don't know his surname?'

'It's not the sort of thing you mention. I don't know any of their surnames.'

'Who else played on the team?'

'Roger, he lives in the countryside near Hoar Cross, just outside Yoxall, and Liam. He lives in Yoxall village.'

Robyn frowned lightly. Henry Gregson's friend Liam lived in Yoxall. It couldn't be the same man, could it? 'Does Liam work at MiniMarkt in Lichfield?'

'Yes. I think so. His partner, Ella, sometimes came along to watch. So did Roger's girlfriend although she hung about the bar area.' Juliet shuffled from foot to foot.

Steph cruised into the kitchen with a packet of cigarettes in her hand. 'Got 'em,' she said. 'Have you told her about what he did?' she asked her mother.

'Not now, Steph,' Juliet said.

Steph turned to Robyn. 'That's half the problem. She won't tell anyone what really happened. It's not too late to say something, is it?'

'It's not too late if your mother wants to press charges,' Robyn said.

'See.' Steph rested her gaze on her mother, who tugged once more at her cardigan.

'This isn't the time, Steph.'

Steph huffed loudly. 'There's never a right time, is there?'

'I'll leave you to think it over. If you want to contact me about anything, here's my card.' With that, Robyn left the house. It was getting late and she still had to prepare for Amélie, but first she had to talk to Liam.

※

Liam was on the shop floor behind one of the tills, serving a line of customers, his face grey and sombre. He saw Robyn enter the shop and called across for a co-worker to handle the customers, and then beckoned her to join him in the staffroom again.

'Any news?' he said as soon as they were alone.

'I'm sorry. Not yet. How are you all?'

Liam's voice was downbeat. 'Astra's refusing to eat. We're at our wits' end. She's in a right mood. Keeps asking for Henry. I don't know when she'll get over this.'

'She will. Give her time. Keep distracting her. Take her out to the park, play games with her. Children are resilient. Eventually, she'll forget about Henry.' Robyn hoped her words didn't sound too callous.

There was silence, then in a heavy voice, Liam replied, 'It's such a shame she'll forget him. He was so good to her. Treated her like his own.'

'Maybe it would help if you take her to visit Lauren. She'll see that Henry isn't at home and gradually, she'll learn that he's gone.'

'We should do that. I'll ring Lauren and see how she feels about it. Why have you come? Not just to see how we are?'

She shook her head. 'I'm here about Tessa Hall. I don't know if you heard but she was found dead at her home yesterday.'

Liam's eyes opened wide. 'You can't be serious. Tessa?'

'I spoke to Juliet, who said you knew her.'

Liam blinked repeatedly, trying to comprehend what he'd heard. 'Tessa?' he asked again.

'I'm so sorry to break the news to you. Especially after what happened to Henry.'

'We weren't friends as such, but of course I knew her. We played together on the same quiz side a few times. Tessa? I can't believe it. Who do you think killed her?'

'We've only just begun our investigations and are looking into a few possibilities. Did she mention a boyfriend to you?'

Liam stuck out his bottom lip. 'I'm not somebody she'd share that information with. I got along with her but we didn't have any cosy chats. Ella wasn't her greatest fan. Tessa was a bit too flirty for her liking, so I kept out of Tessa's way. Didn't want to upset Ella. Tessa was always being chatted up. She was nice, although too full-on for me. I prefer the quiet type.'

'Ella used to attend the quiz nights?'

'Yeah. Now and again, she'd come along with Astra, depending where the quiz was being held. She never participated though. She preferred to support us.'

'You knew Tessa was a nurse?'

Liam nodded. 'Yes. She said she was. Tamworth, I think.'

'Did Henry ever mention her?'

'Tessa? No. Why?'

Robyn smiled tightly. 'Tessa worked at the fertility clinic that Henry attended. I wondered if he had mentioned her name.'

Liam shook his head. 'All I know about the clinic was he didn't want to go. Told me he hated the idea of being probed and questioned about his sex life. He didn't even want children yet. He certainly never mentioned Tessa. That's weird. You don't think their deaths are related in some way?' His mouth opened in astonishment. 'No. That couldn't be the case. They didn't know each other. I'm sure of it.'

'When did you last see Tessa?'

'End of last year. We went to a quiz in Abbots Bromley. We all had too much to drink and we didn't win. We decided to call it a day after that.'

'Forgive me for asking but what's the attraction of a quiz night?'

Liam shrugged. 'It makes for a night out with company rather than sitting in the corner of a pub, drinking alone. Going along to a few quizzes gives you the chance to try other pubs, meet fresh faces. It's the social side that appeals to most people. Not so much for me – I've always liked trivia, especially sport trivia, so I got to test out my knowledge.'

'We only have the first names of your teammates. You don't have any contact details for them do you?'

'No. I had Roger's but after the team folded, I deleted it from my contact list.'

It was the same response Juliet had given. Robyn persisted. 'Do you happen to know their surnames? It would make it easier for us to track them down.'

'Juliet's name is Farrow or something similar, and Roger is Roger Jenkinson, but I don't know Anthony's. It never came up in conversation.' He sighed heavily and shook his head in dismay. 'I'm really sorry about Tessa.'

※

Robyn returned to her car and phoned Anna to see if anything had been uncovered while she'd been interviewing Juliet and Liam. She was about to ring off when she asked, 'Anna, would you say a quiz night in a pub was your idea of fun?'

Anna snorted a response. 'No, but I enjoy playing computer games in my spare time, so I'm not the right person to ask. Mitz likes watching quiz shows and shouting out the answers to the questions. And we both like pubs. Does that help?'

Robyn smiled at the thought of Mitz glued to a quiz show. 'I suppose so. Each to their own, eh?'

She mentally filed away her thoughts about quiz nights not being the most entertaining of evenings for young women or men, and drove back towards Stafford. There was no more she could achieve today, and she had to get back home for Amélie.

CHAPTER TWENTY-FIVE

DAY FOUR – FRIDAY, 17 FEBRUARY, EVENING

Schrödinger purred as he wound himself around Robyn's feet. She ignored his demands and studied the photograph even though she'd committed it to memory and knew every detail of it.

So far, her efforts to contact Peter Cross, Davies' superior, had come to nothing. She wasn't surprised by that fact. He worked for military intelligence and was something of a ghost. Davies had worked for him, and with Davies gone, she had no way of contacting Peter Cross.

A printed A4 sheet contained all the flights that had left Morocco that day. Given he'd left their riad in Marrakesh at six that morning to cross the Atlas Mountains, he'd had sufficient time to travel to any number of airports in Morocco and catch a flight back to the UK. The nearest airport was Marrakesh Menara Airport. He might even have gone to Casablanca Mohammed V Airport, or, at a push, caught a flight from Agadir. All were possible.

She faced the window and fought back the rising anger that came with such considerations. If Davies was alive, he should have bloody well contacted her directly and not put her through this. It was so ridiculously inconsiderate and cruel. And, if he were alive now, she wasn't sure how she felt about him after this. How could he justify what he'd done – the pretence, the lies, the pain? She snatched up the photograph. She was sick of all this. She hadn't got any time for stupid games.

Robyn checked her watch. There was still time to catch her cousin Ross before he went home and before Amélie came over. He was the only person who could help her with this.

※

Robyn found a parking space outside the offices of R&J Associates, behind her cousin's silver Vauxhall. The premises were in the main street in Stafford, sandwiched between an insurance company and an estate agency. She opened the door and entered the narrow hallway, shared by several companies, before bounding up the stairs that led to his office on the first floor.

She waited outside the door before knocking. A raised voice indicated Ross was in.

'I warned you,' he said loudly. 'I'm not putting up with this behaviour for a minute longer.'

She smiled in spite of herself and knocked.

'Come in,' yelled Ross.

She opened the door and slid into the office, shutting the door quickly behind her.

Ross, in a dark-blue ill-fitting suit with tie undone, was looking hot and bothered. He pointed to the basket beside his desk and shouted, 'Down!' The young Staffordshire bull terrier on his large leather chair looked mournful but remained resolutely fixed to the spot.

'For heaven's sake, Duke, get off my chair.'

Robyn patted her thigh. 'Duke, want to see what I've got in my pocket?'

The dog looked over to Robyn then jumped down from the chair, scooting over to her. She fussed over him before giving him a dog biscuit she'd grabbed from the tin marked 'Duke' as she left the house.

'Don't reward his bad behaviour,' said Ross, sliding onto his chair before Duke could return.

Robyn grinned. 'It's your own fault. You let him climb up there when you first got him, and now he thinks it's his chair. You should have been firmer with him when you were training him. Besides, the chair probably smells of you, and when you're out, he likes to feel close to you.'

Duke plopped down on his haunches and stared at her intently.

Ross grumbled something unintelligible. 'I've just got in. You were lucky to catch me.'

'I was going to phone but I was passing anyway and thought I'd take a chance,' she replied, stroking behind the dog's ear.

'So, what can I help you with?'

'No small talk first? You want to get straight to the point?'

'I'm not one for small talk as you well know. You're here because you need my help. And I'm happy to give it to you. What is it this time? Murder, missing person?'

Robyn sat on the chair opposite Ross and rested her elbows on the desk, fingers steepled against her lips. She wasn't sure how to broach the subject but Ross, like her, preferred to get to the point.

'I think Davies is alive.'

Silence fell, broken only by the noise of Duke's claws as he clattered across the wooden floor and tumbled into his basket with a heavy sigh.

Ross stared at her, then picked up a pen and twirled it between his fingers. 'Go on,' he said.

She delved into her bag and slid the photograph of Davies across the table. 'I received this in January. It was postmarked London. At first, I thought it was faked, but now I'm not so certain. It's definitely Davies, but the date and time stamp on it show it was taken the day he was killed. I think it was snapped at a UK airport. If you look closely, you'll see souvenir double-decker toy buses on the stand behind the newspaper rack. It looks like a WHSmith store. The newspapers are all English ones. At first, I believed the picture was photoshopped, but I kept asking myself why? Why would somebody want me to believe he was alive?' She tilted her head backwards and stared into space. 'It makes no sense to me, Ross. I've tried to find out as much as I can. I can't get hold of Davies' old boss, Peter Cross. I'm running around chasing my tail on this. There's a message on the back of it.'

He turned the picture over and read it. '"Fact not fiction". That's brief and doesn't tell you much.'

'It might suggest that this picture is real. I believed Davies was dead, caught in an ambush – but that was fiction, and the fact is that somehow he travelled to an airfield, or airport, and caught a flight back to the UK instead of going across the Atlas Mountains to a meeting with an informant. For whatever reason, he or his superiors allowed me to believe he'd been killed.'

'And his ex-wife and his daughter,' said Ross, shaking his head. 'That's too cruel. Davies wouldn't have allowed that to happen.'

'I wondered about that when I first got the photo. I tried to justify his silence and told myself maybe he didn't know we'd been told he was dead. That we'd been told he was on a top-secret mission and couldn't contact us. I came up with all sorts of crazy notions. Oh, Ross, I have no idea what to think and it's doing my head in. I can't reason why it's happened. All I know is that I've been sent a photograph of Davies taken after his death. He was wearing that exact outfit the last time I saw him.'

'This is crazy, Robyn. Look, I don't want to be rude or disrespectful but maybe you're reading too much into this. It's normal you'd want to believe he's alive and that this isn't faked.'

Robyn tried to keep the ice out of her voice. 'I'm not clinging to false hope to absolve myself of guilt. That's what you mean, isn't it?'

'No, yes. No. You were in pieces after his death. You blamed yourself constantly for going to Morocco. You firmly believed you'd blown his cover. Robyn, I saw you. I watched you sink into the worst depression I'd ever seen. I saw life drain from you until you were an empty husk. You were a mess!'

'I know. I understand. I was in a dreadful state, and yes, I blamed myself for his death. I'm not trying to believe this picture is real so I can feel better about what happened. I'm not even sure I want Davies to be alive. I can't imagine how I'd cope with seeing him or allowing him back in our lives after this deception. I only want to find out who sent this photograph and why. It's eating me up. And then there are the flowers I received on Valentine's Day – anemones. Davies always sent anemones. Who'd know that? I've started to wonder if there's something more sinister going on.'

Ross's chin jutted forward. 'It's times like this I wish I hadn't given up smoking. This is so damn stressful. Robyn, I'm going to be blunt here. Have you considered the fact Davies might have set us all up? It's possible he had a completely different life – a family even – in another country, and he's fabricated this whole death scenario thing to start afresh. It has been known to happen.'

'It crossed my mind.'

'You assumed he was on missions when he left you for weeks on end and he never divulged where any of them were. He might have been living a double life.'

Robyn swallowed hard. She hated the thought she might have been taken for a fool. 'I discounted that theory.'

'Why? It's a good one. Davies never usually told you where he was headed. He always said his missions were secret yet he told you about Morocco. Why?'

'He said it was a low-risk mission. It was just a meeting and he thought it might not even go ahead.'

'Did he beg you to go?'

Robyn thought back to the day Davies tried hard to persuade her to join him in Morocco, cajoling her and tempting her, subtly persuading her. She nodded. 'Pretty much. He really wanted me with him there.'

'Robyn, you know where I'm going with this. Davies wasn't as virtuous as you like to pretend. He and Brigitte split up because he played away on several occasions. She'd had enough of his philandering and lies.'

'It wasn't like that with us,' she replied, stony-faced.

'No, but you had a fair few arguments, didn't you? You rang me on more than one occasion to voice your concerns about him.'

Robyn blinked away memories of the shouting and raised voices. Ross had touched a nerve. It was true she'd had moments when she'd wondered if Davies was being unfaithful.

'I don't want to hurt you. I never would, but let's get this into perspective. Davies could have been living with another woman and might have had his hand forced. He made the decision to choose her. Face it, Robyn, Davies might not be the man you believed him to be, and an anonymous individual wants you to know the truth.'

Robyn swallowed back the lump forming in her throat. She needed closure on this once and for all. 'So you'll help me?' she said.

'You know I will. But I'm doing this purely for you. You've wasted two years of your life mourning this man, and when I uncover the truth, I want you to start living again. I want you to put Davies out of your life, regardless of what's happened to him, and move on, find somebody else. Get out more and stop treating him like some saint, and you have to promise me one more thing.'

'What?'

'You'll get on with your own investigations and let me handle it alone. I mean it. Forget it for now. Get on with your case. Leave it entirely to me and don't pester me about my findings. I'll tell you when I've got something to tell you. Promise?' He waggled his heavy eyebrows at her to signal the end of the pep talk.

Robyn patted his hand. 'Promise. You're the best, Ross. I mean that.'

'Yeah. Sure I am. I'm a big softie at heart.'

'I've got to rush off. Amélie is staying over tonight to meet my new pet cat – Schrödinger.'

His eyes twinkled with mirth. 'You? A cat lady? Who'd have thought it? Hey Duke, you've got a new friend to play with when you go to visit Robyn next. You'll be able to play chase.' He grinned at her, creases forming at the sides of his eyes. 'Go on, scoot. Go see the kid and don't bring that naughty animal any more treats until he's learnt to get off my chair.'

CHAPTER TWENTY-SIX

Robyn glanced across at Amélie, in jeans, fashionably ripped, and a soft baby-pink jumper, arms clasped around her knees, shining pink toenails on elegant pale feet, and mouth slightly agape. Schrödinger was curled up next to her, head tucked into her side, the rise and fall of his tiny body indicating complete peace.

The girl was on the precipice of womanhood and had changed considerably from the round-faced girl with a blob of vanilla ice cream on the tip of her nose, giggling uncontrollably at the camera, while Robyn and Davies grinned wildly for the kind Spanish tourist who'd snapped their photo outside the Houses of Parliament. The picture stood on the mantelpiece over the fireplace that had not contained a crackling fire since Davies' death.

The Devil Wears Prada had been Amélie's choice, borrowed from her mother, Brigitte, who would not have looked out of place in the fashion industry with her sultry French looks, impeccable grooming and ability to wear any combination of clothes and make them look as if they'd been especially designed for her petite frame. Amélie had thrown the DVD on the table with carefree abandon before dropping full length onto the carpet to play with the cat.

'He's perfect,' she repeated as Schrödinger woke and nudged her elbow with his damp nose, deep vibrating murmurs of approval at her light touch along his backbone. 'How come you decided to get a cat all of a sudden?'

'His owner died unexpectedly. He seemed all alone and I felt sorry for him.' Her own words echoed in her head. Was she not lonely too? Was that not one of the reasons she'd taken him?

'Poor little thing. How old do you think he is?'

'At least four months. His eyes would have been blue when he was born and they take up to three months to change colour.'

'And what a colour they are. They're not just orange, they're Day-Glo orange. I know Richard would let me have a cat but it isn't fair, is it? He'd suffer too much.'

Amélie was talking about her stepfather, married to her mother before Davies had met Robyn. Richard, cheery-faced with his exuberant confidence, impeccably attired in freshly pressed shirts and slacks with razor-sharp creases, as if he were permanently about to step onto a deck of a yacht, was as proud of Amélie as if he'd sired her. He would do anything for his stepdaughter, even allow her a pet cat in spite of having a severe allergy to them.

'You can share this one,' said Robyn. 'He's taken to you.'

They'd talked about cats on many an occasion. For all her grown-up ways, Amélie had something missing – Davies. Her sudden adoration of cats came about roughly the same time Davies died. Robyn thought Amélie had transferred her feelings for her father onto the animals, and chosen cats because Davies had always loved them and read stories of *Mog the Cat* to her when she was very young. It didn't require a degree in psychology to work out Amélie's obsession with the creatures. She needed something of her own to love and that would always be there for her. Robyn understood that emotion. It was one she was familiar with herself. Why else would she be showering Davies' daughter with such affection? Because she was the daughter she and Davies never had together.

Amélie had allowed an opening in the conversation to mention Davies. Robyn couldn't resist seizing her opportunity.

'I reckon Davies would have loved him too,' she said.

Amélie rubbed the animal's head with the palm of her hand. 'He would've,' she replied.

Robyn didn't need to say anything else.

A myriad of emotions passed over Amélie's face. She gave a small cough before speaking again. 'I don't like to talk about him too much with Mum. It's difficult, what with her being with Richard. I feel I have to keep my thoughts to myself. I've chatted to Florence about him, of course, but it feels like he's moving away from me. I'm beginning to forget him, Robyn. And I worry I'll forget all about him completely one day. Sometimes, I can't picture exactly what he looked like. I have to look at photographs, and then I feel guilty. Like I shouldn't forget him. He was such a great dad. Even though he was away a lot, he'd be there for me as soon as he returned. And now I know why he was away, he's even more of a hero. Not many girls can say their dad was a spy like a real-life James Bond.'

The words dried on her lips and in that instant she'd transformed back to the vulnerable eleven-year-old who was shell-shocked to learn her father was dead. Robyn dropped beside her on the carpet and put an arm around her thin shoulders, making out the bony ridge of her collarbone.

'You won't ever forget him. Think of the way he'd throw back his head when he found something funny and erupt with laughter so noisy it would make you want to join in. Remember the way he'd kiss your forehead for no reason other than he cared about you. You might forget every detail of him, but you'll always remember something special about him, and that will keep him in your heart and alive forever.'

Amélie swallowed and returned her attention to Schrödinger. 'It's weird because sometimes I think I see him. Do you?'

Robyn tried not to tense at these words. 'That's normal. There are so many people who resemble others. It's only natural you'd see an identifying feature – a tall man with dark hair, glasses like those he wore – and think it's him. I've done it too. Soon after we lost him, I was crossing the road and was convinced I saw him in a crowd but it wasn't him. I chased after the man and when he turned around I could see the similarities, but it wasn't Davies.'

She'd not opened up about this before but if she wanted to gain Amélie's confidence, it was necessary. It had been a horrendous few weeks following his death. Soon after he'd been buried, she'd lost their baby she'd been carrying, and the loss of the two most precious gifts in her world had sent her spiralling downwards into a serious depression and breakdown. Her cousin Ross and his wife, Jeanette, had helped her through it. And now, she was dragging them both back into her mess by asking for help again.

She removed her arm and Amélie spoke again. 'It's horrible, isn't it? I was so sure it was him even though I knew it couldn't be. He did look like Dad, only older and thinner, and he wasn't dressed smartly like Dad. He was wearing a faded sweatshirt. Dad always looked like he was going into an important meeting. Always had the shiniest shoes.' She smiled at the memory.

'See, you remember all sorts of things once you start talking about him. You needn't worry about forgetting him,' said Robyn, hoping Amélie would say more about this unusual encounter.

'I even wondered if Dad had a long-lost twin brother. Florence said that was hardly likely and I was being silly, and maybe I needed to start wearing glasses. She was trying to cheer me up,' she explained.

'Where was this?' asked Robyn, keeping her tone light so as not to cause suspicion. 'Town?'

'Yes, at the CineBowl in Uttoxeter. We were at a friend's bowling birthday party at the end of January, and he was bowling a few lanes down from us. I didn't spot him to start with, but I'd just bowled a strike and was cheering, and I spotted him looking across at me. It was one of those weird moments. He stared right at me. I didn't know what to do. I told Florence and she looked across but he'd gone. I felt silly afterwards. It couldn't have been Dad. I suppose it'd happened because I'd been thinking about him a lot over Christmas. Anyhow, it's not happened again. I've not seen the man and we went to the bowling alley again three days ago.'

'I wouldn't let it bother you. As I said, it happens a lot. It's part of brains refusing to accept a loss. As for forgetting Davies, you won't. If you fancy we can talk and talk about him and it'll bring back all those happy memories. What about the time he decided we should all go camping?'

'And he forgot to bring a tin opener! His face. He turned every bag upside down looking for one. He was so sure he had brought it!'

'And he tried to open the tins with a stone.'

'And gave up and took us to the pub for dinner instead. We had such a laugh.' Amélie's face broke into a huge smile and they both began to laugh. Robyn, grateful to be part of this girl's life, was not going to press her further, but Amélie had given her something to consider – Davies might be alive and was watching them all.

CHAPTER TWENTY-SEVEN

Tony admired his reflection in the bathroom mirror. He was wearing well for a man in his late fifties. His hair was still as thick as it had been in his twenties, albeit silver-grey. His trip to the posh salon in Lichfield had been worthwhile, and the young man who'd cut and styled his hair for an exorbitant fee had done a decent job. The new hairstyle made him look ten years younger. If only his ex-wife, Sandra, could see him now.

He shrugged off the memory and whistled as he splashed eau de cologne on his hands and patted it onto his neck. It had been two years since she'd hightailed it with one of his so-called friends – one who ran a successful business and owned a flashy motor. Tony beamed newly whitened teeth at the man in the mirror. She'd be majorly pissed off when she found out she'd made a bad call. She should have stuck it out with him.

He checked his watch. Tee off time was at eight. It seemed very early to him, but being a novice at the sport and to the golf club, he wasn't going to question the club captain, Jefferson. Not after his secretary had rung to invite Tony to a private lesson. Tony was going up in the world.

It was only a fifteen-minute walk to the clubhouse from his tumbledown cottage in the lane. It would do him good. He'd been a bit short-breathed recently and a brisk walk should help improve his lung capacity. He patted his chest, breathed in the cold air and hoisted his bag of clubs onto his shoulder.

By the time he reached the main street and the golf-club entrance, he wasn't feeling great. The bag weighed a lot more than he'd first believed and had become increasingly heavy as he'd marched down the winding lane. He wiped the perspiration from his brow and made his way to the green. Jefferson had agreed to meet him there. Tony set down his clubs, removed his jacket, rolled it up and slipped it into the side pouch on his golfing bag, then put on his new golfing shoes. He patted his face with the cloth meant for his clubs and looked about. No one was around. It was amazing to think he was now a proud member of this exclusive club. He'd wanted to join for decades but could never afford it. Of course, that had all changed now.

He'd enjoy afternoons playing with like-minded folk. He needed this. Life hadn't been the greatest. He'd had to leave his job because of the pressures on him, and his marriage hadn't worked out. He'd struggled but now things were different. He deserved some comfort in his later years. He had it all planned out: make friends and acquaintances here, practise until he was pretty good at it, then head to warmer climates over the winter months to play: Spain, Portugal, maybe even further afield.

He picked out a club and gave it a swing. His head felt clammy from the walking and his chest was tight from carrying the bag. He stretched and loosened up, then resumed the golfer's stance and swung again. He still didn't feel too good. He should have driven to the club. He didn't hear anybody approach and it was only when his peripheral vision picked up a movement that he lifted his head and studied the figure near him. His brow furrowed.

'He told me about you,' said the person.

'What the heck are you on about? What are you doing here?'

'You shouldn't have made him do it.'

'He wasn't made to do anything,' Tony spat.

'And now, you're going to pay.'

Tony waved his club. The pain was getting worse – like steel bands stretching his rib cage. 'Clear off. I'm about to play a few holes with somebody. They'll be here any minute.'

'They won't. Nobody's due on the course for another hour and the clubhouse is empty. I arranged this meeting with you, not the club captain. Nobody even knows you're here. But they will when they find your body.'

The figure lifted a gun and pointed it directly at Tony, who dropped his club in surprise. 'You're mad. Put that down. We can discuss this.'

The face staring at him smiled – a cruel, cold smile. 'Bye, Tony.'

The blood surged, humming in his head. The pain in his chest intensified and the sweat poured again from his forehead. He opened his mouth to shout but the pain was too fierce and he fell onto his knees.

CHAPTER TWENTY-EIGHT

DAY FIVE – SATURDAY, 18 FEBRUARY

It was 8 a.m. and Robyn stood in front of the whiteboard, blocking out the racket coming from the other side of the office. Matt and Mitz had joined her there and were close enough to have a conversation without shouting over desks. Robyn winced as Shearer yelled something into his phone. He'd been extra vocal since his arrival ten minutes earlier. He slammed the phone onto the table and muttered something to Gareth. Without warning, he pushed back from his desk, leapt lightly to his feet and moved swiftly towards the door.

Gareth was a few seconds behind him. He paused to speak to Matt. 'Bloke dead on a golf course. Maybe he got hit by a golf ball.'

'Roger Jenkinson,' said Robyn. 'Lives just outside Yoxall. He might have dated Tessa Hall for a while. Her friend Juliet said Tessa slept with at least one of the men on the quiz team but doesn't think it was Anthony. Liam Carrington claims he stayed well away from Tessa so that only leaves Roger Jenkinson. Can you find out about him and talk to him, Mitz?'

'Will do. I've spoken to Tessa's parents but they don't know anything about a new boyfriend. I also found out they gave her the deposit for her house and have been paying half the mortgage for her. She's their only child and they wanted to help her out.

Totally devastated about her death. Sara Hall, her mother, could barely speak to me for tears. I thought I might go and visit them personally.'

'Good idea. They must be in a wretched state.'

Robyn's phone vibrated. It was Anna, who, along with David, was at Tessa's house, searching for anything that might lead to the identity of her boyfriend.

'I think we found something relevant – a contract note concerning an offshore account in Grand Cayman for Schrödinger Securities.'

Robyn slapped the palm of her hand on the desk in front of her. 'Photograph it and send it across immediately. Great work.'

'We'll bring back everything we think's relevant.' Anna rang off and Robyn rubbed her hands in satisfaction.

'Matt, Anna's sending across some new information concerning Tessa Hall. She might have been hiding money offshore. Obviously, we need to find out how she got it in the first place. Might be a trust fund from her parents or her lover. Mitz, talk to her folks. This might change how we handle this case. Up until now, we've been looking for a lover or some link to Henry Gregson. Now, we could be looking for somebody who uncovered this information and either blackmailed her or wanted a part of it.'

'You got it.'

Robyn threw her pen towards Matt, who caught it deftly. 'Matt, make the necessary additions.'

Matt gave a mock salute and removed the pen cap with a flourish, adding 'offshore account' next to Tessa Hall's name.

Robyn's attention flitted back to Henry Gregson. She still harboured doubts about Libby's boyfriend Tarik, who'd been in the vicinity on the day. Her instinct screamed he was withholding information, and not only was he in a relationship with Libby, there was also the matter of his brother, Nadir, beaten up at school by Henry and his friends. Seeking revenge for the attack on his brother years before was an unlikely motive, but Robyn had come across stranger cases. If Tarik already harboured a grudge against Henry, he might have been easily persuaded to attack the man. Robyn wasn't yet ready to discount Libby completely as a suspect. She might be behind the murder and have involved Tarik.

With that, Robyn left the busy office, headed for her Golf and programmed JJ Parts in Cannock into her satnav.

It took some considerable time to find the premises at the end of an almost deserted street filled with unoccupied buildings, boarded up and scrawled with graffiti. It turned out to be the smallest of garages, almost no bigger than an ordinary double garage, and shuttered up, with an ugly brick extension attached to its side. The door to it was locked and it was only after incessant banging on it that a short, barrel-chested man in overalls appeared. Robyn held her warrant card to the grimy glass and he unlocked the door.

'Brett?' she asked.

'That's me.'

'I'm DI Carter. We spoke on the phone earlier. I understand Tarik Akar was here Tuesday afternoon.'

Brett squared his shoulders and scratched at his cheek. His button-brown eyes were unusually bright and darted uncomfortably around the bleak office, resting on a tatty grey plastic chair. 'He was here.'

The office, if you could call it that, didn't feel used to Robyn. Apart from the chair, the only other piece of furniture was a shabby square table that looked like it had been rescued from a skip. There weren't the usual notices on the walls advertising services or price lists. An old tyre leant against the tall counter that separated the room from the closed workshop door. Behind the counter was a dusty shelf, housing several small boxes of spark plugs and other accessories. For Robyn, who took her own car for regular services and was used to garage waiting areas, this one felt false. Brett was shuffling uncomfortably as if he wished she'd leave.

'And what was the reason for his visit?'

'He came to collect some parts,' Brett replied, squeezing his nose with his thumb and finger. 'For Mike.'

Robyn pulled out a notepad and pen. 'Can you confirm he came to collect a distributor for a VW Passat?' She watched carefully as he digested her words. She had deliberately set him up, knowing full well that was not what he'd said. Brett fell perfectly into the trap.

'Yeah. That's right. For a VW Passat.'

'And you had to send out for one because you had the wrong one in stock?'

'Yeah.' His eyes had moved from the plastic chair to a pile of boxes stacked in one corner of the room.

'How many mechanics work here with you? It's not a very big place.'

'Only one other guy – Steve. He's out at the moment.'

'Would you mind if I took a look around?'

'There's nothing to see,' said Brett, too quickly for her liking.

'You're not working on anything at the moment?'

He shook his head. 'Bit quiet. Don't do much on a Saturday. Just tidying up. There's been an oil spillage out there. Don't want you to slip over or get messed up.'

Robyn nodded. There was no doubt he was hiding something. The location of the garage, hidden away on an abandoned industrial estate, and the general set-up inside, led her to wonder if there were illegal or dodgy dealings going on.

She thanked him, left the office and drove to the next street where she parked her car between a Ford Escort and a van. She doubled back to the garage on foot, padded silently to the shuttered door and listened to the faint voices and hammering coming from inside. Brett had lied. There were two men inside working on a vehicle. She found a spot in the doorway of a brick building, close to the garage, where she waited, listening to distant traffic and trying not to pay too much attention to the smell of stale urine. Ten minutes passed, then ten more. She stamped away the pins and needles in her feet and then cocked her head to one side to make out a new noise. It was the whirring of metal shutters as they were raised, followed by the growl of an engine starting up.

She dashed forwards, her body blocking the path of the Porsche being backed out. Brett spotted her in the rear-view mirror, braked and dropped his head into his hands. The man working the opening mechanism tried to drop the shutter again, but Robyn pressed forwards, stopping to take in the number plates recently unscrewed from the vehicle on the floor. It took no time to work out what was really happening in the garage. She held up a finger to the man. 'Don't think about running. We'll track you down in an instant.' She tugged at the driver's door handle and opened it. Brett didn't look up.

'If you'd like to get out of the vehicle, sir, we can talk about exactly what happened on Tuesday the fourteenth.'

⁂

It didn't take long to extract a confession. With officers en route to Mike's Motors to arrest the man and his employees, Robyn listened in silence as Brett told her the truth.

'It's Mike's operation. He gets requests for certain makes and models of vehicles to be nicked, and sends out a couple of guys to steal them. I get a call telling me what to expect in the garage, and when. Once the vehicle comes here, we respray it, or make a few modifications, swap the plates for false ones, and then it gets shipped off to Mike's contact.

'Sometimes we have a few issues with the cars. If there's a real problem, Mike sends over one of his mechanics to sort it. We don't have those skills. We took in an Audi Sunday. Needed to turn it around quickly. Got it ready for Tuesday morning as instructed and started it up to put it on the trailer and move it, but the engine cut out. We tried to fix it but it wouldn't go. I rang Mike, who said he'd send Tarik over to look at it. Tarik got here about lunchtime, but the bastard thing wouldn't work. Took him a good few hours to fix the problem. We got it loaded around 4 p.m., after he'd gone.'

'So how long was he here?'

'From twelve forty until almost four.'

'The whole time?'

'Yeah. He didn't go until it was working. Moaned about it taking so long.'

Robyn signalled for the officer by the door to take Brett away. She'd cracked a case, only not the one she wanted to resolve. It appeared Tarik Akar was in the clear and Robyn was facing a dead end.

※

The office was as busy as when she left it. Matt was coming to the end of a phone conversation. Mitz, with his back to the door, was also on the phone, and so deep in conversation he didn't hear Robyn return.

'Okay, thank you very much. If you could send that all over, that'd be a huge help. Thank you, sir.' Matt ended his call and immediately sprang up, notepad in hand.

'Schrödinger Securities is set up in Grand Cayman and only has one company director, Tessa Hall. It has assets equivalent to about a million pounds. If you're going to ask me how a nurse got her hands on a million pounds, I won't be able to answer.' He relaxed against the desk, his chin supported by his open hand.

'She can't have saved it all from her wages,' said Mitz. 'Maybe it's from an inheritance, or a windfall.'

Everything about Mitz smacked of perfection, from his shining black hair and immaculate, squared-off nails to his shirt, impossibly white and neatly tucked into black trousers that appeared to be freshly pressed no matter what time of day. Aspects of his attire reminded Robyn of Davies, who would never leave the house without a belt and gleaming shoes. That, in turn, reminded her of the conversation with Amélie. She forced such thoughts from her mind.

'When was the account set up, Matt?'

'Only last month. January the tenth.'

Robyn flicked through her notes on Tessa Hall, puzzling over where the money had come from.

'What did you learn from her parents, Mitz?'

'They spoke regularly on Skype and Tessa would drive down to see them some weekends. Good, loving daughter. Never been in trouble. She wanted to follow in her mother's footsteps and be a paediatrician but decided she couldn't face years and years at university after school, so opted for nursing. Enjoyed going out. Had lots of friends but after a bust-up with a boyfriend last year, decided to move away to the countryside. Tessa hadn't told them about any new boyfriends recently although she did tell them she'd been given a present – a kitten. I haven't spoken to them about this offshore account, obviously.'

'She had a bad break-up?'

'I asked about that. I don't think so. They were together five years and she'd had enough of the relationship. She dumped him. He was clingy and kept pestering her, so she decided to move out of the area. Mum and Dad agreed and helped her out financially. Since then, he's found a new girlfriend and moved to New Zealand with her.'

Robyn sighed. 'Not him, then. I wonder who bought the kitten. Could be the same person who bought the Valentine's card. We'll have to ask her parents about the million pounds.'

'Want me to go back and see her folks?'

Robyn paced the floor, almost colliding with a desk, and grunted. Tessa was hiding the money for a reason. Why? 'Yes. We have to find out where it came from.'

'I'll be subtle.'

'I know you will. This could all be a huge shock to them.'

'I've not got hold of Roger Jenkinson yet.'

'You stick with Tessa's parents first. And when you get hold of him, see if you can get a surname on the other man on the quiz team – Anthony.'

She glanced at the mess in the far end of her office. Another week of Shearer was almost impossible to bear. This latest development was a huge surprise and she wasn't sure how to proceed. Certainly they still needed to talk to Roger Jenkinson but first they really needed to find out who was Tessa's boyfriend. And as for Henry Gregson, she'd hit the buffers yet again. With Tarik, and probably Libby, out of the frame, she was only left with Lauren and the mysterious jogger to consider. She picked up a pencil and chewed at its end while she wondered what to do next.

CHAPTER TWENTY-NINE

THEN

Clark is scary. Not scary like a huge monster but in a way that can't be described. Clark has become part of the family and the boy doesn't like it one bit.

He is excessively polite, helps wash up the dishes and compliments his mother on her excellent cooking. He brings home sweets for him and his sister, whispering it's best not to tell their mother – after all, sweets aren't good for their teeth.

The boy can't put his finger on what frightens him about Clark. The man is creepy. He watches them through those hooded lids and smiles at them far too often, like he wants to be their friend. Only the day before, the boy had been peeing in the bathroom, and when he turned around he found Clark in the doorway watching him.

'I didn't know you were in here,' said Clark, but he continued to stare, and as the boy tried to ease past him, Clark dropped his hand to the boy's cheek and caressed it with his soft palm. 'Sorry,' he said quietly.

The boy told his mother but she scoffed at him. 'Don't be ridiculous. He's very nice. You're just jealous because he's got your bedroom. Of course there's nothing scary about him. He's a lonely man who's new to the area. You should try to be nicer to him.'

The boy can't make her see what is under her nose. She doesn't see the way Clark studies them, him and his sister. Clark's often at home.

He spends most of his free time wandering the streets with his camera, shooting pictures of local life and the area, or watching television in his bedroom.

It comes to him in a flash. That's what the boy doesn't like. It's the way the man moves about the house without being heard and appears out of nowhere. And when he's alone in a room with Clark, he knows Clark is looking at him.

The noises disturb the boy's thoughts. He goes upstairs and opens his sister's bedroom door to ask her what she thinks Clark is doing, but she's not there. He was sure she'd gone upstairs after their mum went out, an hour ago. Mum's got a cleaning job a few streets away. The boy checks the bathroom but his sister isn't there either. He tries their mum's room but it's empty too. A prickling starts in his scalp and he puts his ear to Clark's bedroom door. He can't hear much. The noises have stopped. Then he hears Clark speaking so softly he can barely make out the words.

'Good girl. Don't move or you know what will happen. Now stay like that.'

The boy presses down on the handle to his old bedroom, inching it lower little by little as quietly as he can. Through the crack the scene unfolds. He can't comprehend what is happening. Clark is bent down on one knee and looking through his camera lens. His breathing is heavy as if he's been running. The camera lens is trained on the little girl in front of him, who is holding a bowl of sweets. She's completely naked. The boy is so surprised he gasps, and Clark turns around. A smile creeps over his face. He lowers his camera.

'Well, hello. Come in. Come and join your sister. We're going to have such fun, aren't we?'

CHAPTER THIRTY

DAY FIVE – SATURDAY, 18 FEBRUARY, AFTERNOON

Robyn used going to the café down the road to buy a sandwich as an excuse to ring Ross. He picked up immediately.

'I need to share something with you. I really wanted to speak to you face-to-face about it.'

'Where are you?'

'Outside the station. About to go to the café.'

'The one that sells the best homemade chocolate cake in Stafford?' he asked.

'That's the one. Want me to place an order for you?'

'I really shouldn't. Jeanette will go bonkers if she finds out I've been scoffing slices of cake. You know how paranoid she is about me having another heart attack.' He paused. Robyn could hear the smile in his voice. 'I'm at the office so I'll be there in ten minutes.'

The phone went dead. The offices of R&J Associates were at the other end of Stafford. It wouldn't take him long to reach her but she'd have time to order cake and coffee for him.

Robyn had placed the tray on the table only seconds before Ross pulled into the space directly in front of the large café window. She was pleased to see the familiar craggy face, unkempt hair and shaggy eyebrows. He was reliable Ross, the ex-policeman with a heart of gold. They ought to bottle his goodness and sell it. There weren't many like him.

Ross waved at her and pointed to the car. Inside, Duke was standing on the passenger seat, staring out at the café with a quizzical look on his face. Ross rolled down the window slightly for the dog, locked the car door and entered the café. Robyn stood to hug him.

He dropped onto the leatherette chair and rubbed his hands together. 'I was going to ring you later,' he said, eyeballing the cake and simultaneously shoving a forkful of it into his mouth. He rolled his eyes and made murmuring noises. 'That is wicked.'

'Amélie stayed over last night. She told me something strange. She thinks she saw Davies. She was at a bowling party in Uttoxeter when she noticed a man who looked like Davies, watching her. He disappeared shortly after they'd made eye contact.'

Ross chewed thoughtfully then wiped his mouth with the back of his hand and picked up his mug of coffee. He peered at it. 'Black?'

'I thought you weren't allowed milk.'

He guffawed. 'You know I'm not allowed milk, or cake. How come you got me cake but no milk in my coffee?'

'I thought black coffee would offset the cake,' she replied, her face deadpan. 'And I scraped some of the cream out of the cake before you got here so you didn't eat so many calories.'

His shoulders rose and fell. 'Sure you did. Okay, let me ask you something. Did Amélie voluntarily give you that information or did you interrogate her?' His mouth lifted at the corners.

'This is serious stuff, Ross. Of course I didn't interrogate her.'

Ross clicked his tongue. 'Robyn, you forget I know exactly how you operate. You've worked with me as both a police officer and as a private investigator. You have a knack for wheedling information out of people. Maybe you wanted to hear that Amélie thought she'd seen Davies and dropped subliminal messages or words into the conversation. Surely, she didn't just blurt out this nugget of information. And if she had been convinced it was Davies, she'd have spoken to Brigitte, wouldn't she?'

Robyn's chin jutted forwards. 'No. She said she doesn't like talking to Brigitte about Davies. She doesn't want to come across as resenting Richard. I honestly didn't employ any techniques, Ross. Even I couldn't guess she was going to suddenly claim to have started seeing men who looked like him in crowds, or at bowling alleys. It's too great a coincidence. I get a photograph that suggests he's alive and around the same time, Amélie thinks she's seen him. Ross, help me. I'm not making this stuff up.'

He squeezed his hands between his thighs and nodded gravely. 'Okay, let me think how best to handle this. I don't want to question her again because it'll spook her. Tell me exactly what she said and I'll investigate it. I'll go to the bowling alley with his photograph and see if I can find a staff member who might recognise him.'

'I wrote down all the details last night when I couldn't sleep. I thought you might ask me for them.' She rummaged in her bag and extracted a sheet of A4.

'I should have known you'd be one step ahead.'

'So, have you found out anything?' Robyn's face was an emotionless mask even though her stomach had been somersaulting ever since he agreed to see her.

'I followed up on the photograph immediately and sent it to a couple of airport security guys I've worked with in the past. One of them suggested it looked suspiciously like Birmingham Airport where he works. If it is the same store, and there's no guarantee it is, we might be able to work out where the individual who took the photograph of Davies was standing.'

Robyn cupped her own mug to prevent her hands from shaking as she asked the next question. 'Is there any chance we could get CCTV footage of that area, for that date?'

Ross prodded his cake with his fork. 'If a crime had been committed, we might have been in a position to gain access to footage. I can't see how it would be possible without a request from a higher authority. I'm not leaping up and down at this discovery because, for all we know, all other airport WHSmith stores could look identical. I've got an idea of how to find out more, and I'll have to see what comes up. I've also put out feelers about Peter Cross.'

Robyn sighed. 'I fear we'll draw a blank there, and he's probably the only person who knows exactly what happened that day.'

'Ah, you have no faith in your amazingly clever cousin.'

He broke off a piece of cake and popped it into his mouth. Robyn, sipping her coffee, waited for him to speak again. She was mindful she needed to return to the office. As much as she needed to uncover the truth about Davies, she had duties to perform and killers to track.

'I've not been on this a full day yet, Robyn. Sometimes these things take months.'

Robyn sat back and breathed out. She hadn't realised she'd been holding her breath. She was satisfied that Ross was in charge of the search, and also looking after her well-being.

'Thank you for believing me.'

'Of course I believe you.' Ross picked up the last piece of cake and studied it with a sigh. 'Ah, that's the problem with all good things,' he said. 'They come to an end.' He shovelled in the cake and wiped the crumbs from around his mouth.

'Now, I must take Duke to the park. So, my dear cousin, head back to your office and don't give this any further thought. I'll keep you in the loop and, Robyn, don't expect too much, will you?'

'I won't. Thanks again, Ross.'

He rubbed at his cheek and said, 'You can kiss me here.'

She chuckled heartily and gave him a playful thump on his arm instead.

'Ouch! That's more like it. My favourite cousin.'

'I'm your *only* cousin.'

'Just as well. I'd be running around like a madman sorting you all out. Imagine all that responsibility!'

CHAPTER THIRTY-ONE

THEN

The house is empty. The boy shrugs off his schoolbag and calls for his mother.

'She's out,' comes the reply.

The boy feels sick. Clark is in the kitchen, making hot chocolate. He stirs the mug slowly then brings the spoon to his thin lips and licks it, his eyes never straying from the boy.

Clark speaks at last. 'Do you want me to make you one?'

'Where's Mum?'

'I suggested she had some time off for herself. She's getting her hair done. I gave her the money for her treat. Nice of me, wasn't it? She's really happy. I told her I'd look after you since your sister is out at her friend's house.'

The boy feels his knees begin to tremble. He knows what Clark really wants.

'Since that was a nice thing for me to do, I think you should do something nice for me in return, don't you?'

He knows he can't refuse. Clark looks shy and pathetic but he isn't. He can cause pain in many ways that can't be detected. The boy has felt that pain. Clark has taken photographs of him naked in various poses, some together with his sister. Clark will not only rip out their tongues if they say anything to their mother, but will plaster the photographs on every lamp post in the town and then everyone will see him and his sister naked and laugh and laugh at them. The boy has learnt the pain of shame. He hates having to pose with his naked sister, arm around her, both of them with mouths taped over, but Clark has threatened them both, over and over, and they know he's dangerous.

He plods upstairs, into his old bedroom, and begins to undress. He peels off his school uniform, letting it drop to the floor. The sooner he does this, the sooner it will be over. Clark follows him into the bedroom and shuts the door, softly.

'That's lovely,' he says as the boy drops his trousers and stands in his underpants. This time Clark doesn't pick up his camera. Instead, he drops his own trousers.

'I think it's time for us to become very good friends,' he says.

He's powerless to resist Clark's demands or to speak out about him. He's only twelve, and who believes a twelve-year-old? His mother certainly won't. They're all used to keeping secrets in this house. He remembers too well the golden rule of silence. For a second, his mind jolts back to a time before Clark. He shuts his eyes and remembers the first time he learnt to keep silent…

Outside is frosty and bright; a new day. Hidden from view in his hallway, he observes a group of schoolchildren prancing down his street, pushing, joking and laughing with each other. He lifts his own schoolbag from the floor, and takes a last look in the hall mirror before opening the front door. He studies the bruise turning yellow at the base of his neck. With quick fingers his mother tightens his tie and pulls his collar high above it. Her eyes alone say, 'We will not speak of this…'

The boy waits for instructions and says nothing. It's always best to say nothing.

CHAPTER THIRTY-TWO

Robyn slipped behind her desk. Anna and David had returned while she'd been out and were hunched over some documents at the far side of the room, deep in discussion.

She pulled out the Henry Gregson file and hunted through every detail. They'd not had one lucky break. Every avenue she'd pursued had led to a dead end. There had to be something she was missing. She reflected on his movements that day. He'd not gone to work. Although his vehicle had been spotted at an automatic number plate recognition point on the way to Lichfield, it hadn't passed through the next ANPR on the main road just outside Lichfield. Why was that? He must have stopped or turned off before that point.

She dragged up a map of the area on her computer screen and tried to determine where he might have headed. He could have driven to any of the houses along the route, or headed north from the roundabout, along the A515 towards Yoxall. She stopped reading. Yoxall was significant. Juliet, Roger and Tessa – quiz team members – all lived near Yoxall, and his friend, Liam, lived in the village. Juliet had been at work that day so it was unlikely Henry had intended visiting her. He might have been heading to Tessa Hall's house. It was a possibility Robyn couldn't ignore. However, if it wasn't Tessa, then it might be one of the others.

Liam had denied seeing Henry that day. Liam's partner, Ella, had been at home with him that morning, before she left to visit her friend, and he'd stayed behind to look after their child. He'd been out and about the village and had several witnesses who'd seen him.

She dragged out the statements and read through them. Ella had corroborated his alibi. She'd returned earlier than planned, and Liam was at home when she got in. It was implausible for Liam to have driven to Cannock Chase, murdered Henry and returned to Yoxall before 2 p.m.; besides, he'd been in charge of Astra. It was unlikely he'd have taken her along to Cannock Chase to shoot his friend. Liam wasn't a suspect, so why was her scalp prickling? She was missing something. She would talk to Ella herself.

※

The village of Yoxall would have made the perfect setting for a countryside television drama, mused Robyn. It stood on the banks of a meandering river and was surrounded by undulating farmland. Pockets of early frost still clung to hedgerows and twinkled on tree branches, creating a postcard-perfect winter scene. Houses set back from the main street were a mixture of old and new buildings, and nestled between were quaint village pubs and antique shops, all next to the twisting A515 that rose gently from the village towards Ashbourne and the Peak District beyond.

Carrington's house was at the entrance to the village and belonged to a bygone era. A small, L-shaped converted barn in aged red brick, it stood in the shadow of a large farmhouse and adjacent to fields occupied by bullocks that snorted at Robyn's car as she pulled up to it. A blackbird sat on the tiled ridge of the barn, observed the intruder and chattered angrily as Robyn rang the bell.

The door opened wide. Ella hoisted Astra onto a slim hip and beckoned Robyn inside with her free hand. Robyn found herself directly in a cluttered kitchen and facing a square table with seating for four, small, slim people. The interior walls weren't plastered as she'd have imagined, but of the same brick as the exterior, making the place feel cool in spite of the heat coming from the nearby radiator. Kitchen units formed a U-shape, covering the back and side walls, and there was little room for the clutter of the ironing board and clothes piled in a basket in front of the fridge. A door to the left of the kitchen had been left slightly ajar, and from her vantage point, Robyn spotted an unmade double mattress on the floor and, alongside it, a single bed with a pink duvet.

'Sorry, the place is a tip. I haven't had a chance to clear up. Astra's had me running about all morning, haven't you, sweetie pie?'

Astra buried her head into Ella's neck.

'Hi, Astra, remember me?' Robyn held up the colouring book she'd brought.

'Oh, Astra, look what DI Carter's brought you.'

The girl gradually craned her neck. She'd been crying again and her cheeks were stained with tear marks. She gawked at the book being offered.

'Do you like colouring?' Robyn spoke gently.

Astra nodded dumbly.

'Me too. Look at all these pictures.' She flicked through some pages and rested on one of a farm. 'Do you know what this is?' she asked.

'Farm,' said Astra, her face brightening. 'That's a cow.' She pointed at an animal.

'Well done. Have you got some crayons?'

Astra nodded again, reaching for the colouring book. Robyn handed it to her and she grasped it tightly, eyes on Robyn.

'Say thank you, Astra.'

'Thank you.'

Robyn smiled at the girl, who was scouring the page, eyes on the animals. 'I have something else for you.'

The girl looked up in wonder as Robyn produced the black toy cat from a plastic bag. 'I have a cat exactly like this. This one's for you.'

Astra let out a small gasp of pleasure and her cheeks lifted.

'You shouldn't have,' said Ella but she was smiling too. 'Thank you.'

'My pleasure. I saw it and thought of Astra.'

'Down,' said Astra, wriggling to escape Ella's arms. She looked from the book in her hands to the cat in Robyn's, placed the book on the table and reached up for the cat. Robyn crouched down and handed it over. The girl took it and held it to her face, rubbing it against her cheeks. 'Cat.'

Astra ran off, up some wooden stairs by the front door, to fetch her crayons.

Ella spoke. 'Thank you so much. That's really cheered her up. She's been behaving differently since Henry died. I think she misses him. He was always dropping in. Every time somebody knocks at the door, she hopes it's him.'

Ella had sounded timid on the phone, but she walked with confidence as she led the way from the kitchen, down two steps into a small sitting room – one window overlooked the wide tarmac drive Robyn had pulled onto, the other over countryside. Ella gave a warm smile, her wide mouth and full lips perfectly proportioned in her almost perfect face. A scar that ran from under her left eye to her upper lip was still visible in spite of thick concealer. Robyn didn't stare at it and instead smiled at Astra, who'd returned with a tin of crayons. She fetched her book from the kitchen and dropped to the floor with it, the cat next to her.

'Beautiful spot,' said Robyn, looking out at the fields beyond. 'Lovely house.'

'We rent it. It's a tad on the small side. There's only one bedroom but there's space upstairs that Astra uses as her playroom. It belongs to the farmhouse next door. The owner – Eugene McNamara – was once a top jockey but he had an accident and went into property development. Now he owns all the outbuildings on this old farm and converted them into houses. He owns all the converted cow barns the other side of the farmhouse too. They're much bigger than this and very grand. They're too expensive for us to rent. This is pricey enough.'

'Rents must be very high around here – prime location,' said Robyn.

Ella returned a thin smile. 'We were lucky. Eugene came from a poor Irish family himself. He lets us have this place for a special reduced rate. He said he remembers what it was like to struggle. So, what can I do for you? I still can't believe what happened to Henry.' Ella turned her attention to Astra, who was now colouring. 'Honey, use the brown crayon for the cow. They're not purple.'

Astra shook her head. 'I want it purple.'

Ella tutted. 'She can be so stubborn. This has been absolutely heartbreaking. Lauren's like a zombie. I don't know what to say to her. Have you made any progress with finding out what happened?'

Astra spoke without looking up. 'Lauren was crying.'

'Yes, she was. And you know why she was crying, don't you, sweetie?'

Astra nodded, put down her crayon and picked up the toy cat, holding it to her, eyes suddenly dewy.

Ella winced. 'I shouldn't have said anything,' she whispered. 'Astra, why don't you take the cat to meet your other toys?'

Astra thought about it for a moment then pushed herself up and moved slowly away, head low.

Robyn watched Astra leave before answering Ella's question. 'We're still following up leads. Unfortunately, it's taking much longer than I'd like. I'm trying to get a better picture of Henry and work out why he went to Cannock Chase.'

'You should really talk to Liam about it. They were good friends and spent a lot of time together at work. I only knew Henry and Lauren socially. Henry was such a nice man. He was one of those people who couldn't do enough for you. Liam liked him from the off. It was his idea to ask Henry to be Astra's godfather. We had her christened last year. Decided we ought to. Henry was so good to Astra.'

'How would you describe him?'

'As I said: good, kind, nice, gentle – all those clichés that people seem to come out with after somebody dies. But he was. He was a really good man.'

'So lots of people really liked him?'

'I'd say so. Liam certainly did, and Lauren was always going on about the kids he trained at Brocton. They all loved him too. It was impossible not to like him.'

'Did you see much of him?'

'Oh yes. He and Lauren came around most weeks. They'd pick up Astra and take her out. Treated her like she was their own. They'd been trying for children of their own for ages.'

Robyn nodded. 'We looked through his phone records and couldn't help but notice he regularly spoke to you and Liam.'

'Yeah. So did Lauren. It wasn't unusual for him to chat to one or the other of us. He was a really friendly guy. Sometimes, if Liam was working, he'd ring me up, see how I was, ask about Astra. He couldn't do enough for her.'

'That's nice. You must miss him too.'

Ella stared at her hard. 'I do. I can't believe he's gone.'

'Can I ask you a couple of questions about the fourteenth of February? Just so I can make sure I've got my facts straight.'

'Sure.' Ella fiddled with a child's cardigan that had been abandoned on the settee, folded it and replaced it.

'You visited a friend that day, didn't you?'

Her eyebrows pulled downwards for a second. 'Yeah. Cassie Snow. At Queen's Hospital in Burton.'

'You told my officer you returned home earlier than expected and Liam was here when you got back.'

'Fast asleep on the sofa, the lazy sod,' Ella said with a laugh, displaying white teeth. 'It's fine for me to look after Astra all day, but he has her for a couple of hours and he's worn out. Want a cup of tea? I'll make us one.'

She bustled back into the kitchen. Robyn followed her and waited while she pulled out two white mugs from a cupboard and held one up.

Robyn refused the unspoken offer. In her opinion, Ella was playing for time.

'You didn't spot Henry's car parked anywhere in Yoxall as you drove through, did you, or maybe when you returned?'

'I don't much like driving. I don't own a car. I caught the ten o'clock bus. I didn't see Henry's car. It wasn't here when I got home. Liam didn't say he'd seen him, did he?' She asked the question casually, filling the kettle, her back turned to Robyn.

'Liam told us he took Astra to the park then on to the butcher's shop, so it's possible he could've missed Henry if he'd visited.'

'Oh yeah. That's possible. You best ask the neighbours over the road, then. They don't miss much.'

'Can you remember the exact times you left the house and came back? Just so I can be sure Henry wasn't here before or after those times.'

'I left at quarter to ten to walk to the bus stop and I was back here just after two.'

'How was your friend?'

She shrugged. 'Bus didn't get in on time, so I missed the connecting bus at the Octagon Centre and was then too late for visiting time. I decided to visit her another day. I went shopping for a while, got bored and came home instead.' Ella fumbled about with a box of teabags before dropping one in the mug. 'Sure you don't want a tea?'

'I'm fine. I won't keep you. Astra's a sweetie. I bet she keeps you occupied. Fancy going back to work when she's older?'

There was a flash of concern as Ella shook her head. 'I'm happy to be a stay-at-home mum. I used to clean at the farmhouse, when she was younger, but now it's more difficult to take her with me and get the work done.' She rushed through the sentence.

'Any plans for more children?'

Ella shook her head. 'One's enough,' she replied.

'One last question. It's concerning Tessa Hall.'

Ella screwed her face up at the name.

'You knew her?'

'Only from the quiz nights. I'd go along to support Liam some evenings. She was on the same quiz team as Liam. She didn't have any time for me, and I had none for her.'

'Why was that?'

'She tried it on with my Liam – flirty cow. She was always drawing attention to herself. I put her straight and she kept out my way after that. She stayed away from Liam and me.'

'Have you seen her recently?'

'I haven't. I was glad when Liam gave up going to those stupid quiz nights.' She pressed her lips together in disapproval.

※

Robyn left the house with an overriding feeling that Ella was hiding something. She'd suggested Liam was really the person to have most contact with Henry, yet the phone records showed Henry had rung her mobile on numerous occasions. Surely they couldn't have talked about nothing but the child? Ella's furtive glances when asked about her movements suggested she was lying. Robyn had interviewed people before who had tried to deflect attention away from a question, and Ella had done exactly that with her comment about Liam being asleep when she got in, followed by the sudden offer of a cup of tea. And there was also the fact she hadn't actually seen her friend and therefore had no concrete alibi.

As Robyn walked away from the house, she glanced over at the farmhouse that overlooked it, and a movement caught her eye. She looked up at the house in time to see a figure retreat from the top window. She decided to try her luck, wandered next door and rapped on the farmhouse door.

Eugene McNamara, Ella's landlord, with impossibly dark hair given his age, was thin-faced and slim-bodied.

'Good afternoon. How can I help you?' He threw Robyn a wide smile, causing creases to form around his twinkling eyes.

Robyn showed her ID.

He sucked a breath in through his teeth. 'Trouble, Detective? Surely not in a quiet neighbourhood like this? Will you come in?'

Robyn declined and kept her conversation brief and formal. Mr McNamara beamed the entire time she spoke.

'I'm looking for witnesses who might have spotted a red Kia outside the house next door, or in the vicinity, on Tuesday the fourteenth, at about ten in the morning.'

McNamara shook his head. 'I can't help you there. I was in London all day – attended a charity gala at the Grosvenor House Hotel. I didn't return until Wednesday morning.'

'Did you know Henry and Lauren Gregson, Liam and Ella's friends?' She described the couple for him.

'I've seen them on a few occasions when I've been outside, but only spoken to them once or twice. Just in passing. They were next door when I went around to collect the rent one time. Why?'

'I'm afraid Henry was murdered on Tuesday.'

'Here?'

'No, sir. On Cannock Chase.'

'Poor Ella. What a shock. And for Liam. I'll pop around and see how they both are later.'

Not wishing to detain him any longer, and wanting to walk the route Liam took the day Gregson was murdered, she withdrew from the doorstep. As she left the house, she turned back and caught McNamara still observing her. He raised a hand before closing the door, and Robyn returned to her car under the impression there was something strange about him.

She drove to the nearest pub in the centre of the village, leaving her Golf in the car park. As she'd left the house, she'd spotted Liam's slippers by the front door. She'd no way of knowing their size by glancing at them, but it reminded her his alibi had yet to be confirmed and, at present, she wasn't completely convinced it was airtight.

She turned her thoughts back to his statement. Several semi-detached, modern houses overlooked the play area, and in one of them, a witness had observed the pair playing at about 12 p.m. From there, Carrington had walked to the butcher's at the bottom of Hadley Street where it joined the A515. Robyn followed the path in that direction, noting it took only five minutes to reach the shop. From this position, it would only be a fifteen-minute walk back to his house.

Having completed the circuit, she deduced Liam could easily have walked through the village, made sure he was seen in the butcher's shop, and then travelled to a meeting with Henry on Cannock Chase. The only fly in the ointment was that he'd been at home when Ella returned. However, Ella might be covering for him, which would explain her reactions to Robyn's questioning. For the moment, this was only guesswork on her part. All she knew for certain was she had to find answers quickly.

※

Darkness was falling as Robyn drove into Stafford and back to the station. She'd called ahead and sent her team home. They needed time with families and friends. She couldn't keep pushing them to their limits.

She shoved open the office door and flicked the switch. The overhead light spluttered into life, illuminating the chaos that was her office. She sighed and threw her bag onto her desk, ambled to the coffee machine that hadn't been turned off and pressed the button for a black coffee.

No sooner had it bubbled into her cup than a familiar figure appeared.

'Couldn't make that two cups, could you?' Shearer said.

'Do I look like a barista?'

'Nice one!' He managed a grin. 'I'll get it myself.'

'Go on. I'll do it for you. Bad day?'

'Aren't they all? I've got one of those "copper" feelings. You know, when you suspect something isn't quite right. It's that bloke who died on the golf course this morning.'

'Not suspicious?'

He shook his head. 'No. He had a heart attack. Can't help but think it's weird he was alone on the golf course. Who plays golf alone on a Saturday morning in February?'

'A keen golfer?'

Shearer pulled a face. 'Nah. His golfing shoes had hardly been worn, his clubs were brand new and unused, and he still had the price tag attached to his jumper. He was definitely new to this. Brocton Golf Club said he's not been a member for long – less than a month.'

Robyn sipped her coffee. The light strip hummed quietly above them. Henry Gregson had lived in Brocton. This man had died in Brocton. Was that a coincidence?

'What's his name?' she asked.

'Hawkins. Anthony Hawkins.'

Juliet had mentioned that one of her teammates called Anthony lived near Stafford. Brocton was near Stafford. Could it be him? She voiced her thoughts to Shearer and told him briefly about the two cases she'd been investigating.

Shearer listened quietly, his keen eyes on her all the time until she finished. 'You think the deaths might be linked?' he asked.

'I don't know. It seems a curious coincidence that Hawkins might know both of my victims, that's all. There's only one way to find out for sure. Establish if he was one of the quiz team and if he knew Henry Gregson. Then take it from there.'

Shearer paced the floor of the office. Outside was so dark and silent. It was as if they were the only two existing in the world.

'I think we should take this to DCI Flint. If these three deaths are connected, we could be dealing with a real threat – a serial killer.'

'We can't know that for sure, Tom. Your man has died of natural causes. We can't leap about making wild claims until we have all the facts.'

'Facts or not, I have a bad feeling about this, Robyn. If you won't tell Flint, I will.'

The look on his face was one of determination. Robyn under-stood why he'd want to report the findings but she was anxious they didn't have enough evidence. Anthony Hawkins might not have any connection to either Henry or Tessa. She needed time to establish that first before running to Flint.

'I'm going to put him in the picture. You can be in on it, or not, but either way that's how I'm going to play it.'

Robyn sighed. 'Give me half an hour to try and prove a connec-tion first. Got a photograph of Hawkins? I need to describe him to Juliet Fallows, who was on the quiz team. Make yourself useful while I'm doing it and find out what you can about the man.'

CHAPTER THIRTY-THREE

THEN

'Gi's it.' The lad with the spiky hair and earring scowls at him and holds out his hand. The boy passes the tablet over. Spiky checks it, rolls it over in his palm and nods, before he passes the money back, flips the yellow tablet engraved with a smiley face into his mouth and chugs from a bottle of water. Then he checks his reflection in the cracked mirror and grins, runs his fingers through his hair and swaggers off to join his mates.

The chain flushes and Johnny Hounslow comes out of the toilet cubicle and winks at him. He passes the notes over and Johnny thumbs through them, lips moving as he counts. He's filled out, with wide shoulders and an even wider stomach. No one crosses Johnny Hounslow. Not because he's a nasty, foul-tempered son of a bitch but because he has a mate who'd sooner stick a blade into someone as look at them. Johnny wasn't the only one who'd changed. He had too. Nothing like having a father in prison and a pervert of a lodger to toughen up a boy, although he doesn't ever talk about Clark. He left their house once the boy began to mature. If ever the boy comes across that man again, he's going to slice him into pieces. He hawks a spitball and gobs it onto the floor, pretending Clark is its recipient, and pats the knife in his pocket for reassurance.

The boy feels camaraderie with Johnny. Johnny's dad left his mum at about the same time as his own dad got banged up in jail, and

Johnny became an out-and-out rebel overnight, hanging out on the streets, getting into fights and now doling out E tablets or cocaine to anyone who'll pay him. It's a good little earner, and who'd suspect a fifteen-year-old kid? Johnny is worth knowing, and he's taken a shine to his schoolmate who knows how to look after himself and is handy with his fists. Together they make a solid team. It had been Johnny's idea to sell drugs at school and it's easy money.

'Nice,' says Johnny, shoving the notes into his pocket. 'Let's go before any of the teachers wake up to what we're doing here.'

They slip back along the corridor and past the classrooms. Lunchtime is coming to an end and they have lessons. He's got a maths test but he isn't bothered about it. He's really good at maths and doesn't need to revise. It's about the only subject he is good at, other than sport.

He and Johnny part company, and as he bounds up the staircase, he sees his sister descending. She's with some stupid-looking boy with glasses who's at least two years older than her. She spots him staring and pulls a face.

He can't help himself – he accidentally bumps into the nerd she's with 'Sorry,' he says, not meaning it. He draws to a halt and stares at Speccy. His sister could do a lot better than this.

'Leave it,' she hisses.

He shrugs, raises his hands and heads off to the lesson, whistling as he goes. He's got enough money to buy a decent bottle or two of vodka and some smokes for later. He'll go round to Johnny's for the evening. No point in going home. He'll only get grief from his mother and sister. He might even be able to flog some alcohol or E to the youngsters that hang about the park. Could be a profitable evening. He calculates how much money he's made and smiles then saunters into the classroom, ready for his test.

CHAPTER THIRTY-FOUR

DAY FIVE – SATURDAY, 18 FEBRUARY, LATE EVENING

DCI Flint stared solemnly from one to the other and back again, fingers pressed together to form a perfect triangle. His round face was, as always, flushed, and his jowls hung over his shirt collar along with an angry red lump, a boil, on the neckline, that looked ripe for eruption.

Robyn had accompanied Shearer to Flint's office, where they now both stood over his desk. She'd been unable to convince Shearer they had insufficient evidence and was now hoping to dissuade Flint from intervening.

Shearer's hairy hands, splayed like giant white spiders, rested on top of the paperwork on the desk. 'For what it's worth, I think we've reasonable grounds to think these seemingly unconnected incidents are related,' he said.

Flint bounced his fingers together lightly, the speed increasing until they performed a final tap that resounded in the silent room. He pushed himself back from the desk and strode to the bookcase filled with binders, tracing the back of each with a finger before speaking. 'You're positive, Tom, there's a connection between these deaths, even though Hawkins died of natural causes?'

'Yes. I think if we dig deep enough, we'll find a connection. I know I'm going out on a limb, but Hawkins' death is suspicious. I know it is. I can't prove it yet, but I will. And once I've done that, we'll have a solid connection between him and the other two victims.'

'I'm not convinced, Tom. This is complete supposition.' Flint continued to stare at the binders.

'I admit it's a hunch, sir, but surely it's worth following up? I don't think we should gloss over Hawkins' death.'

Robyn had had enough. Tom had taken her idea to heart and was pushing too hard. They were wasting time discussing the matter. 'I admit it's strange the victims are connected in some way, in fact, I pointed it out to Tom, but that connection is tenuous at best. Juliet Fallows confirmed Anthony Hawkins was one of their fellow quizzers and knew Tessa Hall. Henry Gregson wasn't anything to do with the team, but lived in Brocton, was acquainted with Anthony Hawkins and maybe knew Tessa Hall from the clinic at Tamworth. I'm a little concerned it's not enough. I've been pursuing different angles and we're searching for Tessa Hall's boyfriend, who hasn't come forward. He's a prime suspect at the moment in that case. I'm looking closer to home for Henry Gregson. Although there are grounds to be suspicious, I don't think we should be trying to join dots between these people without more evidence. It would be folly to give up chasing other avenues to focus on this.'

Shearer interrupted. 'Gregson was found dead on Tuesday, Tessa Hall on Thursday and Hawkins on Saturday. That's three murders in a period of only five days. That's no coincidence.'

Flint held up a hand to quieten Shearer. 'Now, let me explain my dilemma here. You both have excellent instincts, but sorry, Tom, you haven't provided sufficient evidence to substantiate your claims. We have no reason to believe Gregson's death is in any way linked to the other two deaths unless we can turn up something, and we have no reason to believe Anthony Hawkins was murdered.'

Robyn nodded in agreement and was about to call an end to the pointless meeting. Flint continued before she could vocalise her thoughts.

'However, as I said, you both have excellent instincts, so I'll let you pursue the Hawkins case for the moment. That leaves me with the question of which one of you ought to handle it.'

Shearer spoke up. 'I'd hoped you'd let us work on it together, sir. We can pool our information and crack on quicker that way.'

Flint refused with a gesture of his hand and a click of his tongue.

'Then I think Robyn's in the best position to take this on. She's already spent valuable man-hours on the Gregson and Hall cases. I'm more than happy to assist if she needs me,' said Shearer.

'You in agreement, Robyn? Can you handle this on top of the other cases?'

Unwilling to hand over her current investigations to Shearer, she was quick to answer. 'I am.'

'It's all yours, Robyn, but it goes without saying that I want to hear a cohesive argument backed up by evidence on this matter. Also, we must keep any findings away from the press at the moment. They've already been issued information on Henry Gregson and Tessa Hall, but I don't want anything else to get out for now. Nobody is to speak about any of the cases to anyone, is that clear?'

'Sir.' Both spoke at the same time.

Flint's mouth twitched slightly as he commented, 'Putting you together in the same office has helped improve relations. Glad to see you working so well.'

'About that matter,' said Shearer. 'Any news on when we can be rehomed?'

'A week or so. I'm sure you can cope for a little longer. Right, Tom, there's been an arson attack on a shop in Longdon. Owner lives above the shop and maintains whoever did it was trying to murder his family. I was going to ask Jackson to take it on, but now you're free of the Hawkins case, will you look into it?' He ran a finger between his collar and his neck and winced. 'And, Robyn, I want to know the second there's any news.'

Back outside the office, Robyn's voice dropped to just above a whisper. 'I hope you're not wrong on this.'

'Nah, not a chance,' replied Shearer. 'I know I'm right. There has to be an explanation for Hawkins' death too. Maybe someone scared him to death. Given I'm off the case, I'm going to have to let you take the credit for my genius.'

'Cheers for that.'

He gave a lazy grin then looked over her shoulder. 'Ah, there's DI Brown. I want a quick word with him.' He meandered off, hands thrust deep in his trouser pockets, loose-limbed with assured footsteps. Robyn watched him as he departed and wondered if he had a hidden agenda.

Her instincts were on full alert. Shearer wasn't renowned for his helpfulness. Why had he insisted they tell Flint about their findings before they'd unearthed more evidence, and why was he being unusually nice to her? A loud laugh made her turn back. Shearer fist-bumped DI Brown and walked away. The nagging suspicion he was deliberately setting her up for a fall had just been planted. With an exasperated huff, she hurtled back to the office. She had work to do and no time for office politics.

Robyn pumped her fists, her anxieties about Shearer's motives for handing over the case now overshadowing everything.

She drew a deep breath and focused on Hawkins. All the signs had pointed to a massive heart attack. Until she had the pathologist's report, she couldn't treat this as murder. It was, for the time being, a coincidence – one with which she wasn't comfortable, but a coincidence nevertheless.

She checked her watch. It was after ten. She needed to rest. She'd not be able to function properly if she didn't go back home and try to sleep.

*

Back home, as Robyn prepared for bed, she studied her reflection in the bathroom mirror. A few stray grey hairs had appeared. Her face was changing, a little more each day. She wasn't the same woman Davies had fallen in love with. And Davies. Was he alive? If so, how much had he changed? She blinked away such thoughts.

She again considered the possibility Shearer had deliberately manipulated the situation so she'd take over the Hawkins case and hit the buffers with it. Everybody at the station knew he was keen to get promoted. Dumping the Hawkins case to take on a new investigation that might yield quick results would be one way of improving his crime success rate. Would he stoop so low? She hoped not. If Hawkins had died of natural causes, Robyn would have wasted valuable man-hours on the case and tied herself further in knots trying to establish connections between him and Tessa Hall. Is that what he hoped for? That she'd become so entangled in the cases she'd fail to find either murderer?

She scowled at the worn-out face staring back. Look at her! A detective who prided herself on results but who couldn't even get leverage on this case. That wasn't usual for Robyn. She rallied herself with a shake of her shoulders, lifted her head high. Robyn Carter was not going to be thwarted by anyone or any investigation.

She remained awake in bed long after she'd turned off the lights, Schrödinger snoozing next to her, and thought about Anthony Hawkins. While it seemed he'd died of natural causes, it was possible he'd been killed and made to appear as if he'd had a heart attack. She lifted the duvet, trying not to disturb the cat, and padded downstairs to her laptop where she ran 'deaths made to look like heart attacks' through several search engines, noting the results. Satisfied with her findings, she shut the machine down and returned to her room. What she really needed now was a professional opinion, and she'd get that first thing in the morning. Shearer might have thought she would flounder, but she wouldn't. Robyn rarely failed. He should know that by now.

CHAPTER THIRTY-FIVE

DAY SIX – SUNDAY, 19 FEBRUARY, MORNING

Robyn arrived at the office and called the pathologist, Harry McKenzie, before she'd even removed her coat.

'Harry, I have a crazy idea to run past you. If I wanted to kill somebody and make it look like they'd had a heart attack, could I inject them with potassium chloride, emulate a heart attack and get away with the perfect crime?'

'You're not planning on doing away with anyone I know, are you?' The chuckle was hearty.

'I have reason to suspect Anthony Hawkins was murdered but I don't know how to prove it.'

'Anthony Hawkins? He isn't one of mine.'

'Edward Finch is the pathologist on his case. His report shows Hawkins died of a massive heart attack.'

'Did you talk to Ed about it?'

'He left early this morning for a ten-day holiday in Thailand, so I rang you.'

'Oh yes, I forgot he was on leave. The answer to your question is yes, it's possible. An injection of a potassium compound, possibly potassium chloride, can cause severe heart arrhythmias and will mimic a heart attack. We'd have to look for any high levels of potassium or test for them. Potassium chloride can be absorbed by the tissues and generally remain undiscovered.'

'Who would have access to such a compound?'

'People in the medical profession, mostly, although I bet you could purchase it online.'

Robyn's thoughts turned to Tessa and Juliet. Both were nurses but it was unlikely such a compound would be found in a fertility clinic.

Robyn sighed. 'So, it's too late to establish he was murdered?'

'*Nil desperandum*, my dear. I'll scoot to the lab immediately and take another look at Mr Hawkins for you.'

Robyn ended the call, and drummed her fingers on her desk thoughtfully. Potassium chloride. Was Shearer's hunch about Hawkins' death correct? If so, he'd be unbearably smug and Robyn would have even more of a confusing picture to handle than she already had.

Anna called across. 'You have a visitor – a journalist by the name of Justin Forrest. He's downstairs. The desk sergeant put him in interview room two.'

'I'm not talking to any journalists about any of the cases. Tell the sergeant to chuck him out and tell him to go through the official channels for information.'

'Sergeant says he wants to talk to you about Tessa Hall. He insists on only talking to you. Says it's very important.'

Robyn grunted a response. She had no time to play games with the press. She stood up and took off her coat, dropping it onto the back of her chair.

'Come on. We'll find out what it is, and if he's trying to pump us for information, we'll get rid of him.'

※

Justin Forrest was a gangly man with loose limbs, foppish chestnut-brown hair that fell over his forehead and thick-framed glasses masking large grey eyes. He remained seated as Robyn entered, his demeanour that of somebody used to interviews and challenging situations.

'DI Carter,' she said as she pulled out a chair and sat down. 'This is my officer, PC Anna Shamash. How can we help?'

Forrest looked directly at her. 'It's more how I can help you. I've wrestled with my conscience for the last three days and decided I have to do what's right, regardless of the consequences. I suspect you are looking for me. I'm a friend of Tessa's – a good friend.'

'Go on, sir.'

'I met Tessa in early December last year, at the Goat pub in Abbots Bromley. I'd been sent along to write a piece about a quiz contest. Tessa accosted me at the bar after the quiz and asked a load of questions about my job and what it was like to be a journalist. I found her extremely engaging. She was really switched on and lively, and she was very easy to be around. I went back home with her that night, and since then, I've been seeing her regularly. I want you to understand that although we had a sexual relationship at first, it changed into a friendship.'

'I see. And why didn't you come forward sooner?'

'Two reasons. Firstly, I'm married with children and I didn't want my wife to find out about Tessa. We're already having problems, and my wife finding out I had an affair will probably finish us. Secondly, I guessed I'd be a prime suspect. I knew how it might appear to you – the married lover who refuses to leave his wife for his girlfriend. They fight about it. There's an accident. She dies. I've written articles about similar situations. My fingerprints are all over her house. I've been in contact with Tessa for two months. You were sure to track me down at some stage. I figured it was better to give myself up and let justice run its course. I haven't committed any crime – just adultery. I certainly didn't kill Tessa. I'm going to be completely candid here. I know I have to be. I really, really liked Tessa. She understood me and I completely got where she was coming from. We had a very good relationship – lovers and friends.'

Robyn nodded. The man was extremely earnest. 'Where were you on Thursday morning?'

'I had to finish an article for the paper – I write for the *Tamworth News* – so I stayed at home until it was completed, sent it the editor and then went with my wife to the shops to buy a birthday present for my six-year-old.'

Robyn resisted the urge to sigh. If Forrest's alibi held up, she had lost a potential suspect.

'I've got witnesses who can testify to me being at home. I spoke to the next-door neighbour at about six thirty when I took the dog out for his walk. I'm sure if you check the route I took with the dog, you'll find me on CCTV footage. There are cameras all around Tamworth. When I got back, I made two Skype calls. Here, I've written down the times and details of those I called. One was at seven and the other was at seven forty. Those people will be able to verify I was in my home office at those times. I dropped my youngest off at school about eight fifty, so you might be able to find my car going through one of those automatic number plate points that are everywhere. I also have email correspondence sent between six thirty and ten in the morning. I typed up the article and emailed it across to my editor at eleven twenty. Do you think you'll be able to exonerate me? I honestly didn't kill her.'

'We'll have to check all this information first, sir.'

His head bounced up and down eagerly. 'Yes. I know. Please do. I really want to prove I had nothing to do with her death. I was scared rigid to start with. I didn't want to come forward, but by hiding, I was preventing you from finding her real killer.'

'That's very true. Did Tessa contact you last week?'

'I spoke to her last Monday. We arranged for me to drop by and see her on Friday. She couldn't wait to see me. She had some "mega" news to share with me.'

Robyn suspected the news might be that she was pregnant. 'How did she contact you?'

'The usual, by phone.'

'Her mobile contained no contact details at all.'

Forrest nodded. 'She bought a new phone last week. Said she didn't know how to set it up because it was totally different from her old Samsung. I advised her to go back to the shop where she'd bought it, and ask them to show her how to set it up.'

Robyn spoke again. 'Were you aware she'd closed all her social media accounts recently? Have you any idea why she'd do that?'

'We spoke about that too on Monday. I'd visited her Facebook page to send her a message and found out she'd deleted her account. She said it was all part of a "great new plan" and I would have to wait until Friday to find out what that was.'

'So she wasn't concerned about anything?'

'Far from it. If anything, she was the opposite. Kept saying she couldn't wait to tell me her news.'

'Did you have any idea what she might have wanted to tell you?'

'I can't say I did. She gave no clues other than to say it was going to "blow my mind". She was generally upbeat, but she was uber-excited on Monday. I even thought she might have been drinking, or taken drugs, but she laughed when I suggested it. Told me I was an old grouch and to wait until I heard what she had to tell me.' He shifted uncomfortably on his seat. 'Detective Inspector Carter, if possible, I'd rather you didn't involve my wife. I never intended for my relationship with Tessa to be anything other than a fling. Tessa was in complete agreement. She said she was too young to settle down and wasn't looking for a steady relationship. She'd been in one for several years and wanted to "let her hair down". I cared about her but she was a wild spirit. She didn't want to be tamed and I wasn't the man to try to.'

Robyn remembered Juliet Fallows had said something similar. She didn't doubt Forrest's sincerity, but if she required further confirmation as to his whereabouts, and had to contact his wife, she would do so. She told him as much. Forrest sank into his seat, his long frame doubled over.

'I understand,' he said. 'But please check everything I've given you first. You'll see I'm telling the truth.'

'Did she talk to you about her finances?'

'Not really. I know her parents were paying half her mortgage. It came up in conversation when I commented on what a nice house she had. She told me her parents were well off but she resented them helping her out. She wanted to stand on her own two feet. She said she felt beholden, and stifled by them and their demands – and being dependent on them meant she could never really be free of their hold.'

'Their hold?'

'They're very pushy parents. Her mum's a doctor. She wanted Tessa to become a doctor too, and when she didn't make the grades, she was very disappointed. Tessa only took their help and money because it allowed her to live away from home, but she really wanted to break away from them completely – maybe even move abroad. Theirs was a complicated relationship. We had very similar upbringings. My father was a judge, and when I didn't follow in his footsteps he turned his back on me – disowned me. She and I talked a lot about our pasts, and new beginnings. She was so encouraging about what I do. I was flattered. My wife isn't so enthusiastic about it, and with two children to support, she wishes I had a more lucrative job rather than a vocation I enjoy. I found Tessa easy to talk to. In a way, we were more like siblings than lovers.'

'Did you send her a Valentine's card and flowers, sir?'

Justin's brow crinkled in surprise. 'Heavens, no. I told you. The physical side of our relationship fizzled out quickly. We were just two misunderstood people who found solace in each other's company.'

'I see. I'll need to take your fingerprints to identify them at the crime scene,' said Robyn. 'And a DNA sample.'

Forrest looked aghast. 'You don't believe me? I'm still a suspect.'

'It's procedure, sir.'

'Take them,' he replied. 'Do what you must, but keep my family out of this. I beg you.'

Robyn left Anna to deal with Forrest. The prints would go immediately to the head of Forensics, Connor Richards, and the DNA sample would be sent to the lab to find out if Forrest was the father of Tessa Hall's baby.

※

Robyn had sent Matt ahead to Brocton to check out Anthony Hawkins. She hoped Shearer was right. She didn't want to waste time on a case if the man had died of natural causes, but it was her job to examine all the evidence and that's what she'd do.

Her first stop was at Lauren Gregson's. Henry's wife was looking more drawn and vacant than she had the last time Robyn had seen her. Robyn was again shown into the kitchen. It had been tidied up and cleaned. Lauren rested her back against the kitchen units. An opened envelope, addressed to Henry, was on the table.

'How are you, Lauren?'

Lauren's lip trembled. 'Not good.'

'It will get easier. I know everyone says that and it feels like you'll never be able to manage, but you will. Are your parents here?'

'I asked them to leave me alone for a while. Mum's doing my head in. I had a shit night and I wanted some peace.'

'You'll need your parents and friends. They'll be there for you, Lauren. You don't have to do this alone.'

Lauren's eyes filled. 'But I am alone. I'm alone and upset and at the same time, so bloody angry. I'm furious with Henry for keeping secrets and for being where he shouldn't have been, and with whoever killed him and stole the man I loved, and I'm so tired of it all. I want it all to go away and for things to be as they were before this happened. Most of all, I want that. I want this all to be a horrible dream and for me and Henry to be together.'

The tears fell and Robyn felt powerless to assist. Lauren brushed them away with the back of her hand. 'I feel like the universe hates me. Henry's test results came back yesterday and there was nothing wrong with him. What I can't understand is why I didn't fall pregnant. I feel so cheated. If we'd had a baby, at least I'd still have some part of him. It's not fair.'

'You really wanted a baby, didn't you?'

'More than anything. When I first saw how Henry behaved with Astra, I knew he'd make the perfect father. He was so sweet with her and really loved her. I wanted us to have a child for him to love like that. I've always loved children. Some women want careers or to be free agents. Me, I always wanted to be a mother and have three or four or even more children. I was an only child and I hated it. It was miserable being alone. I wanted it to be different for my kids. I wanted a happy, large family.'

'You're still young, Lauren. You still have time to get your wish.'

Lauren sniffled noisily. 'Maybe. I really wanted Henry's children. I tried everything to get pregnant – I read up on what foods to eat, bought ovulation test kits, and even saw a tarot card reader. A friend suggested it was all in my head and I had a blockage. She suggested buying baby clothes and toys and it would change my subconscious – and my body would then accept it wanted to fall pregnant. None of it worked. That's why I went to the fertility clinic. I shouldn't have tried so hard, should I? Then it might have happened naturally.'

She blew her nose and wiped under her eyes. 'Sorry. I'm having a real downer.'

'It's okay.'

'Did you come about Henry?'

'Sort of. I wondered if either of you knew Anthony Hawkins. He lived in Brocton.' Robyn passed Anthony's photograph to Lauren, who studied it carefully.

'He lived in the village?'

Robyn nodded.

'I've never seen him.'

'Are you sure?' Robyn watched Lauren's face carefully for signs she might be holding back.

'I'm absolutely certain I've not met this man or seen him about in the village. Henry might have come across him. He knew quite a few of the locals because of his coaching.' She uttered the words with a tinge of sadness.

The door opened and a deep voice shouted 'hello'.

Lauren grimaced at Robyn. 'My parents.'

'I'd better leave you. I'll let you know as soon as we find anything.'

'Thanks. And sorry about earlier. I shouldn't have dumped on you.'

'It's really not a problem. Take care of yourself. Trust me, this will become less painful.'

Robyn sidled past a middle-aged couple who politely stood aside and held open the front door without asking the reason for her visit.

※

Anthony's house, up a lane at the far end of Brocton village, was a ramshackle mess. From the outside it looked uninhabited. The wooden gate hung limply from its post and squealed in protest when Robyn walked through it on a crumbling pathway that was strewn with weeds.

Matt was inside the dark cottage with Anthony's brother, who introduced himself as William and left them in the outdated sitting room – covered in deep-patterned wallpaper from a bygone age – while he made a cup of tea.

Matt was keen to talk. 'Guv, found out something interesting. The last couple of weeks, Hawkins has been spending money like it's going out of fashion. The neighbours two doors down said he came home in a brand new, top-of-the-range Jaguar last week. The television's new too,' he said, pointing at the enormous screen that filled one wall of the room. 'His wardrobe upstairs is filled with designer clothes and there's a bill in the kitchen for dental work – he had his teeth whitened.'

Robyn looked up. 'Where did he get the money for all of that?'

'Hawkins told people around here an elderly aunt on his mother's side had popped her clogs and left him her entire estate, worth a fortune.'

'What does his brother say about this?'

'He says he has no idea how his brother got his hands on any fortune, especially as we don't have any aunts, or uncles for that matter,' said William, who'd returned unheard into the room, a mug in his hand. 'Sorry, couldn't help overhearing. This is a small place and the walls are paper-thin. I told the sergeant here that it's a complete mystery to me where the money came from. I stayed with Tony at Christmas and he hadn't got two pennies to rub together then. He moaned continuously about being short of cash. I even gave him a hundred quid to get by. I've had to bail him out a few times the last couple of years. You'd think he'd have told me and at least returned some of the loans.' He glowered at his mug, his rotund face crunched up.

'You had no idea he'd come into money, then?'

William's forehead creased heavily. 'Of course I hadn't. I'm totally gobsmacked by the news. I can't believe he kept it quiet. As far as I knew, he received a paltry pension from the prison service. I mean, look around you. Who'd want to live in a hole like this? It was all he could afford after his wife left him and fleeced him for all he was worth. He used to live in a decent bungalow in Yoxall before that. This place was a right come down for him. An old friend lets him live here on the cheap. I'd have offered to let him move in with me but fraternal love has its boundaries, and we'd have fallen out pretty quickly.'

'Could he have inherited the money from any other relatives?' Robyn asked.

William snorted. 'I'm his only relative. I *was* his only relative. That's why I made the effort to visit him at Christmas. I had a few days off work and thought I'd come and keep him company. Pretty shit time of the year if you live alone. He spent the Christmas before that with me, so it was my turn to come here.'

'And was he in good health when you saw him?'

'Sort of. He was drinking heavily, as usual – mostly cheap supermarket whisky. It's come as no surprise to me he's had a heart attack. I warned him about that. It was the stress that drove him to it and stress is a killer. Stress was one of the reasons he gave up his job as a prison warden. He couldn't find another job and then he and Sandra started having marital difficulties until, finally, she ran off with his best friend. Poor sod. He was devastated. I didn't think she'd be such a bitch about the divorce. How wrong I was. She took him to the cleaners. He had to sell his house, give her half of the proceeds and move away. He's been struggling ever since. I told him not to lose heart but he never seemed to make the interview stage let alone a new job. That's what happens when you get to a certain age. You can't find employment.' He took a sip of his tea and lifted his mug. 'Sure you don't want one?'

Matt and Robyn declined the offer.

'I seem to exist on tea,' he replied, patting his rotund belly with a beefy hand. 'That and biscuits.'

'What do you do, sir?'

'I'm a lorry driver. I mostly deliver into Europe. I'm based in Leeds at the moment, but I've lived all over the country and on the

Continent. I got back Saturday night from a seven-day haul. Got the call that Tony had died on my way up the M42.'

'You last saw your brother at Christmas?'

'That's right.'

'Did you meet any of his friends? Did he talk about anyone in particular?'

'Don't think he had too many friends around here. Most of his old friends live in Yoxall, and given they were also Sandra's friends, it was a bit awkward for him to carry on seeing them – besides, they're nearly all couples.'

'Did he mention Henry or Lauren Gregson?'

William shook his head. 'He brought a young woman home while I was here. I don't think she was called Lauren. Goodness knows what she saw in Tony, although he could be suave when he tried. They'd met at the pub in Yoxall. I wasn't feeling too well that day – bit of a cold. Tony went out to some quizzing event – they bore the shit out of me, so I stayed here and had an early night. I bumped into her the following morning coming out of the bathroom. She was wearing one of his shirts. I didn't say much. Bit shocked really. I said hello and told her I was Tony's brother and she smiled and said she knew who I was, then slipped back upstairs with the old fox. Blonde, wavy hair, green eyes. She had a nice face – cheery – and a great smile. He refused to talk about her after she'd gone, even though I pulled his leg about it. Dark horse, my brother. More so than I even thought. Have you seen that brand new car outside?' He shook his head in disbelief.

Robyn rummaged through her folder of photographs and pulled out one of Tessa Hall.

'Mr Hawkins, was this the woman you saw?'

'That's her!' he said. 'Is that Lauren Gregson?'

'No. It's one of the women he knew from a quiz team.'

'He was always good at quizzes. Used to spend a lot of time watching daytime television and endless quiz shows. He always said that one day he'd go on one of those television programmes and win a fortune. Maybe that's what he did! That would explain the money.' William's eyebrows had lifted high.

'If he did, sir, we'll be sure to find out.'

'He kept his paperwork here,' said William, walking over to a scruffy wooden cupboard and opening it. He extracted a pile of papers. 'I'll leave them to you, shall I?'

Matt and Robyn glanced through the piles of receipts, utility bills and bank statements. They couldn't find the most recent bank statement and there was nothing to indicate he had received a large injection of money on those they uncovered. According to his January statement, Anthony Hawkins had less than a hundred pounds to his name.

'We're missing February's statement. Take down the bank account details, Matt. We'll look into this back at the station,' said Robyn.

'I'd like to go home for a day or two, if that's okay,' said William. 'I'll be back to sort out his affairs and I'll leave my details if you need them.'

'Thank you. That would be helpful. We'll let you know when you can make arrangements for Anthony's funeral.'

William nodded sadly. 'And I'd like to know how he got his money. I'd like to know if he did get lucky in the end. That would be good to know.'

'Of course.'

※

Robyn left Matt with instructions to question Anthony's friends in Yoxall and his ex-wife, and she left Brocton. Morning had turned into afternoon and she rang Harry McKenzie as she drove back to the station.

'Just finished with Anthony Hawkins, Robyn. There's absolutely no trace of potassium chloride in his system,' he said. 'I examined his skin for puncture marks or evidence it might have been administered, and there's nothing. There is, however, significant evidence of coronary atherosclerosis. His arteries are very restricted, and checking through Ed's findings, I've also concluded Anthony Hawkins genuinely died of a heart attack.'

Robyn was irked by the news, but now she'd established a connection between Anthony and Tessa, she wasn't too thwarted by it. 'Thanks, Harry. I have another favour to ask you. Can you run a paternity DNA test on Tessa's baby or is eight weeks too soon to establish paternity?'

'I can do that. I think Tessa was almost nine weeks pregnant, so we can definitely run a DNA test on the foetus.'

'I've asked Anna to send you DNA samples from Tessa's sexual partners for comparison to determine the father of the baby. Start with Justin Forrest, but if that comes up negative, I'd like you to compare the DNA with samples from Anthony Hawkins to see if he is the father of Tessa's baby. And can you lift his fingerprints for me and have them sent across to Connor Richards?'

'Certainly.'

'Oh, and if both DNA tests are negative, run one against Henry Gregson's DNA.'

Harry didn't sound the slightest bit surprised at her request. That was Harry all over – practical and accommodating. 'Sure. I'm still at the lab so I'll do it now.'

Robyn now had to work out how best to proceed with the investigation, and she still had one more person she was very interested in interviewing – Roger, the other male member of the team. Juliet had been sure Tessa had slept with at least one man from their quiz side, and Liam had been adamant he'd kept well away from Tessa. She now knew about Anthony, and that only left Roger. She put her foot down to get back to Stafford. There were still questions to be answered.

CHAPTER THIRTY-SIX

DAY SIX – SUNDAY, 19 FEBRUARY, AFTERNOON

Robyn's desk was in disarray as she tapped her teeth with her pen, deep in thought about Lauren and Henry Gregson. Having spoken to Lauren that morning, she was feeling less inclined to believe she could possibly be behind her husband's murder. All she knew for definite was that Henry Gregson had been shot in cold blood, possibly because he was about to reveal a secret. What if the secret was about him fathering a child with another woman? What if Lauren had found out he'd done so? Would that tip her over the edge? Could Henry be the father of Tessa's baby? She'd know soon enough. Her gut feeling that Lauren was innocent tussled with her detective brain that told her she should wait for evidence to support her hunch and not jump to conclusions.

She rubbed the back of her neck. The tension was rising into her skull. She tidied the notes before jotting down three questions:

What time did Gregson leave home?
What time did he text his wife to say he was at work?
What time did he die?

According to Lauren, her husband had departed at about 9.30 a.m. and texted her at just before 10 a.m. to say he'd arrived at work. Robyn's shoulders drooped as she admitted the futility of these questions. Wherever Henry was when he texted his wife, he wasn't at MiniMarkt. Then, almost instantaneously, realisation struck, and she slapped the desk with the palm of her hand. Of course! This sloppy policing wasn't like her at all. She should have jumped on this before.

'Anna, get hold of Henry Gregson's phone provider and ask them to triangulate a location for him at the time he rang that pay-as-you-go phone. There'll be an emergency number to call.'

'No problem.'

Matt, whose forehead was shining damply, interrupted any further ruminations. Back from his interviews, he crashed into the office, bent forwards to catch his breath, hands on hips.

'Couldn't get a space in the car park... Raining... so jogged from car... Bad idea,' he said, in between breaths.

'You should give up the biscuits and sugar,' said Anna, glancing across at the commotion.

'It's not that. Ever since Poppy arrived, I've had to cut back on my training. Missus insists I do my fair share of parental duties. There's simply not enough time to fit in trips to the gym any more. I hadn't realised I'd got so out of condition. Geez. I need to watch it or I'll end up like Anthony Hawkins.'

Robyn digested his words and wondered if Anthony had known that he had any heart disease or health problems.

'Did Anthony have any medication at his house, Matt?'

'Only a box of paracetamol and some cough mixture.'

'Find out anything else interesting about his sudden windfall?'

'He bought the car outright with a banker's draft and had been looking to buy a new house. He'd got a couple of brochures for some very expensive places near Hoar Cross circa £600,000 each.'

'How much money did he have?' Robyn asked.

Mitz called across. 'The bank details you requested for Anthony Hawkins have arrived.'

She crossed the room and read Mitz's screen. A hundred thousand pounds had been deposited into his account at the beginning of February from a unit trust bond. The familiar tingling, a sign she was getting close to uncovering something of importance, began in Robyn's scalp. She marched to the window and stared outside to gather her thoughts once more.

'Okay, folks, time to gather round.' She waited until they were all in position, recapped on all their findings to date and brought them up to speed with regard to Tessa's friend, Justin. 'Anna, did his alibi check out?'

'It does. I spoke to his neighbour and the people he contacted via Skype. He was captured on CCTV footage on the high street at the times he specified, and his car was captured passing through two ANPR points at eight forty and eight fifty-five which was when he told us he did the school run. He wasn't in Barton-under-Needwood. Unless he hired somebody to murder her, he isn't our killer.'

'Another dead end. We're running into a few of those. The Henry Gregson investigation appears to be stalling too. We still haven't found our jogger spotted on the Chase, have we?'

'We've tried every avenue on that score. We'll have to go public and appeal for help.' David looked as fed up as Robyn felt.

'I'll talk to DCI Flint about that then. Okay, let's look at Tessa Hall and Anthony Hawkins. Harry's confirmed Anthony died of natural causes, so we're not dealing with his murder, but we've established a significant connection between him and Tessa Hall.' Robyn paced in front of the whiteboard that had been scrubbed clean.

'We know they had a relationship, played on the same quiz team and, more importantly, both mysteriously came into money. How have they got this money? Were they killed because of it? Or is there another reason? I think the money is relevant. It might even be the key to Tessa's murder.'

Mitz, tilting back on his chair, raised a point. 'Tessa could have given Anthony the money.'

'Why would she do that?' Anna asked. 'That's a ridiculous amount to give somebody you hardly know.'

'Because she really cared about him?' David said. 'She slept with him. Maybe it was more than a one-night stand.'

Mitz spoke up again. 'Or to buy his silence. He might have known about the baby and tried to blackmail her.'

Robyn agreed all scenarios were feasible. 'We have to keep digging. Talk again to those people who knew them both. Find out if they had any idea where the money came from. What did her parents say about the offshore account, Mitz?'

'They were openly shocked. Her mother broke down and burst into tears. Neither had a clue about Tessa's overseas fund.'

'Have you found out who set it up for her? You have to have an official financial advisor for such accounts. It's not like going to a bank and opening an account.'

Mitz shook his head. 'I'm on it. No news yet.'

'I want to talk to Roger Jenkinson now. What have you found out about him?'

Mitz spoke again. 'Got his contact details. Rang him earlier but he didn't pick up. Tried his ex-wife, who said he used to spend weekends out walking in the Peak District or similar. He would sometimes overnight there. That would explain why his phone is ringing out.'

'In February?'

'I said that too. She said he's an outdoors type and heavily into survival skills. He's a market trader. Sells home-grown produce at local markets. Hates being indoors.'

'David, find out the name of Roger's girlfriend and talk to her about him. Juliet Fallows might know who she is. If not, try Liam Carrington. He might be able to help.'

'Got Tessa Hall's phone record here,' said David. 'I looked specifically at those calls made since December last year. There are numerous ones to her parents, and after the end of December to this number, which belongs to Justin Forrest, Tessa's journalist friend. She rang him almost every two or three days. The last call was on Monday the thirteenth of February, three days before she was killed. There's not a lot that stands out, and I've still got to identify some of the numbers, but these three were all rung on the same day – thirtieth December, one after the other, from 11 p.m. onwards.' He pointed at the highlighted phone numbers. 'They belong to Anthony Hawkins, Juliet Fallows and Roger Jenkinson.'

'That's curious. I wonder why she rang them all that day and at that time of night. They'd stopped quizzing by then.'

The ping of an email alert sent Anna scurrying back to her desk, where she checked her computer screen. 'Just received the information from Henry Gregson's phone provider. They've used triangulation to pinpoint where he was when he phoned the pay-as-you-go phone that morning and texted his wife. He was on the main road, somewhere near Barton-under-Needwood.'

'Where Tessa Hall lived,' said Matt. 'Reckon he was visiting her?'

'We'll show his photograph around the village and ask about to see if he or his car was spotted.' Robyn looked thoughtful. If the DNA test proved he was the father of Tessa's baby, they'd have made a breakthrough.

Robyn glanced at the faces of her eager officers and hoped this time they had, then thought about Lauren Gregson's pale, haunted expression, and hoped for her sake they hadn't.

CHAPTER THIRTY-SEVEN

THEN

Johnny's a complete muppet. He's been caught selling a strip of E tablets to a sixth-former outside the school gates. A plain-clothes officer carted him off to the local police station. Johnny isn't one for dropping his mates in the shit. Johnny won't squeal. If he does, he knows what'll happen to him.

The boy's got no income now, which is a pain in the arse. The money he received for being Johnny's minder, even though it was only a fraction of what Johnny took, has been useful. With a sigh, he slumps in front of the television. His mother is at work at the pub. She does four evening shifts a week, along with her day job, in the office of a building company. He's no idea what she actually does there, but she always looks shagged out when she gets home and has no time to cook or clean. The house is a pigsty again.

His mother went off on one earlier. 'Clean it up before I get in. It's about time you pulled your weight. You do nothing but loaf about all day.' That's true, but he can't be bothered. It'll only get messed up again.

He settles on an episode of Brookside *about a bloke's body being found under a patio. He wonders if his dad would be missed if they shoved him under the patio. His father will be getting out of prison soon. There's no way he'll be allowed back into the house. His mother's started seeing a bloke from the pub. The boy doesn't know much about him but hopes he's decent. For a brief second he thinks about Clark the lodger, then, as always, blocks it from his mind. Some things have to stay buried, and memories of Clark are too awful to recall. His sister still has nightmares about the man. Nobody is taking either of them down that route again. As for his father, it's best if he stays away. Things have changed in the five years he's been gone, and he might find himself getting the good kicking he deserves.*

His sister appears from her bedroom and slips onto the settee to watch the programme. Just as he's beginning to get into it, the television goes off, along with the lights.

'Bloody hell. The leccy's gone off. Didn't Mum top up the meter?'

His sister's voice is calm. 'Nah. She told me she was struggling this month. Asked me if I had any money. You got any?'

He snorts. 'As if.'

'I'm not stupid. I know what you and Johnny have been up to. I saw you both going into the toilets again with Kevin Blackford. Kevin was flipping all afternoon,' she says.

He's not sure how to respond. His sister is a clever cookie and she's streetwise. If he denies it, she'll know he's lying. Kevin was an idiot to take the stuff before lessons. One of the teachers could have picked up on it. Still, Kevin is a prize twit at the best of times. They probably thought he was behaving as stupidly as usual.

He decides to come clean. 'I ain't doin' it no more. Johnny got picked up by the cops today.'

She stares into the darkness. 'You want to watch out. He'll drop you in it.'

'No, he won't. He wouldn't dare.' He leans forwards on the chair and rummages for some matches in his pocket.

'Don't you believe it. He may look big but he's a coward at heart. That's why he keeps you beside him. You're like his pet human Rott-weiler. If the police press him, he'll snitch.'

He gives up on the matches and cracks his knuckles instead. 'He'd better be careful then.'

She laughs. 'Yeah, right. You give him a seeing to and you'll be in the slammer alongside him and Dad. You can be really dumb sometimes.'

He rubs his knuckles and glowers. Bloody electricity. Now there's nothing to do and he can't even go and visit Johnny. He'll have to go to the park and join the skaters, have a few smokes. It's boring listening to his sister.

'You know, there's a way we could both make some money,' she says evenly.

'What are you on about?'

She continues in a voice that sounds far older than her thirteen years. 'You and me could take over Johnny's business. You're good at scaring people and I'm good at convincing them. I expect whoever was selling the E to Johnny won't want to be involved with him any more, so there'll be an opening for us. You know who he was getting them from?'

'Yeah, I know.'

'You got any cash?'

He hesitates before replying. A police car races past outside, its blue light illuminating the room and casting an eerie glow on his sister's face for an instant. She's a clever kid – cleverer than him. 'A bit from the last couple of sales.'

'Then we use it to buy stock,' she says.

He thinks about the possibilities for a while, then pulls out a cigarette and lights it, drawing on and letting the smoke fill his lungs. It isn't a bad idea. His dreams to be a footballer took a real bashing earlier. He didn't get picked for the local team on Saturday. He took the coach to task over it. Coach told him he was too aggressive. That was bollocks! He wasn't any more aggressive than the others. Just because he shinned one of the opposition last time, and after the match had headbutted that twat Mark for saying he played like a girl, he'd been dropped. Well, they could stuff it. They were all wankers anyway and the team sucked. See how they got on without him.

'You going to give me one of those, or what?' she asks.

He rattles the packet. 'That's the last one but you can have it.' He tosses it to her.

She lights up and sighs with pleasure.

Eventually he speaks. 'Let's see what happens to Johnny first, and if he gets off, then we'll approach his dealer.'

'Okay, but think about it. It's shit being poor.'

He couldn't agree more.

CHAPTER THIRTY-EIGHT

The trip to Barton-under-Needwood proved to be frustrating and fruitless. Anna, Matt, Mitz and Robyn knocked on doors and spoke to everyone in the vicinity and beyond, but there'd been no sightings of Henry Gregson the day he'd been killed, or indeed at any time. It seemed Henry Gregson had never visited the village.

'I'm done in,' said Matt.

'We'll call it a day.'

'Anyone fancy a pint before going home? I can't face going back to nappies and mess.' Matt looked hopefully at the others.

'I'm in,' said Anna. 'I could do with a very large glass of wine.'

'Guv, you joining us?' Mitz asked.

'Do you know, I'm going to skip it this once. I'll buy you all a round next time. I want to take another look at Tessa's place.'

Matt, Mitz and Anna headed off in the squad car. Robyn, who'd used her own car to get to Barton, stood outside Tessa's house for a few minutes. Tributes had been placed on the pavement in front of it – teddy bears, flowers and cards. She stopped to read the messages from neighbours and acquaintances and strangers, who'd been deeply saddened by the loss of a young life and wanted to demonstrate their respect in some way.

Driving back into Yoxall, she wondered if it would be worth her while touting Henry Gregson's photograph around the village before she called it a day. It was Sunday evening and many people were at home. What did she have to lose? Although Ella, Liam's girlfriend, claimed she hadn't seen him on the Tuesday he'd died, maybe one of her neighbours had.

She tried every house along the main street with frontages overlooking the main road, but drew a blank. Nobody had seen Henry or his red Kia. She trundled further along the main street, intending to try her luck in the open-all-hours shop, and halted by the churchyard. The door to the church was open. For a second she felt an urge to go inside and sit in the calm, away from all the frustration that threatened to drag her down. She traipsed up the path and into the cool interior, her footsteps echoing on the stone church floor.

A voice called, 'Can I help you?' and a corpulent shape sporting a cassock, a neatly trimmed beard and wire-framed spectacles wandered out of the shadows, a book under his arm.

'How do you do? I'm Kevin,' he said, a large hand extended. 'The Rev Kev,' he added and grinned, revealing a wide gap between his front teeth.

'Robyn Carter. DI Robyn Carter.'

'Oh, I see. And there was me hoping I'd found another lost sheep to join my happy flock, although you've missed evensong. I was just tidying up after it.'

'I'm afraid not. I'm here on business. I'm trying to find anybody who saw this man in the area recently.' She handed Kevin the photograph.

He studied it and lifted a finger, tapping the picture of Henry Gregson lightly.

'I think he was here. Last Tuesday. His face rang a bell. I was sure I'd met him before. He was standing in the churchyard, looking lost. I asked him if there was anything the matter and he insisted he was fine. I got the impression he wanted to chat, so I hung about with him for a while, discussing this and that. Thought I might have encouraged him to come inside, but he didn't. Kept glancing at his mobile. Said he had to meet somebody. That's all I can tell you. For what it's worth, I thought he looked troubled.'

'Thank you, Kevin. That's very helpful. I might need you to confirm all this at a later date, is that okay? You didn't happen to see the person he intended meeting?'

'No. I nipped back inside and he'd disappeared when I came back out.'

'Have you been the vicar here for long?' she asked.

'Three years.'

'You don't happen to know Liam Carrington and Ella Fox? They have a little girl, Astra, who might have been christened here a year or two ago.' She described the couple, mentioning Ella's scar.

Rev Kev opened his arms wide. 'I remember them now. They're not regular churchgoers. In fact, I haven't clapped eyes on them here since that day. However, I did christen the little girl. It was a strange ceremony because they didn't have the usual entourage with them. Normally, everybody comes along to a christening but not in this case. There was only the child, the parents and a couple of godparents. That was all.' He slapped his hand lightly against his forehead. 'That's where I've seen the man before. He was godfather to the little girl.'

Robyn offered him her card in case he could think of anything else and left him to lock up. Her hunch had paid off. Henry Gregson had been in Yoxall on February fourteenth. Was he there to visit Liam Carrington? Liam had denied seeing Henry that day. She sat in her car, trying to work out what would be the best course of action. She decided to visit Liam, Ella and Astra to ask again if they'd seen Henry that day. However, when she arrived at the house, it was in complete darkness. Robyn fired up the engine and headed back to her own home.

CHAPTER THIRTY-NINE

The boy wipes the blood gushing from his nose. The three blokes facing him mean business. There's no way he can take them on. The biggest one, bigger even than Johnny Hounslow, stares at him intently as if trying to telepathically drill into his head. His dreadlocks are curled tightly like corkscrews waiting to spring free from his face. Eventually he speaks, a Jamaican drawl, lazy yet filled with menace.

'So, you got the message yet?'

He nods, causing waves of nausea. Dreadlock Man continues with the staring act. His henchmen wait beside him, one brandishing a flick knife that he opens and shuts repeatedly. Dreadlock speaks again. 'Next time, it won't be you. It'll be your little sister and we won't be so gentle with her.'

He swallows. This is bad. This is worse than being picked up by the police. Knife Man keeps opening and shutting the switchblade; click, click, click. He nods again. He wants to speak but his throat is filled with gooey blood. He swallows again then coughs and has to spit it all out, retching as he does so.

'I think he's clear on the subject,' says Dreadlock to his goons. Knife Man glares at him lying on the floor. Dreadlock gives a smile, a proper scary smile, then says, 'Just to drive home the point…'

Before he knows what's happening, something whacks against his back, taking all the air out of him. Skinny Man, the tallest and leanest of the trio, has booted him hard, so hard he thinks his kidneys might have ruptured. His eyes water with pain and he can't breathe.

Dreadlock gives another smile. 'Stay off this patch, kid. My friend here is dying to get hold of your sister.'

They leave him in a heap, bleeding, dazed and confused. They've taken his supply of ecstasy tablets, the bag of cocaine he'd just bought and the money in his pocket. He's nothing at all to show for the weeks of effort and the chances he's taken. He turns over on the ground. The alley is empty now apart from a stray cat that lifts its head from a bin. He tries to stand but everything becomes hazy. The cat speaks, something about lying still while it gets help. He laughs at that – a talking cat – then he blacks out.

CHAPTER FORTY

DAY SEVEN – MONDAY, 20 FEBRUARY, MORNING

First thing in the morning, Robyn and Mitz headed to Hamstall Ridware to talk to Juliet Fallows before she left for work. Her daughter, Steph, dressed in pyjamas and a loose-fitting dressing gown, opened the door and let them in, trailing after them into the kitchen where she sat to finish a bowl of cereal. Juliet, in a white uniform, appeared almost immediately.

'I haven't got long,' she said. 'I have to leave in ten minutes.'

'We won't keep you. It's a couple of things we're following up. Last time we spoke, you mentioned Roger had a girlfriend.'

Juliet's face darkened. 'Why don't you ask Roger about her?'

'We're not able to contact him. We thought his girlfriend would be able to tell us where he is, but we don't know who she is.'

'I only know she's called Naomi. You'll be able to find out about her from the shooting club near Uttoxeter – Bramshall Leisure. She and Roger are both heavily into clay pigeon shooting. They used to be on the same shooting team. Roger often talked about it. They won quite a few matches. Try the club.'

'Thank you. I also wanted to ask you about Tessa again.'

Juliet looked at her watch.

'Tessa made a phone call to you on December the thirtieth.'

'What of it?'

'She phoned you, Roger and Anthony, one after the other, after 11 p.m. I wondered why she'd have made the calls. You said you weren't in contact with the others you met up with on quiz nights. It struck me as odd she rang you all.'

Juliet shrugged, her eyes darting round the kitchen as she tried to think of a response. 'It was about the staff meeting we were having the next day. I'm sure that's why she rang me. She couldn't remember what time the meeting was.'

'She could have found out when she got to the clinic in the morning.'

'She was off work that day. She was only coming in for the meeting.'

'And you didn't speak to or have any contact with the others yourself?'

Juliet looked at her watch again. 'No. I didn't keep in touch with any of them. Look, I told you all this already and I really have to go to work.'

'Of course, and thanks for talking to us.'

Steph stood up. 'I'll let them out, Mum. You get off.'

She waited until they were out of hearing range and whispered, 'If I wanted to report my dad to the police, could I do that?'

Robyn gave her a gentle smile. 'Did he hurt you too?'

Steph nodded and chewed at her lip before speaking. 'It was mostly Mum he hit. I was really scared of him all the time. I didn't dare say anything but since we moved away I feel I can talk about it. I spoke to my best friend and she agrees I should do something about it. He should pay for what he did to Mum. I thought about it a lot after you came last time. Mum won't shop him but she should. She's still scared stiff of him and worries he might turn up one day and beat her up. I don't want that to happen. If he's put away, he won't be able to.'

'I can give you a number to ring to talk to somebody about pressing charges but you really should talk to your mum about it first. She won't thank you for going behind her back. It's a major decision to take your own father to court, Steph. You'd have to be very strong-willed and determined. Don't do anything without talking to your mum.'

'I guessed you might say that. Thing is, she's too frightened to say anything, even now. I'm not.'

'Think about it again and ring me when you've made up your mind. I'll put you in contact with the right people.'

Steph palmed the card Robyn gave her with thanks before shutting the door quietly behind them both.

As soon as she got into the car, Robyn rang David and asked him to contact the shooting club to find out Naomi's surname and contact details.

She and Mitz drove along the narrow lane from Juliet's house that meandered past fields of cows and dairy farms into the village of Yoxall, where it came out almost opposite Liam's house.

'Pull up in that drive, Mitz. I'd like a quick word with Liam or Ella about Henry. He was definitely in the village on Tuesday.'

They drew up outside the house, but Liam's old Audi wasn't on the drive, and when Robyn knocked at the door, there was once again no answer.

✳

Back at the station, David and Anna had been productive.

'Roger's girlfriend is called Naomi Povey. She's a member at Bramshall Leisure where she practises shooting regularly. She won Staffordshire skeet champion in 2016.'

'Skeet?'

'It's a type of clay shooting. She's one of the best at the club and won several competitions. Roger Jenkinson was also a member but he left last year. Before that, he did a lot of shooting at weekends – competition level. I got hold of Naomi and she's on her way here now.'

'Excellent. What about Roger?'

'Still out of contact. Naomi also thinks he's gone off to the Peak District for a couple of days. She says he's sure to return soon because he'll need to prepare his produce for Thursday's farmer's market in Lichfield. He has a stall there.'

'Can't we get hold of him at all?'

'No, guv. He disconnects from the modern world when he's away – doesn't turn on his phone, goes hiking and stays under canvas in fields.'

'Sodding man. He's not making this easy for us.' Robyn stomped about the office, scowling at the other desks cluttering it.

'He isn't making it easy,' agreed David, 'but this might raise your spirits. You know I've been going through those numbers Tessa rang or messaged? Well, one caught my eye after I rang Naomi. It looks like she and Tessa messaged each other several times over a period of two days in January.'

Robyn stopped scowling. She had another lead. 'Great. Let me know the instant Naomi arrives. I want talk to her.'

※

Naomi was at best described as shrewish, with small, mousy features and limp hair pulled back in an elastic band. Her face wore a scowl as if she were sucking lemons. Dressed in unflattering, dark trousers, a baggy top and flat, lace-up boots, she looked far older than thirty-six.

'Thank you for coming in. I'd like to ask you a few questions about Tessa Hall. You do know who I mean, don't you?'

Icy eyes glared at Robyn. 'I know her.'

'Have you spoken to her in recent weeks?' asked Robyn.

The room was filled with a high-pitched laugh. 'Why would I want to talk to her?'

'I was hoping you might tell me.'

Naomi crossed her arms. 'I have nothing to say.'

Matt, who sat adjacent to Robyn, pushed across a photocopied piece of A4 containing a list of phone numbers. One was highlighted in green. 'Is that your phone number?'

Naomi's eyelids fluttered several times before she nodded.

'I'm going to ask you again, have you spoken to Tessa in recent weeks or contacted her?'

Naomi remained button-lipped.

'Miss Povey, you're not helping yourself by keeping quiet. If you continue to refuse to answer my questions, I'll have to consider your silence as suspicious. We're dealing with a murder enquiry here. I don't need to tell you how serious that is. Why did you and Tessa message each other in January this year?'

Naomi almost spat her reply. 'The bitch was seeing Roger. He denied it but I knew he was. I found a text message from her on his phone that proved they were having an affair. I copied down her number and then I challenged her over it.'

'You believed they were having an affair?'

'I know they were. I told her I was going to come over and rip her fucking head off if she kept seeing him. It's not like she cared about him. She was nothing but a tart, throwing herself at every bloke in the pub. I saw her in action when I went along one night – smug little bitch.'

'You threatened her?'

'Yes. It was the only way to get her to understand I wasn't going to give him up.'

'Did she confess to the affair?'

'Eventually. She was so full of herself. She said Roger would always choose her over me so I'd better piss off and leave her alone. I wasn't having that. I've known Roger a long time. I know her sort. I've met plenty like her in my life. She'd have led him on and dropped him as soon as she found a new bloke to chase after. I wasn't going to let her do that to Roger. He's already suffered one horrible break-up. I helped him through that, not her. We're good together. I've been there for him when he's been at rock bottom. I wasn't going to give up without a fight. I told her I'd make sure everyone at her work knew she was a slag who stole boyfriends and husbands. I promised to make her life a misery. In the end, she said she didn't give a shit any more, that she wasn't interested in him. Shows how little she really cared – the bitch.'

Naomi's lips pressed together in a thin line and Robyn wondered how Roger Jenkinson could be attracted to two such different women.

'And I have to ask you this, to eliminate you from our enquiries, where were you Thursday morning?'

'At work at the JCB factory outside Uttoxeter. I went on shift at seven.'

If Naomi's alibi bore out, it was still possible for her to have travelled to Tessa's house in Barton-under-Needwood, some thirty minutes away, kill her and return in time for her shift.

'And for the record, I haven't told Roger I know about his fling with Tessa. Some things are best kept secret,' said Naomi.

Robyn chewed over her words. Here was another person keeping secrets: first Henry, then Tessa and now Naomi. It prompted her next question.

'Do you know Henry or Lauren Gregson?'

'Can't say I do. Not names I recognise.'

'Sergeant Higham, can you show Miss Povey the photographs?'

Matt rummaged in the file he'd brought into the room and slid photographs of the couple across the table.

Naomi studied them carefully and shook her head again. 'I definitely don't know them.'

'They never turned up to any of the quizzes?'

'Not when I was there.'

'Were you at work on Tuesday the fourteenth?' Matt glanced quickly in Robyn's direction but she ignored his look.

'Am I under suspicion for a crime?'

'I'd like to know where you were, please, Miss Povey.'

'I took the day off.' Naomi's eyelids fluttered quickly. 'I got up at eight, did some housework and then went to Tesco to get something nice for dinner. I was cooking a meal for us both for Valentine's Day. Do you want me to drag in the checkout girl to prove I was there?'

Robyn gave a tight smile. 'I don't think that'll be necessary. Going back to Thursday the sixteenth, you said your shift at JCB began at seven.'

'That's right.'

'And before that you'd have been getting ready to go to work?'

'Isn't that what people normally do? Look, where are you going with this?'

Robyn wondered if she should push for more details, but decided she had little to gain by riling Naomi. 'Have you heard from Roger recently? We'd like to talk to him.'

'He was in one of his moods – he gets them from time to time. We call them his dark moods. When they come on, he usually goes up to the Peak District. He spends time outside, getting his head straight. I spoke to him on Friday evening and he was definitely out of sorts. I could tell by his voice. I usually leave him alone when he gets like that. He snaps out of it again. He has a stall at Lichfield market on a Thursday, so he'll be back for that. He can't afford to miss a market day.'

'Any idea where he might be in the Peak District? Does he favour an area in particular?'

'Roger loves all the great outdoors. Me, I hate it. I like shooting clays but I don't like living under canvas and walking over muddy trails in the rain and wind. I've never even been to the Peak District, so no, I have no idea.'

'You've known him a while?'

'About five years. We met at Bramshall Leisure. Used to shoot together. He was the best male shot there. Pity he gave it up. I keep telling him to take it up again, but he can't afford the club fees. I offered to pay them for him, but he won't let me. Says he can't accept charity. Shame, because we used to have a lot of fun together there.'

'If he rings you, will you let us know, please?'

Naomi nodded.

'I think that's everything for now.'

Naomi rose at the same time as Robyn. She only came up to Robyn's shoulders. Her face was expressionless. 'I didn't like Tessa but I had no reason to kill her. She dumped him. I got what I wanted. I didn't need to kill her.'

She picked up her coat and snorted. 'Tessa was always trouble. Even now she's dead, she's still causing it.'

Matt escorted her from the room and earned a glower for his efforts.

As she returned to her office, Robyn reflected on those words and decided Naomi bore enough of a grudge, especially if she knew about the baby, to have murdered Tessa.

CHAPTER FORTY-ONE

With Shearer and his men in the office, and her team fully occupied, Robyn headed downstairs to the staff locker room to change into her running gear. She needed to collect her thoughts, and running usually allowed her to ruminate.

She pounded the empty pavements, past Stafford Hospital, hidden behind thick bushes, and the large university campus, dotted with flats and large brick buildings, where Harry McKenzie worked, before turning into a road that would pass housing estates and Leafy Lane, where she lived. She'd run this same route more times than she cared to remember. It would take her thirty minutes in total; time enough to reflect on what she knew.

Lost in thought, she didn't register her surroundings. As she ran, they became a familiar blur of front gardens, houses and parked cars. Her focus was on Henry and Tessa. Both had kept secrets. Both were dead. Had Henry and Tessa been involved in a relationship, or was Roger the father of Tessa's baby? The questions mounted up and still she couldn't find the answers.

She leapt from a pavement, jogged across the road and bounded onto the opposite pavement that led to her home. She ran on, oblivious to the black BMW parked behind a silver van opposite her house, her mind now on Henry's friend, Liam, and his partner

Ella. Ella had disliked Tessa too. Like Naomi, she'd warned Tessa off her man. Jealousy and love – two very powerful emotions that drove people to commit heinous acts.

Seeing Schrödinger wasn't in his usual spot on the window ledge, she drew to a halt on a whim and decided to check on him. It wouldn't take a minute.

She slipped the key into the door and called for him. When he didn't appear, she went inside, removed her trainers and checked the sitting room and kitchen before heading upstairs. She found him languishing on her bed, where he stretched indolently and then purred contentedly as she lifted him to her face.

'You lazy boy,' she murmured, planting a kiss on his head. Cradling him against her, she stood in front of her bedroom window and gazed onto the garden below. It wasn't much of a garden, but if she put some effort into it in springtime, she and Schrödinger would be able to enjoy it in the sunshine. She was about to return him to the warm spot on the bed when a movement outside caught her eye and she froze. A man in dark clothing was slipping back out from the garden, through the side gate that led onto the street.

She put down the cat and bounded down the stairs to catch up with the intruder. She raced out the front door in her socks and onto the pavement, but was in time only to see the rear end of a BMW pull away and join the main road.

She cursed loudly and returned inside, pulled on her trainers and checked to see if the back gate had been forced open. It hadn't. However, it was unlocked, and Robyn was certain she hadn't left it like that. With shaking hands, she rang Ross.

'Hey,' said Ross.

'Somebody broke into my back garden and was hanging about outside the house. I came home unexpectedly and frightened them off, I think. Might have been a burglar, but I've got a bad feeling about it. The back gate was unlocked. I ran after him but he'd gone.

I couldn't see anyone, only a black BMW. It pulled out of my road and into traffic, headed towards the town centre.'

'Registration?'

'I didn't get it. Shit, Ross, I was so shocked I couldn't think straight and I wasn't quick enough. I caught sight of the person but only for a second. Ross, I think it could have been Davies. He was about the same height and had dark hair.'

'Robyn, calm down. If it'd been Davies, why would he have sped off?'

'Oh, for fuck's sake! You're right. I'm behaving like a madwoman. It's because of what Amélie told me.'

'Well, you can put that out of your mind. I'm over at the CineBowl at the moment, and I've shown his photograph to almost everyone who works here. No one has recognised him, or seen him here. Amélie was imagining it. Much like you. It happens.'

'Yeah. I guess so.'

'You probably disturbed somebody casing out your place for a robbery, or a chancer. I'm going to come round and install some top-of-the-range spy cameras. I'll put one inside the house and another outside. That way, if anybody else comes around, we'll see who it is.'

'Would you? I'll pay you for them.'

'I'll give you a generous, ex-employee discount,' he joked. 'Seriously, I'm concerned somebody's got into your garden. That lock on the gate is one of the most sophisticated on the market, and totally impregnable. I can't see how they unlocked it.'

'Do you think he could be somebody connected to Davies? The photo… the flowers… and now he's checking out my home.'

'Let's not jump to conclusions. We'll treat it as a potential break-in for the moment. I'll see if there are any fingerprints or other clues left behind. Don't worry. I'll come over immediately. I've got your spare house key, so you don't need to stay at home. I'll fit the spy surveillance cameras. You know how they work, don't you?'

'Are they the same ones we used when I worked with you?' Robyn had spent a year working with her cousin before returning to the force and it had been exactly what she needed to get back on her feet.

'The very same.'

'Oh, fuck it, Ross. I don't need this shit.'

Ross's voice was calming. 'Come on, Robyn, this is nothing compared to what you've faced in the past. We're probably reading too much into it. You might have forgotten to lock the gate, what with your mind on other things. It could have been no more than an opportunist who tried your gate, found it open and wandered in to see what he could steal. He saw you and ran away.'

Robyn huffed. Had she locked the gate? She couldn't remember the last time she'd used it. Was it when she took the wheelie bin out, last Wednesday? They'd been really busy with the investigation that day. She might have forgotten to secure the gate in her haste to get to the office.

'What about the BMW? It seemed to speed off.'

'Cars go up and down your road all the time at speed. Might not be connected in any way at all.'

Robyn rubbed at her forehead. Her hand was clammy now with sweat and exertion. 'Yeah. You could be right. I'm getting worked up. It was such a shock. That's all. If I hadn't stopped off, he might have broken into the house.'

'Well, he'd not have stolen anything. You've got that top-of-the-range house alarm fitted, haven't you? That would've gone off.'

'It wasn't turned on. I didn't alarm the place because of the cat.'

'Robyn!' Ross sounded exasperated. 'You need to take more care.'

'I know. I wasn't thinking clearly. My mind's been on the investigations.'

Ross sighed. 'There's a setting that allows pets to move around the house freely and not trigger the alarm. I'll programme it for you. First, I'll head to the office, collect the cameras and then get cracking. Want me to get that gate lock changed while I'm at it?'

'Would you? It'll give me peace of mind. Thanks, Ross. You're a diamond.'

'Take it easy, Robyn,' said Ross, his voice filled with concern. 'I don't want to see you go backwards again.'

'I won't. Not with you on my side.'

Robyn disconnected and shoved the phone back in her pocket, furious that she'd been sideswiped like that.

As she jogged back into the station car park, she tried hard to turn her attention back to the investigations and put the intruder and black BMW out of her mind.

✳

Robyn was copying a report when David joined her by the photocopier. His brows were knitted together.

'We got hold of Roger Jenkinson at last. He's on his way to be interviewed. I came across something of interest on the general police database about him. He was an animal rights activist. He was charged back in 2004 for protesting against Newchurch guinea pig farm,' he said.

'I remember those protests. There was an outcry about testing on the animals. It was all over the news.'

'He was also suspected of digging up the remains of one of the guinea pig farm's ancestors. That charge didn't stick. He's known to police for various break-ins and property damage on farms, notably those associated with controversial methods of raising animals, overcrowded turkey sheds, that sort of thing. His wife filed for divorce in 2014, on the grounds of unreasonable behaviour. Claimed Jenkinson threatened her with physical violence and was abusive.'

'A man with an aggressive nature who was also a member of a shooting club. That rings some alarm bells for me, David.'

'Then this will ring them more.' He tapped at a note in his book. 'He was also accused of possession of a firearm in 2014. Used it to ward off an intruder, who reported him to the police. Police, due to insufficient evidence to support the intruder's claim, dismissed the accusation. Jenkinson firmly denied the incident and no firearm was found on his property. I've requested further details. I'll let you know as soon as I get a response.'

Robyn collected her copies and slid back behind her desk. Outside, the skies had darkened again and rain splattered against the windows, leaving silvery trails that slid down the panes of glass like thick slugs. She hated days like this. They sapped her energy. Anna, at the back of the office, pushed away from her desk and approached Robyn.

'You might like to read this. It's an unofficial statement from the landlord at the Goat pub in Abbots Bromley. He hosted the final quiz that year. I rang him when I was checking to confirm Tessa and Justin had met at the pub as he said. I left a message for the landlord to call me. He only got back to me this morning. He said he wouldn't normally have remembered such a thing but was excited about a journalist covering his quiz. He saw them sitting in a corner together after the quiz, before leaving the pub together, and then he told me about Roger Jenkinson and Anthony Hawkins. They had an argument. Landlord had to break it up before it got out of hand. It's all there.' Robyn read the statement before shaking her head in dismay.

The desk phone trilled. David picked up the receiver. 'Yep. Thanks. Jenkinson's here. Interview room one, guv.'

Robyn signalled across the room. 'Matt. Come on. Let's see what he has to say for himself.'

※

Roger Jenkinson was a stocky, wide-shouldered, self-assured individual, with ruddy cheeks and a thick thatch of dark hair. His air was one of defiance, legs apart, arms folded.

Robyn began by asking where he'd been while they'd been trying to contact him.

'In the Peak District. I like to lose myself up there some days. I don't take my phone when I go. It's a good place to take stock of your life. Got back about ten this morning.'

'You camped out up there?'

'Yes.'

'It's an unusual time of the year to go camping. Wasn't it very wet and cold?'

He gave a disparaging snort. 'I'm hardy. Rain doesn't bother me. Nor cold. I had my thermals. I dried out in the pub – the Farmhouse Inn. Had a pint and a bite to eat there.'

Robyn made a note to check out his whereabouts.

'They might not remember me there,' he said. 'Place was busy.'

Robyn ignored the comment. 'I'd like to ask you a few questions about Tessa Hall. You knew her from quiz nights, didn't you?'

'I did.'

'And you are also aware she was murdered last week.'

He nodded.

'I wanted to ask you about your relationship with Tessa Hall.'

'I didn't have a relationship with her.'

Robyn shook her head. 'I'm afraid that isn't true. It would be best to be honest with us, Mr Jenkinson. When was the last time you saw Tessa?'

'I don't want to discuss it.'

'Are you refusing to assist us, sir?' Robyn's eyes narrowed as she spoke.

Roger remained silent. Robyn let him stew for a couple of minutes, noting the slight beads of sweat that formed on his upper lip, before speaking again.

'Did you send Miss Hall a Valentine's card? Before you answer, please be aware we have extracted fingerprints from it.' She didn't need to explain any further.

Roger Jenkinson spoke so quietly she could hardly hear his response. 'Yes.'

'You were having a relationship with Tessa Hall?'

He gave a brief nod. 'I've been seeing her whenever possible since last December.'

'It strikes me as odd that you didn't come forward as soon as you heard she'd been murdered. Instead, you suddenly departed for the Peak District.'

'Once I found out Tessa was dead, I needed to be alone. I couldn't talk to anyone about it. I wanted some time to think and try to understand what had happened. I loved her. I couldn't believe she'd been killed.' Roger's demeanour changed. He suddenly looked less self-assured.

'As I understand it you've also got a steady girlfriend – Naomi Povey. If you loved Tessa Hall so much, why were you still with Naomi?'

'I tried to finish with her but it's been really difficult. Naomi's like a bloody limpet. You try to get rid of her but she clings on. I tried dropping hints, being offhand with her, and even told her we should break up, but she keeps turning up at my house as if nothing's wrong. I ought to have told her straight about Tessa but I was a bit worried about how she'd react. Thing is, I still have feelings for Naomi too. I didn't want to hurt her. She was really nice to me when my wife left me. We had a fair bit in common – we were both on the same shooting team at one point – and for a while I even thought I loved her. But once I met Tessa, that changed.'

'Does Naomi know about Tessa?' Robyn asked even though Naomi had told her she'd not challenged Roger about the affair.

'I planned on telling her last week, but Naomi made a huge fuss about Valentine's Day and bought me presents, insisted we spent time together that day and, oh, God, it was just too hard to tell her. I should have. I know I should have, but Naomi's so intense, and it wasn't the right time. Tessa knew I was having difficulty getting rid of Naomi, and we were both concerned she'd turn psycho on us if we didn't handle her properly. Tessa said to leave it for a little while longer, keep out of Naomi's way, let her get the message, and then tell her.'

'Naomi can be volatile?'

'Bloody hell, can she? If she loses her temper, you know about it. She can be very fiery. I used to like that in her. I'm not so keen on it now.'

'I understand you've also had your hot-blooded moments, sir. In 2014, you were accused of possessing a firearm and threatening an individual.'

He sighed dramatically. 'I should have known you'd bring that up. We're talking about that nutcase who was on my property. He was the one in the wrong, not me. He climbed over my fence and wandered across my field. When I told him to clear off, he said he was entitled to walk across it because it was common land. I didn't feel like arguing the toss, so told him to piss off or I'd shoot him. I waved a stick at him. He was too far away to see what it really was. It scared him enough that he ran away, but he stumbled trying to get back over the fence, and hurt his ankle. Next I knew, the bastard had gone to the police and reported me for threatening him and causing him injury! Where's the logic in that? I denied it. The police didn't find any weapons in my house. I wasn't charged. End of.'

His face had turned deep red with annoyance and Robyn allowed him a few seconds before she calmly asked, 'Do you currently own any firearms?'

'Course not.' A thin spray of spittle flew across the table as he spoke. 'Search my house. You'll not find anything there. Now, can I go? It's been a totally shit week.'

'In a moment. When was the last time you saw Anthony Hawkins?'

'Anthony? Why are you asking me about Anthony? He had a heart attack, didn't he?' He fixed his hard blue eyes on her.

'How did you know he had died?'

'I found out this morning. I rang a mate, Paul, to arrange to meet for a pint later. He's a member of that posh golf club at Brocton. Said Anthony had snuffed it playing golf – heart attack.'

'Could you describe your relationship with Mr Hawkins?'

'We got on. He was a bit bossy at times. He used to be a prison warden and he liked telling us what to do. I don't always like being told what to do.'

'Did you fall out with him?'

'Not really.'

'You were overheard at the Goat in Abbots Bromley, in late December, threatening to kill him.'

Roger spluttered. 'Hang on a sec. I was drunk. I didn't mean anything. He was being his usual pompous self and I got angry with him. It wasn't serious.'

'So you are saying this was nothing more than a spat, but you can't remember what it was about.'

'It was the usual. Anthony told me I was out of order. I said something about it being a good job we weren't going to be playing together any more. He went on about my shit attitude to life in general – all petty stuff in the cold light of day – less so after several pints. The landlord told us to clear off and we did. I went home, sobered up and forgot about it. This was all ages ago.'

'Is that why the team broke up? Because you fell out?'

'No. We'd decided to split up anyway. It was only a bloody quiz team! That night I was sick of him.'

'So it was about your attitude to life?'

'Something like that.'

'It wasn't about Tessa Hall?'

Roger Jenkinson went very quiet. The beads of sweat on his lip were more evident now.

'I'll ask you again. Was it about your attitude or was it because you'd found out Anthony had slept with Tessa?'

'Oh, for fuck's sake. I don't have to put up with this. It doesn't matter what it was about. I was pissed. Got it? It didn't mean anything. Anthony wasn't murdered so this isn't relevant.'

Robyn still had to learn where he'd been the morning Tessa Hall was murdered. 'So, where were you on Thursday the sixteenth of February?'

He shuffled in his seat. 'You're barking up the wrong tree. I didn't kill Tessa. I met up with an old work colleague who lives north of Leeds. I arrived there about eight thirty. Spent the morning with Andy – that's Andy Ford. We both used to work for Moo Dairies.' He waited for Robyn to make a note and smirked when she finished. 'He'll vouch for me. And, of course, I spent the afternoon and night with Naomi.'

He sighed heavily. 'And if you want to know where I was on Saturday morning when Anthony dropped dead, I was somewhere in the Peak District – probably on my way to Kinder Scout – a plateau in the Dark Peak. There was a group of exercise instructors – from the Nuffield gym in Sheffield – walking up there. I spoke to a couple of them. We decided the weather was too shit to go any further. Ask them. They'll probably remember me. I don't want you to think I scared the old bastard to death.'

There was a pause while Roger scratched at his face and stared into the distance. His eyes glittered when he next spoke.

'You were right. The argument in the pub was about Tessa. That twat Anthony was bragging about how he'd slept with her. He'd seen me with her and was mouthing off. I told him to shut up.' He flexed his knuckles as he spoke. 'May I leave now? I've got stuff to be getting on with.'

As he stood up, Matt's attention was drawn to the man's scuffed walking boots.

'What size shoe do you take, Mr Jenkinson?'

'Ten.'

Robyn caught the look Matt threw her and spoke. 'Sit down again for a minute. Do you know Henry Gregson?'

'I won't sit down. If I'm not being charged with something, and I presume I'm not, then I have work to do at home.'

'Answer the question, Mr Jenkinson, or I'll find some excuse to hold you here.'

'No. Never heard of him.' He stared at her, nostrils flaring.

'Thank you, sir. Now, would you please allow Sergeant Higham to take a DNA swab and your fingerprints for elimination purposes, and then you'll be allowed to go.' She didn't linger to listen to any protests. Matt would set him straight.

Robyn stomped back into the office. If Roger Jenkinson had been with Andy Ford on Thursday morning, it was unlikely he'd have murdered Tessa. It would take two hours to reach Leeds from Barton-under-Needwood – longer at that time of morning with the heavy traffic, and his friend lived further the other side of Leeds. That still left Naomi. Could the woman have been so jealous of Tessa, she'd killed her?

'David, can you talk to Andy Ford, an ex-employee of Moo Dairies, to confirm Roger Jenkinson was with him on the sixteenth?' She threw the notepad she'd used onto his desk.

'Yes, guv,' David replied.

Mitz was frowning at his screen. He called Robyn over. 'Matt was dealing with Anthony Hawkins' bank details and trying to track that huge amount of money deposited into it. He contacted Fidelity, the company behind the unit trust bond, and they've released the information he requested. Anthony Hawkins only triggered part of the fund. The initial deposit to set up the bond was one million pounds. He still has £900,000 left in it.'

Robyn drew a sharp breath. Anthony Hawkins and Tessa Hall both had a million pounds squirrelled away. How had they come by it? This changed everything. Could his death have been unnatural? Jenkinson's words triggered a thought. Had somebody scared Anthony Hawkins to death? Was that actually possible?

She rang Harry McKenzie straight away.

'Not got those DNA test results yet, Robyn. Another case arrived soon after you rang yesterday and that had to take precedence. I've put an assistant on it for you and we should get back to you very soon. I know how important it is for your investigation.'

'Thanks, Harry. I won't keep you. I wanted to know if it's possible for a person to physically die of fright. I suspect it is. However, I'd rather hear it from a professional.'

Harry cleared his throat. 'This is about Anthony Hawkins, isn't it? In his case it is definitely possible. If a person is already at risk, and has narrowed arteries such as those we found in Anthony Hawkins, he or she might never experience any symptoms, but when faced with an incident that causes the adrenalin levels to rise rapidly, and destabilise the plaque that's built up within the arteries, could well have a sudden heart attack.'

'What sort of incident would cause such fear?'

'You're the detective, Robyn. What do you think? I'd say something fairly major – a car accident, brush with death, or someone holding him up at gunpoint, that sort of thing.'

'Harry, thank you. You're a gem.'

Her own heart was now racing. She called across to Anna and Mitz. 'Anthony Hawkins was alone on an empty golf course when he died. According to Shearer's report, the man hadn't booked a round of golf. Now, Anthony Hawkins knew the club rules: that a tee off slot had to be booked with reception. A breach of the rules would result in him being asked to leave the club, so why didn't he book one?'

'So do you think he'd arranged a meeting there, guv?' Anna asked. 'The golf clubs and outfit were just for show?'

'No. If that had been the case, he wouldn't have changed his shoes for a round of golf. If he'd arranged a meeting, he'd have worn ordinary shoes and certainly not taken his clubs. I have a hunch he was lured to the course to be killed. I suspect his killer arranged the meeting on the golf course, and Hawkins turned up, expecting to play a round of golf.'

Anna nodded. 'That makes sense.'

'Now, consider this: how could the murderer be certain the golf course wouldn't be in use? To be sure neither of them would be spotted by another group of golfers, teeing off at the same time, he'd surely have contacted the club reception. It's the only way the killer could have known the course would be empty. Did somebody phone the club and ask if the course was free Saturday morning?'

Anna's pen flew across her notepad. 'I'll look into that,' she volunteered.

'Thank you.'

'What's made you think Anthony Hawkins was murdered? He died of a heart attack,' Mitz asked.

'Something Harry said. He told me a serious shock – one brought on by fear of dying – could kill a person with atherosclerosis. He mentioned it could happen if somebody pointed a gun at such a person.'

Mitz nodded as he followed her argument.

'I wondered if the same person who killed Henry Gregson persuaded Anthony Hawkins to come to the golf course in order to shoot him, but when Anthony Hawkins caught sight of the gun, he keeled over in fear, and saved the killer the job. Is that a leap too far?'

Matt caught the back end of the conversation as he entered the office. 'That bloke Roger Jenkinson is definitely aggressive. I almost had to hold him down to get his fingerprints. What's a leap too far?'

Robyn told him about the latest revelation and ran through her theory again for his benefit.

'It's certainly feasible. We still need to work out why.'

'It could be to do with the same secret. Henry Gregson, Tessa Hall and even Anthony Hawkins were keeping something secret, and let's not forget Tessa and Anthony had suddenly come into money. Keep digging, folks. There must be something else that connects these men and Tessa Hall. We're getting closer. I'm sure we are. Once we get those DNA results back, we might have the answer to this confounding case.'

CHAPTER FORTY-TWO

THEN

The young man is sick of trying. Today was the third job interview he's had and it's obvious that the suited bloke, who spent most of his time staring at notes, was never going to employ him.

Back home, his mother's getting ready to meet her new fella. She's all giddy like some teenager and he feels a mixture of happiness and nausea. She's not like his mum at all. His sister obviously thinks the same. She pulls a face.

Ever since the night he was beaten up by the trio of bad-assed drug dealers, he's been forced to keep on the straight and narrow – no more selling drugs to the kids at school and, consequently, no more income. Johnny Hounslow is still in a secure centre near Stoke, and he thinks he should visit him but can't be bothered. What's he going to say to him? Johnny will get out soon and that'll be that. He'll probably end up working at his dad's factory. Lucky sod.

Of course, the cops wanted to know what happened that night six months previous. A drunk, who'd been asleep in the alley, saw what happened and called for help. He didn't know why the three huge guys were kicking a kid to death, but terrified they'd do the same to him, he hid behind the bins until they left. It was thanks to the old drunk that he was still alive. The trio had caused some serious damage to his kidneys and face, and if he'd been left for too long in the alleyway, he'd have probably choked on his own blood, or his kidneys would have packed in and he'd be on regular dialysis now. His sister was really upset. She blamed herself and said it was all her fault it had happened, but of course, it wasn't.

At the moment, he couldn't care less. Life sucks big time. He's spent the entire summer looking for work, along with every other sixteen-year-old now out of education. So far, no one has been impressed by his qualifications or his attitude – he's had a few interviews and got nowhere. It's bloody disheartening. Why don't they want him? He is bright and wants to work. What more do they want?

He'll have to try harder if he really wants employment, and at the moment, his dole money isn't enough for fags and booze and having a good time. He's going to end up like his old man – a loser – if he doesn't get a grip.

His mother's flouncing about in yet another revealing top. This one's black with sparkling sequins on it. She looks like a deflated disco ball. 'What'cha think of this one?' she asks.

His sister stops working the gum in her mouth, puts down her magazine and looks her mother up and down. 'That's the one. Wear that. You look great.'

His mother's face breaks into a rare smile. 'Thanks, sweet cheeks.'

His sister goes back to her magazine. As soon as his mother leaves the room he speaks. 'Really? You like that one?'

'Nah, but she's happy and she'll stop parading about in every single outfit she owns. She's doing my head in.'

He laughs and turns up the television. The football is on. As he watches the teams walk out onto the pitch, he wishes once again he'd made it as a footballer. There'd be no stopping him if he had that sort of money.

His sister's chewing again, her jaw moving silently.

'How come you've got a magazine? You nick it?' he asks.

She puts down the magazine and gives him a patronising look. 'I got it from a friend who'd finished with it. No point you looking at it cos you can't read anyway.'

He scowls. 'Shut your face.'

'Gosh, I'm so scared,' she replies in a bored tone.

He throws a cushion at her and she dodges it, laughing at him. 'Here, there's an article in it about this gorgeous guy who became an escort and earned loads of money taking old, rich women out. Why don't you have a go at that?'

'Why don't you shut up?'

'Nah. Forget that idea. No one would want to go out with you. You don't know anything unless it's about football. You don't even have a girlfriend cos all you talk about is footie. Blah-blah-blah football.'

He ignores her. He knows lots of things. He just happens to like football a lot.

Eventually she gives up taunting him. He sits back in the chair and watches the teams battle it out on the field. His mind is only half-focused on the match. His sister has given him an idea. He can make money if he doesn't concentrate on the usual, conventional channels. It's a case of thinking outside the box.

※

He scrubs up well. The suit makes him appear older – about eighteen or nineteen. The old biddy in the charity shop let him have it for five quid. Not bad. It must have cost its original owner a packet. Mum gave him some money towards it. He told her he needed a suit for a job interview and that he wasn't getting any work cos he didn't look smart enough.

His sister cut his hair. She'd done a decent job too. 'You look like Jason Orange from Take That,' she said, returning her scissors to her bag. 'You should make effort more often. You actually look okay.'

'Take That? You listen to some right crap.' He'd thumped her cheerfully on the arm and, whistling, had washed his hair and styled it with some of her hair gel.

He looks at his reflection one last time. He does look a bit like Jason. Pity he doesn't have Jason's singing voice. He tries out a few notes but there's no doubt he can't sing. Still, he has brains. He doesn't need a recording contract with a band.

፨

The bookmakers is busy, filled with men watching sleek horses thunder across large television screens, betting slips in hands, the air filled with hope. He stands against a counter, head over a betting slip but actually observing the comings and goings. He's going to get rich on the Premier League. Winning isn't down to luck. It's about odds and probability. All he has to do is work out if the odds are in his favour and that's down to maths – his favourite subject.

The football season will start in a couple of weeks with Manchester United playing Aston Villa, and he's going to use every hour he has until then to ensure he bets wisely on the matches. He might not be able to play football but he can still strike it rich from the game.

CHAPTER FORTY-THREE

Ross had been true to his word. The gate lock had been replaced and two spy surveillance units were set up – one outside, in the guise of a house alarm box, and another hidden behind a photo frame in Robyn's sitting room, facing the settee and the window behind it. She could access both from an app on her phone and had found she could even catch the odd glimpse of her cat as he sat on the window ledge. She'd set her house alarm and was feeling less jittery after the events of the day before when she'd spotted the intruder.

Robyn and Matt were going to start the day with a visit to Brocton in the hope they could unearth information at Anthony Hawkins' house, which might give them a clue as to who he was meeting on the golf course. Robyn stopped off first at Lauren Gregson's house and was delighted to find Astra there.

'Ella and Liam thought it would be a good idea if she came over. She's been awfully miserable. We thought it might help her, and me. I haven't seen her since…' she swallowed. 'Since before we lost Henry. Gives Ella a break and helps to take my mind off everything else.'

Astra was eating an apple, a piece in her small fist making its way to her mouth. She put it down immediately when she spotted Robyn, reached for the toy black cat next to her and lifted it towards her. 'Look,' she said.

'You've brought your new cat with you,' said Robyn.

The girl's face was still ghostly pale but she seemed a little more content. She nodded.

'How do you know it's new?' Lauren asked in surprise.

'I gave it to her. I recently inherited a black cat and it's wormed its way into my affections pretty quickly. I spotted that one in a shop and thought Astra might like it. She was so upset about Henry.'

The corners of Lauren's mouth lifted. 'What a lovely gesture. She's a little poppet, isn't she? Henry and I would have loved a little girl like her.'

Robyn reflected on the child she might have had, had she not miscarried, her thoughts interrupted by Astra.

'Henry is gone,' she said, solemnly.

'That's right,' said Robyn, crossing the room and dropping down beside her. 'But you have Lauren and she needs lots of cuddles from you. She misses Henry too. Can you look after Lauren?'

Astra gave her a sincere stare and nodded, then toddled across to Lauren, threw her arms around the tops of her legs, and hugged her tightly.

Lauren gave a soft laugh. 'Thank you, poppet. Tell DI Carter what we're going to do later.'

'Watch a film,' said Astra.

'What are we going to watch?' Lauren stroked the girl's head tenderly.

'*Aristocats.*'

'That's right, a Disney film all about cats, and this one is going to watch it with us. Why don't you finish your apple and I'll talk to DI Carter, then we'll play dressing up?'

Astra obediently returned to the table, where she pretended to feed a slice of apple to the cat.

Lauren sighed. 'I hope I can find another house nearby. I wouldn't want to lose contact with Astra.'

'You're moving?'

'I have to. I can't afford the rent here on my own. The landlord's been amazing and says I can stay a while, paying only half the rent, until I find another place. My colleagues at the estate agency have been on the lookout for a new place for me. Everyone's being very kind. I asked Ella if there was any chance one of those barn conversions she rents is coming free soon, but she says not. My parents want me to move back home. I really don't want to do that. It'll be horrible without Henry, but at least here I have my independence, some friends, my job and Astra.'

'Henry had no savings or life insurance?'

Lauren smiled weakly. 'Not something we thought about. You don't at our age, do you? We had a little saved up for a rainy day, but that day's come. The funeral expenses will eat it away.'

Robyn and her team had already examined the Gregsons' finances and discovered nothing untoward. There was no hidden money in an offshore fund or bond.

Robyn made small talk for a while longer before leaving to catch up with Matt. Her last image was of an excited Astra pulling out clothes from a dressing-up box Lauren had specially made for her. The possibility that Lauren had anything to do with Henry's death was becoming less and less likely. There was nothing to gain financially from his death, and there didn't appear to be another man in Lauren's life. What would induce Lauren to have her husband killed? The only motive Robyn could come up with was jealousy. If the DNA test results proved Henry to be the father of Tessa's baby, she'd have to consider Lauren as a suspect. She hoped it wouldn't come to that – at least for Astra's sake.

米

Robyn walked up the lane to Anthony Hawkins' house, which appeared even more dismal than she recalled. The gate squealed in protest when she pushed it open, and inside the cottage there was already a damp smell, usually associated with old, uninhabited houses. She wrinkled her nose at it and called out. Matt was in the kitchen going through drawers. She joined him.

'No diary or calendar?'

'Nothing. There wasn't anything on his phone either,' said Matt. 'No appointments or diary app. It's a right antiquated piece – no Internet even – only good for calls and text messages.'

Robyn left him and entered the sitting room. It was a sad affair: a shabby chair, a single bed-settee covered with a woollen blanket to mask the stains on it, dark shelving filled with dusty books with faded spines. The flat-screen television was at odds with the room, and perched on one of the shelves was a shiny Bose sound system. Anthony had been amassing new purchases. It would only have been a matter of time before he'd have left this place and found somewhere more suited to his new lifestyle. A table next to the window was cluttered with receipts and paperwork. She shuffled through it all and finally found what she hoped for – a notepad. Although Anthony had noted Saturday's date and the time, there was no mention of the person he was meeting.

'Got it,' she called.

Matt appeared almost instantly.

She held up the notepad. 'No name.'

'Oh crap. This is hopeless.'

Robyn flicked through the pages of the notepad. There were other scribbles in it, messages and dates that made little sense to her. 'At least we know he definitely made arrangements to meet somebody at the golf course, and that person is likely to be his killer. We'll take the notepad. He's written other bits of information on it, which might lead to something. He didn't have a computer, did he?'

'No devices at all. I don't think he was into technology. There's no modem in the house.'

'Okay, we'll call it a day here.'

As they pulled away from his road, Robyn thought again about the likelihood of all the murders being connected. If they were, she still had to establish why. The other thought that bugged her was that Shearer's hunch had been right. It was looking more likely that Anthony Hawkins had been murdered, and Shearer would be even more insufferable once he found out.

CHAPTER FORTY-FOUR

THEN

The bloke on the doorstep looks nothing like his father. This guy is smaller, weaker, a sad apology of a man with eyebrows like grey caterpillars and worn-out, yellow teeth like an aged wolf's.

'Hi, son.'

He sneers. 'Bit late in the day to call me that. I haven't seen you in six years. You've hardly been a father, have you? What do you want? Mum's out.'

'I know she is. I wanted to see you. See how you were doing.' His father studies his brown shoes with frayed laces.

'I'm fine so thank you for your concern and goodbye.' He pushes the door but his father shoves his large foot in the way, preventing it from shutting.

'Please hear me out,' he pleads.

'I don't really want to hear you at all.'

His father shifts slightly. 'I know. I can't expect you to forgive me. I wanted to make it up to you though.'

He snorts. 'And how do you intend doing that?'

'I met someone who might be able to assist with your project,' he says.

'What project?' he asks, eyebrows high in mock amusement.

'I still have friends with influence. One of them told me you've been hanging about the betting shops in town and asking blokes to place bets on football teams for you, then sharing the profit when you win.'

He crosses his arms. 'So what if I have? It's hardly a project, is it?'

'Let me come in and I'll explain. I picked up a lot while I was banged up in jail. I have skills now and I can help you become wealthy. But if you're not interested in what I have to say, I understand.'

He studies the man who had once beaten him on a regular basis. Could he trust somebody so volatile? At the same time, his brain whirs with possibilities. Maybe the old man had learnt how to cheat the system while he was in jail, and would it hurt to hear him out? His father stands patiently.

In the end, curiosity wins out. 'Come in, but only for a few minutes. If I don't like what you tell me, I'll throw you out myself.'

'Sure. I understand. You look like you can stand on your own two feet fine,' says his father as he crosses the threshold into the house. He hesitates for a second. 'Doesn't look like I remember it,' he says eventually.

'Nothing's like it was. You've got two minutes to explain what you mean.'

His father nods. 'Sure. I heard you've been placing bets on the football games.'

'And?'

'And it's a mug's game. You'll lose more than you'll make, and even if you win big on a match, you'll lose it all again. I met loads of blokes when I was banged up who wasted money on betting. We all did it inside. It was a way to pass the time. We'd bet on almost anything: football matches, horses, snooker games – you name it, we'd bet on it.'

'If that's all you have to tell me, you can bugger off.'

His father looks at his feet again. 'No, that's not it. I want to help. I did a lot of thinking while I was inside. You get too much time alone. You get too much time to realise how you've affected others and how you've ruined their lives. I did wrong. I was quick-tempered, always hit first and thought afterwards. It was the drink. I know that's not a good excuse but the drink changed me. I wasn't a bad man. I was a man who couldn't control his drinking. It became an addiction. Your mum tried to tell me I had a drinking problem but I didn't listen. I don't think alcoholics want to hear the truth. We hide it away. We can only focus on the next drink.' He licked his lips again, shifted again uncomfortably. 'I'm over that. I don't drink any more. I really am a different man. I found God in jail and I'll never be the man you knew again.'

He resists the urge to snigger. His father's too sincere about this to laugh at him, however ridiculous this sounds. His father finding religion! He wants to interrupt and tell him to leave, but his dad keeps talking, trying to explain.

'This is my way of making amends. I know a bloke, Sid, who runs the betting shop near the railway station in Stoke. He's a good man. I met him at our local church. He and I got chatting. He knows all about me, and about your mum, sister and you. I told him how I ended up in prison. I explained how I'd screwed up my life. I don't suppose you'd understand but I'm not proud of myself. I let you all down. Anyhow, I've been keeping my ear to the ground, asking about you and trying to find out how you're all doing.'

'We're doing fine. You don't need to check up on us.'

'I wasn't checking up. I wanted to know how you all were. I missed you.' He sighs, shakes his head and continues, 'Sid's in his early sixties now. He's willing to take you on at his betting shop. You won't be able to handle the bets yet cos of your age, but he'll pay you for work out the back, show you the ropes and you'll learn a career – a proper job. If you're any good, you'll be able to take over when he retires in a few years' time. The real money is behind the counter, not in front of it. I told him about you and how you'd done well at maths at school. I also heard you'd been placing bets, getting others to make them and splitting the winnings. You've made a few good calls. I told Sid about that too, and he'd like to meet you.' He gives his son a weak smile. 'I don't expect you to forgive me but maybe this will go towards helping

us become friends. I'm a changed man. Not drunk a drop since I went inside. I'm not the man you remember. This is the new me.'

Something about his father's demeanour embarrasses him. The man seems weaker, less confident and more subservient. He wants to please. It's written all over his craggy face. It would be so easy to plant a kick into the old man's abdomen and get payback for all the hurt he caused in the past, but he's too defenceless. Something about him suggests he'd allow his son to bash him up. He'd roll over and accept it. It's pathetic.

He watches Paul Scholes slam the ball into the back of the net on the TV and considers his father's words. Working at a betting shop appeals to him. He'd enjoy that. He looks at his father, so eager to make amends. It'll never happen but he will take him up on the job offer. What's he got to lose?

CHAPTER FORTY-FIVE

It was almost two thirty when Robyn and Matt got back, and she heaved a sigh of relief that Shearer and his team weren't in the office.

'Finally got hold of Andy Ford,' said David. 'He confirmed Roger Jenkinson was with him in Leeds on Thursday morning. Only one discrepancy – he didn't arrive at eight thirty. It was just after nine.'

'Which gives Roger Jenkinson just sufficient time to murder Tessa and travel to Leeds.'

'It'd be tight.'

'But possible. Best keep an open mind about this man. I'm not ruling him out yet.'

Anna had spoken to the receptionist at Brocton Golf Club, who confirmed there was no record of the golf course being booked on Saturday morning, the day Anthony Hawkins had died, but remembered taking a call from someone asking if it was available. The line had been so bad she couldn't tell if it was a male or female voice and they were cut off before she could make a booking. They didn't ring back.'

'Could you trace the call?' Robyn asked.

Anna shook her head. 'It was from a withheld number.'

'So, we believe this mysterious person rang up to ensure nobody was playing on the golf course on Saturday morning, enticed

Anthony there with the intention of murdering him, and might have scared him to death. It sounds a little far-fetched but it's all we have at the moment, and given Anthony Hawkins had come into a vast amount of money – a similar amount to Tessa Hall – we have reasonable grounds to treat his death as suspicious.'

The call from the front desk interrupted the meeting. Mitz took it, his eyebrows rising at the news.

'Guv, one of Tessa Hall's friends, Juliet Fallows, is in reception and insists on speaking to you – alone.'

Robyn put aside her pen and marched towards the door, a fresh spring in her step. Maybe Juliet was about to throw even more light onto this case. 'Keep at it, folks. We're making progress.'

⁂

Juliet was standing by the window, arms wrapped around her body even though it was warm inside the room. She spun around and spoke as soon as Robyn entered.

'Steph told me she'd spoken to you about Gerry, my ex-husband – well, soon-to-be ex-husband. She's got a right bee in her bonnet about it and wants to press charges. I can't dissuade her. Please, can you? Can you tell her how much pain it will put her through to go ahead with it, and how we'll have to face up to Gerry in court? Explain how dreadful it will all be – dissuade her. Please.'

Robyn beckoned Juliet over to the table. 'Come and sit down, Juliet.'

Juliet's head shook rapidly. 'Please, just talk to her. She likes you. She'll listen to you. I can't let her go through with it.'

'Steph said her father hit her too. It's a serious allegation, and if Gerry was abusing you both, it ought to be reported. You shouldn't hide from it. He may well go on to attack others in his life.'

Juliet hung her head. 'It was only the once,' she said. 'Gerry hit her the once. That was the day I found the strength to leave him. I'd been planning to run away with the kids for ages. Somehow, I could never get the courage up. I was too weak and part of me believed I deserved the treatment he gave me. He'd be so apologetic after each time – so sincere – I actually believed he'd change. Or he'd try and reason why he'd hurt me and that I'd deserved it. He only ever went for me. It wasn't even frequently, only now and again, and when nothing would happen for a few months, I'd begin to think we'd come through it. Then, for no reason, he'd fly off the handle.

'He'd never hit either of the children before. I don't even think they knew about what was happening. Until they got older, they didn't understand it was Gerry who'd broken my wrist, or blackened my eye.

'That night was different. I caught him swinging for Steph. I went for him and he turned on me instead. I can still see Steph's expression as she watched her own father punch and kick me. She tried to make him stop. I yelled for her to get out of the room. If I'd lost consciousness, I had no idea what he'd do to her. She ran off. When he'd finished, he stormed off to the pub. I told the kids to collect what they needed, cleaned myself up, packed a bag, called a taxi and we went to a hostel. I got support there. I pulled myself together and we moved away to stay with a cousin for a while before coming here, to the countryside, far away from Gerry.

'We've moved on and I'd like to keep it that way. I don't want to see Gerry ever again.' Her eyes shone damply. 'You understand, don't you?'

Robyn covered Juliet's hand with her own. 'I understand. I can send an officer specially trained in this field to talk to her. That would be better than me saying anything. This isn't my area of expertise, and I want you both to have the best advice possible.'

Juliet spoke sharply. 'No. No. That's not what I want. You have to stop Steph going ahead with this. I never want to see him again.'

Robyn attempted to see it from Juliet's point of view but she was mystified. 'You won't have to face him or talk to him, if that's what's bothering you.'

'You don't get it. I don't want this to happen. I have a plan and we'll be rid of him forever. I just need to wait for my decree absolute to come through and then it'll be over.'

'Being officially divorced won't change what he did to you, or how Steph feels. Gerry will still have rights and access to his children. You'll have to let him see them. You can't get rid of him. What if Terence decides he wants to see his father?'

Juliet let out a soft groan. 'No. This isn't going the way I planned it. We're going to get away for good and start a life abroad, somewhere where he can't ever find us. I want them to forget about him altogether. I had it all worked out. This will mess it all up. Steph can't start proceedings against him.'

Robyn wasn't sure what she meant. She had a home, a job, and she'd already started a new life in Hamstall Ridware. Why would she want to go abroad? Then it struck her. There'd only be one way Juliet could take her children away, and why she wanted Gerry out of her life before he found out about it. Like Tessa and Anthony, Juliet also had money hidden away.

Robyn watched the frantic woman pace the room before speaking calmly. 'Juliet, tell me about the money.'

CHAPTER FORTY-SIX

DAY EIGHT – TUESDAY, 21 FEBRUARY, AFTERNOON

Robyn asked Anna to join her and Juliet in the interview room. She arrived with a smile and a cup of tea for Juliet.

'Tell me about the money, Juliet,' Robyn asked again, once Juliet had taken a sip of tea.

Juliet's face remained impassive, and then with a sudden movement her shoulders slumped forwards and her head lowered.

Her voice was little more than a whisper when she next spoke. 'I should have guessed it would come out in the end, especially with Tessa being murdered and then Anthony dying.' She rested the tips of her fingers against her forehead. The silence seemed to stretch for a long time with only the incessant tick, tick, tick of the clock on the wall filling the void.

'What do you mean, Juliet?' asked Robyn, her voice even and low.

'We were members of a lottery syndicate,' Juliet said with a slow sigh, 'and our numbers came up in December.'

'Was it a big win?'

'Huge. It was a rollover week. Over six million jackpot.'

'Gosh, that's quite a win,' said Anna. 'You must have been ecstatic.'

Juliet appeared not to hear her. With her head hung low, she refused to meet their eyes.

'It's not that simple. When you suddenly come into such a life-changing amount, it comes with complications, and none of us were prepared for those. We didn't know how to handle them, or how to spend the money. We'd won it but we couldn't spend or enjoy it.'

'What do you mean?'

'For me it was Gerry, my ex. If he'd got wind I had a fortune, he'd have pushed for half of it. I didn't want Gerry to have a bean, not after how he treated me. I told the others how I felt – I wanted to keep it secret until I was well shot of that man. I applied for a decree nisi. I'm waiting for the decree absolute, and then we're leaving for good – Spain – I want to go to Costa del Sol. The kids will love it there. Steph will easily find a job somewhere and Terence will finish school soon anyway. There'll be enough money for us to live on.

'It turned out a few of us had valid reasons for keeping it under wraps for a while. Roger was having relationship problems with Naomi, and didn't want her to find out. Anthony's brother was going to stay with him over Christmas and Anthony wanted to wait until he'd left before he started spending his money. And Liam didn't want the lottery people to find out he was part of the syndicate because the ticket had come from his shop. He wanted to wait for the dust to settle. Tessa was the only one who was happy to spend her share but we dissuaded her. We made a collective decision to keep shtum about it. Gossip gets out so quickly when you live in rural communities, so we made a pact that all of us would keep quiet until the dust had settled.'

'Were all the lottery tickets bought at MiniMarkt?'

Juliet fidgeted uncomfortably and avoided Robyn's gaze. 'No, it depended on who bought them. Ella volunteered to buy them and she got them at MiniMarkt.'

'Why Ella? She wasn't part of the syndicate.'

She shrugged. 'She asked if she could. It was no biggie. It didn't matter who bought the tickets as long as we had them.'

'And you weren't worried she'd steal the money?'

'No. Why would she? If we won anything on the lottery, Liam would get a share. She had no reason not to buy them.'

'It seems a strange arrangement. How did it come about?' Robyn asked.

'It all started when we won our first quiz together. We won forty pounds. Anthony suggested instead of dividing it among us, we should buy lucky dip lottery tickets with it and have a chance of winning proper money. It seemed a good idea. We were all struggling for money one way or another, so why not? After that, we either put in money ourselves or used any quiz winnings to buy tickets. We won sixty pounds at the beginning of December and decided to blow the lot on lottery tickets. One of those won.'

'So, what happened to your share of the lottery jackpot? Is it in your bank account?'

Juliet shook her head. 'First, Ella phoned the lottery commission, claimed the ticket and arranged anonymity for us, and then Anthony set up everything through a financial advisor – somebody he'd known for years. The lottery committee placed the money into a collective account, and from there it was distributed into individual offshore accounts, one for each of us, except for Anthony, who had his share transferred into a bond. He didn't trust banks one bit. We met the advisor – Dario – at Anthony's house. He was really nice and very professional. He explained how we could "hide" the money until we were ready to use it, and where it would attract the best interest but not attract attention from the tax office. He'd done the same for many wealthy clients. It seemed the sensible solution and allowed us to keep our winnings under the radar until we wished to spend them.'

'Do you have Dario's full details?'

'I've got his card.' She rooted through her handbag, pulled out her purse and extracted a business card. 'The kids don't know. I didn't want them to find out until I'd officially divorced Gerry. It won't hurt them to learn the value of money before they suddenly discover they've got mountains of it to spend on whatever they want. Steph's recently got a part-time job at one of the cafés in town, and Terence, he helps out at the Heart Foundation shop on a Saturday.' She gave a proud smile. 'They've come a long way in the short time since we left Gerry.'

'Was anyone else part of the syndicate or just the quiz players?'

'Only the five of us: me, Tessa, Anthony, Liam and Roger.'

'And no one knew about the big win?'

'Nobody. I didn't tell anyone and I can't imagine the others would have either.'

'Did you discuss the win in a pub where someone might have overheard you?'

'No. Definitely not.'

Robyn took the business card from the table and stood. Could the lottery money be the reason for Tessa's and Anthony's deaths?

'If you don't mind, I'm going to leave you here for a moment with PC Shamash. I'll be back in a moment,' she said.

She headed back to the office and spoke quickly to Matt, David and Mitz.

'Tessa Hall and Anthony Hawkins were both members of a lottery syndicate that won several million. What do you think to the idea that somebody might have found out about the win and be targeting the winners? Killing them off, one by one?'

'You mean some nutcase who has it in for people who are lucky?' David asked. Robyn considered his words. It was feasible.

Mitz thought carefully before speaking. 'I can't see it myself. It's not like the killer can get their hands on Tessa's or Anthony's money, is it? What would they have to gain?'

Robyn gritted her teeth and made an exasperated noise. 'It's a crazy idea, isn't it? It's not reason enough for murder.'

'Anything's possible.' Matt offered open palms and a shrug of concession. 'We've come across stranger situations.'

Mitz spoke again. 'If it were the case, we'd need to offer the others in the syndicate some sort of protection.'

'I can't see DCI Flint agreeing to that. You know how short-staffed we are,' said Matt.

Robyn screwed up her face. 'I know. He wouldn't be keen, would he? Especially as I don't have a strong enough argument to persuade him.'

'Sorry, guv, I don't think he'll swallow this particular theory. Want us to have a word with the other syndicate members, see if we can find out more? Maybe somebody had a grudge against Anthony and Tessa, and the lottery win tipped them over the edge,' said Matt.

Robyn thought that was better reasoning than she'd offered.

David swivelled round in his seat and offered his thoughts. 'But then, that would depend on the person knowing about the win. Who knew about it apart from the syndicate involved?'

'Naomi Povey, Roger's girlfriend, might have known, although Juliet thinks Roger wanted to keep it from her. Ella Fox, Liam's partner, certainly knew about it because she phoned the lottery commission to claim the winning ticket. That leaves any other loved ones the syndicate members confided in, anybody they might have blurted it to, and a financial advisor. Here are his details. We'll need to interview him.' She passed Mitz the card.

He studied it and started tapping his keyboard, searching for information.

Matt picked up the conversation thread. 'There are a few potential suspects. If we're right, it'd have to be somebody who knew all the people involved and also about the win.'

'Juliet said they were all keeping quiet about it for the time being.' Robyn ran back through what Juliet had told her.

'A lottery win doesn't seem a powerful enough reason to kill somebody, or indeed two people. There must be more to it,' said Matt, his forehead creased in thought.

'You're right. There are too many people keeping secrets in this case. I'm going to see if I can squeeze anything further out of Juliet.'

'I'll get hold of this chap – Dario Pelligrini.'

Robyn marched back towards the interview room. The team had pointed out the flaws in her argument. It made little sense for anyone to kill off the lottery syndicate members. She entered the room again with a sense of determination. Juliet was looking more composed.

'Sorry to have left you. Are you feeling up to answering a few more questions?'

'I suppose so.' Juliet shifted in her seat. Anna gave her an encouraging smile.

'I'm somewhat concerned that two people involved in this lottery syndicate have died. It's imperative you tell me anything you can think of that might help us track down the person responsible. It's very important, Juliet. I have to stop this person in case they strike again.' Robyn didn't want to unnecessarily scare Juliet but she needed more information. She had to have good reason to go to DCI Flint and request protection for Juliet, Liam and Roger. 'Can you think of anybody outside of the syndicate who might have known about the win?'

Juliet repeatedly shook her head. 'No. I can't. I don't want to talk to you any more. I want to go now. I only came to ask you if you'd speak to Steph for me.'

Robyn dropped her voice. 'Of course. I didn't want to alarm you. I wouldn't be doing my job if I didn't ask you all these questions.'

Juliet wouldn't look at her. She pushed back her chair and marched towards the door. She hesitated there and Robyn thought she might say something; instead, she took a deep breath, opened it and walked out without looking back.

'She didn't say a word while you were out,' said Anna. 'Not a word.'

'I'm pissed off with all these people keeping silent. Somebody knows something. We'll get there. I'm not giving up yet.' Robyn stared at the shut door, convinced Juliet had been about to talk again and enlighten them further. She sighed in annoyance, trying to decide if Juliet's life might be in danger. If she didn't share her thoughts with DCI Flint and something happened to Juliet, or the others, it would be her fault. She squared her shoulders, turned around and headed for Flint's office. She wasn't going to take any chances.

⁂

'Sir, I really think—'

'I'll discuss it with you tomorrow.'

With that, DCI Flint rang off. Robyn clenched and unclenched her fists several times until she felt calmer. DCI Flint had been out of the office, and the brief conversation with him over the phone had resulted in him refusing to do anything until he'd thought about the matter.

Once she'd put down the phone, David called across. 'We've got a match on the DNA we sent to Harry McKenzie's lab. Turns out Roger Jenkinson is the father of Tessa's baby.'

'What about the fingerprints?'

'Just got off the phone with the lab. The prints lifted from the Valentine's card and others found in the house are also Roger Jenkinson's.'

Robyn sighed. Roger Jenkinson, a man with a temper, who'd owned guns in the past and had rowed in the pub with Anthony over Tessa Hall. Had he killed Anthony because of his relationship with Tessa? Was he also responsible for Tessa's murder in some way?

Was Robyn looking at a crime of passion, or was it related to the jackpot win? Or was there something else she had yet to uncover? At least it ruled out the possibility of Lauren killing her husband because he'd fathered a child with another woman. It was too late to do any more today. She was fatigued, drained and fed up. In the morning, she and Matt would talk to Dario Pelligrini. He knew about the win – and that made him a suspect.

※

Robyn returned home to find Schrödinger eagerly waiting by the front door. She had hardly opened it before he wrapped himself around her ankles, weaving a figure of eight, all the while purring like a small car engine.

'Well, hello you,' she said, turning off the newly installed alarm. She scooped him up and he nuzzled against her face, his whiskers tickling her cheeks.

It wasn't fair to keep him inside the house for such long periods of time without anybody here with him. He'd have got used to having Tessa around and now he was alone for hours on end. For now, however, he seemed content to sit on her lap as she stroked him and thought about the investigation, and she was very grateful for his company.

CHAPTER FORTY-SEVEN

THEN

It's the first time Sid's left him in charge of the betting shop and he feels bloody marvellous. He whistles as he clears the desk, ready for another day of takings. Sid's had to go to the doctor's. He hopes the old boy's okay. He's been looking a bit drained recently.

Sid's been like a proper father to him. He looks up to the betting shop owner, who played football for Birmingham City in the fifties and who regales him with tales about his time on the squad. Sid didn't scoff at him when he divulged he too had wanted to play football and still wished he had made it.

He points the remote control at the large television screen against the far wall and turns it on. It's Ascot week and there'll be plenty of bets placed today. He spots a regular punter on the opposite side of the street. He'll be in later. He comes in every day. He's one of those addicted to their visits to the shop. Sid treats them all with respect whether they're winners or losers. That's the thing about Sid. He has time for everyone, including a messed-up kid who had ambition and just needed a lucky break. He owes Sid big time. He runs his thumb over the shop door keys, presented to him a week before.

'You should get the key to the door when you're twenty-one, but I'm happy to give you the key to my shop now,' said Sid, slapping him on the back and then shaking his hand. 'Congratulations, lad.'

He'd never felt such happiness. After eighteen months of training, watching how the business operated, swotting up on every possible sport, and sitting with Sid most evenings soaking up every ounce of the man's knowledge, he was now officially the betting shop manager and had the door keys to prove it. There's one condition – he's not yet to accept bets. He's not old enough to legally do so. He has to direct punters to another assistant if they wish to place a bet. That's fine by him – he's still the manager.

He flicks through the channels and leaves it set up on Channel 4. Sheila, one of the three assistants, arrives quietly through the back door and appears at his elbow.

'Morning, boss,' she says cheerfully, making him grin widely.

She bustles about, getting everything ready for the first customers of the day. Now she's here, he'll leave her to it and go out back to work on the figures for yesterday. He stops to pick up a paper and takes a quick look at the horses running in the afternoon races, and becomes lost in thought. He doesn't hear the door buzzer and he only looks up when he hears a cough. The girl on the other side of the counter smiles at him and for a second he's transfixed by her shimmering, pink, glossed lips. He feels himself redden.

'Yes. Can I help you?'

The girl pushes a slip towards him. 'Can you put that on for me?' she asks.

She's about twenty, dressed in a pale purple bandana and loose-fitting drawstring trousers bearing an ethnic print. Her ebony hair is gathered back from her face in a headband. He takes in the glittering, silver-grey eyes, and before he realises it, he's spoken.

'I have to work on some figures so I'll get Sheila to take your bet. I don't suppose you'd like to go for a drink afterwards to celebrate your win?'

She laughs. 'How do you know this horse will win?'

He waves the slip at her with a knowing smile. She's chosen well. She's gone for the King George VI race and picked Swain, ridden by

Frankie Dettori. It stands a really good chance and won the year before. 'I'd have made this choice. Swain is going to win,' he says confidently.

Her cheeks lift and she observes him, lips tugging into another smile. 'Okay. If I win, we'll go out.'

✳

His sister blinks at him and wafts air over her freshly painted toenails.

'It's a miracle she's still with you,' she says. 'You must bore her rigid. "Football, blah-blah, racing, odds, blah-blah, percentages, commission, blah-blah, profits,"' she continues in a monotone voice before giggling. 'Poor Kayley must have had six weeks of torture hanging out with Mr Mega Boring!'

'Shut up,' he says amiably. 'Some of us have to hold down a proper job and happen to be interested in it. At least some of us can hold down a job.'

She sticks out her tongue at him. 'Not my fault I got sacked in the first week.'

'Course it wasn't. It's perfectly okay to tell some stuck-up bitch she's a scabby cow, even if she's your supervisor.'

Her mouth turns down. 'Well, she is a cow.'

'I agree,' he says, grinning. 'Might have been an idea not to have drawn a picture of a cow covered in spots, with her name under it, and then posted it on the office noticeboard though.'

'She asked for it,' she continues, tightening the top on the nail varnish bottle and easing back on the settee. 'Didn't she, Johnny? Anyway, I'm going back to Spain with Johnny when he leaves. I'm going to work in bar and get loads and loads of tips from customers, just for being beautiful.'

Johnny Hounslow has changed beyond recognition. He's about six foot three, broad-shouldered, with muscular arms and well-defined pectorals. His dirty-blond hair is cut short and spiked, and he wears a permanent look of menace. The boy isn't keen on his sister going out with Johnny, but she seems happy with the arrangement.

It's been almost a month since Johnny turned up at the bookmakers. He'd not recognised Johnny but Johnny had recognised him.

'Bloody hell! What are you doing here?' he'd said. 'I thought you'd be a gang leader, a notorious drug dealer or have ended up in the slammer like your old man. You were a right tough nut at school. Look at you now – a pen behind your ear like some accountant and dressed in a shirt and tie!'

Johnny, suntanned, in jeans and a T-shirt that stretched across his wide chest, now looked like he could handle himself in any dodgy situation. He no longer needed a minder.

They ran into each other again at the pub later that day. He couldn't avoid Johnny, sitting beside the bar, slugging whisky. Johnny called him over.

'Come and join me. I'm celebrating. Just back from Marbella. Been working there for over a year and made a bloody fortune on my last job.'

'You been working in Spain?'

'I'm a builder now. Piece of piss it is too. You just need some muscles. There's loads of work over in Spain. Hundreds and hundreds and hundreds of Brits who need work done on their villas and want new swimming pools or patios or new kitchens. And the birds love a bit of muscle too, if you know what I mean?' he said with an empty laugh.

He never knew quite what it was Johnny was supposed to be celebrating, but after downing almost a bottle of whisky, they'd tumbled out of the pub and back to his mum's house, where Johnny had crashed on the settee.

He looks across at Johnny now, slumped beside his sister, and wonders when he's going to return to Spain. He feels uncomfortable knowing what they're up to in his sister's room. He hears their noisy lovemaking through the paper-thin walls. He feels responsible when their mum is out, and she's been working extra shifts at the pub, so they've hardly seen her the last month. She's still his little sister and not even sixteen yet, and he hopes Johnny isn't using her. He's voiced his concerns to her but she doesn't get it, or she doesn't want to get it. She's crazy about the new, macho Johnny, and that saddens him. He ought to talk to Johnny and sort it out. Get him out of her life before she becomes even more serious about the jerk. He doesn't want her to go to Spain. He can't imagine life without her around.

He hears a car horn. Kayley's arrived. She insisted on driving so he can enjoy a few drinks. He smiles at such thoughtfulness. It's her birthday and yet he gets to drink.

'You'd better go. Don't want to be late for the all-important football match,' says his sister. 'Much nicer than taking her to a romantic restaurant for her birthday.'

He refuses to be put off by her snide remarks. He's managed to get his hands on a pair of the much sought-after tickets for the cup final match between Millwall and Wigan at Wembley. Kayley is remark-able and he can't believe his good fortune. She's the only woman he knows who can name all the top teams in the league and their playing grounds. Although they've only been seeing each other for a few weeks, he's thinking about asking her to move in with him, find a flat together, somewhere nearby so his sister can still come around to visit. He checks his pocket for the tickets.

'Go on. Before she drives off without you,' says his sister, chuckling. Johnny ignores him and begins to kiss his sister's neck. He wrinkles his nose up at her and leaves them to it.

CHAPTER FORTY-EIGHT

DAY NINE – WEDNESDAY, 22 FEBRUARY, MORNING

'We need one last push here, folks,' said Robyn. In spite of all her concerns, not the least of which was no news from Ross about Davies, she'd enjoyed the best night's sleep in ages, deep and dreamless, and woken to find Schrödinger curled on top of her stomach, like a small, furry hot water bottle.

She'd also found time for a twenty-minute run before arriving at the station and was feeling more upbeat about the investigation than she had recently. She'd blown Schrödinger a kiss as she left. He'd sat on the window ledge, orange eyes like welcoming beacons, observing her movements. It was comforting to know he'd be there later.

'The lottery draw was on the nineteenth of December and the jackpot of six million was deposited into a bank account set up by this man – Dario Pelligrini. He's now a person of interest. David?'

David was also clear-eyed and eager to speak. 'Got the info on Dario Pelligrini – one of the financial directors working at SFE, Staffordshire Financial Experts, based in Lichfield. He's been an independent financial advisor for the last twenty years. Lives in Brocton with wife, Ailsa, also a financial advisor at the same office.'

Robyn's eyes opened in surprise. 'Brocton – same village as Anthony Hawkins and Henry Gregson. And his wife works with him?'

Her mouth twitched involuntarily as a rush of adrenalin pumped round her veins at the news – they'd uncovered another connection between Henry Gregson and the quiz team. She thought back to Juliet Fallows' comment, that gossip spread in small villages, and considered the likelihood that either Pelligrini, or his wife, had let slip about the lottery win to Henry Gregson. 'Then we'll start with them. Matt, you and Anna go to Barton-under-Needwood and do a final check for witnesses who might have spotted anyone suspicious near Tessa Hall's place the day she died. I can't believe nobody saw anything. It's a busy village with over four thousand inhabitants and lots of movements. There must have been people passing through the place to get to the A38, even at that time of the morning. Take Roger Jenkinson's photograph with you and ask if he was spotted in the vicinity that day.'

Matt, head propped in one hand, suppressed a yawn. 'Sure. I could do with a walk and fresh air.'

'Bad night?'

'Every night's a bad night at the moment. Little'un's got a chest infection now.'

'Oh, poor little soul,' said Anna, half-expecting a cheeky retort.

Matt was rarely downhearted. Instead he threw her a sad look. 'Yeah. It's tough seeing her suffer like that, coughing and wheezing. Bit frightening really.'

Robyn couldn't help but feel for him. 'You want to get off for a couple of hours? Check on her?'

Matt refused. 'I'll be no use hanging about the place. Missus is taking her to the doctor later.'

'If you change your mind, let me know,' Robyn replied. 'Offer's there.'

He gave a grateful tilt of his head.

Robyn announced, 'I'd also intended talking to Liam Carrington once more. I'll leave that until we've visited SFE. Mitz, have a word with Anthony Hawkins' brother, William. Ask how well Anthony knew this Pelligrini chap – and determine once and for all if he could possibly have known Henry Gregson through cricket or football connections. Right. Focus. Let's nail this. Good luck.'

She didn't spot Tom Shearer, who'd entered the office.

He sidled over to her. 'Nice. Good rallying of troops.'

Her positive energy began to drain. 'You got much on?' she asked, deflecting him from asking too many questions.

'Yeah. Moving our stuff again. Flint's allowed us to set up in the briefing room for the next couple of days until our new office is ready.'

'You asked him outright?'

'I figured we'd outstayed our welcome here. Besides, it's crazy having two of us trying to run several investigations at the same time.' He smirked. 'So we'll take our kit and be off. Thanks for having us.' He waggled his fingers at her and meandered away.

❋

SFE were based on the top floor of a two-storey, purpose-built office block. The bottom floor had been given over to a small advertising business. A plaque attached to the front door invited clients to buzz and wait. Robyn pressed the button, announced who she was and waited for the door to swing open. She and David climbed the thick-carpeted staircase and were met by a woman, attired in a tight black silk skirt that shimmered as she moved, teamed with a pristine white blouse and gravity-defying, skyscraper-heeled shoes that flashed the trademark red soles of Louboutin. She ushered them into an open-plan office populated by a handful of sharp-suited people, staring at screens and murmuring quietly into hands-free sets.

'I'm Ailsa Pelligrini,' she said, holding out an elegant hand and flashing an enormous diamond cluster ring.

'DI Carter. You're expecting us.'

'Yes, my husband will be with us in a moment. He's just speaking with a client.' She directed them to the far end of the room, past the desks and computers revealing graphs and flashing dots and lists of names with which Robyn was not familiar.

The glass office was furnished simply with an oval, glass-topped table and six cream leather chairs. A water cooler stood at one end and next to it, a table of glassware.

'Can I offer you a drink of anything?'

Robyn declined. She and David sat down on the plump cushions and waited in silence. They didn't wait long. Within minutes, the door opened and a suntanned man with striking Mediterranean looks strode in.

'Dario Pelligrini,' he said, his clipped southern accent similar to his wife's. He drew out the seat at the head of the table and studied the officers.

'Thank you for agreeing to see us. It's in connection with Anthony Hawkins.'

'Ah. We suspected as much, didn't we, Ailsa? I won't beat about the bush. This is slightly awkward for us.'

'In what way?'

'Well, you've undoubtedly discovered we handled a substantial amount of money for Anthony and have come to question the legality of the situation.'

'Are you saying you didn't adhere to the financial code of practice?'

'Far from it. We did everything by the book. It was, however, an unusual set-up. I took it on because I've known Anthony for years. I'm sure other financial advisors would have asked more questions than we did, and spent longer on it. Anthony wanted accounts set up fairly quickly and we obliged.'

'Tell me what exactly happened.'

'Anthony dropped by the office last December. Said he and some friends had won a fortune on the lottery. They didn't want the lottery money to be paid into individual bank accounts. I went through a series of options and we settled on opening a holding account. From that, funds were to be distributed into individual offshore accounts. Now, I'm guessing that's why you're here, but I can assure you, we did nothing illegal. We merely exploited some loopholes in the British tax system, set up companies and sent monies to the new accounts. We are a reputable firm, and fully aware of our country's laws and tax rules. Anthony chose to invest his share in what we call a fixed-rate bond, allowing him to draw down a percentage of the fund, tax-free each year. It was an excellent rate of income that would have afforded him a good lifestyle for many years to come.'

'So, Mr Hawkins came to you for advice and then he and the other members of the lottery syndicate employed you?'

'In a nutshell. Both Ailsa and I worked on setting it all up. There was a significant amount of paperwork to prepare.'

'Did you know who else was involved in the win?'

'I met up with the other syndicate members soon after Anthony told me about the win. I explained the options to them, but after that initial meeting I didn't see them again. Everything we needed from them to set it up came via Anthony – signed paperwork, relevant details, passports, proof of ID, all the things we have to check to prevent fraud. He thought it'd be easier for everyone if he dealt with it.'

'You're undoubtedly aware he died on Saturday?'

'Yes. Very sad we were to learn about it, too. I've offered our condolences to his brother. They weren't the greatest of friends, but he's the only surviving relative, and because Anthony died intestate, he will inherit the fortune. Anthony had drafted a will and was going to leave the money to charity. I was an executor, that's how

I know of its contents. He hadn't yet made it official. Anthony will be turning in his grave now – all that money and no time to enjoy it, and worse still, his brother will get his hands on it.'

'Would you say you were close to Mr Hawkins?'

Dario's head tilted from side to side quickly. 'Not close exactly. We'd known each other a long time. Used to play cricket together, many moons ago. That was before I did my knee in. Can't play any more. I go along and support the youngsters these days.'

Robyn's pulse quickened slightly at the mention of the cricket club. 'Are you acquainted with a man known as Henry Gregson? He helped with the junior teams.'

Pelligrini gave a quick nod. 'I know him. Poor fellow got murdered. We visited Lauren two days ago. She was in such a state. Ailsa took her round some lasagne but I doubt she ate it.'

Robyn looked at Ailsa, her hands folded in front of her on the desk. 'You knew Lauren well?'

'We played tennis together last summer when she first moved to Brocton. She's a lovely lady. We went to Lichfield Garrick a couple of times too. I sometimes get free tickets for various plays and Dario isn't a fan of the theatre. Lauren was good company.'

'Did either of you talk to Henry or Lauren about this lottery win?'

Pelligrini shook his head. 'Absolutely not. Client confidentiality is everything in this profession. We wouldn't want to lose clients through loose tongues, would we, Ailsa?'

She gave a tight smile, her red lipstick standing out against the white of her porcelain complexion, and shook her head.

Robyn imagined he'd charged the team handsomely for all his work, and his accounts would reveal exactly how much. She struggled to believe Dario Pelligrini was behind the murders. Outside the offices, she'd spotted a Bentley convertible with a private number plate that clearly belonged to him, and judging by his attire – the pure wool, bespoke suit, polished leather shoes and Patek Philippe watch – he had no need to get his hands on the jackpot money. Nevertheless, she had to ask the question.

'May I ask how much you and your wife earn per annum?'

'That's a leading question.'

'But one I'd like answered. It'd be much easier than me demanding to see your books.'

'Fair enough. I have nothing to hide. We each take an annual salary in excess of a hundred thousand a year. We also own shares in the business, and annual pension contributions of approximately seventy thousand per annum are paid into each of our accounts. It's a lucrative occupation if you have sufficient numbers of the right sort of client. We make most of our money from annual commissions, and they mount up over the years. Last year, the business turned over four million. You can always talk to our accountant if you require further details.' His voice had retained its easy tone but his eyes had turned icy cold.

'And finally, I'd like to ask you about your movements, Mr Pelligrini. We have to establish where you were on Tuesday the fourteenth of February.'

'Rome. Stayed at the Rome Cavalieri. You can call the concierge there – Fabio. He'll attest to that. He knows us well. We always stay there when we're in Rome. And we ate at their three-star Michelin restaurant that night if that helps with your enquiries. We were there until Sunday. Thought we'd make it a romantic mini-break. Caught the afternoon flight back.' He glanced at his watch, and his eyebrows rose as if to signal the end of the conversation.

Robyn stomped back downstairs. Although she couldn't place either of the Pelligrinis at two of the crime scenes, she might have established a connection between Henry Gregson and the lottery win. Whereas Dario had been adamant he would never have spoken about the lottery winners to anyone, Ailsa had remained silent on the subject. It was possible she'd let it slip to Lauren.

'I'm in the wrong job,' mumbled David as they left the building. 'That's an obscene amount of money to earn.'

Robyn thought about Pelligrini's smug expression when he'd divulged how much money he had earned. He'd been very self-satisfied. 'You're in the right job, David. We both are. We're going back to the station via Brocton. I want a quick word with Lauren. I suspect Ailsa might have told her about the lottery win.'

As they pulled away, her phone lit up with a text message from her cousin Ross:

My investigations aren't turning up any answers yet. Hope you are having more luck than me.

She gave a half-smile. Ross hadn't mentioned Davies by name. Her cousin was a very cautious man and believed all messages could be hacked or read. She replied and then deleted the texts as he'd taught her. She was lucky to have Ross on her side.

CHAPTER FORTY-NINE

THEN

He can't believe what he's seeing. Sid is lying on the floor, his face scrunched up in pain. He's been taking pills for a heart condition for a while, and at first, he thinks Sid's had a heart attack, until he sees the gun. He looks from the gun to the man holding it, a man he knows all too well.

'Johnny, what the fuck are you doing?'

Johnny waves the gun at him. 'Shut up. Stay back. Sid here was about to speak, weren't you, Sid.'

He looks from Johnny to Sid and then to Kayley. Bile rises in his throat.

'Kayley?' he whispers, shaking his head to clear it.

Her face is impassive. The northern accent he found attractive has vanished. 'That's not my real name.' Her words make no sense. This is Kayley Frost. He's shared her life with her for almost two months. He knows all about her: her family back in Wigan, her childhood, her schooldays, her love for sports even back then, and her current job as a researcher for a local radio station. They've been looking at flats to rent together. What's going on? None of this makes any sense to him.

Johnny speaks up. 'Tell us, old man, or I'll put a bullet in you.'

Sid lifts a weary head. His face is the colour of putty. His thin hair is damp with perspiration and lifting his head seems to be too much effort for him. 'Go ahead. I've nothing to live for. My God will look after me.'

Johnny lets out a growl and kicks Sid, who grimaces but doesn't cry out.

He shouts, 'Leave him alone. He's sick. He doesn't deserve this. What do you want?'

'The combination to the safe, you dumb prick. If only you'd just been sensible and told Kayley what it was when she tried to prise it out of you, we could have avoided all this unpleasantness. She's been trying to get you to tell her for weeks.' Johnny's face is a mask of contempt.

Kayley cocks her head and a sarcastic smile plays across her mouth.

Suddenly it all falls into place. That was why she asked if he had any special birthdays or sequences of numbers he liked. She told him she always used her birth date and year for any numeric code. He'd thought it a little strange at the time but didn't deliberate. Now it makes sense. She'd been asking him all sorts of questions about being a bookie: how much the shop takes on average in a week, about the most popular and best fixtures to bet on, and what happens to all the money they take from punters. His heart weighs as heavy as a stone. He's been an utter idiot and told her everything, from which days the security van collects the winnings to how much today's takings were likely to be. The glut of spread betting on cricket fixtures recently had meant they'd been raking in money. And that explains why he couldn't find his keys to the shop the week before. It was Kayley who retrieved them from behind a cushion on the settee the following evening. She must have stolen them and made a copy, and that's how they've got into the betting shop's back room. It dawns on him with such ferocity it almost winds him.

Kayley has never been interested in him. He's a victim of a hustle and she's gradually been pumping him for information about the book-maker's so she and Johnny could rob it. What a bloody fool he's been.

She knew Sid was working alone at the shop this evening. He shouldn't be there. It had been a last-minute decision, made on the way to the pub, to drop into the betting shop and chat to Sid once he closed up. Sid always hung back half an hour after closing time to make sure it was all tidy for the next day. He was going to ask Sid for a loan for a deposit on a flat he'd seen – a surprise for Kayley. Johnny and Kayley hadn't been expecting him to appear, but had taken his sudden arrival in their stride.

He has no more time to consider what's happening. Johnny is staring at him. 'Combination or he gets it,' he growls, pointing the gun at Sid.

'Don't tell them, son,' says Sid. 'I'm too old to worry about death.'

Son? True. Sid's been more like a father to him than his own father, who's now buried in a local cemetery. He can't let anything happen to Sid. Sid's been good to him. Trusted him. Given him a chance to become someone and make an honest living. Without Sid, he might have chosen the wrong path and ended up heaven knows where. He won't let anything happen to his boss and mentor.

'Twelve, zero, ten, nineteen, eight, six.'

'That's more like it,' says Johnny with satisfaction. 'Kayley?'

He takes in the thin rubber gloves. She's been part of this all along. Kayley and Johnny. How long had they been planning this together? Her sudden appearance at the bookies, her bet on Swain, Johnny turning up soon after – it had been no coincidence. And what about his sister? Johnny has played them both for fools.

She doesn't open the safe. Instead, she shakes her head. 'Make him do it.'

Johnny ponders the idea and smirks. 'Yeah, why not? Go on! Open the safe, Bookie Boy, or you know what will happen.'

He glowers at Johnny, tempted to smack him in the face as he eases past him, but knowing any sudden movement will result in Sid's death. Kayley gives him a blank stare, devoid of any affection. Sid lets out another groan and he hastens to the safe, punches in the code and the door springs open with a click. Johnny pushes him to one side with the butt of the gun. For a millisecond he considers wrenching the weapon away from Johnny, but Kayley is watching him, with those cool, white-grey eyes that he'd once found bewitching. He wonders if they're contact lenses, fake like her hair colour and her.

Johnny grabs some of the notes neatly piled on shelves. He makes a honking noise. 'Looky here! We're rich, babe.'

A small smile tugs at her lips. 'It'll do to start with.'

Johnny puts an arm around her waist, yanks her towards him and kisses her full on the lips.

His veins fizz with anger. How could she do this? He's about to challenge them both when a small sound like air escaping from a tyre stops him. He races across to Sid, whose eyes have shut. It's too late to save him. Sid's had a massive heart attack. Johnny stops shoving notes into his sports bag and looks over.

'Oh crap. The old bugger's died. We'll have to get a move on, sugar. Don't want to be had up for murder.'

Kayley shrugs. 'We didn't kill him.'

He cries out. 'Of course you did! You frightened him to death.'

Then Kayley laughs – a sound that chills him. 'Course we didn't. We weren't here. There's nothing to prove we were here. There's been no break-in, and the CCTV camera in here was switched off – thanks for telling me how they worked.' She laughs again. 'There's nothing to prove we've been here but there's lots to prove you have. The police will take you in. You've got a bit of a reputation for being a bad boy anyway, haven't you? I'm sure they'll think you nicked the money from the safe and poor old Sid caught you in the act. Your fingerprints are everywhere. Ours aren't.'

Johnny checks the now empty safe. 'Right, babe. Let's go.' He hoists the bag on his shoulder. 'Be seeing you,' he says with a grin.

'Not if I see you first,' he growls.

Johnny halts and bears his teeth. 'You think you're so bloody clever, don't you? You and your sister. What a slag she is. She couldn't wait to be laid.'

A guttural sound begins in his throat and he launches towards Johnny, who points the gun at him. 'Go on. Want some of this, do you?' He waves the shooter at him and he backs down, nostrils opening and closing repeatedly.

'You want to know why I set you up? Because you thought you were cleverer than me. You thought you could take over my nice little drug business. It might have been a few years ago, but I haven't forgotten that you stabbed me in the back. You were supposed to be my mate, but you dumped me. And while I was taken into the nick and grilled by the copper, all the time keeping quiet about your involvement in it all, you and your sister were muscling in on my business. You made a laughing stock of me, you know? Wrecked my street cred with the main men. I had to start all over again. Try something new. Bit of hustling. Found myself a partner I can trust this time,' he said, nodding in Kayley's direction.

'I don't forget disloyalty. I looked after you back then. Made sure you had money. Thought I'd befriend you. What a mistake that was. I don't take shit from anyone these days. I've been sorting myself out and biding my time. I had a few accounts to settle. Yours was one of them. It's been a laugh. You're such a wimp these days. Look at you! Strutting about in your shiny suit, talking crap about fixtures and odds, pretending you're an honest bloke. You're pathetic! Anyway, looks like you'll have to find a new job now.' He nodded across at Sid. 'So, cheerio. Been nice to catch up with you. Got to run. Don't bother trying to grass us up. We'll be well gone by the time you contact the police, and I'd keep quiet about the missing money if I were you. This looks like an inside job – no break-in, you see?' He holds up a back door key. 'She's right. You'll be their prime suspect. Adios, dumb ass.'

Johnny elbows the door open and Kayley slips through it. He turns back and speaks once more. 'And in case that isn't enough reason for you to keep your trap shut, let me warn you: if you mention me or Kayley to the cops, I'll kill your little sister.' He points the gun at him. 'Bang!

Just like that. Comprendez?' Johnny nods to himself before disappearing through the side door into the alley behind.

He slides to the floor next to the man who'd put his faith in him. The man who'd handed him the back door keys to his shop, and who'd treated him better than anyone else ever had. He lifts Sid's hand in his own and blinks back tears.

'I'm so sorry,' he whispers. 'So, so sorry.'

CHAPTER FIFTY

Lauren was alone, unwashed hair scraped back from her pasty, make-up-free face; the first signs of a cold sore developing on her lips. She invited them into the kitchen, where Robyn spotted a pile of clothes and a roll of bin bags.

'I was trying to put Henry's clothes together for the charity shop, but I couldn't. I'm not ready to have him ripped from my life yet.'

'Have you nobody to help you with that?' Robyn asked kindly.

'My mum volunteered but I sent her away. I wanted to do this alone. She'll be back later. She's with Dad making the arrangements for his funeral. I couldn't face doing it. I tried but as soon as they opened the book and asked which coffin I wanted for him, I broke down. His sister doesn't want anything to do with it either, so Mum and Dad are handling it.'

'You've spoken to Libby?'

Lauren nodded miserably. 'She said her mother was in such a bad way, she couldn't be sure she'd even attend his funeral. That can't be right, can it? They were siblings. How can you turn your back on your brother like that?'

'I know this is really tough for you but we're making progress with our investigations and I have a couple of questions that might help us greatly.'

'Sure. Anything to find out what happened. I am tortured at night by what happened. I had a horrible dream last night: I was there with Henry, in the car, laughing and chatting, then suddenly I saw a shotgun pointing at us. My heart pounded but I couldn't scream, and then I woke up. It was horrific. It was a good thing Mum was here. I don't know what I'd have done if she hadn't been.'

'You know Ailsa and Dario Pelligrini?'

Lauren screwed up her face. 'Yes, of course. I play tennis with Ailsa and Henry occasionally met up with Dario at the pub, after cricket. Why?'

'Did Ailsa tell you about some clients she'd taken on – a lottery syndicate?'

Lauren chewed her lip for a moment. 'She did. It was supposed to be very hush-hush. We went out to the theatre in Lichfield and on to a meal afterwards. We had a couple of cocktails and then she ordered a bottle of champagne with the meal. We both got a bit drunk. She told me she was celebrating because they'd taken on the lottery syndicate and were arranging accounts and funds and all sorts of stuff I didn't understand, and it was going to net them a huge income. She'd been setting up a special holding account for them that day.'

'Did you tell anybody about this? Did you tell Henry?'

Lauren's eyes grew big as she nodded. 'I'd had way too much to drink and I blabbed, but I knew he wouldn't tell anyone. He was so trustworthy. I found it amusing because they'd named the account Astra Holding. I made some comment about the name and we both laughed at the thought of little Astra Carrington winning the lottery. Why? Is it important? Should I not have told him?'

'How did he react when you told him?'

'He laughed.'

'Did you notice any changes in his behaviour immediately afterwards? Did he ask you for more details?'

Lauren shook her head. 'The subject didn't come up again. He was quieter than usual, but he claimed it was because of the problems we were having – you know, with me not getting pregnant.'

'So he was quieter than usual?'

Lauren tilted her head back and shut her eyes briefly. 'Yes. The following day I got cross with him because he wasn't listening to me, just staring at the cereal packet and ignoring me. I asked him what was wrong and he said he felt under pressure all the time to get me pregnant. We had an argument over it. He stormed off to work but he was fine when he came home later that day.'

Robyn and David left the house buoyed by the interview. They'd made the breakthrough at last. From what they'd discovered, they could assume all three deaths were related. She would present her findings to DCI Flint, arrange protection for the other team members and then track down the murderer.

※

Robyn dropped David back at the station and hastened to Yoxall.

Liam Carrington, in jeans and a jumper with something sticky down its front, looked surprised to see her.

'Come in,' he said, running a hand over his forehead. 'Just getting Astra a snack.' Astra came running out to see who was at the door, and seeing Robyn, gave her a smile.

'Hi, Astra. Did you enjoy the film with Lauren?'

Astra nodded and slipped her hand into her father's.

'I happened to be at Lauren's when Astra was visiting,' she explained.

Carrington's head bobbed up and down. 'I took your advice. I think it helped them both. Astra certainly seems less agitated.' They headed into the kitchen, where he'd been putting together a cheese sandwich. He placed the top slice of bread onto it, cut the sandwich into four and handed Astra the plate. She took it and shuffled onto a seat by the table, picked up the black cat and hugged it, ignoring the food.

'On your own today?'

'Yeah. Ella is teaching an exercise class at the village hall. I try to work my shifts around her. She usually holds two classes every Wednesday – one in the morning and one early evening.'

'What sort of classes does she put on?'

'Self-defence,' he replied. She noticed a slight shift in his stance but said no more.

Ella's scarred face sprang to mind. 'Can I ask what happened to her? I couldn't help but notice the scar. Was she in an accident?'

'Some drugged-up kid after money. He slashed her face when she refused to hand over her purse. That's why she took up self-defence. She teaches it to women to help them stay safe.'

Astra seemed subdued again and was staring into space.

'Come on, honey. Eat it up. For Daddy,' he said.

Astra took a piece of the sandwich, nibbled on it and then put it down on the plate and shook her head, her curls bobbing around her head.

'Don't want it, Daddy,' she said.

He sighed. 'I hope she isn't sickening for something. Okay, Astra, go and play next door. Daddy will come and make up the jigsaw with you in a minute. I'm going to speak to the nice police officer now, okay?'

She slipped silently from her chair, and moved through the door towards the sitting room without glancing up. Robyn decided she really was a very quiet little girl – too quiet.

She spoke again. 'I really wanted to talk to you anyway, about the syndicate.'

'What's to tell? You obviously know about it,' he snorted. Robyn remained impassive and waited for an answer to her question.

'We put the odd bet on, using any quiz winnings, and one week it came good for us.'

'That's an interesting choice of words. The lottery isn't quite a bet, is it?'

He cricked his neck, playing for time. 'No, I suppose not, but it is a gamble. You hope to win money by choosing numbers. It's a gamble that paid off.'

'You didn't have a special system of numbers, did you?'

'We threw caution to the wind and bought lucky dip tickets.'

'I understand the winnings were deposited into a holding account called Astra Holdings.'

'What of it? We had to call the account something. It was the first name that came to me and the others agreed on it.'

'Juliet told me the ticket was purchased from the MiniMarkt where you and Henry worked. Did you buy the ticket?'

He shook his head. 'No. Ella bought it that week. She got it in MiniMarkt. It's against the shop rules as an employee, let alone manager, for me to buy lottery tickets from my own shop.'

'Mr Carrington, have you any idea who would have wanted Tessa Hall and Anthony Hawkins dead?'

He shook his head. 'I really don't know. I haven't had anything to do with them since last December.' He held up his hands, a defensive gesture. 'It's a mystery to me. Didn't Anthony die of a heart attack?'

'We believe his death to be suspicious.'

Liam looked at her with open surprise. Robyn bided her time then asked, 'Did Henry Gregson mention the lottery win to you?'

Carrington pouted before answering. 'No. Why would he?'

'He was your best friend. He also knew a local lottery syndicate had won a huge amount of money and it was being transferred into an account called Astra Holdings. I figured he might have said something to you.'

'You figured wrong. The subject never came up.' Liam Carrington gave her the longest look. 'Are you suggesting Henry's death is somehow connected to the lottery win? That's ludicrous. Why would anyone kill him because he knew a syndicate had won a few million pounds? Doesn't make any sense.'

That was one question Robyn couldn't answer. That knowledge shouldn't have got Henry killed. She asked a few more questions and was about to leave when she saw a pair of shoes placed by the door and remembered she hadn't asked him an important question.

'What size shoes do you take?'

'Ten. Why?' Liam asked.

'Just part of our enquiries, sir.'

After the door closed behind her, her mind wouldn't settle, and she drove only as far as the village hall, parked up and wandered to the side door that was slightly ajar. Loud grunts and shouts came from inside as Ella put her class through their paces. Robyn peered through the gap in time to observe Ella demonstrate a manoeuvre to counter a gun-wielding attacker. With legs a blur, she expertly propelled a kick that knocked the object from the volunteer's hand high into the air. The women applauded.

As she drew back, Robyn decided to investigate Ella Fox further.

CHAPTER FIFTY-ONE

DAY NINE – WEDNESDAY, 22 FEBRUARY, EVENING

Robyn tilted back on her chair, relieved her office was back to normal. The desks and cables and boxes had all disappeared, and she could think again. She was waiting for DCI Flint to call her through to his office when there was a commotion in the corridor and Matt burst through the door.

'Guv, we've found a witness who saw somebody near Tessa Hall's house on the sixteenth. They're in interview room one.'

Robyn slapped the report and photograph onto her desk with a satisfying thump and raced off.

The woman waiting for her was glowing with excitement at being in the station. She jumped up when Robyn came in and for a minute Robyn thought she might curtsy.

'Hi. I'm Tory Goode. Victoria really, but nobody calls me Victoria, and Vicky doesn't suit me.'

'Good evening, Miss Goode,' said Robyn. 'Thank you for coming all this way to speak to us.'

'It's a pleasure. When Sergeant Higham asked me if I minded dropping by, I thought it's the least I can do. Especially if it helps to catch a murderer.' She whispered the last word.

'Can you tell me what you told him about the visitor you saw near Tessa Hall's house?'

'Oh yes, sure. It was last Thursday the sixteenth. It was dead early, about six. I was talking to my mum. She always phones me the same time every morning. I'm an early bird because I have to travel to Birmingham every day. I like to go before the traffic builds up. Anyway, Mum calls every morning. She's getting on, you see – seventy-three and lives alone – she likes to start her day with a quick chat. Mum was going on about some illness or another, as she does, and I happened to peer out of the window to see if there'd been a frost. When there is, I have to get out earlier and scrape my car windscreen, you see? Anyway, it was dark outside but I caught sight of a person in a dark hoodie, with the hood over their head, jogging up the road towards where that young woman was murdered. The hood slipped off and she turned around for a minute under the lamp post out there, and that was when I saw her.'

'Her?'

'Yes. It was a woman.'

'Can I ask you why you didn't come forward before with this information?'

'I didn't think it was important. I thought she was just a jogger. She didn't look suspicious in any way. She wasn't carrying a machete or anything.' Her chin jutted forwards and she shook her hair back.

'I don't wish to be rude. I'm a little surprised, that's all. You didn't see the television appeal or read about it in the newspapers?'

'No. I don't like the news. There's always loads of horrible things happening. I don't watch it. It was lucky I was in today or I wouldn't have spoken to Sergeant Higham. I'm normally at work, but today I took time off for a dentist appointment.'

'Did you know Miss Hall, the lady who died last week?'

'No. Never met her. I've only been in the village six weeks. I hardly know anybody yet.'

Robyn gave her an understanding smile. 'If you saw this woman again, would you recognise her?'

'Probably.'

'Excellent. I'm going to ask you to make a statement now. I'll send in an officer and they'll write down exactly what you saw and you'll sign it. Okay?'

'Is that it?' Tory looked deflated.

'No. I might need you to identify the woman you saw. Are you up for that?'

Tory sat upright in her chair. 'Yes. I'd be happy to help.'

'Thank you. I'll get back to you.'

Robyn rose, trying not to wince as the woman thanked her again and began telling Matt how much she enjoyed watching television police dramas.

She strode back to the office, lost in thought. Another jogger! A jogger they'd been unable to identify had been spotted on Cannock Chase. Could it be the same person? She thought briefly of Ailsa Pelligrini; however, she couldn't work out what motive the woman would have for murdering Tessa, or Henry for that matter. She shut her eyes briefly and thought of Ella Fox, kicking at an imaginary attacker. She couldn't work out why Ella would kill Tessa but it crossed her mind that Ella might have a motive for killing Henry. Henry knew Ella had bought lottery tickets. If he'd put two and two together about their winnings, he might have confronted the pair, asking for money. Had Ella wanted to protect their winnings and killed him? Then there was Naomi Povey, who had no solid alibi for the morning Tessa was killed, and who was off work on Valentine's Day. She had reason to hate Tessa, but Henry? Robyn sighed. So many questions, and what she really wanted were answers.

CHAPTER FIFTY-TWO

THEN

He's on his back on the hard single bed with its scratchy blanket, staring at the ceiling. Of all the poxy things that have happened in his life, this is the worst. He's been put in solitary for his own safety. The prison guard, Mr Hawkins, took pity on him when he found him bloodied, bruised and naked in the shower block. He shifts uncomfortably at the thought of what had transpired. His backside is so sore he doubts he'll ever be able to sit properly again. Hawkins wasn't soft but he had a streak of humanity in him. He'd helped him up and taken him to the medical centre, where they'd stitched him up.

Hawkins is the only screw he has time for. He doesn't treat him like the other officers do, with cruel taunts and harsh words. Even the other prisoners treat him like he's a real criminal – funny, really, because of all the sorts in here who claim they're innocent, he genuinely is. They've taken against him, in spite of his efforts to keep his head down and stay silent. His cellmate in particular has it in for him and has made his life a living hell.

While he was at the medical centre, Hawkins had sat with him. The old guy reminds him a bit of Sid. They'd chatted a bit. Hawkins told him he was going to retire soon and would be glad to be out of the place. He was going to live in the country as far away from people as possible, and that some of the things he'd seen in prison had sickened him. In return, he'd unburdened himself and told Hawkins about Sid, Johnny, and Kayley, and how they'd stitched him up good and proper.

Hawkins had stared at him hard and said, 'Don't tell that to anyone in here. You know your trouble, lad? You try too hard. You show weakness. The other blokes in here, they can smell fear. They home in on weakness like sharks sniff out blood. If you tell tales like this, you'll get more than a beating up. These guys are hard, and I mean hard. You need to toughen up and keep your head down if you want to survive the next few months. You're a bright lad. I've noticed that about you, so you know what I'm saying. Don't try and make friends. Take my advice.'

Hawkins has arranged for solitary confinement until things calm down back at the cells. He'll be moved from the cell he was sharing and into another when another con, up for parole, leaves. He hopes his next cellmate is not such a thug.

Prison has been bad. His life had been pretty shit up until now, but prison has been a whole lot worse. He's only been here five weeks, and already he's got another pile of horrible memories to add to the others. His sister comes to see him every visiting time. She knows he's blameless but no matter how much she tries to convince him to tell the truth, he refuses. He isn't going to have her hunted down and sliced open by Johnny Hounslow. Three days earlier, she'd visited and sat opposite him, her eyes blazing.

'But he doesn't deserve to get away with it,' she argued.

'It doesn't matter. I can't lose you. You know he'll come after you. I can stick this out. I don't want anything to happen to you.'

Her eyes had brimmed with tears. She'd squeezed his hand tightly. 'It's so unfair.'

It was. Life was unfair but he was a survivor. While his sister was by his side, he'd survive. She advised him to keep his head down. Keep silent. They were used to keeping silent. Said she'd think of him every day.

The hatch door in the huge metal door opens. The prison officer with the shaved head calls his name and he struggles to stand to attention. A tray of food is pushed through the hatch. It's stewed mince and smells worse than dog shit. He wrinkles his nose as he collects it.

Shaved Head – Mr Burns – snarls at him. 'Don't look so bloody po-faced. It could be a lot worse. Count yourself lucky it was Hawkins found you. If it'd been me, I'd have left you there or locked you in with Kurt the Knife, and watched while he played with you.' The hatch snaps shut.

He places the tray on his bed and crosses the room, where he bashes his knuckles repeatedly against the wall until he can no longer feel the pain. Hawkins was right – he has to toughen up. It's a technique that'll not only prevent himself from crying but to make him feel hate – hate like he's never experienced before. One day, it'll serve him well.

CHAPTER FIFTY-THREE

Robyn was woken by her mobile phone. She pushed Schrödinger away to reach it, glancing at the time as she did so. It was coming up to 5 a.m.

'Carter.'

The voice at the other end was tearful and quiet. 'It's Juliet Fallows. I can't sleep. I had to ring you.'

Robyn sat up, fully alert. 'Is everything okay, Juliet?'

'No. I'm okay but it isn't okay. Oh, God, I'm not making any sense, am I?'

'You're fine,' said Robyn smoothly, hoping to calm the woman. 'Take your time. What's this about?'

'I shouldn't be ringing you, but I can't keep silent about this. I've been thinking about Tessa and Anthony. I should have told you everything when you asked me, but I didn't dare.'

Robyn was still struggling to comprehend what Juliet was saying.

'What's worrying you?'

Juliet let out an almighty sigh. 'It's to do with the lottery win. I should have come clean. The money shouldn't be ours.'

'I don't understand, Juliet. Why not?'

There was silence, during which time Robyn wondered if Juliet was going to hang up. Eventually, she spoke. 'We won the pub quiz like I told you and decided to use the sixty pounds winnings for lottery lucky dip tickets. We'd had too much to drink that night and were joking about what we'd do if we actually won the lottery. Liam told us about a couple whose numbers had come up. He has an incredible memory for numbers and he was convinced their ticket had won a rollover jackpot in November. The couple were away on one of their regular holidays, and he was certain they wouldn't even be aware they'd won. They always relied on Liam to tell them if they'd won or not, by passing the ticket through the shop machine. They had a routine, and instead of getting a weekly ticket, they'd buy monthly lucky dip ones that covered them for every draw that month. At the end of each month, they'd hand Liam the ticket to check it out. Liam said they sometimes won a tenner or even a little more but mostly they lost, and he'd throw the ticket in the shop bin, give them a new one for the next month, and off they'd go again.

'A few more drinks later and we were working out ways of getting our hands on that winning ticket. If Liam was right, he could tell the couple they hadn't won, pretend to throw the ticket away, keep it, and we could pocket the winnings.

'Liam wasn't keen on the idea. Said it wasn't moral. Anthony took him to one side and had a man-to-man chat with him. It worked. He agreed to the plan.

'Two weeks later, Liam told us he'd got the ticket, and it was, as he thought, a winner. We became the official winners of the rollover jackpot. We decided to keep quiet about it like I told you, and then on December the thirtieth I got a phone call from a man who said he knew everything but was giving us all a chance to confess and hand back the winnings, rather than report us. Tessa rang me two minutes after I hung up. She'd had a similar call and had been alarmed by it. We both telephoned Anthony. He was convinced it was a prank call and there was no possible way anybody could have known what we did. He told us not to be so silly and to relax.

'I gave it a week, then two, and there were no further calls. I decided Anthony was right. And then last week Tessa was killed, and soon after, Anthony died.' There was a lengthy pause before she spoke again.

'I should never have got carried away like that. I was so excited at the prospect of all that wealth. Who wouldn't want to get their hands on a million pounds?'

'Did the man who rang you tell you his name?'

'You asked me once about Henry Gregson. I've been wondering if it could have been him.'

'Juliet, you'll have to come to the station and make a statement. You can't keep the money. You know that, don't you?'

'I know we can't. It's been eating away at me. It was so wrong of us to even think about cheating that couple like that. I'm such a lousy example for my children, aren't I? I want to make this right now. I want to make amends. I'll come in later today.'

'I'd like to send an officer around to keep an eye on you while we investigate further. Or, if you'd rather, we could move you somewhere out of harm's way.'

'No, that's silly. I have to go to work this morning. I can't let them down at such short notice. I'll go to work and come straight to the station as soon as I finish.'

Juliet hung up. Robyn dialled DCI Flint's number and brought him up to speed.

'I'll arrange for officers to watch her house,' he said. 'What about Liam Carrington and Roger Jenkinson?'

'I'm going to bring them into the station, sir, for further questioning. We might need to keep an eye on them afterwards.'

'I'll sort it first thing.'

Flint disconnected, leaving Robyn alert and eager to get started. The puzzle was at last taking shape. If Henry Gregson knew about the ticket being stolen, was that enough to get him killed? Robyn suspected it might be. She had a lot of work to do. Leaving the cat slumbering, she padded downstairs. It was going to be a long but productive day, of that she was sure.

CHAPTER FIFTY-FOUR

Juliet Fallows slipped out of the clinic where she worked and slunk along the road, turning past the Volkswagen dealership into the side road behind the workshop. It was a grim day and she was feeling especially tired. She hadn't slept one wink for worry. At least she'd now come clean. Even if she had to face the consequences, it had been the right decision to make.

Behind the clinic stood a grand retail park of several furniture and electronic stores, supermarkets and cafés. She checked left and right to ensure nobody had spotted her and slid into the alley behind the garage, out of sight, as planned. The call she'd received an hour earlier had made her pulse race. She didn't want to sneak out but she wanted this to be over. It was doing her head in.

The clattering and high-pitched noises coming from the garage drowned out all other sounds, and she didn't hear the person approach until they were close to her.

'Oh, for Christ's sake. You made me jump,' she said. 'My nerves are bad enough at the moment.'

'What did you tell the police, Juliet?'

Juliet was taken aback. The icy stare was unnerving.

'It had better not have been the truth.'

Juliet's blood ran cold. The barrel of the gun was pointing at her. Her mouth opened and shut. How could she have been so stupid as to agree to the meeting? She'd have to lie to get out of this. There was nothing else she could do. She tried to speak calmly.

'I already told you when I rang you up yesterday. They know about the syndicate but I didn't tell them everything, okay? I'm not that stupid. They don't suspect anything.'

'I don't believe you. You've told them what happened, haven't you? I know you. You're weak. You'll have caved in and told them.'

Juliet's voice rose. 'No, I haven't. I need this money. I'm not going to give it up. Not now we've come this far. You know how important this is to me. I was a bit vulnerable, that's all. They put me in one of those interview rooms and it freaked me out. They kept on at me. In the end I had to give them something to go on.'

'You stupid cow. You've probably put them onto us.'

'You'd have done the same if they'd interviewed you.'

'I wouldn't have been so dumb as to turn up at the station in the first place.'

'I didn't tell them the truth,' Juliet whimpered.

'You still told them too much,' came the reply. The figure lowered the gun, turned and walked away from Juliet. She watched the retreating figure move away and breathed in deeply. She'd leave today. She'd collect the kids and go. It didn't matter where they went as long as they were together. She couldn't stay here any longer. As she prepared to leave as well, the figure stopped and turned back towards her.

The gun fired once and the bullet smashed into Juliet's nose, sending fragments of cartilage and blood spinning into the air like bloody raindrops. The noisy drilling next door obliterated all sound of gunfire, and the murderer casually walked away from Juliet's crumpled body.

CHAPTER FIFTY-FIVE

Robyn was in a determined mood, and now her office was free of Shearer and his officers, she felt more in control of the investigation. Juliet's phone call had been another boost, and she was making sure she scrutinised every last detail of those in and connected to the lottery syndicate.

'We have new information. The lottery ticket that won the jackpot was stolen from a couple who regularly shop at MiniMarkt. They are probably unaware they won.' She summarised Juliet's confession. 'I'd like to find out who they are so we can pass the names on to the lottery syndicate and get the money to the right-ful winners. What's important is that it gives us a motive behind Henry's murder. Henry was going to blow the whistle on the team. How he found out about the stolen ticket remains a mystery. He might somehow have put two and two together, or given he was friends with Liam and Ella, one or the other might have confessed the truth to him. My instinct says one of the team, or one of the team's partners, killed Henry. I want us to look very carefully at each of the syndicate's alibis again for the three days in question. Anna, will you look into Ella Fox? She claimed she was visiting a friend the morning of Henry Gregson's murder – Cassie Snow, who was in Queen's Hospital in Burton She didn't get to the hospital because she missed a bus connection and was then too late for visiting time. Could you confirm Cassie was in hospital and, if possible, the bus times? Here are the details she gave me. Also, and this is going to be trickier, see if Ella actually caught the bus from Yoxall to Burton.'

'On it,' came the reply from Anna.

Robyn logged on and searched for Ella Fox, figuring two heads were better than one. A more general search yielded no results. The woman didn't have a social media footprint at all. Robyn found that really strange – a stay-at-home mother – surely she'd be online, posting photographs of her child, even if it were within the privacy of mum-type Facebook groups. It didn't feel right. She must have other friends – from the exercise class she gave and from the village itself. Was she really that much of a loner?

She stared at the whiteboard and wondered just what to make of it.

Anna bounded from her desk.

'We were lucky. I emailed a shot of Ella across to the bus depot. The driver for that morning was in the office and remembers her clearly – the scar, he remembers the scar.'

Robyn nodded. 'Okay, so she got on the bus and went to Burton.'

'Cassie Snow was definitely in hospital on the fourteenth. Appendicitis.'

'So Ella probably did go to visit her?'

'Looks that way. There's only one thing. According to the bus depot, there's no reason for Ella to have missed her connection. The buses were running on time that day and she ought to have been able to catch the connecting bus that goes to the hospital.'

'That's interesting.'

'I've also pulled this from the police database. An Ella Fox was attacked and robbed on her way home from work in Nottingham in

May 2011. An anonymous caller saw a young man run away from the scene of the crime. They never caught the man who assaulted her or found the knife used. She was badly injured.'

'She lived in Nottingham?'

'Last known address was this.' Anna passed a note to Robyn, who read, 'Lee Potter, The Stables, Amble Lane, Beeston. And this is Lee's contact number?'

Anna nodded furiously.

'Great stuff.'

Robyn rang it immediately. Lee Potter sounded distant and vague.

'Mr Potter, my name is DI Robyn Carter of Staffordshire Police. It's concerning somebody you might have known or indeed still know. It's nothing alarming.'

'Go on. I'm at work but go on.'

'Ella Fox.'

His voice dropped. 'Is she all right?'

'Yes, please don't concern yourself. I was making enquiries about the terrible attack that took place in 2011.'

There was a pause as he moved away from where he was speaking, wind rustling down the phone. When he next spoke it was clearer. 'Yeah. It was horrific. Poor Ella. She didn't deserve that.'

'What happened exactly?'

'She was on her way home from the nursery school where she worked, when she was attacked. Police suspected it was a random attack. She told them her attacker looked like he was spaced out on drugs but couldn't describe him – just young and scruffy. He stole twenty pounds. Twenty quid and in return she gets a lifetime of looking like that.' He sucked his teeth.

'What was your relationship, if you don't mind me asking?'

'We were living together. Thinking of making it more permanent too. The attack changed everything. She wasn't the same person after that. It wasn't so much the fact her face was carved up, but she shut down, rejected me. Like she couldn't bear me to look at her. I still feel bad about it. I didn't want her to leave. It was entirely her choice.'

'You haven't heard from her since then?'

'Nah, she went off with her brother and that was the last I saw of them. He was a bit odd. Lived in Stoke but was always hanging about our place like he had a crush on her. He couldn't seem to function without her. He was always tipping up for money, or because he was drunk. I don't miss him.'

'I was unaware she had a brother. I don't suppose you have a contact address for him?'

'Nah. No chance. Only put up with him for Ella's sake. Like I said, I didn't much care for him and he mostly kept out of my way. He'd visit Ella when I was out. I always knew he'd been though. Ella used to have this sort of guilty look on her face. They had different fathers, so I don't know his surname, but his first name is Liam.'

CHAPTER FIFTY-SIX

THEN

The young man may as well still be locked up. Friends and punters he'd served at the betting shop and laughed with over the last two years now observe him warily as he walks about town, barely acknowledging him.

He misses Sid badly. He'd always been so positive and seen the good in everyone. He'd been an honest man. That was the trouble with life – it made no difference if you were honest and kind – life was bloody unfair.

He's alone in the dingy bar, a half-pint in his hand. Here, he isn't haunted by memories of beatings, abuse, ever-deepening sorrow and deception. Here, he doesn't think about Johnny's cruel sneer, or Kayley's ice-cold, Arctic-grey eyes, or his sister's face when she told him about the abortion. Johnny Hounslow had ruined too many lives. Here, he plots his next move. He knows what that'll be. Prison has toughened him up. Hopefully, it's toughened him enough for this plan to work.

He sits undisturbed in the furthest corner of the pub and calms his mind, emptying it of all the memories. Here, alone in the pub, there's nothing to interrupt his thoughts and he can sit in complete silence.

The hunt for Johnny Hounslow has been his priority and he's combed the area the last couple of weeks, talking to old schoolmates and those who knew Johnny, in an attempt to find out where he might be. Johnny's father hadn't even known he was in the area, let alone hanging out only a few streets away.

Kayley Frost is impossible to track down. Nobody of that name has ever worked at the radio station. He isn't surprised. She went to a lot of trouble to pretend to be somebody she wasn't. He doesn't have any idea how to find her, but he knows if he can locate Johnny, he might come across her. Two days ago, he had a breakthrough when he bumped into Kevin Blackford on the high street in Stoke. Kevin, who still looked fifteen years old and wore the same glasses he'd worn at school, was busking, a cap at his feet. The young man dropped fifty pence into it and stopped to chat. Kevin finished his song and sat on the wall, guitar by his feet.

'I don't often come into Stoke town centre. I usually stick to Newcastle-under-Lyme. Funny me seeing you here,' said Kevin, as he rolled a joint.

'How come?'

He scratched his head, pulled something out of his hair and studied it before dropping it onto the ground. 'Well, I saw Johnny only last Tuesday. He drove past me in that black Porsche of his. You two used to be inseparable at school. See much of him these days?'

'You recognised him?'

Kevin sucked on his joint and scowled at the passer-by who frowned at his actions. 'Sure. I've seen him quite a few times over the last couple of years. I once even spoke to him in a pub, but he walked off, like he didn't know me. Guess he's not into druggy friends.' He laughed and removed a bit of tobacco from his brown teeth. 'Now, whenever I see him, I keep my head down. He looks like he'd plant one on me if I said anything. He's often out and about in Newcastle-under-Lyme, and since that's where I usually perform, I see him.'

Kevin sniffed and wiped his nose on the sleeve of his grubby jumper. A loose thread hung from it. He looked up and grinned. 'Don't suppose you fancy going for a pint, do you?'

He shook his head. 'Too early for me, but I'll stand you a beer if you like, later.'

Kevin nodded. 'Great. See you over there at five,' he said, pointing to the pub opposite. 'Best get back to this. Who knows, one day I might get discovered and get my own recording contract.'

The young man slapped Kevin on the back and left him to his singing. Kevin was always a bit off the wall. His thoughts quickly moved from Kevin to Johnny. So, the bastard was in the area. That was exactly what he needed to hear.

He sips his pint and waits. He's arranged a meet for 9 p.m. and he's only got half an hour to wait. The guy who's meeting him is an ex-con like him. He's integral to the plan and had better show up with the goods. The young man shivers in anticipation – he's never owned a shooter before.

CHAPTER FIFTY-SEVEN

By mid afternoon. Robyn had obtained birth records proving Liam Carrington and Ella Fox were related.

'I want both Liam Carrington and his sister, Ella Fox, brought in for questioning immediately,' said Robyn aloud. 'They're somehow involved in this. Has Juliet Fallows rung in yet?'

'No, guv.'

'She said she'd come by the station as soon as she finished work. Call the clinic in Tamworth and see where she is.'

Anna squirmed in her chair. 'I might be about to throw a spanner in the works. Got a response to the email David sent asking for more information about Roger Jenkinson and an incident with Michael Judd, the man who trespassed onto his land. Here's Michael's statement.'

Robyn read through Michael's statement that detailed his actions that day and paused at one section:

I didn't know the land was private. I thought I was on a public footpath. Mr Jenkinson shouted to get off his land. I put up my hands and said, 'I don't want any bother.'

'Of course you do,' said Mr Jenkinson. 'Or you wouldn't have climbed over my fence and onto my land. You know what I'm going to do to you?'

He pointed a gun at me. 'Don't shoot,' I said.

'Bit late to say that now, you shitbag. You come onto private property, no doubt to rob me, and don't expect me to defend myself? You're stupid. You know what this is?'

I nodded. 'It's a gun.'

'Well done, Einstein. It's one of the best – it's a Smith & Wesson. And I'm a great shot. I can blow your head off with one little pull of this trigger and my eyes closed.'

He raised the gun and I ran. I ran as fast as I could. I ran back to the fence and scrambled back over it. He shouted something else I couldn't make out and I fell from the fence, stumbled and twisted my ankle.

He walked up to the fence, his gun still in his hand. 'Run, you bastard, before I splatter what's left of your brain everywhere,' he said.

And I did.

'Henry Gregson was shot with a Smith & Wesson, wasn't he? Do you think Roger Jenkinson could be his murderer?' Anna's face creased in frustration.

'Oh, you're kidding me,' groaned Robyn. 'We'll have to bring Roger back in and ask him again about the gun. He might still own it. David, instruct the officer currently outside Roger Jenkinson's place to bring him in. Looks like we'll be in for a full house. Hope we've got enough interview rooms.'

David departed to do her bidding. Robyn racked her brains to fathom why Liam and Ella would be attempting to pass themselves off as a couple. And what about Astra? Surely she didn't belong to both of them? There were lots of parts to this investigation that continued to bug her.

David raced back into the room. 'Roger Jenkinson's not at home.'

'Where is he?'

David shrugged. 'The officer watching the place said he must have slipped away, over the fields. It's a huge property, plenty of places for him to get lost in.'

Robyn groaned. This was rapidly turning into a farce and all she needed now was Shearer smirking in the corner.

As if on cue, Shearer stuck his head in. 'Came to see if you missed me,' he said, sidling up to Robyn.

'Not now, Tom. I'm up to my neck.'

'Heard that was the case. Flint made some comment.' His eyes glittered.

'Tom, go away. I really haven't time for this now.'

He raised his hands in mock obeisance and backed away, leaving her rattled. How dare Flint make any comment to Shearer about her work or otherwise? She fumed for a moment until Mitz put down the internal phone and spoke quietly. 'Liam and Ella are on their way. Should be here in half an hour. Naomi Povey's already here.'

'When the others arrive, we'll start by interviewing Liam Carrington.' She opened a drawer, pulled out a silver foil pack and popped a couple of headache pills.

Mitz studied her actions then asked, 'You want me to take over?'

'No ta. I'll be fine.' She brushed off his concerned look and refocused on the notes in front of her. Now, to add to her workload, she had a missing suspect. Where would Roger Jenkinson have gone? Or had he been murdered? This all seemed too much to deal with. Was Flint deliberately letting her handle this in the hope she'd break? Were he and Shearer discussing how far they could leave her floundering before they waded in? She squared her shoulders. That was never going to happen.

'Put out a call on Roger Jenkinson, Mitz. I want him apprehended as soon as possible. Check all the farms and homes in the area. His car's still outside his property. He can't have gone too far if he left on foot, not unless he had help from somebody.'

※

Tory Goode, the witness who claimed she'd seen a jogger near Tessa's house on the morning she'd been killed, was sitting behind the one-way mirror looking into the interview room.

'I didn't know this sort of thing actually happened,' she whispered. She'd calmed down a little, worn out by waiting around, but was still enthusiastic about helping to identify the woman she'd spotted in Barton-under-Needwood.

'The women can't see you but you can see them. If you spot the woman you saw on the sixteenth of February at 6 a.m. let me know. Are you clear about that?' Robyn asked.

'Yes. I'm clear.'

Anna gave the woman a smile.

Robyn gave the instruction and David opened the door and five women entered the room and moved to their positions, where they waited, facing the glass. Tory took her time in studying each woman.

'Miss Goode, do you recognise any of the women on the other side of the glass?' asked Robyn.

Tory chewed her lip and craned her neck forward. 'I don't know. I can't be sure.'

Robyn waited, hoping for a more positive identification, but Tory sat back and shook her head.

After Tory left, Robyn entered the interview room and was soon joined by Naomi Povey. She walked to the chair, pulled it out from under the table and sat down, all the while scowling.

'I'm going to have you for harassment,' Naomi spat. 'I'm not happy at having to take part in an identity parade.'

'Thank you for your assistance. I won't keep you, Miss Povey,' said Robyn. 'It's only a couple of questions.'

'I'm not sure I feel like answering any more of your questions. I've got better things to do with my time.'

'I'm afraid it's necessary for our enquiries. When was the last time you saw Roger Jenkinson?'

Naomi flushed. 'A few days ago.'

'We're concerned about him. He's disappeared. I wondered if he'd contacted you.'

'I can't help you with that. I haven't seen him since last Tuesday.'

Robyn gave a knowing smile. 'Miss Hall, have you any idea where Mr Jenkinson might be at this moment?'

Naomi scowled. 'No. I'm not his minder. He doesn't have to tell me where he is or what he's doing and check in every hour.'

'I wonder how much he actually tells you. I suspect he's kept quite a few things from you.'

'Crap. He tells me everything. We're a team – a solid team.'

'I was led to believe he wanted to end your relationship.'

'You're wrong.'

'Did he ever suggest you and he split up?'

Naomi let out a soft snort. 'We had our ups and downs. He might have said something in the heat of the moment but he'd never have left me for her.'

'But he wanted to, didn't he?'

'I don't know what you're talking about. He stopped seeing that tart after I phoned her. It was over. Got it? Over.'

'I'm afraid that wasn't the case. Mr Jenkinson continued to see Tessa even after you tried to break their relationship up.'

Naomi's head shook from side to side. 'No. No. That's not possible. I'd have known if he was still seeing her.'

Robyn persisted. Naomi was definitely beginning to crack. 'Again. I'm sorry to contradict you, but we lifted his fingerprints from Tessa's house, and off a Valentine's card he sent her.' She watched Naomi's reaction very carefully. The woman was in denial, her eyes blinking repeatedly.

'No. This isn't true. He can't have. He was with me on Valentine's Day. We spent it together. He loved me. Only me.'

'Mr Jenkinson kept a few secrets from you, Naomi. Or maybe he only thought he'd kept them from you. Did you find out he was still seeing Tessa, and murder her?'

Naomi spluttered, 'No. I didn't. Check with my work colleagues. They'll tell you I was at work that day. I went nowhere near her house.'

Robyn waited for Naomi to digest what she'd been told before she dropped the next bombshell. She was banking on Juliet's information that Roger was keeping Naomi in the dark about the lottery.

'Did he tell you about their lottery win, or did he keep that a secret from you too?'

Naomi's mouth flapped open. 'What lottery win?'

'He didn't tell you he and the others had won over six million pounds in December?'

There was silence followed by a chuckle and then further chuckling. 'Go on. You're winding me up.'

'Mr Jenkinson and his fellow teammates won a jackpot amount of money on the lottery, and that is why I'm concerned for his well-being. He could be in danger.'

The woman bristled suddenly. 'You needn't worry about Roger. He can handle himself. I don't know where he might be, so if that's everything, I'm leaving. If you drag me in one more time without good reason, I'll report you for harassment.'

With that, she slammed her chair back with force and marched out of the interview room. Robyn looked across at the glass and spoke to Anna, still watching and listening behind it.

'Get someone to follow her, will you? I have a feeling she knows exactly where Roger is. I want an officer watching her movements. I'm going to interview Liam Carrington.'

As Robyn exited the interview room, she glanced along the corridor towards the double doors that led into the station foyer. Through the glass she spotted two figures – Liam and Ella. He had one hand on the back of her lustrous hair, holding her head into his chest and shoulders. Robyn observed the couple standing in silence, arms wrapped around each other as if welded together. An officer approached and spoke to them. Liam withdrew. Ella reached for his hands and they stood again for a moment like two children about to play, no word passing their lips. It was obvious now looking at them. They looked so similar: their foreheads, noses, even their mannerisms. It was clear they were related. Robyn turned away. It was time to get to the bottom of the mystery.

CHAPTER FIFTY-EIGHT

THEN

He can't believe it. The man standing beside the bar is none other than Mr Hawkins, the prison officer who'd helped him survive jail. He's much older, obviously – grey-haired and a bit fatter than he was back then – but he's still got the same cocky air of authority.

The young man's been in the pub all evening. He had to get away from the house. A final demand for the electricity plopped through the letter box this morning and he doesn't know how he's going to make ends meet again this month. He's maxed out on his credit card and his damn car needs two new front tyres. They're down to the tread and he's sure to get prosecuted if the cops stop him and check.

He simply doesn't earn enough. The trivia machine is his last-ditch attempt to win some money. He's made the half-pint of beer stretch out for an hour so he can play. The questions are easy: What city is the capital of the country Turkey? He presses answer B, Ankara, and the machine lights up and plays a triumphant tune to indicate he's won ten pounds.

Hawkins potters over to him and hands him a pint. 'Here. You deserve it.'

Buoyed by his success, he smiles and takes the drink from him.

'I remember you, lad. Been a while, but I never forget a face. I always said you were bright. I've been watching you. You're good at this. Fancy another go – you and me against the machine?'

Hawkins is suitably impressed. He buys him more drinks and together they beat the machine twice more, pocketing twenty pounds each. He's cheerful now. He'll have sufficient money to put towards the electricity demand – might keep the bastards off his back a little longer. Luck has been on his side today, and all the while, Hawkins has been buying him drinks and slapping him on the back, telling him what a great player he is. He's not brought up the past at all. He's okay, is Hawkins.

He's about to leave the pub and go back to his cold house when Hawkins beams at him and says, 'Listen. You're a top quizzer. Your talent's wasted. I have a proposition for you. How would you like to be part of a proper team and win some serious money?'

He's never been part of anything. It seems too good to be true. He's not sure, though. He's not too comfortable with people. Hawkins must have read his mind because he says, 'We won't bite. We're a lot like you, really.'

Like him? Lonely, insecure? Hawkins nods again, his smile never leaving his face.

'Come on,' he says. 'What have you got to lose? Come and meet them and see what you think. You'll really enjoy it. And you must stop calling me Mr Hawkins. I'm not a screw any more. Call me Anthony.'

He feels the crisp notes rustling in his pocket. It would be nice to have some more disposable income. He looks into Hawkins' cheerful face. It'd be good to make some new friends too.

'Go on. When do you want me to meet them?'

CHAPTER FIFTY-NINE

DAY TEN – THURSDAY, 23 FEBRUARY, AFTERNOON

Liam Carrington, slumped in a chair, didn't acknowledge Robyn's entrance.

'Mr Carrington,' she said.

He ignored her.

'We can make this a lot easier if you'd just cooperate with us. I'm going to ask a series of questions and you're not obliged to answer them, but it would assist our enquiries if you did. Do you understand?'

Carrington finally looked up.

'On the morning of February the fourteenth you were at home with your daughter, Astra. Is that correct?' She waited for a response, and when she got none, she spoke more loudly. 'Is that correct?'

His answer was little more than a mumble. 'Yeah.'

'And you did not at any time that morning speak to or see Henry Gregson?'

'No.'

'Did he visit your house?'

'No.'

Robyn sat back. 'I think he might have done. I think he called to visit you soon after Ella left.'

Carrington twitched momentarily. It was all Robyn needed. She homed in on it.

'I think he wanted to discuss something with you. Did he, Mr Carrington?'

He looked down at his hands. Robyn wasn't going to let him off the hook now she had him.

'Henry Gregson was spotted, you see? We have a witness who saw him. Now, you can tell me the truth or I can find it out anyway. It'll be better for you in the long run if you tell me what you know. After all, you have your daughter Astra to consider in all of this.'

His Adam's apple rose and fell but he remained silent.

'Okay, let's try this scenario. Henry came to visit you and you argued about something. He left, and you became even madder about what had happened. You asked Ella to come home to look after Astra, then you arranged to meet Henry on Cannock Chase, where you murdered him in cold blood. Is that what happened?'

He shook his head. 'No,' he said, quietly.

'I can very easily obtain a warrant to search your house. We'll search your phones and computers and we'll get to the bottom of this, so it would be a lot easier if you just come clean now.' She waited for a response, and when none was forthcoming, she continued.

'Did you ask Ella to cover for you? Say you were there when you weren't?'

'No.'

'But she would if you asked her, wouldn't she? She'd look after you and make sure you had an alibi. After all, blood is thicker than water.'

He hissed quietly through his teeth and then stopped and resumed his sullen expression. 'Okay, I asked her to stretch the truth. I knew you'd suspect me if my alibi wasn't tight enough, but I honestly didn't kill Henry. I loved that man. I really did. I'm not the easiest person to get along with and I don't find it easy to make friends. Henry was solid. He was my friend.' His eyes filled and he bent forwards, head in his hands.

Robyn was rattled for a moment. The man was genuinely upset. The silvery tears trickled down his face. He wiped them with his sleeve, and she allowed him a few seconds to collect himself before speaking again. She wasn't going to be swayed by this emotional outburst. 'Ella's your sister, isn't she? I wonder if anyone knew that. Maybe Henry discovered your secret.'

He shook his head slowly from side to side, sniffing back tears.

'Did he, Mr Carrington? Did Henry find out Ella was your sister and threaten to tell everyone?'

'You're so wrong,' he said, quietly, before drawing himself back upright in his seat.

Robyn puffed out her cheeks. 'Well, then maybe you could explain what mysterious secret Henry was keeping. We believe he was texting his killer and threatening to expose them just before he was shot. Whoever committed this crime had a secret so big it was worth killing for.'

He crossed his arms, fidgeted and stared at his feet.

'Did you agree to steal a winning lottery ticket from two MiniMarkt customers?'

Liam remained silent.

'Juliet Fallows told us about the ticket. It's pointless to remain silent. Did Henry find out about the theft and threaten to shop you all?'

Again, she was met with silence.

'Did you go to Cannock Chase on February the fourteenth, Mr Carrington?'

'No. I didn't. I was in Yoxall all day.'

'I think, at this point, I should ask you again if you would like a lawyer to be present. I understand you refused one earlier. Would you like a lawyer, Mr Carrington?'

'Yes.'

'Let it be noted for the tape that we're pausing this interview until Mr Carrington has spoken to a legal representative.'

She rose without further comment. Liam Carrington remained in his seat, head hung to his chest.

As soon as the door was shut, she spoke to Mitz.

'What do you reckon?'

They walked back to the office.

'He's guilty of theft and deception, but I can't be sure he's guilty of murdering Henry Gregson.'

Her lips pulled into a grimace. 'I got that same feeling. I wish I had something concrete on him. I hope we can get more out of Ella Fox. I'm flying by the seat of my pants here. If one of them doesn't crack soon and confess, I'll be stuffed. There's insufficient evidence at the moment to convict him of murder.'

Ella was brought into the room next.

'I'm saying nothing without a solicitor so don't bother asking me anything,' she said, looking Robyn directly in the eye.

'We only want to ask you a few questions, Ella,' Robyn said.

She was met with stony silence.

'We understand Henry visited Liam the day he died, while you were out.'

Ella fixed her eyes on a spot above Robyn's head.

'We also believe Liam wasn't at home when you returned at two and that you lied for him.'

There was no flicker of acknowledgement.

'It would be quite understandable for a sister to protect her brother.'

Ella's face gave nothing away. She wasn't going to speak. Robyn tried more questions but was met with the same response. She ended the interview and had Ella taken away until her solicitor arrived. She rubbed her forehead and sighed heavily.

David tapped on the door and entered. 'The receptionist at the Tamworth clinic claimed Juliet went into work first thing but left mid-morning because she didn't feel well. She isn't answering her mobile. I sent a unit round to her house.'

Robyn put her hands on her hips. 'Oh, for fuck's sake. So we've lost Roger Jenkinson and now Juliet. What the hell is going on?'

'They could be in on this together,' said David with a helpless shrug.

'Or both dead. Either way, I've made a complete bollocks of this case. Liam Carrington and Ella Fox are being completely uncooperative at the moment too. Can this get any worse?' Robyn resisted the urge to scream in frustration. She'd been in difficult situations before. She had to be logical, that's what Davies would have told her. She attempted to calm her heart rate with some deep breaths.

'Right, here's what we'll do. First, get a search warrant for Liam and Ella's house. Next, track down Roger and Juliet. If Juliet's involved in any of the murders, it means her claim that they stole the lottery ticket is a lie too. We'll stick to the facts we have and see if we can make anything stick. Right. Let's get going. Time isn't on our side.'

CHAPTER SIXTY

THEN

He loves quiz night. It's the one night he feels he's a winner. His sister still isn't sold on him being part of the team and doesn't trust Hawkins one bit even though she's never met him before or spoken to him until now. She doesn't like him because Hawkins was one of the prison officers who used to keep him locked up behind bars.

'He's too nice all the time,' she says, leaning against him on the settee. 'Reminds me a bit of you-know-who.'

They never mention Clark by name. It's taboo. He knows what she means. Hawkins is always so smiley and friendly – too friendly – but he's nothing like that man. He wouldn't commit any of those indecent acts.

The team members were most enthusiastic in welcoming him. Now, they praise him for his quizzing abilities that help them win on occasion. For the second time in his wretched life, he feels he belongs – he fits in at last. Sid's memory is still with him, and on occasion he talks to Hawkins about what really happened that day at the betting shop. Hawkins believes him. Says it was a travesty what he went through and he should never have had to suffer like that.

'Have to go, babe,' he says. 'Playing in Sudbury tonight. You coming?'

She shakes her head.

He knows why she's so downbeat. They fell short with the rent money again. He really tried to make sure they had enough, but the fridge packed in and they'd had to shell out for a second-hand one that still cost them everything they'd saved. She'd had to perform the unspeakable again with McNamara to get them through the next month. He pulls her to him tightly and wishes he could bring in more so she wouldn't have to go through it again.

She kisses him and pulls away. 'I think I'll have a bath and an early night, instead. Good luck,' she says. 'I really hope you win.'

CHAPTER SIXTY-ONE

Robyn paced the floor, her stomach churning. Flint had approved a search warrant for Liam Carrington's house, and a small unit, headed by Mitz, was on its way to Yoxall. Now she had to tackle another concern – Anna. Unable to locate anyone to follow Naomi, she'd taken the task upon herself, and Robyn was not happy.

'I asked her to find an officer to follow and watch Naomi, not do it herself.'

David spoke. 'She rang in a while ago. Signal was lousy. She said Naomi Povey went straight home and was inside with the curtains drawn. She intended waiting outside Naomi's house until we found another officer to replace her. Then she lost her signal again and when I dialled her number, her phone went to message – bloody dead zone.'

'Didn't you try her on the comms unit?'

'She didn't take one with her. She shot off like a jackrabbit. Used her own car.'

Robyn tutted loudly, and striding into the corridor, she rang Anna's mobile and left a message. 'Anna, ring me as soon as you get this message.' She returned to the office, brow furrowed, speaking to no one in particular.

'What was she thinking of? She shouldn't be staking out Naomi Povey alone.' The thought of Roger Jenkinson, desperate and possibly dangerous, troubled her deeply. 'Where are the officers who're searching for Roger Jenkinson? Can't they send someone over to Bramshall?'

'There was a sighting in Uttoxeter, near the racecourse. Somebody matching his description was spotted next to the grounds. They were all deployed to that area.'

Robyn heaved another sigh.

David spoke again. 'DI Shearer's team are all out on another investigation, and there's nobody else available. That's why Anna took off after Naomi herself.'

As much as she admired Anna's dedication to her job, Robyn didn't want her to take unnecessary risks. It was Robyn's responsibility to keep an eye on her team. She'd had doubts about Roger Jenkinson and not followed them up quickly enough. Now, she chastised her own stupidity. There had been clues – his history of violent outbursts, his size ten feet, being Tessa's lover, and his argument with Anthony Hawkins. Was there a possibility Roger Jenkinson was their perpetrator and he'd run, because he was afraid of being caught by the police? He had to be located – and quickly.

'Head over to Bramshall, David, and join her at the house. Use a squad car and radio in once you arrive. I'll feel happier knowing she has backup.'

David scooted off, leaving Robyn with Matt. They'd still had no luck with Ella Fox. She'd played the silent game. Nothing Robyn had asked or said had produced a single word from her lips. Her solicitor, a starch-faced woman with grey hair scraped so tightly from her face it gave her a permanent look of surprise, had advised Ella to make no comment.

'Matt, got Tory Goode's statement?'

'All here.' He patted the bundle of papers.

Robyn pursed her lips. The interviews with Liam Carrington and his sister were hopeless. She'd been unable to prise any information from either of them. She crossed her fingers that her latest hunch was accurate and a search of their home would yield black fibres that matched those at both murder scenes.

She steeled herself, entered the darkened room adjacent to the room and tapped on the glass. 'Bring them in.'

Matt, standing on the other side of the glass, nodded. The door opened and five women walked in and stood in a line.

Tory was sitting once again in the room with Robyn. She leant forward and nodded. 'I'm pretty sure that's her. The one wearing jeans and a white jumper. She walked like that too. Confident-like.'

'Miss Goode, are you confirming that you recognise the first woman in the line?'

'Yes, I am.'

She had identified Ella Fox.

※

Robyn ran through her deliberations with Matt, voicing what was in her head.

'If Tory Goode is correct, Ella Fox was somewhere in the vicinity of Tessa Hall's house on the sixteenth. Unless she has a good explanation for being there, we have to consider her a likely suspect. She admitted she disliked Tessa and had warned her off Liam. There was a fingernail found at the scene of the crime, which might be evidence we can use, but it takes time to get DNA results and we don't have that much time. Forensics found no weapon and no fingerprints that match either hers or Liam Carrington's at the crime scene, so to sum up, we have no concrete evidence she was ever inside the house.

'Let me run a theory past you: Ella Fox left home undetected before 6 a.m., drove Liam's Audi to Barton-under-Needwood, parked out of sight and pretended to jog to Tessa's house. Either Tessa was expecting her or was unfazed by Ella's arrival, and opened the door to her. Whatever was said secured Ella's entry to the property, where she attacked and killed Tessa.'

Robyn dragged her hands over the back of her neck. 'What I can't fathom for the life of me is why? It can't be over Liam. Tessa wasn't involved with him. And it can't be about the lottery money because Tessa didn't tell anyone about it and wasn't spending it. It's not enough, is it, Matt? Her brief will laugh and say it's conjecture. In less than an hour, she'll be out of here. I can't hold her for much longer. Any suggestions? I'm getting desperate.'

'I'm as stumped as you. We have to find something else that connects her to that location and crime, especially as we have nothing that places her at the other murder scenes. Can we speed up the DNA findings on the fingernail?'

'Forensics are overburdened, just like us. It's going to take five to ten days at best to get a result.'

'How about I head to Yoxall and join the search team there? Might help.'

Robyn rubbed her neck, keeping her hands in place. Ella's presence in Barton-under-Needwood might be perfectly innocent. Another vision of Astra passed through her head. She couldn't get this wrong. 'Yes. That's a good idea. I'm not keen to even hold her for twenty-four hours if we have nothing more than this. She's got a child to look after. Matt, what if she and Liam Carrington aren't involved in this at all, and Roger Jenkinson and Juliet Fallows are our perps?'

'I don't think so. '

'What makes you so sure?'

Matt's eyes twinkled. 'You have the best instincts of any copper I know.' He headed for the door, pausing to grab at the packet of biscuits from Anna's desk, then halted. 'What if we tracked Ella's mobile for the days in question?'

'Already done. She must have left it at home each time she went out. It didn't move from the house. If she's guilty, she's been pretty clever, leaving it there.'

'Then we need some way of extracting a confession from one of them, or pray for divine intervention.' With that, he left.

A few minutes later, DCI Flint appeared at the door.

'DI Carter.'

He drew himself to his full height and stared ahead at the office door. 'There's no easy way of saying this. Juliet Fallows was found dead behind a VW garage in Tamworth a few hours ago. She was shot in the face. It took a while to identify her body. She wasn't carrying any identification. Early indicators are it's the same type of bullet used to kill Henry Gregson.'

Robyn stared hard at him. Juliet hadn't run off, nor was she in hiding with Roger Jenkinson. The same person who'd murdered Tessa, Anthony and Henry had undoubtedly murdered her too. A dull thudding began in her temple. Flint waited for her to speak but she kept her counsel.

'I've requested all details and information to be sent directly to you and your team. Officers have been dispatched to inform the next of kin and will handle all that side of it. I want you to concentrate on catching the murderer. That's all.'

'Yes, sir.'

He walked away, his head high, without any further words. Robyn cursed the fact she hadn't had sufficient evidence to prevent Juliet's death. It was crushing to think she might still be alive if Robyn had acted more quickly. She balled her fists and kicked out at the wall with a low growl. Then she dropped onto the nearest desk, head in hands. If only she'd acted sooner. She thought of Terence and Steph and how she'd let them, and Juliet, down. She shut her eyes and tried to banish their faces but they remained fixed in her mind's eye.

She had no idea how long she'd sat there. She waited until the anger began to subside and she could draw on her reserves. She had to lead her officers and she had to catch the killer, or killers. She'd bang them to rights for certain. She owed it to those relatives left behind, to her team, and to herself. Her mobile rang and dragged her back to the present. It was David.

'There's no sign of Anna, guv. Her car's not here and there's no one answering the door at Naomi's house.

'Ask about. See if anyone saw anything. I'm on my way.'

CHAPTER SIXTY-TWO

THEN

Henry knows the truth – or he thinks he does. He found out about the syndicate because somebody – Ailsa Pelligrini – let it slip to Lauren, who mentioned it to him, and now he's put two and two together. He sold Ella our actual lottery tickets, because I'm not allowed to sell to a relative, and knows full well we played the same numbers every week, and that we never purchased lucky dip tickets.

Henry doesn't say a word while I confess I'd stolen a winning ticket and passed it off as the syndicate's. I don't tell him who the ticket really belonged to. I say it was a man I hadn't seen before. When I finish explaining why I did it, he gives me a kindly look – a look full of support and compassion – and a volcano of sorrow erupts from within. The desire to be like him, to have a normal life, hope, and love is too much to bear.

The thing is I never wanted to steal the ticket, but everyone was so pleased at the thought. They really wanted me to help them. Mr Hawkins – Anthony – put an arm around my shoulders and whispered, 'You're the only one who could do this. Do it for us all. Sid would have wanted you to help us. Sid gave you a chance, didn't he? Now we need you to give us one.'

I was startled by the mention of Sid. Would he have wanted me to help these people? I figured he would. They all looked at me with such expectation in their eyes, I felt my resolve weaken. And then there was Ella. I had to do it for her and Astra. I wasn't bringing in anywhere near enough money to look after us all. I'd had another demand for council tax I couldn't pay, and Ella had gone round to McNamara to pay him like she usually does when we can't afford the rent. The thought of her with that man made me want to vomit. Anthony smiled again and I sort of nodded.

'That's the spirit. We knew we could count on you.'

Suddenly everyone was smiling and looking at me differently. They needed me. For the first time, since Sid, I felt wanted and appreciated. I decided there and then I'd do it. I'd help us all to a better life.

The following day, I knew I couldn't pull it off. It would be too risky. I phoned Hawkins and told him so. His voice was ice-cold. 'Oh, yes you will, lad,' he hissed. 'If you don't, I'll tell everybody about your past. I'll phone up that store of yours and tell the owners that you stole from your employer, Sid – a man who'd given you a chance to prove yourself – and that you left him dying, to make good your escape. I bet MiniMarkt don't know about your past. How old were you when you were convicted? Oh yes, only seventeen. Your record will have been wiped clean after five and a half years, and you've never told them about it, have you?'

I'm panicked. It's true. MiniMarkt have no idea.

'That's not what happened,' I stuttered. 'You know I didn't steal from Sid.'

'No, lad. I know you were a nasty little shit who robbed a good man, and who got what you deserved. You were a whining, pathetic individual in jail and you're still pathetic now. I'll ruin your life. I'll tell everyone on the team what you really are and you'll be ostracised again. You know how that feels, don't you? Imagine what somebody like Roger would do to you if he finds out about your past. He can't tolerate wimpy tosspots like you. I only have to "accidentally" divulge some information about you and your disgusting antics in jail, and

you'll be watching your back ever more. So, what's it to be? Do I make that phone call to MiniMarkt, or do you toughen up again and get hold of that ticket?'

※

Now, I can't bear to think about what I've done. Looking at Henry, I realise I've made a monumental error in trusting those people. Henry has been more of a friend than any of them. He asks about the others who have benefited from my theft. In my heightened state of emotion I tell him, explain they're none the wiser, that they're honest people. He throws me a sad look.

'When money is involved, people can become very dishonest.'

He requests their phone numbers, and, eager to rectify my wrongdoing and to win back his trust, I pass them to him, all the while terrified that my world will unravel. I have to trust in Henry.

He's going to ring them, one by one, and tell them they have no right to their share of the jackpot. He'll tell them the ticket isn't rightfully theirs and they should return the money. He's going to give us all a chance to prove our worth.

CHAPTER SIXTY-THREE

DAY TEN – THURSDAY, 23 FEBRUARY, EVENING

David had got hold of a set of spare keys for Naomi's house from a neighbour. Robyn arrived to find him by the front door. He shook his head.

'No sign of anybody.'

Robyn followed him into the kitchen and took in the dirty dishes in the sink and a half-drunk mug of tea on the kitchen top.

'Somebody left in a hurry,' she said.

'Naomi?'

'Could be. There's only one mug. Neighbour see anything?'

'Nothing.'

Robyn heaved a sigh and shut her eyes, trying to picture exactly what might have taken place.

'Is Naomi's car still in the street?'

'Yes.'

'Then she might be in Anna's car and even taken her hostage. I know it sounds crazy but it isn't like Anna to not stay in touch. Something's happened to her.'

She marched out to the back garden, surrounded by fence panels. There were no places to hide here. She turned on her heel and walked back through the house and down the front path, following it to the road, hunting for signs of a struggle. A couple of metres down the road an object caught her eye. She donned plastic gloves and lifted it. She recognised its plastic protector. She called for David who raced towards her and let out a groan. Robyn was holding Anna's mobile.

She'd rung DCI Flint on her way to Bramshall, and as the first blue lights appeared down the street, she faced the sickening reality that one of her own was in danger. This ought to eclipse everything. Her search for Anna should take precedence. Although Flint's voice had echoed her own concern, he'd insisted on the contrary.

'Robyn, I'll arrange extra assistance immediately but I want you to leave this to them. Return to the station and continue with your investigation. You can't hold Liam Carrington and Ella Fox for much longer. I understand your anxiety but we'll find her.'

Where could Anna be? If Robyn were Naomi Povey or Roger Jenkinson, where would she hide? It was impossible to second-guess their movements. DCI Flint was right. She had to get back to the station. She would have to leave this to the officers involved in the manhunt for Anna, Naomi and Jenkinson.

'David, I want you to keep me updated on this. Keep communication channels open at all times.'

She drew away from the now busy street as more police cars arrived, heart weighing in her chest. She forced her focus back onto the case. They had three definite murders to deal with and one suspicious death. While Roger Jenkinson might be guilty of murdering Henry Gregson, there were still two suspects back at the station who were somehow involved in the lottery ticket theft and possibly even the other murders. Ella Fox had been in Barton-under-Needwood the morning Tessa was killed. Robyn desperately needed more evidence. She couldn't charge either Liam or Ella until she had it, and she couldn't return to the search for Anna until she'd got to the bottom of their involvement. With a determined expression on her face, she drove towards Yoxall. She might not be able to look for Anna but she could help speed up the search at Carrington's house.

Within fifteen minutes she pulled onto Liam Carrington's drive. The curtains weren't drawn, and lights in every room revealed figures hunched over cupboards, tables and drawers, sorting through the couple's life. Mitz was at the back of the property rummaging through the tiny cluttered shed. Petrol cans and boxes of tools were strewn outside on the patch of lawn behind it. Robyn checked in with them. She couldn't bring herself to tell Mitz about Anna. It would serve no purpose other than to upset him.

'Nothing so far. It's filled with man-junk,' said Mitz, picking up a paint stick used for repairing paint chips on cars. 'There are boxes and boxes of cleaning cloths and car shampoos and waxes. I've been asking myself if Carrington owned a fleet of cars or if he was moonlighting as a car valet.'

Robyn gave a half-hearted smile. She glanced at the Audi A4 on the drive. 'You checked it, didn't you?'

'Yes. Inside, and the boot, and underneath it in case something had been taped to the underside. It's clean,' said Mitz, picking up a bottle, unscrewing the cap and sniffing.

'It's unusual these days for couples to only have one car between them. It's quite an old model too. Done almost 150,000 miles. It'd be a right pain if it broke down. They'd have to use public transport or get a taxi. I wouldn't trust such an old car,' he said.

Robyn blinked suddenly. Anna had checked all the automatic number plate recognition points closest to Cannock Chase around the time of Gregson's murder. She'd been looking for privately owned vehicles passing through them, in the hope one would belong to the killer. Nobody had been searching for a taxi. She called the station and spoke to the duty officer.

'Is there anyone who can run an ANPR check for me?'

'Tom Shearer's the only person available. He came in about ten minutes ago. I'll put you through.'

Shearer was surprised to hear her voice but listened without comment while she explained quickly why she needed to second him. 'So, can you check through the footage of all the cars that passed through the ANPR points around Cannock Chase on the fourteenth? See if any of them were taxis. Ring me back when you find one.'

'I wouldn't do this for anyone else,' he said. 'But seeing as you asked so nicely—'

'Thanks, Tom. I owe you.'

'Yes, you do,' he said before disconnecting.

Robyn marched across the tarmac drive and directly into the kitchen, acknowledging the officer searching through cupboards.

Matt was in Astra's playroom in the attic, hunched over, his huge frame filling the small space as he lifted boxes and toys and scoured for the evidence they so desperately needed.

The low walls of the room had been painted in a cheerful yellow. A picture made of scrabble letters that spelt the name Astra was fixed to the end wall, below it a fat cushion, and various scattered books. This was her reading corner. The room was small but every fitted cupboard in the spaces in the eaves was crammed with children's paraphernalia – toys, books, games and clothes. An enormous teddy bear with a smiling face and large bow tie sat propped up next to a chest of drawers. It was surrounded by numerous plastic toys and activity centres, most of which were tired hand-me-downs.

'There's so much stuff,' said Robyn.

'Poppy's the same. She's got more clothes and possessions than either of us. You can't help it. You see something and buy it for them. You just want them to have the things you didn't have,' Matt explained.

Robyn opened one of the drawers and felt her heart lurch at the tiny outfits she found. If only, she thought. She felt around, moved the endless neat piles of jumpers and cardigans and shook each one of them. Matt dealt with cupboards filled with piles of boxes. He pulled them out patiently, sorting through the contents. Once she finished with the drawers, Robyn had run out of places to search. She lifted the gaily-coloured rug and felt along the wooden floor for loose boards. There was nothing.

Matt began to pack up the boxes again. Robyn stared at the cheerful bear. She'd owned a teddy bear but it had been nowhere near as huge as this one. She wandered across to it. It was far too large for a child to lift. Astra probably climbed on it. She picked it up. It was surprisingly soft and lighter than she imagined it would be. It was strangely comforting, and for a second she felt an urge to hug it. She gave it a quick squeeze before putting it back but stopped in mid-motion. It hadn't felt right. It hadn't felt squidgy enough. There'd been something hard inside it. She lifted the bear again and searched the seams along its back. The stitching here had been repaired with a different-coloured thread, a shade darker than the original. She licked her lips, suddenly dry. They wouldn't hide a gun inside a child's toy, would they? There was only one way to find out. 'Matt,' she said, her voice filled with hushed urgency. 'I need a pair of scissors.'

With trembling fingers she unpicked the stitching until she'd created a gap large enough to push her hand inside the bear. She eased it through the stuffing until she grazed plastic. Her eyes widened. This was crazy. She gripped the object and drew back her hand. The disappointment was crushing. She held a round plastic device.

Matt let out a heavy sigh. 'I know what that is. It's from the Build-a-Bear workshop store. It's for a recorded message that's put inside the bear before it gets stuffed, sewn and completed. We had a bear made for Poppy and one like that inserted. When the child squeezes the bear, it sets it off. Poppy's says, "I'm Arnie, I love you."' He took the object from Robyn and shook it. 'This one's broken.'

Crushed and frustrated, Robyn cast about the room. If there was no weapon concealed in this house, she'd have to work hard at getting confessions from her suspects. It was all too much – Anna had disappeared, Roger was on the loose, and she couldn't find enough evidence to convict any suspects. She straightened up. Defeat wasn't a possibility. She'd strip this place if she had to in order to find something that would give her answers. Her eyes lighted upon a pale-pink box marked 'Treasures'. It was three times the size of a large shoebox.

'Checked that?' she asked Matt.

He confirmed he had. 'Keepsakes,' he said. 'Her first baby boots, book, toys. That sort of thing.'

The tugging at her heart drove her to peer inside. The pain of losing her own child had never left her, and she had no idea what made her look inside a box filled with memories of a healthy baby, other than a desire to know what it would have been like, had her own child lived. The pale-pink baby boots took her breath away. They were so tiny. The white Babygro embroidered with three silver stars was so soft Robyn wanted to hold it to her cheek. She replaced the item before the overwhelming sadness that was bubbling inside consumed her. She lifted the box by its handles to make room to search under the carpets and checked herself. For a box that contained only light items, it felt a little on the heavy side. She replaced it and lifted the lid once more. This time she removed each object: the boots, the Babygro, a hairbrush and toy felt giraffe. She pulled out a newborn's blanket and a soft rattle bearing a picture of a rabbit. Underneath she found a book entitled *Astra* and two silver teaspoons. With the box empty, she lifted it again and shook it.

'I think there's something in here,' she said.

'I can't hear anything rattling about. It could just be weighted so it doesn't collapse. It's only made of cardboard.'

Robyn studied the interior of the box and let out a gentle sigh. Matt was right and it would be awful if she were wrong again. She'd already destroyed a beloved teddy bear. This was a precious item and she didn't want to do the same to it. The slight kink in the corner of the base made her challenge these thoughts. She would be able to lift enough of the base to confirm it was, as Matt had suggested, weighted, without ruining the box. She scratched carefully at the slightly elevated corner, using only the tips of her nails until she felt it give and could get leverage on it. Pinching it between her fingertips, she lifted it. It had been firmly pressed into the base of the box. Robyn persisted, driven by her intuition. There had to be something other than baby memorabilia inside the box. *A weighted strip?* She brushed that idea away. The cardboard base eased from the edges of the box, making it easier to peel back. Robyn could concentrate on nothing but the task, all the while wondering what she'd do next if she were wrong yet again.

Time stood still as Robyn took in the enormity of her find. A bubble-wrapped object lay beneath the false bottom. She lifted it to the light, veins fizzing.

'Holy shit! You were spot on,' said Matt in an awed tone. 'It's a gun.'

The Smith & Wesson Webley in her hands was surely the same weapon used to kill Henry Gregson. It hadn't been dumped, as they feared. She had the evidence she needed. She could finally close this case. She'd get back to the station immediately. She was about to speak to Matt when a shout from the couple's bedroom drew their attention.

'I might have something here.'

Robyn and Matt raced towards the room, now in disarray, with bedding upturned and clothes heaped in a pile on the floor. An officer was wrestling a panel away from under a set of fitted drawers. 'It's loose,' she explained as the panel came away.

Robyn bent down and felt inside the space under the drawers. Her fingers immediately brushed against a plastic bag that she withdrew and passed to Matt. His face broke into a broad smile.

'One mobile phone, undoubtedly belonging to Liam Carrington,' he said, holding up the Nokia. 'I suspect it's the same pay-as-you-go phone Henry Gregson called the morning he died.'

CHAPTER SIXTY-FOUR

'Do you recognise this, Mr Carrington?' Robyn held the mobile phone up.

Liam nodded.

'DI Carter has shown Mr Carrington a pay-as-you-go mobile phone,' Matt said clearly for the recording device.

Robyn spoke again. 'Could you confirm your response for the benefit of the tape recorder please? Do you recognise this mobile phone?'

'Yes,' said Carrington.

'Did you use this mobile device for conversations with Henry Gregson?'

'Yes.'

'When was the last time you used it?'

'On the fourteenth. Henry rang me.'

'Why did he ring you on this number and not your usual mobile?'

'I had to keep the calls secret. I didn't want Ella to find out.'

'Why not?'

'I didn't want her involved in any of it.'

'When you say you didn't want her involved in any of it, what do you mean by that?' Robyn stared intently at Carrington.

The man licked his lips and spoke. 'I'd cheated the system. I took a winning ticket from a couple in MiniMarkt, told them they hadn't won anything, and pocketed the ticket myself. I couldn't claim the jackpot without arousing suspicion, so I pretended the syndicate, of which I was a member, had won it. Henry found out and was going to give me up to the police. I didn't want Ella to find out – it would have freaked her out. That's why I got the second phone, so Henry could ring me on it and talk it over. We had several conversations about it. I was hoping he would change his mind and not shop me.'

'But he threatened to do so.'

'He came to my house while Ella was out and said he'd decided to tell the lottery people and the MiniMarkt owners.'

Robyn folded her arms and studied Carrington's face. He licked his lips again. She nodded towards Matt, who placed the gun on the table in front of Carrington and his solicitor.

'Is this the weapon used to murder Henry Gregson on the fourteenth of February?'

'Yes.'

'Can you explain why it was found at your home, inside a memory box?'

'I put it there. I hid it. After I killed Henry.'

'You admit to killing Henry Gregson?'

'Yes. I arranged to meet him on Cannock Chase. I hid behind a tree and waited for him to arrive. He didn't see me at first. I walked forwards and waved at him. He lowered the window to call me over and I shot him. Then I drove home and hid the gun.'

'You drove to Cannock Chase?'

'Yes.'

'And what time would this have been? You were spotted around the village at twelve.'

'I don't know. After Henry said he was going to tell the lottery people about me stealing the ticket, I lost track of time. I rang him while I was walking about the village. Astra was tired that morning and had dozed off in her buggy, so I put her in the back of the car and drove to Cannock Chase without thinking about it.'

'And you pulled into the car park, walked up to where Henry was waiting for you, shot him and drove home?'

'Yes, except I didn't go to the car park. I drove to the clearing where Henry was waiting. There's a lay-by close by. I pulled over there,' he said with some satisfaction.

Robyn continued staring at him. 'That's indeed very true. There is a lay-by close to the clearing where Henry Gregson was found dead, but you did not drive to it. Your car did not go through any of our automatic vehicle recognition points. If you had taken that route, it would have shown up.'

'I went a different route,' he said quickly.

'There are points all around that area. It would have been impossible to have approached the lay-by without your car being seen.'

'I did go there. You can't prove I didn't. I killed them all.'

'Are you also confessing to the murders of Tessa Hall, Juliet Fallows and Anthony Hawkins?'

'I am. I killed them and I shot Henry.'

'But you said you hid the gun in the memory box after you shot Henry?'

Liam blinked rapidly before answering. 'I took it out again to kill Juliet. Then put it back.'

Robyn nodded then spoke. 'I'm afraid I don't believe your version of events.' She pushed forwards a photograph.

'DI Carter is showing Mr Carrington a photograph taken at one fifteen on fourteenth February.'

Liam's face gave nothing away.

'This is a photograph of a car that passed through one of the automatic vehicle recognition points at one fifteen. As you can see, it's a taxi from A111 Taxis, based in Burton-on-Trent. The driver remembers the passenger who booked this taxi from Burton-on-

Trent to Cannock Chase via Yoxall quite clearly and was able to give us a detailed description. The company also has records of the same individual who booked a trip from Cannock Chase to Yoxall an hour later. They have records of the times this passenger was picked up and deposited. If you look very closely at the photograph, which has been enlarged, you'll see that passenger. Mr Carrington, can you explain why your sister, Ella Fox, was in that cab?'

CHAPTER SIXTY-FIVE

THEN

Henry phoned the quiz team members as he threatened to do. It transpired I wasn't the only one driven by greed and desire for wealth because they chose not to believe him. Everything would have been fine too had it not been for Tessa. She'd been ruminating over Henry's phone call and had decided to leave the country for a new start. She intended ringing each member of the syndicate to tell us of her decision and advise us to do the same in case the call hadn't been a hoax.

As it happened she rang me first, and Ella answered the phone. Ella calmed her down and advised her not to tell the others of her plans. There was no point in alarming them. She told her the phone call was definitely a ploy to cheat her of her money. She'd talk to me.

And she does.

'You total half-wit,' she snaps. 'You've probably ruined everything.'

'No, I can fix it. I'll talk to Henry. He won't let me down. He loves us. He adores Astra. He won't spoil it for us. Everyone has a price. He and Lauren want to have fertility treatment. It's really expensive. I'll offer him the money so they can start the programme. He won't be able to refuse.'

She offers a smile that distorts her face, pulling it into a grimace, exaggerated by the horrid scar.

'At last, you're using your brains. Make sure he takes the money. I'll call on Tessa and make sure she keeps silent about her intentions.

If this all becomes exposed, you'll be the first to pay for it. I knew they couldn't be trusted.'

※

Ella leaves to visit a woman she knows – Cassie – who's in hospital. Five minutes later, the pay-as-you-go mobile rings. It's his number. I answer.

'On my way,' is all he says.

Astra is colouring a picture of me and Ella and her, all holding hands, in front of a big house. She's drawn a massive sun above the roof, but when I tell her it's too large, she gives me a happy smile. I hope she'll help win Henry over. He spies her when he comes in, and she drops her crayon immediately and races into his arms, shouting his name in delight. He crouches down and chats quietly to her and I think it's going to be all right.

'I've decided to notify the lottery authorities,' he says from his position on the floor, without any preamble.

I'm at a loss for words. This isn't how I planned the conversation. I was supposed to offer him a share of the jackpot, for IVF treatment. I know how badly he and Lauren want children.

'No, please don't,' I say. I don't know how to convince him. My thoughts tangle themselves and words stick in my throat. Finally, I blurt out, 'This isn't just about me. It's about Ella. She desperately needs the money for plastic surgery. Don't do this to us. She can't go through life the way she is.'

He distracts Astra by handing her a red crayon and asking her to draw his car. As she does so, her face screwed in concentration, he speaks.

'I'm sorry for Ella but there are lots of people who manage with disfigurements far worse than hers. I can't stand by knowing you've stolen from somebody and duped others to be part of your plan. I'm sorry, Liam. I have to report it.'

'But I'll go to jail. What about Ella and Astra?'

'I doubt they'd be found guilty of anything. They're not party to this. You ought to take responsibility for the entire unfortunate incident.

Confess and say no one else other than you knew that ticket was stolen. That way, you won't be involving the others you hoodwinked.'

'No, you don't understand. I can't leave Ella alone.'

His face changes, lines crease his forehead and suddenly he seems so much older than his years. 'Of course you can,' he says. 'She'll be fine.'

'No, you don't understand. She needs me. She can't live without me. I look after her.'

'She'll get help – she has us – and I'm sure she'll find a job to see her through.'

'I don't mean look after her in that way,' I yell. 'I help her when she has the nightmares and is shaking and crying with fear. It's me she turns to when she can't get out of bed for fear he'll find her.' Of course, I'm lying. She doesn't get the nightmares any more. They stopped years ago but I'm not thinking clearly – desperate for Henry to suddenly see sense, tell me it's okay and he won't report me – and words tumble without me having any control over them.

He sighs. 'A doctor will be able to help her. She needs professional help. With treatment she'll get over the attack, Liam. She's stronger than you think. The knife attack was random. That person won't be looking for her.'

'I'm not talking about the knife attack. I mean Johnny Hounslow. She still has nightmares about killing him. She sees him in her nightmares, coming back for revenge.' My mouth falls open. What have I said? Henry blinks slowly like a reptile. His face closes.

CHAPTER SIXTY-SIX

DAY TEN – THURSDAY, 23 FEBRUARY, NIGHT

Robyn's eyes were squeezed shut. Mitz hadn't spoken since they'd set off together, him behind the wheel, face set tightly. She'd had no need to justify her decision not to tell him about Anna's disappearance. He'd been a policeman long enough to understand how the system worked. His priority had been to search Liam Carrington's premises, but with Ella and Liam in custody, both he and Robyn had joined the hunt for Anna.

It was half past eleven and they ought to have felt exhausted but both were completely fixated on finding Anna. The roads were eerily empty of traffic, the world filled with dark shapes and shadows broken only by the beam from their headlights as it swept along the roads, the constant roar of their car engine the soundtrack to a silent movie.

Robyn replayed the conversations she'd had with Naomi Povey, searching for a clue as to her whereabouts. The woman hadn't known about the lottery money. Had she been angry with Jenkinson when he finally showed up or had she forced Anna into accompanying her to wherever he was hiding? Mitz's voice interrupted her thoughts.

'I really care about her, you know?'

Robyn looked across at his face, worn out from the horrendously long day but still handsome even with a dark five o'clock shadow. 'I know. She feels the same.'

Robyn could see the worry etched across his forehead and she cared too much about him to hide that knowledge from him.

He didn't reply but his face softened a little. Robyn returned to her musings. Anna had been in her car, possibly on the phone to David, when something caught her eye. She'd opened the car door. At some point, she'd dropped her phone. Anna had skilled reflexes and was trained to protect herself. It was unlikely she'd have been attacked, and if she were, she'd have fought tooth and nail. Besides, Robyn and David had hunted for signs of a struggle, blood splashes and torn clothing, and found nothing outside Naomi's house. Could Naomi have used a firearm to threaten Anna? A flicker of something made Robyn sit up. The main beam swung to the left, illuminating a verge and startling a rabbit, eyes caught in the spotlight, whiskers twitching in fear. The beam trained back onto the road, the rabbit now behind them.

Open fields gave way to high hedges and coal-black tree trunks with branches like black coral overhanging the lane. Roger might have raced off to the Peak District to hide out there. He knew the area very well and would be familiar with remote areas where he could remain hidden for days. Naomi, on the other hand, hated the outdoors. She'd have gone somewhere she felt safe. Where might that be? *Firearms.* Roger Jenkinson and Naomi Povey shared a love of shooting and had both spent many hours at the shooting club at Bramshall. She stabbed at her smartphone, hunting for information on the club, and scrolled through the pages on events, gift vouchers, corporate events and parties, then drew a sharp breath. The club offered cottages for hen and stag parties.

'Mitz. Head towards the shooting club – Bramshall Leisure.' She put a call in to David to meet them there and closed her eyes again. This time she prayed with all her strength she was right, and they weren't too late.

※

The sign to the club was at the start of a single-track road and blocked by a locked, five-bar wooden gate, a code panel to the side.

'We'll walk it,' said Robyn. 'The car will only alert them to our arrival if they're here. Put in a call to the station, tell them where we are and get them to alert the owners of our presence. Ask them for the entry code though. Give it ten minutes, and then follow me. If you've got the code by then, bring the car. I'm going on ahead.' Placing a foot on the lower bar of the gate, she jumped over with ease and ran light-footed up the track, guided only by the beam from her torch.

The skies were clear and a half-moon aided her navigation. She could see the roof of a large building – the clubhouse – and raced towards it. The area was vast, some seventy acres, she'd read. She pushed away thoughts of how insurmountable a search it might be.

She left the track, dropped down a grassy bank and approached the clubhouse from the rear. Pressing her face against a glass window, she made out items for sale in a shop – protective clothing, skeet vests and high-vis jackets were hanging closest to the window. The shop would be alarmed. Little chance Naomi was in there.

She skimmed the side of the building looking for any signs of entry. There was nothing. The car park in front of the building was empty. She slipped away along a path marked 'Cottage One', desperate for more luck. Around her was stillness broken by the occasional sounds of the night – an occasional rustling in the under-growth, a distant bark of a farm dog or fox – each noise bringing her to a halt. From somewhere behind her came the quiet purring of an engine. Mitz was en route to the clubhouse, creeping along the track, headlights off. She turned, signalled him briefly with the beam of her torch so he would know which direction she'd taken.

The wide path meandered past shooting ranges bounded by wooden railings and soon opened out to a monochrome world, a patchwork of dark and light fields and thick dark copses of woods. Below her, a body of water glistened in the silvery light of the moon, and set beside it was a stone cottage. Robyn's eyes, now accustomed to the dark of the night, spotted a sliver of dull orange glow that escaped a crack in drawn curtains. Somebody was inside the cottage. She left the path to take a more direct route. She moved gracefully, her many years of exercise paying dividends as she leapt down the hillside as surefootedly as a mountain goat, her breathing controlled, senses on high alert. She let out a silent breath and crouched down in the damp grass, getting a feel of the place and working out how best to handle the situation.

A light scrabbling alerted her to Mitz making his way towards her.

'Here,' she hissed.

He dropped down on his haunches beside her and handed over a pair of night-vision goggles.

'See, that's why I love having you on my team,' she quipped. 'You think of everything.'

'That's Anna's car,' whispered Mitz. 'Over there on the far side.'

'We should wait for backup. We'll be able to handle it better with more men. Radio in and confirm her location and request assistance. And Mitz, don't worry. We'll get her out.'

Mitz was picking his way back to the squad car when the cottage's front door suddenly flew open with a clatter that made him turn back, and a figure dashed out of the house, arms pumping as it made its escape.

Both he and Robyn sprinted from their positions towards the fleeing individual who stumbled in the darkness, fell to their knees, and then pushed back up and ran again. Robyn slipped and slid as she tried to gain footing on the slope, her ability to navigate the ground lost in her anxiety to reach the person. 'Anna,' she called.

The figure paused, turned towards her voice and raised a hand. 'Help.'

'We're coming,' shouted Mitz.

Both hurtled towards her. Spiteful branches on prickly bushes ripped at Robyn's skin as she propelled herself down the slope. Anna, a blur of movement, was scrambling up the slope in their direction. She'd only covered a few metres before a roar went up inside the cottage and another figure, this time Roger Jenkinson, filled the doorframe. His head turned left and right and his eyes locked onto Anna's fleeing form. He raised a gun.

Robyn yelled, 'No!'

There was a flash of the explosion a split second before she heard the gunfire. Anna dropped to her knees, arms thrown up, and fell forward.

'Anna!' Mitz's cry filled the sky and a thousand birds from the lake joined him with flapping and screeches that resonated around the hillside; a thousand plaintive cries that ripped through the night air and tore into Robyn's soul. She pounded down the hill. Mitz made for Anna. Robyn set her sights on Roger Jenkinson as he sprinted for Anna's car.

'Stop. Police,' she shouted. 'It's over, Jenkinson.'

Her words were lost, drowned out by the screeching of wildfowl. Never had she run so fast. She stumbled and tripped and rolled a few feet to the bottom of the hillside, then bounced up and hurtled after the man, now climbing into the car. He started the engine and drove off, Robyn in his wake, sprinting for all she was worth. She refused to give in and dug deeper, urging her legs to propel her faster, but the car pulled away from her, up the track to freedom.

Robyn drew to a halt. Her lungs were ready to explode, her heart shattered. Emotion blinded her eyes and clouded her thoughts, and then, through the fog of tears that had welled, she spotted distant blue flashing lights, picking their way down the track towards Anna's car.

There was another route to the cottage. The assistance Mitz had requested had arrived and taken both roads. They'd surely capture

Roger Jenkinson. He wouldn't escape this time. She turned towards the cottage, door still open and light pooling in front of it. *Naomi.* She might still be in hiding. The thought galvanised her into action and she hastened to the cottage, hoping the woman hadn't also fled the scene. It was plausible she was biding her time to make good her escape. The door led directly into a sitting room filled with beams and farmhouse charm that held no appeal for Robyn at the moment. Outside, the birds were settling back down on a dark grey lake, unaffected by the tremendous loss on the hillside. Robyn stood in the shadows and waited silently. The noises outside ebbed, and in their place came a soft thud. Naomi was still here.

Robyn moved stealthily around the perimeter of the wall, eased into the adjacent room and stood back against the wall. She silenced her mind, relaxed her shoulders and listened. There it was again. A muffled sound. It wasn't coming from this room. It was further away. She sneaked back into the sitting room and again tiptoed to the next door, coaxing it open inch by inch. She found herself in an open-plan kitchen. To the left was another door.

She crept silently forward, alert and ready for the unexpected and prepared for Naomi to burst from the room, wielding a second gun. The door was latched shut. She thumbed the latch gently, inhaled slowly then pushed hard and threw the door back as hard as she could. It exploded against the wall with a crash and Robyn threw herself onto the floor, anticipating a shot. There was none. As her eyes adjusted to the darkness of this room, she made out the broken shutter hanging loosely on the back window that knocked against the window with the breeze.

'Guv,' Mitz's voice came in rasps, 'I've been shouting for you. It's not Anna up there. It's Naomi and she's fine. The bullet missed her altogether.'

'Does she know where Anna is?' asked Robyn.

'Yes. They left her outside a clinic in Uttoxeter.'

CHAPTER SIXTY-SEVEN

THEN

He's lost in the past, wondering if everything will ever be okay again. He's made such a mess of it all. The memories flood back now. It's like he's eighteen all over again. Liam shuts his eyes and remembers that night long ago…

⁂

The young man has chewed his thumbnail down to the quick. Ever since his fruitless trip to Newcastle-under-Lyme, he's felt edgy. He needs to forget about Johnny and move on with his life.

He'll have to deal with it another way, but as yet, he can't think what that way might be. He puts the television on low volume. It's 8 p.m. and his sister is already in bed. She's not been sleeping well lately. It's partly this course she's chosen to do – some qualification so she can look after children – which has brought back all the memories of the abortion. She's lost weight and isn't eating. Mum's worried about her too and has threatened to take her to the doctor, but she refuses to go. Mum's got enough on her plate without hassling her offspring. She's had a recent job appraisal that hasn't gone well. She's anxious about retaining her position and has been in a filthy bad mood for the last few days. It's a relief she's working at the pub tonight. At least he hasn't got to listen to her complaints.

On television, a doctor is giving a family gathered around a bed some bad news. He flicks through the channels and heaves a sigh. What a crap life this is. He should be doing something more on a Saturday night than watching rubbish on television. The hammering on the front door comes as a surprise. He mutes the television and answers the door without any thought other than to stop the noise that will wake his sister. There's a rush of air accompanied by an angry roar, and a sharp pain in his hand as the door flies open, smashing him backwards against the wall. His feet scrabble against the floor as he tries to stand before he's pounced upon. Johnny Hounslow has the advantage and strikes before he can gain leverage. He's flattened against the floor, a fist raised above him.

'You fucking wanker. Thought you could track me down, did you? I heard some twat was looking for me, an old schoolmate who wanted to see me before he left to go abroad. I knew it was you. He described you perfectly. I warned you to stay away from me. I told you what I'd do to you and your sister.'

He tries to throw Johnny off but fails.

Johnny sneers. 'Fucking tosser,' he says again. He circles his legs helplessly, kicking out wildly, but his feet don't connect with his attacker. His arms are pinned onto the floor and he can't wriggle out from under the weight pushing them back, and then, Johnny hoists him up by the front of his sweatshirt and slams his head against the wall. Splinters of light burst like popping fireworks in his head. He fights the pain. He mustn't lose consciousness. Johnny drops on top of him, hatred oozing from him, and his thick forearm across his windpipe. He grins malevolently and pushes harder, crushing his neck. He can't breathe.

'I'm going to fucking murder you,' Johnny snarls.

He has to save his sister. Tell her to get out. Johnny is mental. His legs flail, his brain is on fire. Johnny leers at him. 'Toss-er.'

The edges of his world darken as he's starved of air. He thinks he sees his sister – an angel in a nightshirt. She's holding a shining black *wand. He wants to tell her he loves her but he can't speak. A golden light surrounds her and he feels at peace. He shuts his eyes and allows oblivion to take him.*

光

Sitting now, on the floor with Astra, he wishes he could turn back time. If only he'd been stronger and had been the one to murder Johnny, things might have turned out differently. He owes his sister so much and has given her the only things he possesses – his undying love and his silence.

CHAPTER SIXTY-EIGHT

Mitz had been adamant about accompanying Anna to hospital in the ambulance. The paramedics had checked her over and said she was fine, but Robyn had insisted Anna be taken to the hospital for a complete check-up and observation. Mitz held Anna's hand as she lay on the gurney. Robyn stood on the ambulance step like a proud mother hen.

'I'm sorry,' said Anna again.

'If you apologise again, I'll have you fired,' said Robyn. 'You were only doing what I'd have done, and stupid as it was, I can't blame you for your actions. However, you are not, under any circumstance, to ever put us through this again. I'm going to chain you to the desk and your computer for all future investigations.' She smiled.

Robyn moved off the ambulance tailgate. It was time for Anna to leave. She raised a hand.

'No high jinks, you two. Especially you, Anna.'

'Promise,' said Anna, wearily.

'I'll make sure she behaves,' Mitz said. Robyn caught the look that passed between them and nodded goodbye.

The ambulance moved away. Robyn watched until it disappeared from view then continued standing, hands thrust deep into her pockets. The church clock struck three before falling silent. She let the silence wash over her, allowing the calm of the night to seep into her tired bones, before she slid back into her car. The night wasn't over for her yet. Roger Jenkinson and Ella Fox still had some explaining to do.

※

Roger Jenkinson was a blubbering, miserable wreck of a human, full of remorse for his actions that had been driven by fear and greed.

Robyn and Matt sat side by side in the interview room, waiting while he dabbed at tears.

'I've not known what to do since Tessa was murdered,' he said. 'It knocked me for six. I'd only spoken to her on Monday and she sounded so happy. She said she had something important to tell me. Something really special.'

Robyn said, 'Miss Hall was expecting a child. We have confirmed you were the father. I imagine that was the news she was going to give you.'

Roger made a guttural noise in his throat and choked back a sob. 'Deep down, I guessed it would be that. We'd talked about running off together, pooling our winnings and starting a family. I was waiting for the right time to let Naomi down gently.' He shook his head, unable to continue.

'I'd like to know what happened earlier today, sir. Before and after you abducted PC Shamash.'

'It wasn't intentional. Ever since Tessa, I've been anxious. When I heard Anthony had died too, I figured there was something amiss – two of our quizzing side dead in the space of two days – it seemed too much of a coincidence. I thought I'd take matters into my own hands and lay low. Naomi didn't know about the money. I didn't want her to find out. It's been hard enough to try and split up with her. If she knew about the money as well, I'd never have managed it. She was pissed off with me for going to the Peak District without telling her and has been pestering me ever since to meet up. I told her you suspected me of murdering Tessa and asked if I could hide out at her house for a while until it was all resolved. Of course, she agreed. I thought I'd be out of harm's way there. I took my guns for protection and moved into her house, but then your officer turned up and parked right outside.'

He shut his eyes to remember exactly what had happened…

☆

Naomi pulls into the street, gets out of her car and slams the door shut. She marches into the house and calls for him.

'You're right. The police do think you killed Tessa,' she says. 'They asked me if I knew where you were.'

'You didn't tell them though, did you?'

She smiles at him. 'Roger, of course not. We're a team. I look out for you and you look out for me.'

Naomi drops her coat on the back of the kitchen chair. 'You eaten?'

'I wasn't hungry,' says Roger, taking up his usual position in the siting room, where he has full view of the comings and goings outside. He's sure the bastard who killed Tessa will be after him too. It's probably the same person who rang him to tell him to give the lottery money back. Well, he can get stuffed. Roger isn't frightened of him. His gun is in the armchair. If anyone wants to try and take on Roger Jenkinson, they'll be in for a surprise. Suddenly, a silver Vauxhall pulls into view and draws up outside the house. He recognises the police officer. He's seen her at the station.

'Fuck. The cops are here.'

Naomi rushes into the room. 'It's that female PC. The bitch has followed me home. Bet she's hoping to catch you here.'

This messes things up. Roger bites his thumbnail and considers his options.

'Got it,' says Naomi, snapping her fingers. 'We'll pretend you've taken me hostage. Get her to climb out of her car and then we'll steal it. She won't be able to chase us on foot, will she? She seems to be alone so we shouldn't get followed. We'll head over to Bramshall Leisure. The cottages there are all empty. We can hide out until they find out who really killed Tessa. Have some "us" time. It'll be like the old days when we both used to shoot together.' She offers him a smile and kisses his forehead.

That's one good thing about Naomi, she always stays cool in a difficult situation. He agrees.

The officer is on her mobile when they approach her car. Roger holds the Smith & Wesson to Naomi's head and she looks suitably terrified. The woman catches sight of them in her mirror. Roger motions for her to climb out. As she does so, her mobile tumbles to the ground but she doesn't notice it. She's looking at Roger and asking him to put down the gun.

He's hoping to entice her into the house, tie her up and then escape with Naomi, but he hasn't banked on the officer, who suddenly launches at him with considerable strength and attempts to wrestle his gun away from him. He panics and shoves her hard. She falls backwards and strikes her head on the pavement.

'Oh fuck… fuck… fuck.'

Naomi shushes him. 'Quick, help me get her into the car before anyone sees us.'

Luckily it's a quiet road. There aren't many houses, and those that are there are well shielded by trees and bushes. Nobody is likely to have witnessed the events outside Naomi's house; besides, most people are at work.

'We'll take her to the health clinic in Uttoxeter. Leave her outside. Somebody will find her and help her.'

They drive at speed and dump the officer, then race off towards Bramshall Leisure. Naomi is looking very pleased about the whole *situation. He isn't. He's even more nervous. He forgot to retrieve the female officer's mobile phone from by the car and it's too late now to go back.*

'We're good together,' she says, putting a hand on his knee. 'Really good.'

Roger's sense of paranoia has increased. Not only does he believe a killer is after him, but now so is half of the Staffordshire police force. He's tetchy and anxious, and all the time Naomi's treating it as if they're out for a Sunday drive. The silky, soft tone she's adopted is irritating him, as is the stream of questions she's begun asking. He keeps silent and gradually he senses iciness. He isn't feeling up to dealing with one of her moods. He just wants to hide – away from police, murderers and an over-inquisitive girlfriend.

'You sure you don't want to tell me something, Roger?' she asks as they pull into Bramshall Leisure and turn off down a track towards one of the cottages.

He shakes his head. Naomi throws him a look but he ignores it. Hopefully she'll shut up. They draw to a halt and walk the short distance to the first cottage. Naomi knows the code to the small box by the front door that houses the door key, and extracts it. Together they slip unnoticed into the house.

No sooner has he set down his gun than Naomi starts again. 'You've been keeping something from me, Roger,' she says, her hands on her hips.

'I don't know what you're on about.'

'Oh, you do. The police detective told me.'

Roger sighs. He really doesn't need this.

'When were you going to let me in on it? You were going to, weren't you? Or were you hoping to hide it from me, and drop me for that slag, Tessa? What was it you really liked about her, Roger? The fact she was such an easy lay, or that she also had a share in the lottery jackpot?'

The argument escalates. Naomi won't shut up. She's furious with him for keeping the lottery win secret, even when he tries to explain they all kept quiet about it because the ticket was stolen. He attempts to convince her he kept silent for her safety, and tells her he thinks that whoever killed Tessa probably killed Anthony, and is after him too. She loses it big time then. Says he's a lying, cheating bastard who deserves to be shot.

'I thought you were keeping out of the way of the cops. If I'd known I could get killed too, on account of your greed, I'd never have helped you. You utter prick. I've stuck by you even though you two-timed me, kept me in the dark about the lottery win and treated me like shit some days. I loved you and I stuck by you but I'm not hanging around to be shot. You can handle this fucking mess on your own. I'm going home. I'm taking the car.'

'Don't do that. What if there's more than one of them after me? I'll never be able to get away if I don't have a car.'

'Fuck you,' she screams and marches towards the door. He grabs her and drags her kicking and screeching back into the room. It's all getting out of hand. His life is in danger and his girlfriend is trying to leave him in the shit. He's beginning to lose his grip on reality. He can't stay in the middle of nowhere without some form of transport. He yells something at her that angers her even more and she lands a kick in his groin that floors him, and strides towards the door.

'I hope he blows your fucking brains out,' she sobs.

He makes it to the door and spots her making her getaway. The stupid bitch is headed towards the car. He races back, reaches for his gun. He'll aim to miss. It'll frighten her enough to make her return to the house. She'll see sense then. He fires. Naomi drops to the ground. He hears voices. There's somebody else out there…

❋

Roger had nothing further to say to the detective. He'd told her everything as it happened. 'Is the officer okay?' he asked. 'I never intended to harm her.'

'She's okay,' Robyn replied. 'I'm afraid I have more bad news. Juliet Fallows was killed earlier today. Is there anything else you can tell us that might help us unearth this killer?'

Roger Jenkinson paled further and shook his head. 'If I'd found out who was behind Tessa's death, I'd have shot him,' he said.

CHAPTER SIXTY-NINE

DAY ELEVEN – FRIDAY, 24 FEBRUARY, EARLY MORNING

Ella gave a twisted smile. 'You'll never understand,' she said. 'They deserved it. They all bloody deserved it.'

'If you explain, I'm sure I would,' Robyn said.

There wasn't a flicker of regret or recognition of the crimes she'd committed. Ella Fox had confessed to killing Henry Gregson, Tessa Hall, Anthony Hawkins and Juliet Fallows, but showed no remorse or guilt.

'They badgered Liam into stealing the ticket, and when he refused, Hawkins threatened him. Hawkins, who'd pretended to be his friend and hooked him up with all the others, was going to make sure Liam lost his job and destroy our lives. Where would we go after that? How would we be able to look after Astra? Liam didn't want to steal the ticket. We spoke about it after the night they asked him to take it.' She recalled the evening with clarity…

※

Liam stumbles through the front door and into the kitchen, where Ella is waiting.

'Hey, babe,' he says. 'You okay?'

Hot tears stream down her face. 'Not really. He was so rough this time. I can't do it again, Liam. We have to find money for the rent next month. It was bearable when it was quick sex, but he's started playing games. He blindfolded me, Liam. Like Clark used to.' The trembling begins again.

He rushes towards her, his face distraught, and pulls her into a tight embrace. 'I'll kill the bastard,' he says, teeth bared.

'No. Don't! We'll try and find somewhere else we can afford.'

They stay entwined, so close their hearts beat as one. Finally, he whispers, 'There is one way out of this.'

He tells her of the plan. How the team members want him to steal the lottery ticket and how it would be possible to do so. He explains the looks, the smiles and the support from his new friends.

'Liam, love. They're not your friends. I see how they laugh behind our backs. I see the nudges and hear the soft sniggers. They're using you. You, my love, are too gullible.' She kisses his nose. 'Don't do it. It'll go wrong. A security camera at work will pick you up and you'll get caught. Tell them to get stuffed. We'll find another place to live. There must be somewhere we can afford. I can't face sleeping with McNamara again.'

Liam kisses her head, his heart heavy with sadness. 'I'll phone Hawkins and tell him I'm not doing it. I'll look for a flat for us to rent somewhere else. It won't be as nice as this place, but as long as we're together – you, me and Astra – we'll be fine.'

❋

Ella shelved the recollection, stared ahead and continued her monologue. 'After Liam had taken the ticket, he couldn't sleep or eat. He cried about it, almost every night. They didn't care what effect stealing the ticket had on him, but I did. I detested them all – especially that Anthony Hawkins, who sucked up to Liam, all the while taking the piss behind his back. He was behind it all. He knew everything about my brother. He exploited him.'

'I don't understand how.'

'Liam spent six months in prison for a crime he didn't commit. Hawkins was one of the prison officers who worked there – he learnt everything about Liam. When he came across him again, he knew exactly how to push his buttons and manipulate him. He knew Liam had real difficulties connecting with his peers. He'd seen first-hand how Liam retreated when around other people, yet wanted to be accepted. More than anything else, he's always wanted that. He's only ever wanted to be loved. Hawkins was never a true friend. None of them were. They suckered him onto the team purely for his intelligence and then they bullied him into taking that ticket. They are all guilty as hell.'

While Robyn could comprehend Ella's jealous hatred of the team who'd befriended and then browbeaten her brother, she still couldn't fathom why Ella had gone to such extremes to murder them. She asked the question.

'If Henry had snitched as he threatened to, every one of them would have crumbled like the cowardly bullies they really are, and made Liam the scapegoat. He'd have ended up in jail. He can't go back to that place. He suffered such atrocities last time – disgusting, barbaric, humiliating indignities. He'd die. I know he would.'

'But murder, Ella, brings a severe penalty, and as an accessory, Liam will be charged and go to jail for a long time. The penalty for murder is heftier than for theft.'

'He's blameless. It was my idea to kill them and I acted alone without his knowledge, so he can't be charged.' Ella's head bounced from side to side, her eyes unfocused. Robyn persisted.

'Even if that were so, he'll still be charged with stealing and defrauding the lottery.'

'A good lawyer will get him off. Astra needs him.' Ella smiled suddenly.

Robyn didn't want to argue any longer. 'I'm going to leave you for a minute, Ella. Would you like a cup of tea or anything?'

Ella refused, her gaze now resting on a point above Robyn's head, a smile on her lips, mind far away. Robyn nodded at David and left him watching over her.

In the office, Matt had been dragging up everything he could on Liam Carrington and his sister. He'd been talking to staff at MiniMarkt and searching for the couple whose lottery ticket had been stolen. He was on the phone when Robyn put her head around the office door. He covered the mouthpiece and whispered, 'Got something.'

She edged into the room, mindful she'd spent days working non-stop on this investigation, and stretched, trying to galvanise her stiffening muscles back to life. Matt put down the phone.

'The owners of the ticket have been identified as Mr and Mrs Roper. They were victims of a break-in last December. Mrs Roper got up in the early hours to get a drink of water and in doing so, disturbed a burglar. He attacked her with a blunt instrument, which police believed to have been a crowbar or similar, used to gain entry to the property. Her screams roused Mr Roper and caused the burglar to run off, empty-handed. Mrs Roper received a fractured shoulder and severe damage to her face – shattered cheekbone. A team from Lichfield was assigned to the case.'

Robyn thought about the first time she'd interviewed Liam at MiniMarkt and the frail lady with the dark mark on her cheek, and recalled how Liam had directed Robyn into the back room when he spotted the woman and her husband. It hadn't been for reasons of privacy after all. It had been because he couldn't face the couple.

'That's too much of a coincidence. Liam Carrington supposedly steals the ticket from the couple in the shop, and they're broken into soon afterwards. I don't like this one bit. What details have you got?'

Matt pulled up all the information she needed. Robyn stared at the screen and read through the statements. There remained one explanation for what had taken place, and it could also be the real reason Liam Carrington had experienced sleepless nights and nightmares. It would also account for why Ella felt she had to murder to keep the secret safe.

Robyn ran her theory past him and he agreed it was a likely explanation. She issued him with instructions to call the Ropers and ask the important question that would provide the answer.

She prepared to re-enter the interview room. She'd be in serious trouble if she was wrong, but it was a chance she was willing to take. She slid back into position.

'Thank you for waiting. I need you to help me out, Ella. I'm still puzzled about how Liam got his hands on that winning ticket. He was asked to check it so he put it through the lottery machine and pretended it hadn't won. Then he threw it in the bin and retrieved it later. That's right, isn't it?'

'Finders keepers,' said Ella, with a faraway look on her face.

'And this made him very upset?'

'He didn't like stealing.'

'But Liam had already spent time in jail for stealing, hadn't he? He was convicted of theft in 1998 when he was seventeen.'

'He didn't steal anything.' Ella's voice rose. 'He was framed. He didn't do it. He loved Sid. It was Johnny Hounslow who stole the money from the safe. Johnny Hounslow and his slutty, evil girlfriend.'

Robyn's eyes widened. She wasn't sure what else she'd uncover. For now, she had to keep Ella on the right track.

'I doubt pinching a ticket would have upset him enough to give him nightmares, especially as he was going to get his hands on a vast amount of cash that would transform your lives.'

Ella lowered her gaze.

'Here's what I think occurred. I don't think he got his hands on the ticket in the shop at all. He broke into the Ropers' house to steal it. No doubt he had an idea where it would be kept. He'd have chatted to the Ropers and asked questions. They're a friendly pair. He'd have advised them to look after the ticket, and they'd have told him where they put it for safekeeping. Or maybe you uncovered that piece of information for him.'

A tap on the door interrupted her. Matt came in and whispered to her. It was what she needed to hear.

'Liam went to their house, attacked Mrs Roper and stole the ticket. We'll find something that will place Liam at the Ropers' house. Lichfield Constabulary has kept every piece of forensic evidence on file. All they require is a suspect. Now they have one. It's over, Ella. You can stop protecting him.'

Ella levelled her gaze at Robyn. Her words spewed out, almost unintelligibly. 'Look, I didn't want to kill Henry. He was Liam's only real friend and Astra loved him so much. I had to do it. I had to for Liam's sake. You can understand that, can't you? Henry was going to notify the lottery people. I couldn't allow him to do that.

'This was not my fault. Hawkins and his teammates were responsible for Henry's death. They drove Liam to steal the ticket, and as a consequence, Henry had to die. I wanted them all to pay for their part in the deception and his death. They were desperate to share in the fortune so they also deserved to share the blame.'

Ella shrugged again, her face impassive, and began humming.

CHAPTER SEVENTY

THEN – LIAM

No sooner does Henry leave than I ring Ella and confess. She doesn't call me stupid. She doesn't shout at me. She says one word. 'Okay.'

'What do I do?' I ask.

'Look after Astra. Take her to the park in an hour. Walk around the village and say hello to a few people. Call in at the butcher's shop and buy something for dinner. Behave as if nothing has happened. It'll be fine. I'll talk to him. He'll listen to me.'

'Ella, I'm sorry.'

'I know,' she replies. 'Don't worry. Look after Astra.'

I do as she suggests and play with my little girl, fix the wooden dog she drags along the floor while she observes me, talk to her, tell her we'll go out in a minute. I take the mobile phone with me, wrapped in a plastic bag. I'm going to throw it in the bin near the butcher's shop. It'll serve no further purpose. Ella knows about my treachery so I have no need to keep my conversations with Henry secret.

As I walk down the road to the playing fields, holding onto Astra's hand, I'm sure I see Ella pass by in the back of a taxi. It can't be her. She's at the hospital in Burton with a sick friend called Cassie, who I've never met. I have Ella on my mind.

Time floats by, like I'm on heavy medication or out of my skull on booze. I have no real sensation of what I'm doing. I merely go through the motions, and after we return home, Astra watches the television while I prepare her lunch. She giggles at Dora the Explorer *and chats as if nothing is wrong in the world. I hope it's always like that for her. At some point, my eyelids become too heavy to stay open and I drift off to a dreamless sleep until Ella wakes me.*

'Is it okay?' I ask.

'It's sorted,' she says. 'We just have to stay silent.'

CHAPTER SEVENTY-ONE

'I have to admit I had my doubts, but you really pulled this together, Robyn,' DCI Flint said, head nodding up and down with approval, his neck fat squeezing behind his collar like a concertina. Robyn was reminded of one of the nodding dogs found on car parcel shelves.

'Only doing my duty, sir. Couldn't have got anywhere without my team. I'd like to have it noted officially that they all contributed in the investigations, and without their diligence, we would not have had such a good result.'

'Duly noted,' said Flint, with a twinkle. 'It's also noted that you are rapidly becoming one of my best officers. Have you ever considered further promotion, Robyn?'

She had, on many occasions, but a vision of her old DCI, Louisa Mulholland, sprang to mind, and as much as she admired the woman, she didn't want to lose sight of what she had – a great team. Their commitment to both the job, and to her, were what kept her motivated each day. She didn't want to be in a position that distanced her from investigations and work in the field. This was where she belonged.

'I have, sir.'

'Should you wish to pursue that avenue, I'd be happy to recommend you.'

'Thank you, sir. I really appreciate that.'

'And how is Anna?'

'She's fine, sir. The wound was superficial and she's itching to get back to work already. I had to insist she take a couple of days off with Mitz.'

'Good. Okay. Right. Thank you, Robyn. It was a fine job.' He patted the thick file on his desk. 'Witness statements, evidence and confessions. Couldn't have got a tighter case. And another murder charge to be taken into account – Johnny Hounslow. I see Ella Fox is pleading diminished responsibility.'

'That's correct, sir. She's undergone psychological assessment, and the clinic report suggests she suffers from anxiety and mental trauma. She was a minor at the time and acted purely to save her brother's life. I think any judge will have difficulty sentencing her. Liam Carrington confessed to purchasing the gun from a man in the Stag in Stoke-on-Trent in 2000, and then staging Johnny Hounslow's death so it appeared to be an accident. He's more likely to be charged. Add to that the attack on Mrs Roper, and he'll be banged up for a very long time.'

'Gruesome. What on earth makes people act in such despicable ways?'

'Fear and greed. They're often the reasons. Although I think in Fox and Carrington's case, there was something more – a murky past maybe – something else in the shadows. They have an unusual relationship.'

'And the child?'

'Astra's in care at the moment, but I understand Lauren Gregson is getting advice about trying to adopt her.' Robyn's heart lurched as she thought of the little girl, last seen holding an officer's hand and clutching the toy black cat. Robyn might have been able to take in Schrödinger and look after him, but she hadn't been able to do the same for the sweet little child with the beautiful eyes.

Flint grimaced. 'I can't figure people out,' he said.

'We're not supposed to. We find and deal with those who cross the line, sir. If we thought too much or too often about what we do, we'd all go mad.'

He heaved a sigh. 'Wise words, Robyn. So, once again, well done and remember what I've said.'

'Thank you.'

Robyn left the office with a sense of worth. The outcome was as good as she could hope for. The lottery jackpot was being returned and the Ropers had been notified they were the real winners. Roger Jenkinson was facing a mandatory five-year sentence for possession of firearms and had been charged for obstructing a police officer. Naomi, who'd convinced him to take Anna to the health clinic in Uttoxeter, had been cleared of any major wrongdoing, although she had been cautioned for perverting the course of justice. Following a full confession, Ella Fox was facing charges for the murders of Henry Gregson, Tessa Hall, Anthony Hawkins and Juliet Fallows, as well as that of Johnny Hounslow.

There would be more conclusive evidence if needed: the fingernail in Tessa's kitchen might have her DNA on it, the black jacket stuffed into a box in the shed with fibres that would undoubtedly match those found at the scene of Henry Gregson's death, and the Nike LunarGlide 8 hidden at the bottom of McNamara's wheelie dustbin. They'd been her brother's – a brand new pair he'd purchased from eBay at a huge discount. Ella had scooped them up when she stopped off to collect the gun, and stuffed them with socks so they fitted her feet. Robyn had almost admired her logical thinking and attempts to deflect from her guilt. However, try as she might, Robyn still couldn't dismiss the blank look on Ella's face. Some event or curse of nature had turned Ella Fox into one of the

cruellest murderers Robyn had come across. Ella's confession had
been thorough, right to the end.

'So you killed all those people to protect your brother?'

'Yes. But I also did it for me.' She had turned her face towards
Robyn. The scar on her face rose like a thick, flat worm. Even
under the concealer, Robyn could see its uneven, thick surface.
'The others were little more than greedy bullies, but Liam and I
deserved that lottery money. We were entitled to it. Liam's share
was for his and Astra's future. Mine was for salvation, to rescue me
from my past.' A solitary tear trickled down her cheek, tracing the
line of the scar. She let it fall.

※

As Robyn meandered into her office, it was to applause. Shearer
was alone, sitting in her chair.

'Congratulations! I just heard. That was some achievement.'

'It was touch and go for quite a while there.'

'I knew you'd pull it all together.'

'Did you, Tom?' she said, quietly.

He beamed a lopsided grin. 'Of course I did.'

In spite of his apparent openness, she couldn't gauge his sincerity. That was the problem with Shearer. Just when you thought he
was being nice, he'd drop you in it. It was as if there was always a
hidden agenda with him. Had he been hoping she'd fail? She may
never know. Whatever his thoughts or motives, she felt he had to
be kept at arm's length.

'Then thank you.'

'Fancy a celebratory drink?'

'I'd love to but I have to get home to Schrödinger.'

His brow dropped and the grin left his face. 'It's a cat. It'll be
perfectly fine without you for an hour. It doesn't need a bath and
bedtime story, does it?'

His attempt at humour was weak and he knew it. He stood before she could reject his proposal again and spoke softly as he left the office. 'You did brilliantly.'

Robyn's phone buzzed. It was a message from Ross.

Can you meet me in the café in ten minutes? I have some news.

CHAPTER SEVENTY-TWO

Robyn couldn't control the flipping in her stomach as she pushed open the café door and joined Ross at the table without first buying anything. As usual, her cousin's face was unreadable.

'No cake?' he said, lip jutting out.

'You can have as much cake as you want in a moment. First put me out of my misery. You know how much this is messing with my head.'

Ross rested his arms on the table, and the elbows of his navy-blue blazer rode up to display the cuffs of a mauve shirt he'd owned for at least a decade.

'Tell me,' she said.

He picked up a sugar packet from the bowl on the table and shook it. 'I've got closer to finding Davies' boss, Peter Cross. His ex-secretary has agreed to meet me but she's going on vacation tomorrow and can't see me until she returns. I've made an appointment for the third of March. I'm unlikely to track down Peter Cross until I've spoken to her, and she categorically refuses to discuss him over the phone.'

Robyn gave a brief smile. He'd done well. She hadn't been able to make that much progress in the time she'd been looking into the mystery of the photograph.

'And there's some more good news. I've located the florist your flowers came from and spoken to the very person who arranged for them to be delivered to the station.'

She could barely think for the hammering of her pulse in her temples, nor could she ask the question. Had Davies ordered them? Ross tapped the sugar packet on the table, allowing the contents to settle. His lips twitched.

'Ross! Tell me.'

'They're not from Davies.'

'Oh.' Her energy suddenly drained from her and she couldn't establish if she was upset or relieved by the news.

'You disappointed?' Her cousin returned the sugar packet to the bowl.

'I don't know. I think so. No. I'm sort of glad. If they had been from him it would have proved he was alive, and I really don't think I'm prepared for that news yet.'

'I was sort of glad too. I'm hoping this is all one big set-up and it'll all go away again, and although I don't like anyone messing with your head, I'd rather it was that than your life being overturned again. I don't want to find out Davies has been alive all this time. I'm not sure how I'd react if I found him. I think I'd like to drive my fist into his face for all the hurt he's caused.' He sat back and folded his arms. 'Still, it hasn't come to that yet, has it? So, don't you want to know who sent you those anemones?'

'I suppose so. I can't imagine who else it could be. I didn't think I was on anybody's radar.'

There was a glint in his eyes as he answered. 'Oh, you are. You're on somebody's radar all right – Shearer's.'

Robyn's mouth fell open. 'You're joking.'

'Seen the actual order. Tom Shearer sent you a dozen scarlet-red anemones for Valentine's Day. So, that's my part of the deal completed. Where's this cake you promised me? And you might like to get an extra slice to take back to the station. For DI Shearer,' he said with a wink.

EPILOGUE

As Robyn pulled up on her drive in Leafy Lane, she acknowledged for the first time in many weeks the heavy loneliness that ordinarily haunted her was not present. The automatic timers had come on and her home looked welcoming. The curtains were wide open and she could see the pastel-coloured soft furnishings in her sitting room. The television, thanks to another automatic timer, flickered, adding to the impression the house was occupied and somebody was watching the dancers on stage performing a rigorous routine. Then, as she clambered out of the car, head filled with thoughts of Davies and Tom Shearer, a shape appeared at the window.

She smiled as it opened its mouth and meowed at her, and then marched up and down the window ledge, eager for her to come in.

She'd decided Schrödinger was going to stay. Amélie had sent a text earlier asking if she could come and visit at the weekend to see them both. He had a profoundly calming effect on Robyn's ragged nerves, and in the short time she'd had him, she'd come to love him. Besides, what harm could come of having a lucky black cat?

She alarmed her car and entered the house, murmuring softly for him. Schrödinger leapt from the ledge to greet her. She bent to caress him.

❋

Outside, the man hiding behind the lamp post opposite her house slipped into the darkness. He'd transformed since she'd last seen him. Could he really approach her after all this time and tell her the truth? He thrust his hands deeper into his coat pockets and moved swiftly away. He had to exercise extreme caution. He was a hunted man and he couldn't face capture again.

LETTER FROM CAROL

Dear everyone,

I really hope you've enjoyed reading *The Silent Children* and are keen to find out what will happen next.

Robyn's not had the easiest of times, but now she has Schrödinger and he'll provide comfort and companionship while she tackles her next investigation.

If you did enjoy the book, and want to keep up-to-date with all my latest releases, just sign up at the following link. Your email address will never be shared and you can unsubscribe at any time.

www.bookouture.com/carol-wyer

The Silent Children has been a difficult book to write as it tackles the thorny subject of abuse. I gathered a lot of my material from a lady who wishes to remain anonymous: she married for love but found herself in a hateful relationship in which she was at first verbally abused, then physically. She was unable to speak about it for many years, but it was only after a prolonged incident where she feared for her life that she reached out for help.

I fear there are many people – men and women – who find themselves in abusive relationships, unable to speak out or escape, and who, like Juliet Fallows, wonder sometimes if they deserve to be treated this way.

If you enjoyed reading *The Silent Children*, please would you take a few minutes to write a review, no matter how short it is? I would be most grateful. Your recommendations are most important. If you'd like to keep up-to-date with all my latest releases, just sign up at the following link. Your email address will never be shared and you can unsubscribe at any time.

Thanks,
Carol

 www.facebook.com/AuthorCarolEWyer

twitter.com/carolewyer

www.carolewyer.co.uk

ACKNOWLEDGEMENTS

As I come to the end of another DI Robyn Carter book, I am grateful not only to Natalie Butlin and Lydia Vassar-Smith for their endless patience and guidance, but to everyone at Bookouture for their stupendous efforts to ensure *The Silent Children* was ready for publication on time.

I would also like to thank all those who have kept me motivated throughout the process. Special thanks go to Angie Marsons and Patricia Gibney, two outstanding authors, who gave freely of their time to offer advice and huge amounts of support when I was flagging on those long, endless nights.

More thanks go to the truly incredible Kim Nash, publicist extraordinaire and tremendous friend to all of us.

There are so many people who support an author as they battle with deadlines and plot holes, long nights and frustrations, and I am no exception. There are days when a review from a kind reader or blogger can make all the difference, and I would like to thank all of the book bloggers who have put a spring in my step on a dark day. There are far too many to mention and I'd need several pages to list them all, but I'll start with Annette Angelx, Joanne Robertson, Trish Tishylou Hill, Shell Baker, Alison Daughtrey-Drew, Sian-Elin Flint-Freel, Linda Hobden, Linda Hill, Kaisha Holloway and Sue Hampson. I'm sorry I can't mention you all, but you are so important and hugely appreciated.

And finally, my heartfelt thanks to you, the readers. Your comments, reviews, messages and emails about my books keep me writing. Thank you all.